She has written numerous drama adaptations for BBC ... as well as some highly-acclaimed original drama. *Miss Treadway & the Field of Stars* is her first novel.

'A fabulous depiction of a London where the "Swinging Sixties" hides a darker, more complicated story of prejudice and struggle. I loved the strong women and evocative writing from an author offering more questions than clues'   HELEN SIMONSON, author of *Major Pettigrew's Last Stand*

'A fabulous period piece, expertly evoked, that looks at race, identity, isolation and acceptance, and everyone's need to find love'
Daily Mail

'Well researched and well crafted'   *Observer*

'A deftly assured debut, full of layers and characters that come alive in a few vivid sentences. I can't wait to read more from Miranda Emmerson'   *Red*

'A zippy read set in the Swinging Sixties'   *Good Housekeeping*

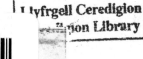

MISS TREADWAY & THE FIELD OF STARS

Miranda Emmerson

4th Estate • London

4th Estate
An imprint of HarperCollins*Publishers*
1 London Bridge Street
London SE1 9GF

www.4thEstate.co.uk

First published in Great Britain by 4th Estate in 2017
This 4th Estate paperback edition published in 2017

1

A catalogue record for this book is
available from the British Library

ISBN 978-0-00-817060-8

Printed and bound in Great Britain by
Clays Ltd, St Ives plc

MIX
Paper from
responsible sources
FSC˙ C007454

FSC™ is a non-profit international organisation established to promote
the responsible management of the world's forests. Products carrying the
FSC label are independently certified to assure consumers that they come
from forests that are managed to meet the social, economic and
ecological needs of present and future generations,
and other controlled sources.

Find out more about HarperCollins and the environment at
www.harpercollins.co.uk/green

For Chas

Chapters

An American in Hampshire

by James Wingate

How Iolanthe Green is charming the Home Counties

Iolanthe Green is perching on the arm of an antique wing chair. She is dressed entirely in red, dress cut rather high by our fusty English standards for a shooting party on a country estate. Several times her laughter rings out, filling the salon and library, ruffling the edges of the antimacassars. Her face is almost entirely concealed by what one can only describe as a mane of dark curls.

'Do you think it's real?' the housekeeper asks me when I enter.

'Do I think what's real?'

'The hair. I've never seen anything like it.'

'Not Lord Vellam's average guest,' I observe. 'Will she shoot?'

'She's American,' the housekeeper mutters. 'They're born shooting.'

But shooting parties and country house estates were not a feature of Iolanthe Green's early years. The celebrated actress was born into a humble Irish-American tenement home in Boston, Massachusetts. After ten years playing small parts on and off Broadway it was at the age of thirty that she first came to the public's attention playing Cathy in Leopold Grisci's 1955 film adaptation of *Wuthering Heights*.

This summer she has been reunited with Grisci as she takes the part of Lady Macbeth in his experimental retelling of Shakespeare's play. And it is Grisci's film that has brought her to the estate of one of the richest men in Britain, where a remarkable sixteenth-century ruin in the grounds of Halsted House is playing the part of Macbeth's castle.

It's August when we meet, the weekend after the glorious twelfth, and I find Miss Green enjoying all the pleasures of this extraordinary estate as she takes a break between filming and starting rehearsals for a new production of *The Field of Stars* which opens in the West End in October.

Cont. page 14

Iolanthe Green reported missing

DISAPPEARANCE OF A WEST END STAR

Iolanthe Green, whose performance in *The Field of Stars* this paper so admired last month, has disappeared, leading to the cancellation of two performances.

Miss Green left the Galaxy Theatre at twenty past eleven on the evening of Saturday October 30th and was seen to walk south down the Charing Cross Road. A member of staff from the theatre assumed that she had chosen to walk back to her rooms at The Savoy as the temperatures were unusually mild that evening.

Miss Anna Treadway, a dresser at the Galaxy, told our reporter, 'I saw Miss Green leave the theatre as usual. I said goodnight to her and she replied. She did not seem dispirited or depressed. She's been very nice to me since she arrived. I'm terribly worried.'

Metropolitan Police Inspector Edwin Knight said in a statement to the press: 'We would be grateful to the public for any information regarding Miss Green's whereabouts. Members of the public who may have seen Miss Green at any time since Saturday evening are asked to call WHI 1212 so we can register your information.'

A Beloved Daughter of County Cork

'Look out into the darkness,' Iolanthe had told her. 'Look out into the darkness and you'll see them.'

'Do you look?' Anna asked.

'Sometimes. Sometimes I forget not to. Always at the curtain, at the end. The old ones with their bags of liquorice. The dates who look at me, the dates who look at him. The students; herringbone jackets, no tie. The ones who look lustful. The ones who look bored. Some of them, you can see they're thinking about something else entirely. You, up there on the stage, you're nothing more than the reflection of a bulb.'

'What are they thinking about?' Anna asked.

'All the stuff that's going wrong. The stuff they can't fix. What they're always thinking about.'

Anna paused in the action of pinning Iolanthe's hair and caught her eye in the mirror. The older woman was sitting in her underwear, quite still and unselfconscious as if Anna were a lover or a sister.

Anna moved Lanny's hand to hold a roll of curls while she picked through a bowl of oddments for more hairpins. 'It must be very strange,' she said. 'Everyone looking and seeing something different. As if you were a funhouse mirror.'

This made Iolanthe laugh. 'That's just what I am. Different for everybody. The Lanny who sits here will die as soon as she walks through that door. And a new Lanny will be born. Stage-door Lanny. Interview Lanny. Getting-the-drinks-in Lanny. I walk through the door and I start afresh. No hang-ups. No neuroses.'

Anna cast a questioning glance towards the surface of the mirror and Iolanthe seemed almost to blush. 'That's the idea, anyway. Live in the moment. Don't get caught in the net.'

*　*　*

Out in the darkness of the upper stalls, tiny pinpricks of light caught Anna's eye. Opera glasses, trained no doubt on Iolanthe, bouncing back light. Towards the stage she could see long rows of pale faces tilted upwards. From where she stood the stage looked tiny and the sound was flattened and distorted, muffled by the footsteps of the actors and the crew. Look at us all, she thought. Look at all us monkeys sitting in a great black box. Less than ten of us facing one way; nine hundred facing the other. One person speaks; the many hundred stay silent. And at the end all but the speakers will bang their little paws together. How did we all learn what to do? What made us so obedient?

Anna watched Lanny stride upstage and gesture to the crude oil painting of a woman in 1920s garb which hung above her on the living-room wall. In the semi-darkness the scene-shifters were quietly rolling the fairground set into place behind it.

'… I had the inspiration … the ability … to be anything.'

Lanny paused and gauged the level of attention, the silence in the space. In the upper circle there was a fit of coughing. Anna saw Lanny's face twitch just slightly with displeasure. She drove her next speech across the heads of the stalls and right into the upper circle high above. Her annoyance rang through in her delivery, her anger directed not at her fellow actor but at the audience members themselves.

'This whoreish existence that you despise me for … I chose it. I had everything before me and I chose the life that would fit me best.'

Archie flicked three switches down and the stage went dark. Anna blinked in the blackness waiting for her eyes to refocus, and when they did she saw the shape of Lanny hopping towards her, pulling her heels off as she came.

'Awful audience,' she pronounced darkly, shoving her feet into black Oxfords. 'Fuck 'em.'

Anna stripped Lanny of the negligee and opened her orange flower dress wide so she could step into it. Lanny popped the poppers shut and Anna cinched the belt as the lights rose on half a carousel and strings of fairy lights and bunting. Anna ran her hand quickly over the line of the dress, feeling for mistakes, then squeezed Lanny's arm, telling her she was okay to step on out. And out she bounded, literally kicking her heels up, high on all kinds of wild energy.

In the corridor on the way back to the dressing room Anna met Dick, whose job it was to man the counter at the stage door.

'There's a journalist downstairs. Wingate. Says he's got a meeting with Lanny. Interview? I told him he'd need to hang around till five.'

'Okay,' Anna told him. 'I'll warn her.'

'And Cassidy called again.'

'Cassidy?'

'American guy. Third time this week. Is she seeing someone?'

'No one she's mentioned. Is there a message?'

'Just to say he'd called.'

As act three drew to a close, Anna made lemon tea in the little kitchenette at the top of the stairs and buttered some bread. She watered Lanny's plants and Agatha's for good measure. She cleared the rubbish from the dressing table. The wrapping from a malt loaf, sweet papers, ticket stubs from a lunchtime showing of *The Great Race*.

Lanny wasn't big on culture but she liked the pictures. Every few afternoons she'd take herself off to a matinee at The Empire on Leicester Square. *What's New Pussycat? How to Murder Your Wife.* Nothing too serious, nothing tragic. Anna had tried to persuade her to go and see *The Hill*, but Lanny had laughed in her face.

'A film about a bunch of sweaty men trekking over a mound of earth! Seriously? Is that what passes for entertainment with you art school types?'

'Art school! I went to secretarial college in Birmingham.'

'Yeah, but you have the whole black stockings, polo neck, pony tail thing going on. You're just missing a beret and a pack of French cigarettes.'

'You're calling me a pseud!'

'I'm not. It's a look. I'm fine with it.'

'Lanny. I am not a pseud!'

'No, I get that. Just because it walks like a pseud and talks like a pseud ...'

Anna smiled at the memory of this derision – for in truth she was rather pleased with the art school reference – then she set to sweeping magazines, knickers and old socks off the chaise longue.

Lanny was back in her dressing room by ten to five. So anxious was she to get out of costume that she tried to pull her jacket off without unbuttoning it first. Anna took her by the shoulders and sat her down, then she unbuttoned and unzipped the woman as if she were a child. She hung the costume on the rail and found Lanny a pair of jeans and a shirt which she'd thrown into the corner of the dressing room a week earlier.

'The jeans don't fit,' Lanny told her.

'Would you like a skirt?'

'I'd like not to be so fucking cold all the time. This country just makes me want to eat. All I could hear through my final speech was *hack hack sniff sniff cough cough.*'

'British audiences sniff when it's cold.' Anna's eyes searched the dressing room for whatever Lanny had worn into work that day. She found it under the make-up table, a green silk dress lying in a creased heap. Anna shook out the expensive rag and handed it over.

'You know you have an appointment at five?'

'Do I? Who with?'

'Some journalist. He's been downstairs for hours.'

Lanny pulled on a pair of heels and sat at the dressing table to drink her tea. 'Would you hang around for a bit?'

'For the interview?'

'Yeah; sometimes journalists can be a bit ... sleazy. I haven't got the energy for all that crap.'

'Of course. Also someone called Cassidy called.'

4

Lanny nodded. 'Did he leave a message?'

'Just that he called.'

'Okay,' Lanny said. 'Okay.'

* * *

Anna showed James Wingate up the many flights of stairs. He was in his fifties, Anna thought, with a gaunt, handsome face. He wore a slim-fitting navy suit with a turquoise silk tie and smelled of cigarettes.

Wingate started talking before he was even in the room. 'Miss Green, thank you so much for seeing me between performances.' Lanny – who had arranged herself modestly on the chaise longue, legs covered by a lap blanket – sat very still and looked at Mr Wingate.

'My dresser didn't tell me who it was.'

'That's because she has no idea who I am.'

Lanny stood, letting the blanket fall from her lap. She tugged at her green silk dress, pulling the fabric free from its belt so that it hid the curve of her breasts. Nobody spoke.

'I'm sorry. I didn't know that I was meant to know,' Anna said at last. 'Shall I get you both something to drink?'

'Mr Wingate interviewed me for *Harper's Bazaar* – this past summer – just as I was finishing filming on *Macbeth*.'

Wingate sat down on the chair provided for him and drew out his notebook and a small stack of papers. 'A coffee would be delightful,' he said without looking up.

Anna went to the kitchenette by the green room and rifled through the cupboards for coffee. Did snotty journalists drink Nescafé? Leonard – the company manager – found her staring at the jar.

'Lanny ripping the audience to pieces?'

'No more than usual. Someone called James Wingate wants a cup of coffee.'

'Wingate? Ugh. Okay. Take a cup, go across the road to the 101 and get them to put real coffee in it. Might be worth a nice write-up in *The Times*.'

'Seriously?'

Leonard held up his hands. 'This is the idiocy we live with. Make the best of it.'

The windows of the 101 were steamed white against the cold and the afternoon custom seemed mostly to consist of taxi drivers, off shift, who sat at separate tables silently contemplating the melamine.

A radio muttered on a shelf above the head of the proprietor. 'Teams of police are this evening continuing to search a vast area of moorland on the Cheshire–Yorkshire border.' Anna tuned it out and leaned across the counter.

She slopped some of the coffee down her skirt as she climbed the stairs back to the dressing room and Wingate barely acknowledged her as she handed him the cup. He was leaning in towards Iolanthe, brows furrowed, head tilted to one side. 'I assume you wanted to be in films as a girl? Don't all young girls want something of the kind?'

'I … Well, I don't know. Let me think. I knew from an early age that I'd have to earn my own money. Supporting myself. No one was going to do that for me.'

'Because you didn't come from money.'

'Well, no. But also by the time I was eighteen my father and my mother were both dead.'

'And brothers and sisters? I don't think we covered brothers and sisters at our last meeting.'

'It was a very small family.'

'Just you, then.'

'Well, no. Not exactly. But I was the one who had to earn.'

'You supported your parents?'

'No. I didn't mean … I guess … Everybody worked.'

'Sorry, I'm just a little unclear here. You are or you aren't an only child.'

'I had a brother.'

'Okay. Good.'

'I'd rather not …'

'You don't like talking about him?'

6

'Yes. Well … no. I don't. Can we talk about the films?'

'Is he proud of you? Is he jealous of your success? I mean, what does he do?'

'He doesn't do anything.'

'At all?'

'He's dead.'

Wingate sat back in his chair and slowly crossed his legs. 'I'm so sorry, Iolanthe. I didn't know.' Anna glanced up to check that Lanny was okay but the woman was staring at the floor, looking a bit perplexed, as if she was trying to remember something.

'That must be very hard for you,' Wingate went on.

'I don't know …' Lanny sat in silence for a minute. When she spoke again she addressed herself to the rail of clothes on the far wall. 'He was killed in 1946 when he was stationed in Japan. He was riding in a Jeep and it turned over on a bad road. He'd been too young to fight and around where we lived … well, boys were getting fake IDs and signing up at sixteen and I think Nat saw it as a mark of shame that he hadn't … He was seventeen years old. It was his first posting.

'It's very strange. It's very strange to find yourself all alone at twenty-one. And to think … well, whatever I do in my life now … I mean … other people, they do it for their parents, they do it to make their parents proud. But I couldn't do that; that was gone for me.' And Lanny sat in silence as if she'd forgotten they were there.

'So tell me, Miss Green, your parents … they were from Ireland originally.'

'My parents? Oh, well, no. Second generation. My grandparents were from County Cork. I think they left in 1880, 1885, something like that.'

'Not because of the famine, then?'

'No. More general.' Lanny waved her hands in the air. 'You know, the whole making a better life thing.'

'And have you ever been back to Ireland. I mean: have you visited?'

'No. I have never had that pleasure or that privilege.'

'Do you know where in Cork they were from?'

7

Lanny's voice rose a little. 'Anna. Anna! I'm so sorry, James. There's something nagging at the back of my mind. Do I have some-one in tonight?'

'I don't think so.' Anna stood. 'Do you want me to double-check who's got the house seats?'

Lanny waved her hand frantically. 'No. No. No. It doesn't matter. I'm being silly. Sit down. Pre-show nerves.' She directed this last remark to Wingate whose eyes were rather wide.

He waited a moment and then began again. 'I only wondered. Partly, I suppose, because Green is not a typically Irish name. I wondered if it had been changed along the way?'

'Green? No. I think if I'd chosen a stage name I'd have gone for something a bit wilder.'

'I wondered if it had been anglicised. If you were once all O'Gradys or MacGoverns.'

'Well … that's very interesting. You see, my daddy was Green, but I didn't know my grandaddy at all because he died so young. And, well now, I assume that we were all Greens – not my mother's family of course, they were Callaghans – but I never really asked. I mean, it's not something that you think of, is it? "Daddy, is that definitely your name?"' Lanny laughed, showing Wingate all of her teeth.

'Are you tempted now to go digging around and find out?' Wingate asked her.

'You've got me interested, James, you really have.'

'Might you make a pilgrimage?'

'To Ireland? Perhaps. If time allows and they want me back.' Iolanthe laughed and Wingate joined in with her. He tasted his coffee, made a face of disgust and deposited it at his feet. Lanny's eyes wrinkled into a smile. She held his gaze for a moment.

*   *   *

After the show that evening, Anna stood by Lanny's side as she always did and watched her clean off all the muck. The dark black liner, the red lips and the mascara made her glamorous and sultry, but she was far more lovely underneath it all. Her eyes were round

8

and deepest brown, her eyebrows thin and delicate. Her nose was too broad for her face and underneath all the panstick it was covered in light brown freckles, which always made Anna think of her as a little girl from a storybook. Lanny's lips were a soft, deep rose and her teeth snaggly, the inheritance of a childhood without money.

Lanny pawed at a mole on her cheek, which sprouted a single hair. 'I look so old these days.'

Anna smiled at her in the mirror. 'I think you look lovely. Like a woman from a Rossetti or a Waterhouse.'

'I don't know what those are.'

'Rossetti? He was one of the Pre-Raphaelites. Waterhouse as well. They were painters in Victorian times who painted these big romantic pictures of women from literature. All flowing locks and big, bold eyes and lips.'

'It sounds pornographic.'

'Well, it is, in a way. It's very sexual. But I wanted so much to look like those women when I was younger. My father had a book with plates in it. I wanted to be the Lady of Shalott or Pandora or a mermaid. But you really do … Without make-up …' Anna shook her head. 'You look more real somehow.'

'Well, I am more real.'

'I suppose.'

Lanny's hand sneaked across the dressing table and picked up the mascara. 'A little something, just for going home,' she said.

'What's it like, living at The Savoy?'

Lanny met Anna's eyes in the glass and her own eyes wrinkled into a smile. 'It's exactly what you'd think, child. Everything is very shiny, the breakfast is excellent and everyone looks terribly, terribly bored.'

Anna laughed and helped Iolanthe into her dress and coat. A little pile of post lay unopened on the dressing table. Lanny pushed the envelopes into her bulging handbag and then paused in the act of picking up yesterday's *Standard*. She glanced down at the headline.

SNOW ON MOORS HAMPERS SEARCH
Brady and Hindley remanded

They'd hardly been off the front pages this past month. First the boy's body, then the girl's, now a second boy had been found.

Anna watched Lanny's train of thought. 'I know,' she said, 'I've been having nightmares.'

'About the kids?'

'After they found the girl. Under the earth. Who'd leave a child like that?'

Lanny's face creased a little in pain. 'I don't want to think about it.'

'Sorry,' said Anna. 'Let's not.'

They walked in silence down the many flights of stairs. Outside the theatre Lanny belted her coat against the cold and drew on gloves. Anna paused at the corner and watched her walk away. Lanny looked over her shoulder just once and waved a hand.

'See you Monday,' she called.

'See you Monday,' Anna called back.

And then she was gone.

Walk On and Walk Off

Monday, 1 November

At half past five Anna was ready for Lanny's arrival. A cup of lemon tea sat on the table waiting. Lanny's clothes were ironed and hung ready for her in neat rows. The play began at seven and the cast were expected to be in place at the very latest by the half-hour call, which came at six twenty-five. Lanny normally liked to arrive early. She had make-up and hair to do. She wanted to drink her tea and go to the toilet. She wanted time so if anything went wrong with her costume it could be fixed.

Any moment now Lanny would come running in, throw down the newspaper, empty her pockets of sweets, peel herself out of her dress.

'Fucking cold!' she'd cry. 'And the cabs! No one knows how to drive in this country!'

'Did you look the wrong way again?' Anna would ask.

'I looked the right way. But all the assholes just kept driving in the wrong direction!'

Or perhaps tonight she'd be contemplative, slip into the dressing room without a word. If she was in a quiet mood Anna had learned to come and go without a sound. Fetching and carrying everything that might be needed as Lanny stripped herself. Sometimes Anna would find her standing naked before the mirror, touching her hand to her breasts or her belly or her thighs, lost in thought. Anna would look, too hard to be a human and not look, but then she would look away. She tried to imagine her way into the body of Iolanthe. The mind, she corrected herself. Iolanthe resided in her mind.

Half past five became six. Anna went downstairs to see Dick but Lanny hadn't signed in yet. Leonard popped his head in to ask if she thought Lanny had been getting sick.

'I don't think so,' Anna told him. 'She just seemed her normal self.'

Anna waited. Lanny's tea grew cold. At six twenty-five exactly the call came on the backstage tannoy:

'*Field of Stars* company. This is your half-hour call. Thirty minutes, please.'

Leonard burst in again. 'We can't raise her at The Savoy. She isn't there. Agatha is dressing to cover Lanny. Minnie is dressing to cover Agatha. Can you go and cast an eye over what she's doing?'

Anna helped the young understudy to get into her clothes. Minnie was talking all the time. Running the lines at high speed over and over again. Anna gave her a hug.

'It isn't Shakespeare,' she told her. 'No one knows the words. You can say anything at all and they'll still think it's part of the play. Walk on, walk off and try to look like you know what you're doing. Don't worry. You'll be fine. I'll see you later for the quick change.'

She walked back to Lanny's dressing room. The cup of tea sat on the table untouched. Was Iolanthe ill?

Of course, everyone expected Lanny to arrive by the interval. She must have gone off for the day and got stuck in traffic. That's what made most sense. But the interval came and went and there was no Iolanthe.

Leonard phoned round the hospitals in case there had been an accident. He phoned The Savoy again and spoke to the desk clerk. Iolanthe hadn't been in her room since Friday night.

The show came down at ten to ten. The audience cheered Agatha, though many had left at the interval since catching sight of Iolanthe Green had been their main reason for buying the tickets. Leonard called a meeting on the stage. The cast sat on chairs in a circle. Anna sat with the other dressers and the crew on the floor. Leonard told everyone about his call to The Savoy.

'Iolanthe has to be considered a missing person. I've already called the police. If she hasn't turned up by tomorrow morning they'll be coming down to interview us here. The show will keep running but management are going to keep an eye on cancellations. If we're not playing to at least forty per cent attendance they may take us off in another week. Don't worry about that now, but I need to give you that warning so you're prepared. No one of Iolanthe's description has been admitted to any of the big hospitals. I'm going to see that as a good thing. You all did well tonight. Go home. Get some sleep. Company meeting at four tomorrow followed by a line run if it's understudies again. Okay. Off you go!'

* * *

On Tuesday the papers were full of Iolanthe's disappearance. The *Mirror* asked if Brady and Hindley had inspired a copycat murder in London. The *Sun* wanted to know if Iolanthe had fallen prey to a gang of Soho people smugglers. The *Daily Express* asked its readers to join police in hunting for the glamorous starlet. The *Daily Telegraph* wondered if fragile, unmarried Miss Green had run away from the pressures of fame.

On Wednesday afternoon, as the company of understudies gathered for yet another line run, BBC Radio News arrived to interview Leonard about Lanny's disappearance. Anna stood in the green room beside the transistor radio and listened to Leonard intoning his worries and incomprehension at six o'clock and then again at ten. Each time she heard someone familiar speak, or read someone she knew quoted in the paper, they – the people involved, the events – became less familiar. She was starting to see it as a story herself. The story of how Lanny disappeared.

On Thursday *The Times* wanted to know why women weren't safe to walk the streets of Theatreland and the *Guardian* wanted to know why so much attention was being paid to one wealthy actress when in the past week alone two hundred ordinary people had gone missing without any great fanfare at all.

On Friday, as Londoners gathered to burn effigies of Guy Fawkes, police were called to a disturbance at a flat in Golden Square. When they arrived they found a young male prostitute called Vincent Mar lying on the front steps having sustained a terrible head wound. The police arrested a middle-aged man who was the tenant of the flat they'd been called to attend. The man's name was Richard Wallis and he happened to be a Junior Minister of State for Justice in Her Majesty's Government. By the time Wallis had been released – without charge – late on Saturday night, the papers had got hold of the scandal and Iolanthe was about to be knocked quite definitively off the front pages.

Monday, 8 November

In West End Central police station, up on Savile Row, Inspector Knight had been co-ordinating a well-resourced search effort for Iolanthe but now he was running out of ideas. Statements had been taken and double-checked, posters had been mounted in prime locations, hospitals had been phoned and visited. Nobody, it seemed, absolutely nobody, had seen Miss Green.

Over the course of a fraught weekend, in which he had seen nothing of his wife or children, Knight had been instructed firmly by the Home Office that he was to scour Soho for other possible assailants of young Mr Mar who had – to the relief of many – failed to regain consciousness after the attack. But the majority of Knight's men were assigned to the hunt for the missing actress.

The Sunday papers had attempted to try and convict Mr Wallis right there on the newsstands and pressure from the offices of government was increasing. So at 9 a.m. on Monday, Inspector Knight called into his office a detective sergeant by the name of Barnaby Hayes.

'The government is defecating in its collective knickers, Hayes.'

'I'm sure it is, sir.'

'I have until next Sunday to find at least one fully fashioned scumbag who might have tried to kill, rob or bugger Vincent Mar. I also have to hope the bloody man's about to die, because if he wakes up and recounts a night of ecstasy with Mr Wallis we're all fucked.'

'Sir.'

'The worst of it is I still have to pretend to care about Iolanthe Green when any fool can see that the woman's obviously done herself in and hasn't had the decency to leave her body somewhere handy.'

'Yes, sir.'

'You're the closest thing I have to competent in my department, Hayes. Don't fuck up and don't talk to any press.'

'Sir.'

'Find the body. Close the case. We have better things to be doing.'

Barnaby Hayes picked up the small pile of manila files and carried them out of the office to his desk. He was a meticulous and careful officer, a player by the rules. He had distinguished himself in the eyes of Knight by working long hours and never once trying to cut corners or claim he'd done work when he hadn't. His name – as it happened – was not Barnaby at all, but Brennan. He had cast this particular mark of Irishness away from him when he joined CID.

He opened the files and rearranged their contents. He knew from bitter experience that not everyone in the department was as assiduous as he was and he could see no other way ahead but to start from scratch and re-interview everyone connected to Iolanthe. He cast his eyes down the list of eyewitnesses from the Saturday she had disappeared. The name at the top of the list was Anna Treadway. He dialled her number.

Miss Treadway

Anna Treadway lived on Neal Street in a tiny two-bed flat above a Turkish cafe. She went to bed each night smelling cumin, lamb and lemons, listening to the jazz refrain from Ottmar's radio below. She woke to the rumble and cry of the market men surging below her window and to the sharp, pungent smell of vegetables beginning to decay.

At seven o'clock most mornings of the week she would make the walk to buy a small bag of fruit for her breakfast. Past the Punjab India restaurant, where the smell of flatbread was just starting to escape the ovens. Past the vegetable warehouses with their arching, pale stone frontages. Past the emerald green face of Ellen Keeley the barrow maker. Past the dirty oxblood tiles of the tube station where Neal Street ended and James Street began. Past Floral Street where the market boys drank away their wages and down, down, down to the Garden. Covent Garden: once the convent garden. Now so full of sin and earth and humanity. Still a garden really, after all these years.

The roads around it were virtually impassable most mornings, a deadly tangle of horses, dogs, cars and old men whose thick woollen cardigans padded out their frames until they looked like overstuffed rag dolls with pale, needle-pricked faces. Men who pulled great barrows – like floats from a medieval carnival – piled with sweet-corn and plums, leeks and potatoes and fat red cabbages that gleamed and glistened like blood-coloured gems. Men who balanced on their heads thirty crates of lavender that swayed and bowed as they walked and left the perfume trail of distant fields everywhere they went. Covent Garden, so sensual and unkempt: a temple to something, though no one could tell you quite what. Money. Nature. London. Anna sometimes thought that it acted like a city gate, announcing London's size and grandiosity to all who visited there. Look at us, it said, look what it takes to feed us all. How mighty we must be when roused. How indomitable.

Through the garden and into the house she went. Into the vaulted space of the indoor market and through the crush of tweed jackets and donkey jackets and macs.

'Sorry, love.' 'Mind yourself.' 'MUSTARD GREENS!'

In this world of men a woman's voice could become lost, clambering high and low to find its place between the layers of bass and tenor sound. 'Black— Goose— App—.' The syllables of the woman in the dark red pinafore were eaten by the whole, swallowed down like soup in this dark, confusing dragon's belly of a place. Anna handed the woman her pennies and the woman gave her a paper bag of blackberries in return. How strange, Anna thought it was, to pay for blackberries when she had gone every September as a child to the railway cutting at the bottom of town to fill her skirt for free.

'Everything can be given a price if someone chooses,' her mother said. 'It doesn't have to make sense to us, Anna. So little of the world makes sense.'

Back home in the little flat, she shared her early-morning rituals with an improbably blonde American called Kelly Gollman who worked as a dancer in a revue bar in Soho and who rented the better of the two bedrooms from Leonard Fleet, Anna's boss who lived in the flat above.

Anna had never seen Kelly dance and Kelly was careful never to ask her if she might one day come into the club. Both had the uneasy feeling that they were not on the same level as the other: Kelly taking her clothes off for boozy businessmen and Anna carrying clothes and cups of lemon tea for proper actresses in a theatre with dark gold cupids above the door. Anna had the kind of job that one could tell one's parents about *and* she was English *and* she had a leather-bound copy of Shakespeare on her bedside table.

Sometimes, if Anna was home late or Kelly early, they would meet in the little kitchen and make toast together at midnight. Anna would compliment Kelly on her clothes and her hair and her tiny waist and Kelly would laugh and demur and enjoy it all immensely. In the early days of living together Kelly had gone out of her way to compliment Anna in return, but since she found Anna's way of dressing rather severe all she could find to talk about was books.

'You must have read so many books. I see those library copies coming and going off the table and I … I can't imagine.'

And Anna would smile modestly and nod. 'I'm easily bored.'

'I'm sure I haven't read a book since school. I just can't get through twenty pages without wanting to throw it out the window and do something more fun.'

Anna would shrug and smile. 'It's not for everyone.'

Kelly stopped mentioning the books. She stopped commenting on Anna's cleverness. She smiled and nodded but often her eyes were cold and still. She did not trust Anna – quiet, bookish Anna – and she did not want to be friends with someone she didn't trust.

Anna was not overly sorry when Kelly withdrew from her attempts at friendship. She had dreaded having to share a flat with someone who would try and drag her out at all hours of the day and night, try to feed her drinks or marijuana and suggest they double-date with this man or that, his friend and his other friend. Men were obstacles to progress, the murderers of time and intellect. Anna did not do men, not in the romantic way at least.

The Turkish cafe two floors below their flat was the same cafe that Anna had waitressed in from the ages of twenty-three to twenty-six. She had, when she first arrived in London, worked as a receptionist in Forest Hill and before that she had lived in Birmingham while she trained as a secretary. Before that had been school somewhere, though no one was ever quite sure where. Anna's accent was obstinately RP. Ottmar Alabora, the manager of the coffee shop, had always meant to pin Anna down on where exactly it was that she came from, but somehow the moment always eluded him, or he would get her on to the subject and then she'd be called away to service and he didn't like to seem insistent. He tried not to pay too much attention to any of his waitresses, but particularly not to Anna.

'We don't need another waitress,' his wife Ekin had told him when she caught him, in Anna's first week, ordering a new uniform from Denny's.

'We're struggling in the evenings. You're not there. And then I was thinking of putting more tables outside in summer. If you don't serve people they walk away. Or leave without paying.'

'But it's November. Who's going to sit outside our cafe now?'

'She's a nice girl. She's starting on evenings. You'll like her. If you don't like her we'll let her go.'

So Ekin came and sat in the corner of the restaurant and watched Anna work. She had a nice way with people – Ekin could see that. She was attractive but not in a blousy way. She wore her skirt at the knee and her sleeves below her elbows. Her long hair hung in pigtails and she wore no make-up. When she served Ekin her coffee and cake she smiled and thanked her for the position. Ekin turned to look through the hatch at Ottmar, who raised his eyebrows at her. Ekin made a face, but only to let him know she wasn't angry. Anna was nice enough; she could stay.

All the same Ottmar carried around a secret shame. He had offered Anna the job in a moment of temporary madness.

She had come in one Tuesday at half past one in her best suit and had ordered coffee – Turkish coffee – which she drank without sugar. She had carried with her a copy of the book she had treated herself to from the basement of a Charing Cross bookshop and Ottmar had read over her shoulder words he loved though hardly knew in English.

> *'Oh, come with old Khayyám, and leave the Wise*
> *To talk; one thing is certain, that Life flies;*
> *One thing is certain, and the Rest is Lies;*
> *The Flower that once has blown for ever dies.'*

Anna sat quietly, politely, as he read aloud from her book and then she turned and smiled at him and he felt unutterably foolish. He cleared her plate, though he never normally waited on the tables, and then he begged her pardon.

'I got … I got carried away. Not so many people read poetry.'

'Even here?' she asked.

'In my coffee house?'

'In London. In Covent Garden. I thought it would have been full of poets.'

'If it is they are not coming into my coffee house. London is full of …' Ottmar waved his hands, tipping the spoon from Anna's saucer. He bent down to retrieve it from under a table then knelt for a moment on the tiled floor. He looked up at Anna and she stared back at him. 'London is full of … hare-brained people. Chancers. Gamblers. Opium fiends.' He laughed to himself at his own exaggeration.

'You make it sound Victorian.'

'Do I?'

'Like something out of Conan Doyle.'

'I don't—'

'He wrote Sherlock Holmes.'

'*The Hound of the Baskervilles.*'

'That kind of thing.'

'My uncle read me Omar Khayyám. In Arabic. Not Turkish or even English. I tried so hard to understand it. I would ask him what it all meant but he always said the pleasure was in the finding out … the discovery. He said you can keep some poems by you your whole life and they will only reveal parts of themselves to you when you are ready to hear them. So at twenty I would understand one little part of it and then at forty something else. I'm probably not making any sense.'

'Not at all. You're making lots of sense. I think … I think that would make me impatient. I don't want to understand poetry when I'm fifty. I want to understand it now. What if I don't make it to fifty? Do I have to be cheated out of all that understanding?'

Ottmar smiled apologetically. 'I think perhaps you do. We can only grow old in days and weeks and months. There is not a short cut. Nobody can know the world at fifteen.'

'When I was at school it used to drive me up the wall listening to the teachers go on about the folly of youth. If someone is ugly you don't say to them: "Hey you, stop being ugly over there!" so why is it okay to mock the young for being inexperienced?'

'I was not meaning to mock you, miss!'

'No! Sorry. I didn't mean you were. I meant that it sometimes feels hard to be young when no one has a good word to say about youth.'

Ottmar set down her cup and saucer. He frowned at someone out of her line of sight. 'If we are grumpy it is because we had to leave the party and you are still there.'

'And the party is a stupid party?'

Ottmar laughed. 'Yes. A very stupid party. Very loud and drunken and disgusting.' His eyes crinkled in all directions. 'But so much fun!'

Anna laughed and Ottmar felt his heart glow in his chest.

'Will you have anything else, miss? We have cake. We have sweets. We have baklava.'

Anna held her book at arm's length and glared at it. 'I spent my lunch money on something else to cheer me up. But your coffee was wonderful.'

'Why do you need cheering up? Is it a stupid boy?'

'A stupid boy of fifty.'

'Too old for you. Forget him.'

'I was called to interview at Jamiesons on Waldorf Street. And I borrowed five pounds from my landlady to buy this suit because it said: "Professional position. Business attire is requisite." But when I got there, there were fifteen girls in the waiting room and I had hardly sat down when Mr Jamieson said: "You mustn't be too disappointed. We had no idea we'd be so popular." And that was that. With lunch and fares I'm out by six pounds and five shillings and I can't conjure that kind of money out of the air.'

'You need a job?'

'I only have a short-term contract and it's almost over.'

'We have a job.'

'Do you?'

'Waitressing. It's not professional, I'm afraid. I'm not sure what you'd do with the suit.'

'I don't mind. I mean, I have waitressed before. How many days would you want me?'

'All week. Six days. You could start this weekend. In the evenings. If that was convenient.'

'That would be very convenient. My name is Anna. And thank you so much.'

'I think you should have some baklava to celebrate.'

'I'm sorry. I've nothing left to spend.'

'It's on the house,' said Ottmar expansively. 'Our waiters eat for free.'

This was not strictly true.

* * *

Anna caught the bus from Forest Hill to Cambridge Circus every evening at 5 p.m. She worked from 6 p.m. until 11 p.m. and then stayed on until midnight helping to clean up and tidy and sitting around with the other waiters and waitresses playing pontoon for matchsticks and drinking the ends of bottles. Then she walked down to Trafalgar Square and sat for an hour in a shelter on the east side near St Martin-in-the-Fields waiting for a night bus to take her near to home. She became fascinated by the statue of Edith Cavell and would stand at the base of it in the freezing cold of a December morning, looking up.

Patriotism is not enough. I must have no hatred or bitterness for anyone.

Sometimes those words made her cry. The tears would come uncontrollably and they would not stop. And in those moments Anna found forgiveness and it made her free. But they were only moments. Forgiveness is a hard thing to hang on to.

The Deplorable Word

Monday, 8 November

Orla Hayes climbed the stairs and pulled on a jumper and another pair of socks. She put her head round the door of Gracie's little room and pulled the quilt and sheet and blanket up to her chin. She stood for a moment looking down at Gracie's fat, beautiful face; listening to the sound of the breath that came through lips slightly parted; allowing her hand to brush strands of dark hair away from her closed eyes. Nothing on earth must be allowed to disturb Gracie, for if Gracie was fine then so was all the world.

She left her little one sleeping and crept downstairs to turn off the fire, though it was only ten o'clock and the nights were becoming bitterly cold. Her fingers were tingling now and her nose and the tips of her toes. She had wanted another hour of light and reading or else to darn Gracie's socks before she went to bed but the cold was going to be too much for her.

She pulled the blue-flowered quilt out of its cubbyhole and made the sofa into a bed, arranging her cushions as she always did. She briefly lit the gas and warmed half a cup of milk, which she mixed with sugar and drank down straight. Then she ran to get warm while the effects of the milk could still be felt and pulled the quilt right up to her eyes. The window in the kitchen whistled and shook in the wind. Brennan was late home tonight and she wanted to be asleep when he came in.

She must have been lying there more than an hour when she heard his keys rattling against the door. Then a click and a scrape of wood and brush against the floor and a gust of cold blew across her face and fingers. The door shut again with a soft crunch.

Brennan Hayes paused for a minute, standing on the mat, listening to the silence in the flat. Then he crept into the kitchen, poured water into a glass, left his boots by the understairs cupboard and softly plodded up towards his bed. Orla listened to him do this just as she had done on hundreds of other nights and she waited for him to speak to her, though this he never did.

The little carriage clock ticked on the windowsill in the darkness. She guessed it was nearly midnight; he was rarely home earlier than half past eleven these days. In six hours Gracie would be awake, sitting on her mother's stomach, poking her awake and she would grudgingly agree to light the fire again and make them both tea and porridge and the radio would be playing 'Make It Easy on Yourself', which always made Orla want to cry. And after seven he would come downstairs, washed and shaved and in his smart, clean uniform and he would drink a cup of tea at the kitchen table while Gracie told him some crazy story about monsters and eyes and tigers walking her to the shops and then he would kiss his daughter on the forehead and say goodbye and he would be out of their lives again for another fifteen hours or months or even years … because in every real sense he had been cut adrift and it was she who had done the cutting.

Tuesday, 9 November

At twenty past seven Brennan Hayes walked out of the house, squeezing the door closed behind him. He could still just feel the warmth of Gracie's head where he had kissed her. The sky was dark grey and rain spotted his uniform. He turned north onto Finsbury Square and then headed west towards Smithfield Market. Fleet Street. The Strand. Charing Cross Road. Leicester Square. Piccadilly Circus. Savile Row. And at the end of it all – at the end of the road crossings and the grey-suited shuffle and the noise of angry bus drivers and the taste of petrol on his tongue and the spiky cold air of a London morning which thrilled him and froze him in equal measure – at the end of it all lay a different name, a different voice and a different life.

* * *

'Excuse me. My name is Anna Treadway. I've been called in for an interview at eleven.'

The desk sergeant continued to stare at her sleepily. Anna felt compelled to continue but couldn't think what else to say.

'Shall I go and sit over there?' she asked, nodding to a wooden bench by the door.

The desk sergeant frowned for a moment, as if this was a truly ingenious question to ask. Then he looked her in the eye as if seeing her for the first time: 'Yes.'

Anna retreated gratefully and sat down, squeezing herself to the very edge of the bench – against the armrest – in case some strange or large or terrifying other should arrive at any moment and be told to sit with her.

Iolanthe had been missing for ten days and Anna could not shake the feeling that not enough was being done to find her. She'd been all over the fronts of the papers for a few days, and posters had appeared on the lamp posts asking for information, and Anna had found herself thinking how ridiculous it all was, and what a waste that Lanny wasn't here to enjoy all the fuss. But then the boy had been injured in Golden Square, the headlines had changed and she hadn't seen or heard from a policeman in over a week until the call last night.

She thought about Lanny's story of her father, her mother and then her brother dying. She was the very last of her little family. Surely she was meant to carry on – to have children, even. Iolanthe was forty but it might still be possible. If she met someone soon she could have the chance of a child. Maybe she could adopt. She had asked Lanny once about men: was there anyone, was there someone back home in the States?

'I've never been a great one for relationships. And I'm not too good at sex and nothing else. I grew up really fast, really young.

25

Went straight over that drippy crush stage and into the cold, hard world. Men are dangerous, Anna, you never know what they're really thinking.'

'I suppose. I'm not any good at relationships either. I quite like having my own life.'

'That's it. That's it exactly. I have my life.'

'Miss Treadway? Is it miss?' A tall man carrying a bunch of folders under one arm was calling her from across the hallway. She raised her hand, nerves rendering her momentarily dumb. The red-haired policeman advanced on her with an outstretched hand: 'Good morning, miss. I am Detective Sergeant Barnaby Hayes. We're in interview room four. Would you follow me, please?'

Anna followed Hayes along a beige corridor and then another. In the distance she could hear the murmur and rattle of a works canteen, but for the most part the station was oddly silent. Voices murmured and muttered behind half-closed doors; file drawers squeaked and rolled in and out in offices as they passed.

'Here we are.' Hayes knocked on the door and when no reply came back they entered. The room was windowless, but held a table and three chairs. The walls were painted pistachio green and the floor was black linoleum.

'Cup of tea?' Hayes asked.

'Yes. Please. Milk, no sugar. No, actually, sorry … sugar please. Two.'

'It's comforting, isn't it?' Hayes smiled at her. 'June!' he cried down the corridor and a door somewhere unseen opened.

'Yes, Sarge, what'll it be?' a voice came back.

'Two teas for interview room four, please. Normal for me. Milk and two for the young lady.'

'Your wish is my command.' Hayes shut the door.

Sergeant Hayes spread the folders out in front of him and pulled out half a dozen forms and bits of paper.

'Now, I wanted to go back over your statement and then I also wanted to ask you about this interview. The one from *The Times*.'

'I was there for that. I was in the room.'

Hayes blinked at Anna with a look that signalled genuine interest. 'Right. Well … First things first. Would you describe Iolanthe Green as a stable person, Miss Treadway?'

'Define stable.'

'Really?'

'I mean, how stable is stable? She was stable enough … in the grand scheme of things. But she was human. I mean, she was a bit highly strung and a bit, um, prone to moodiness. But then, when I say these things sitting in an interview room, they suddenly sound much more serious, much more terrible, than I think they are. She was … there's no good way I can put this … she was female and she had female insecurities and she was an actress and she had those insecurities too but that makes it sound like I'm trying to say she was mad when really I just think she was rather ordinary.'

'So, you're saying she was essentially ordinary?'

'Yes. Ordinary woman. Ordinary hang-ups. Ordinary … intelligence. You know, Sergeant …'

'Hayes, miss.'

'You know, Sergeant Hayes, actors and actresses are very, very ordinary people. They do a job and half the time the people around them yelp like castrated cats, howl with pleasure and tell them that they are the saviours of the world. But most of them, the ones who don't let the publicity drive them mad, know that they are very ordinary people, with a basic technical ability: like a plumber or a welder. Except that half the world has decided that this type of welding is akin to performing miracles.

'Iolanthe wasn't clever. Not book clever, I mean. But she wasn't stupid either. She knew that what she was involved in was a kind of popular conjuring trick. And she knew that her career would be finite and that she had to make the best of it and save for the future. She didn't spend her money on fancy things. The Savoy gave her that room for publicity. She was sent clothes by department stores and designers. She wore costume jewellery and never caught a cab if she could help it. She told me once that she had been born into poverty and had half a mind that she would die that way too. She took her money and she sent it back home. Every month, every shilling she could spare, she squirrelled it away somewhere.'

There was a knock and Hayes rose to let in June, who was carrying two cups and saucers.

''Bout time too,' he noted drily.

'Up your bottom, Sarge,' said June, winking at Anna, who was slightly outraged at this piece of rudeness in such an austere setting.

As June shut the door behind her Hayes started to arrange the papers into a chequerboard in front of him.

'You spoke about Miss Green sending money home to be deposited. And we have talked with Miss Green's agent in New York and with their in-house accountant who very kindly gave us select details of the accounts Miss Green deposited her earnings into. Now I don't have a record of amounts but I do know that over the years Miss Green deposited money into a series of accounts with a variety of names attached to them. We have three accounts in the name of Iolanthe Green. One account in the name of Yolanda Green. Two accounts in the name of Nathaniel Green. And one account in the name of Maria Green. Would you happen to know anything about these other names, Miss Treadway?'

'Well, Nathaniel was her brother but she said … I heard her say that he died in '45 or '46. Just after the war … in Japan. He had a car accident.'

'And yet he has two savings accounts still open. One held at a bank in Boston and the second at a bank in Annapolis, Maryland. Any ideas?'

'None. She always said she had no family … Her mother and her father died in the forties or late thirties and her brother died just after. There wasn't anyone else … though I suppose aunts and uncles?'

'Her agents knew nothing about her wider family, it seems. They only have addresses and phone numbers for Iolanthe herself. They never met anyone else from her family. Though we have to suppose, given the shared surnames, that all these people belong to the same family. In the interview she said she came from Cork.'

'Her grandparents came from Cork. She'd never been there. I never saw a card or a letter in the dressing room that looked like it came from family … I mean, she got them from fans, from other actors, from her agency, from the studios she'd worked with …'

'Did you notice anything which might suggest that she was in contact with people in Ireland? Did she want to visit Ireland? We're wondering if … well, sometimes people find themselves under pressure and they run. We're wondering if Miss Green might have run away to Ireland.'

'To be honest she'd never mentioned the place. Not before the interview.'

Hayes smiled and changed the subject. 'I gather she was a big star but I have to confess I'd never heard of her. Perhaps I recognised her face …'

'She is a star … of a sort. She's had top billing in at least one film. But she isn't Julie Andrews or Elizabeth Taylor. And she probably made it too late. If you're a woman you have to make it at twenty and then stay there and even then … It's a very uncertain business. My theatre manager, Leonard, he says she's got maybe another three years in pictures and then she'll need a stage career. That's why her agent wanted her to do this play.'

'Was she depressed about all this? About the uncertainty of it all?'

'She never said she was. She always seemed very philosophical about it. She just wanted to work. I mean, she worried about money. She always worried about money.'

'This interview she gave … have you read the transcript? I mean the bit they printed in the paper.'

'Not really. I was there for nearly all of it and it rather annoyed me. The way they printed it after they knew she was missing.'

Hayes drew out a newspaper cutting.

'I'm going to read from it. I want you to tell me if anything might have been left out, or added, or if there's anything you don't remember her saying … Okay. There's a load of silliness at the beginning: "lies back on her green velvet chaise longue", "tale of heartbreak and longing", blah blah blah. Then it begins. "*Wuthering Heights* was my big break, though. It really made my name. From my humble beginnings among the Boston Irish I could never have imagined I'd be so successful in Hollywood. California seemed like another planet, not where a girl of my humble origins belonged at all." How does it sound so far?'

'Well, the gist of it makes sense. I don't remember Iolanthe saying it quite like that and he's leaving out a lot. But it's sort of rightish.'

'Okay. She goes on: "In many ways I'm doing all of this for my little brother Nate. He was killed in Japan at the end of the war and it broke all our hearts. My poor mother never got over the shock of losing him. By the age of twenty-one I was all alone in the world." Okay?'

'I'm pretty sure her mother died before her brother did. The chronology's wrong.'

'Anything surprising?'

'Not really.'

'"I ask Miss Green about her connections with Ireland. 'My grandfather's family – the Callaghans – claimed to have pledged allegiance long ago to Perkin Warbeck when he made his claim to the English throne. And I like to think that a piece of that rebel heart lived on in all of us, helping us to fight a little harder for the things we believe in.'" How's that?'

'I can't imagine Iolanthe knowing who Perkin Warbeck was. But … I don't know. They did talk about Ireland. And I was cleaning things and moving around. Maybe I wasn't paying enough attention.'

'It goes on: "I ask Miss Green what she's enjoying most about her time in London. 'Oh, James, it's hard to choose. I've lived in Boston and New York and Los Angeles but there's something really special about London. Some magic ingredient. I think it's the coming together of so many different, vibrant people all in one spot. I've loved the parties I've been invited to here: at Ronnie Scott's, the Marquee and the Flamingo. The music you have in England is amazing. I think there's something in the Celtic heart that responds to that beating of drums, that essential rhythm of the night.' I tell her that our diarist was thrilled to spot her coming in and out of Roaring Twenties on Carnaby Street on several nights last week, but Miss Green just blushes and stands to fix her make-up. She has another show to do. I let her rebel heart prepare."'

'Yuck.'

'Well, yes. But is it accurate?'

'I've no idea. I didn't know Iolanthe went to clubs. As far as I was concerned she was trotting off back to The Savoy every night at eleven. I don't … I'm sorry. I can't honestly say that she didn't mention this because I might have missed it, but it doesn't bear much resemblance to the conversation I heard.'

Barnaby Hayes stared down at the clipping in front of him and wrinkled his brow.

'Is that helpful?' Anna asked.

Hayes looked up at her and smiled a smile of frustration. 'Well, it's all helpful if it's true, isn't it?'

'Is it, though? Does it get you any closer to what happened to her?'

'The thing about truth, Miss Treadway, is that it's not always the friend of narrative. My job is to figure out your friend, Miss Green, and to construct a likely narrative that will help us to determine if she left of her own free will or was taken. And there are two ways I can go about this. I can invent a number of plausible narratives and try and hold them up against the facts until I find the one that fits. Or I can listen to all the facts – with no particular narrative in mind – and then assemble the known knowns in such a way that they reveal the basic truth of the matter.

'And I have to tell you that in my experience the human brain only wants to do the former. It wants to think like a scientist. Hypothesis. Experiment. Results. It doesn't want to look at all the facts in all the world and wait for a pattern to emerge. Because that is a ridiculously hard thing to do. It's the sort of thing that only geniuses can achieve. Normal people need a narrative. And currently your Miss Green refuses to offer much of one.'

'Why do women usually go missing?'

'Because their husbands beat them. Or they have affairs and decide to run away. Some of them are murdered. But not many. Mostly it's violence. At home.'

Anna watched Hayes scanning the pieces of paper and was briefly jealous of the job he did. She couldn't remember the last time she'd been asked to use her mind for anything much at all beyond the dressing and undressing of actresses.

Hayes sighed. 'Let's go back to the names. Yolanda, Nathaniel, Maria. We know Nathaniel was the brother. Killed in Japan. Yolanda and Maria?'

'Well, one of them must be the mother. Or an aunt.'

'But if they're dead …'

'… then why is she giving them her money?'

'Unless it's just tax avoidance.' Hayes shook his head then he looked Anna hard in the eye. 'You talked to Iolanthe more than most, didn't you?'

'Probably. At work anyway.'

He tore a piece of paper off the bottom of one of his notes and wrote down two numbers on it.

'This one's work. This one's home. If you think of something; doesn't matter what. Ireland. Names. Clubs. Money. Men. Will you call me? Please? I would like to find her alive.'

Anna took the slip of paper and filed it in the pocket of her handbag. Then they sat for a moment in the silence of the room, looking at each other. It occurred to Anna that there was an odd kind of intimacy to a police interview. She couldn't remember the last time she'd been alone in a room with a man, certainly not a man who looked to be the same age as she was.

Hayes gave her a slightly embarrassed smile. 'I hope we find her,' he said. And then he stood and almost seemed to be bowing but offered her his hand instead. Anna took it and shook it and wished that her own wasn't so slippery.

'It was nice to meet you, Sergeant Hayes.'

'And you, Miss Treadway.' Hayes opened the door to let her out into the corridor.

* * *

On Sun Street, Orla and Gracie made oatmeal biscuits because having the oven on made the kitchen warm and then Gracie drank milk at the table and drew a monster in blue and purple crayon with eyelashes that licked the edges of the page. Orla made them toast and beans for lunch and drank cup after cup of tea to ease the passing of the hours.

After lunch they bundled up in everything woolly they owned and went to watch the trains in Liverpool Street station. When Orla had the money she would treat Gracie to a cup of hot chocolate from the buffet or a tube of fruit pastilles from W. H. Smith. In leaner months she would pack a little picnic of biscuits or butter sandwiches and they would wait for a bench to perch on and play I Spy and Twenty Questions and Botticelli – the characters in the latter taken entirely from the pages of children's books, for Gracie only knew the worlds of Andersen and Grimm and Lewis.

'Are you a princess but only after marriage?'

Gracie thought about this. 'No,' she said at last, 'I'm not Cinderella.'

'Are you furry and mistaken for a witch?'

'What's that?' Gracie frowned at her mother as if Orla was being grown up and clever just to annoy her. 'I don't know.'

'The cat. Musicians of Bremen. The robbers think she's a witch. I've got a proper question! Are you royal?'

'Yes,' said Gracie with a haughty arch of one eyebrow, 'I'm a queen.'

'Of course. Okay, okay. Did you send your neighbour a little gift which could have doomed him?'

Gracie blinked and stared out towards the chuffing, chugging, waiting, steaming trains and watched the great black hands of the great white clock sweep round. Orla felt a pang of regret that she had made the question so hard because she could feel sadness leaking out of her daughter. Was she – as a mother – meant to coddle her daughter or challenge her? She never really knew for sure, so in her own haphazard way she would do first one then the other, just as she felt inclined at that moment in time.

'I don't know,' Gracie said in a very small voice.

'Sorry. Was that mean? I'm the Emperor of Japan with his mechanical nightingale.'

'Okay,' said Gracie, clearly fizzing with annoyance. 'Have another question.'

'Are you queen of a dying world?'

Gracie fixed Orla with a long, withering look. 'Yes, clever Mummy. I am Queen Jadis and you win ...' she threw her arms up towards the ceiling, 'everything.'

'You're really narked with me, aren't you?' said Orla.

'You make it too hard. I'm *four*.'

'I know. Mammy knows.'

'You shouldn't make me cross.'

'Shouldn't I?'

'I can make the world blow up.'

'Really? And how do you do that?'

'I say the deplorable word.'

'Well, you should do it. Go on, Gracie, blow it all to bits. Just tell Mammy one thing first. What is it?'

'Bum,' said Gracie. 'Bum is the deplorable word.' And she held her mother's stare for half a minute until Orla's face cracked into a bright-toothed smile.

The men in their camel-coloured coats swept past and the trains honked and blew out steam that seemed to scorch the cold air above their heads. Mother and daughter held hands and watched all the people in the world pass by, aware only of the features and topography of their strange and dazzling bubble life together.

Not Going Out

At half past ten Rachel brought the remaining customers their bills on little silver plates with tiny pieces of Turkish delight around the edges. At ten to eleven Ottmar turned on the main lights in the coffee house, flooding the space with a harsh yellow glow. By five past eleven the bills had been paid and Ottmar was ready to lock the doors.

Rachel and Helen cleared the tables, blew out the candles, stacked the plates by the sink and started to sweep and scrub the restaurant clean. In the kitchen Mahmut scoured the surfaces and washed down the hob. Ottmar brought the radio up to the hatch and tuned to the Light Programme for the last hour of Jazz Club. All but one of the overhead lights was turned off and the cafe sank back into a gentle night-time space where the silver mirrors on the walls threw strange shafts of light across the floor and the ghostly, mesmeric sound of Stan Tracey playing 'Starless and Bible Black' seemed to echo, bounce and flutter against every wall. The people in the cafe moved slower now, feeling the night soaking into them, filling their arms and legs with darkness and a dreamy quiet that felt like drunkenness and sleep.

Ottmar sat on a stool at the counter behind the hatch and arranged in a series of little metal bowls a late supper of eggs and flatbread and spinach and yoghurt. He cut up the end of the coffee cake and arranged a pyramid of squares on a blue china plate and then he carried the plates and the forks and the dishes of food and laid them out on two of the longer tables which he pushed together.

He noticed a blank, black human shape standing at the glass doors to the front.

'Helen!' Ottmar called and Helen let Anna in. Ottmar waved his hand for Anna to join him at the table as the others cleaned and swept around him. Anna pulled off her coat and gloves and scarf and flung them down over the back of a chair.

'How are you doing today?' Ottmar asked.

The question made Anna want to cry, though she didn't really know why. 'I went to look for her.'

'For Iolanthe?'

'I walked the Strand and the banks of the river … past The Savoy. I looked for her in St Paul's Cathedral. I had this sense of her seeking refuge from something. I walked in there and I started to believe that I would see her sitting at the end of a pew or hiding in the shadows. But once I'd looked around it didn't feel like somewhere where anyone would go seeking refuge. So much grandeur. So much pomp and frilly woodwork, lights and gold. It looked like a theatre. And that's the last place Lanny would run.'

'You're sure she ran away?' Helen asked her.

'I have to believe it.'

'From what, though?'

'From us?' Anna shrugged. 'I don't know. Money trouble.'

'Men,' said Rachel.

Anna shook her head. 'I went to meet a policeman today and he asked me questions and he showed me the interview Lanny did and it's full of mistakes so I don't even know if we can trust it but it said she'd been going out to the clubs. Like the jazz clubs and the ones down Carnaby Street.'

'Does that seem likely?' Ottmar asked.

'Not really. She never even talked about clubs or music or men or any of that. But then the man from the paper claimed that she'd been seen coming out of Roaring Twenties more than once.'

Helen and Rachel threw their rags and brushes into the corner of the kitchen, stripped off their aprons and used the edges to scrub the smell and slick of grease from their hands. Mahmut brought out a pot of coffee and a bowl of sugar and sat at the end of the table slapping his face violently with his hands as if to beat out the tiredness. The music from the radio changed and now the notes rippled through the air like the smell of grass on a clear spring day. The lights seemed to burn a little brighter above them and slowly, imperceptibly, the pace of their movements changed. Anna poured herself a cup of coffee and ate a plate of spinach and yoghurt, which tasted like midsummer and helped to draw the chill from her bones.

Ottmar's mind drifted free of the assembled group and took him back to Melanippus's vast living room in Nicosia with its white marble floor and long dark leather seats. In a former life he'd written book reviews for a Greek magazine in his native Cyprus. The only Turk on the staff, he'd spent his evenings smoking cigarettes and talking about art and philosophy and life with all the other twenty-somethings who dreamed of flying away to a life of avant-garde delights in Paris or Berlin. Melanippus, the editor, would play jazz until four in the morning: Duke Ellington, Count Basie, Artie Shaw. Ottmar had so desperately wanted to belong and for a little while he had. And now, here in his cafe at midnight with The Harry South Big Band playing 'Six to One Bar', he knew that he was not quite locked out of that world; just downgraded to a cheaper room.

Anna had sunk into a kind of sulk. Her broad shoulders fell forward and she stared at the corner of the table while her fingers worked apart a piece of bread. 'It's too strange, Ottmar. We talked every day. But then I think about the things we talked about and there's her clothes and her looks and we joked about men and people in the company but she never told me anything about ... before. Where she came from. Everything was always in the present. She never mentioned family. She never mentioned her past.'

Ottmar made a slight face as if to say that Iolanthe was not the only one. Anna chose to ignore this. 'She had all these bank accounts in different names. Maria and Yolanda and Nathaniel. Nathaniel, her brother, isn't even alive any more – but she's paying money to him all the same.'

Ottmar frowned. 'You mean Iolanthe?'

'What?'

'You said Yolanda.'

'Well, yes. She was Iolanthe but she paid money into the bank account of a woman called Yolanda Green.'

'But they're the same name. Iolanthe is a Greek name, yes? But in Spain, she'd be Yolanda. Iolanthe; Yolanda: same name.'

'Oh.' Anna was taken aback by her own ignorance. 'I didn't realise. I … Thank you.' She stared at Ottmar and he couldn't quite read the emotion in her look. 'I went to the police station today and it felt real again. And I realised that all those stories, all those articles and interviews, they'd turned this thing – Lanny's disappearance – into something else. They took it over. Made it unreal. I'd come to feel that Iolanthe belonged to some other world. A world of newspapers and radio. Almost as if she wasn't real. Wasn't our problem. But she is real. And she is our problem. She was this person that I knew and liked … and something horrible has happened to her.'

*   *   *

Anna dreamed that night that she was standing on the Strand in the darkness. A line of red double-decker buses queued on the other side of the Aldwych, their windows dark. She knew she had to get home but she couldn't remember where it was she lived. Forest Hill? No, that had been years ago. Where did she live now? She tried to call up the name of the roads she'd lived on. Aberystwyth Close. Horns Lane. Bearwood Road. Havelock Walk. None of these seemed right. A figure approached out of the darkness. It was a man. A policeman. But his uniform was strange: a black suit with a mandarin collar and bright buttons down the front. He wore a peaked cap with a badge she did not recognise and carried a thin black stick. When he opened his mouth to speak she expected to hear a language other than English pass his lips.

'I think the buses have stopped for the night now, miss.'

Anna peered at his face, which was hard to see, and shifted rather from glance to glance. He had red hair like that young man she had met … she couldn't quite think where.

'There are night buses. I always used to catch the night bus,' she assured him in as definite a voice as she could manage.

'Where to, miss?'

'I can't remember. I'm so sorry. I can't remember where I live.'

The policeman smiled at her. 'Well, how do you imagine you'll get home if you don't know where it is you're going?'

The next moment they were standing together just north of St Martin's near where she used to wait for her bus to Forest Hill. Anna felt an odd sensation of pinching in the palm of her right hand and looking down, she realised with horror that she was holding hands with the policeman. She pulled away quickly, though he seemed unwilling to let her go.

'I'm sorry,' she told him. 'I'm so sorry. I have to get my bus.'

She walked north up Charing Cross Road without once looking back, but she found then that her stop had vanished and with it the statue of Edith Cavell. Anna stood in the spot where Edith's monolith should have been and then gazed warily up at the sky in case perhaps the statue had been rocketed into space and would descend again at any moment, crushing her where she stood. Fifty yards away the policeman raised his hand and waved to her as if to attract her attention to some new emergency. He seemed to be calling to her and Anna strained to make out the words.

'Your bus is coming, miss!'

Anna turned and there it was, a great red metal tower charging onto the pavement towards her as she stood watching, paralysed, already doomed.

Anna woke, the sheet around her clammy with sweat. She untangled herself and got out of bed. There was a thunder of feet coming down the stairs outside the flat and Anna could hear Leonard's voice speaking quickly and urgently. The footsteps passed by and she stood for a minute in the dark living room listening for what came next. The street outside was quiet; no traffic on Shaftesbury Avenue at this time. Footsteps climbed the stairs again and paused for a moment outside the door of the flat.

'Leonard?' Anna spoke his name almost without meaning to.

'Anna?'

She fetched a dressing gown from the back of her door and pulled it tight around her. Leonard stood on the stairs outside the door dressed only in pyjama bottoms, his hair sweeping madly to one side, his eyes bloodshot.

'What happened?' Anna asked.

'Benji's sister's sick. We've been up for the last hour trying to call people and now he's gone to find a cab. Can I come in? No. Sorry. Scratch that. You need to get back to bed.'

'No. It's fine. I was having a rotten night anyway. What time is it?'

'It's five or half five. Do you want to come up? I've got proper coffee. Might even manage a bun.'

Anna had no great desire to sink back into her clammy bed. 'Not like there's a show tomorrow.'

'Well, quite.' And Leonard led the way.

Very Dark, the Georgians

For the first few months after Anna took the waitressing job at the Alabora she hadn't minded the toing and froing from Forest Hill to Covent Garden because it seemed romantic – London seemed romantic, with its twisting parks and grime-covered frontages; its dark-stained river flanked by rictus-mouthed fish who held with their tails a trail of softly glowing lights: the epitome of grand metropolitan strangeness. It was a shifting city of light and dark; of strange shadows cast across the Thames at twilight, of grimy dark underpasses and roads which shone like sheets of metal on a summer's day. The players in the theatre moved in packs, now lightness and colour, now darkness and gloom. Women in white and red and blue, flowing like a moving tricolour along the riverbanks and shopping streets, handbags swinging, heels clicking and clacking like discordant castanets. Then the men of the city in their work attire, the endless bowler hats, mackintoshes and dark striped suits – the extraordinary conformity of the ruling class, as if bankers and lawyers and politicians were actually some great branch of the Army or police.

After the first few months the endless travelling started to take its toll. She never got to bed before four and the bathroom above her was busy with noise by half past six – jolting her from sleep, dragging her from her bed, so that her head banged with cold and tiredness at two in the morning when the night bus was running late and her feet were aching in her broken shoes. But that was before she met Leonard.

She had just started to work lunchtimes as well as evenings at the Alabora and so had been introduced to a whole new selection of regular faces. Leonard Fleet owned the flat at the top of the building and worked in a theatre on Charing Cross Road. At least three times a week he would pop home for something or other – a book, a script, a pound for a night out – and he would use this journey as an excuse to eat lunch at the Alabora. The Alabora served a strange mixture of Turkish and English food and most lunchtimes you could choose from egg and chips, spinach and pea omelette, kiymali ispanak or kofte with simit and yoghurt. Leonard was an egg and chips kind of man – most of the customers were – but he liked the smell and sight of the Turkish food and he would drink the coffee and eat the little baklava that Ottmar always popped onto his saucer when he spotted that Leonard was in.

This particular lunchtime he was seated at the back of the restaurant, away from the draught near the door, and chatting to Ottmar through the hatch. It was February and the restaurant was only a quarter full because the wind was bitter cold and the shoppers and theatregoers were staying at home. A family came to the door, dark-haired with olive skin: Romanian perhaps or Bulgarian. There was a younger woman, an older woman and a baby in a perambulator. Ottmar hurried forward to open both the doors and let them in. The grandmother thanked him and pointed to a table where they'd all sit. The baby was tiny, maybe only two weeks old and swaddled in at least three knitted blankets against the cold. Ottmar nodded to Anna and she went to take their order.

The grandmother was the only one who spoke. The baby in the perambulator snuffled and the younger woman rubbed her still-gloved hands together and perused the table.

'Does the kiymali ispanak have lots of meat or just a very little bit?'

'I think about half and half with the spinach, ma'am.'

'Good. I will have a plate of that. And my daughter-in-law … My daughter-in-law does not like foreign food. She will have an omelette.'

At this the daughter-in-law started to protest but was quickly silenced by the older woman. 'If you eat, the milk will come.'

She shot Anna a fierce look for reasons that Anna could not discern. Anna decided to ignore it. 'And to drink?'

'A pot of tea. We will have that first, please. My daughter-in-law is freezing.'

'Of course.'

While Anna was waiting for the tea she became aware of a struggle going on at the table by the door. The younger woman was trying to stand up, presumably to leave, and the older woman was pulling and pushing her back into her seat.

Leonard leaned towards the hatch and asked Ottmar: 'What do you think they are?'

Ottmar leaned heavily over the wooden sill. 'Georgian,' he whispered. 'Very dark, the Georgians.'

Anna carried the tea over to the two women, wondering as she did so whether Ottmar had been speaking about their skin or their temperament.

The younger woman had given up on her attempts to leave and had instead shifted into the far corner of the table away from her mother-in-law. Anna set the cups and saucers down and settled the pot away from the pram. The mother-in-law reached out and touched Anna lightly on the wrist. 'Thank you, my dear. We did not mean to disturb the other customers.'

Anna refrained from pointing out that the other customers seemed to be enjoying the floor show. She simply smiled at the woman and left.

The older woman poured tea for the younger one and heaped sugar lumps into the cup, though no milk. A minute later Anna heard a cry and rushed out from the kitchen to find that the older woman had just pulled the younger woman's hand out of the cup of scalding water.

'Get her a dishcloth with cold water,' Ottmar told Anna, and she did.

At the table Anna passed the wet dishcloth to the older woman, who attempted to wrap the younger woman's hand. Anna stood across from them and moved all the scalding objects out of the way. The younger woman nodded dumbly as her hand was wrapped and then she looked up at Anna, her face streaming with tears.

43

'I am going to kill my baby.'

'Shhh. Shhh,' the older woman soothed.

Anna was surprised to hear that the younger woman had no foreign accent. Instead her voice had a soft twang of east London to it.

'If I don't stop myself I'll choke him in his sleep.'

'Shhh.'

'How old is the baby?' Anna asked.

'He is nineteen days,' the grandmother said.

'I think your daughter needs to see a doctor.'

'The doctor tells her to sleep—' the older woman started.

'But I cannot sleep,' the younger interrupted. 'If I sleep, the dreams come.'

'I knew a girl once,' Anna said, 'I knew a girl who was very young and when the baby came it seemed to make her mad. But she was not mad before.'

'I know,' the older woman told her, 'I know of such things happening but we cannot make it stop. She will not feed him. She will not eat. She says she's going to kill him if I leave them alone.'

'Then you cannot leave her,' Anna said.

The older woman's eyes overflowed with tears. 'I will not leave her. I do not leave her any second of the day. I don't know how to make her better.'

Anna shook her head. The older woman's face contorted into something more like control. 'What happened to your friend? The young girl and the baby? Did she stay mad for ever?'

'No. She didn't. I don't remember … I only knew her for a little while. A year after the baby came I heard that she was well again. She went back home.'

'And the baby? The baby survived?'

'Well, yes. I suppose. They took him away.'

'Why did they take him away?'

'Well, she was so young, you see. They were always going to do that.'

'No father?'

'No one who wanted to be a father.'

The older woman looked gratefully at Anna, as if she were relieved simply to be spoken to.

'Would you still like me to bring your food?'

The older woman shook her head. 'I pushed her out of the house too soon. I think we need to go home.'

Ottmar and Leonard were listening from across the little room. Ottmar shook his head at the woman. 'No charge,' he called out. 'No charge.'

When they had gone Anna went and sat by Ottmar on the stools by the hatch. Ottmar introduced her to Leonard, who asked: 'What were you saying to her? You seemed to be telling her a story.'

'I knew someone ... someone else who had a baby and then went a little mad for a while. It happens. I wanted her to know it happened to other people too. Their doctor ... I don't know what you do if your doctor doesn't understand what's happening. I mean, who else do you ask?'

'God?' Leonard suggested, but he seemed to be saying this almost as a joke.

Anna looked at him carefully. He was in his forties, middling in height with dark hair and a little hint of beard and moustache. He wore a navy V-neck with a flowered shirt beneath and bottle-green cords. She could not quite place him in terms of class and station. He seemed to be something of an oddity.

'Well, I suppose if they have a god perhaps that's better than nothing,' she said at last. 'Though I don't know. Can you lean on something that offers no resistance?'

Leonard looked at Ottmar and raised his eyebrows. 'She's sharp.'

Ottmar grinned in turn at Anna. 'Our Anna is a heathen. But a very clever heathen. Very clever indeed. No time for boys, our Anna. Work and study, books and words, always in her mind. She's reading Lermontov. Very keen on Lermontov right now.'

Anna looked embarrassed. 'I do like him very much.'

'He's a poet?' Leonard asked her.

'Poetry and a novel. A very good novel. Very modern and shocking. Upsetting in the strangest way ... I could lend it to you, if you like,' Anna offered.

45

Leonard studied her face through the hatch. She had a sharp chin with full cheeks and large dark eyes. She also had what people would call a strong nose and mouth.

'You're not Russian, are you, Anna?'

'Russian! No.'

'There's something about your face. You have something … un-English about you. I was thinking Polish or German …'

'German!' Anna laughed.

'Who knows? The Germans have all evaporated. The Baumanns are Bakers and the Krugers are all Crabtrees. I mean, if you were German it's not as if you'd say …'

Anna shook her head. 'Definitely not German. My mother's family have a line of French relatives … generations back. None of us look quite the thing.'

'Well,' Leonard nodded, 'that explains it.'

Ottmar leaned through the hatch and fixed Leonard with a smirking grin.

'My dear friend Leonard …'

Leonard shot Anna a look. 'He wants something.'

'This poor young lady has to make the most terrible journey to and from my cafe every day. And I was thinking …' He trailed off hopefully.

'What? The second floor?'

'You only have one tenant.'

Leonard looked apologetically at Anna. 'The second bedroom is a shoebox. You can barely fit a bed in there. I don't even like letting it out.'

'But it would be so convenient. She would be just upstairs.'

'Do you want to live in a shoebox?' Leonard asked. And Anna thought about it. She did not relish the thought of living in a shoebox but a flat on the corner of Shaftesbury Avenue …

'What's the rent?'

'Three pounds, six shillings a week. Bills included.'

It was the same as she was paying for a room in Forest Hill but then she'd save on bus fares. 'Who would I be sharing with?'

'Well, the tenant in the main room changes. Normally I rent to actresses or dancers. I'd try not to lumber you with anyone too awful.'

Anna looked at Ottmar who was twinkling away at her expectantly. 'Okay,' she said. 'That would be most acceptable.' She offered Leonard her hand through the hatch and he stood and then bowed and then kissed it with a great flourish of gentlemanly decorum.

For the first few weeks of their acquaintance Anna couldn't tell whether Leonard was interested in her sexually or whether he simply wanted to take her under his wing. He made a fuss of her as she was moving in, bringing her little gifts and lending her clothes hangers and coffee and a table for the side of her bed. And then one morning, when she was on the way upstairs to let him know that the hob wouldn't light at all and there was something up with the gas, she found him standing at the threshold to his flat kissing an older man with slick grey hair and a banker's dark striped suit. Leonard broke away when he spotted her over his lover's shoulder and for a moment he said nothing but his eyes searched her face for clues to her reaction. Anna wasn't quite sure what to say so they stood on the stairs for a while and stared at one another.

'Good morning, Miss Treadway,' Leonard said at last.

'Good morning, Mr Fleet.'

'Can I help you?'

'There's something up with the gas. The hob won't work.'

The grey-haired man in the stripy suit smiled briefly at her. 'I'm sure Leonard can fix that for you.'

Anna nodded and shot him a brief smile back. 'I'm sure he can.' And with that she padded quietly back down the stairs.

The very next day Leonard asked Anna – for the first time – if she'd like tickets to one of the matinees at his theatre. He offered to show her round backstage afterwards and take her to tea at Bunjies if anyone was playing that afternoon.

Anna was feeling sensitive to the fact that she had, as she saw it, thrown herself on the mercy of Ottmar and Leonard. She found that it was not in her nature to trust for too long. Her temperament seemed to fall into phases, like seasons of the year. She would blossom for a little while, establish friendships and socialise and then she would retreat and regroup, becoming watchful, even fearful, for months at a time. After the great leap from the anonymity of Forest Hill to her new life in Covent Garden she was experiencing a familiar feeling of fear, a sense of foreboding that such luck and apparent serendipity would be punished by a fall from grace. Every week Leonard would offer Anna a ticket for this or that performance and every week she gently but firmly refused his offers.

One evening she was clearing up after the dinner service when Ottmar cornered her, his face clouded with signs of worry.

'Sit down,' he told her. 'We'll have a little talk.'

They took seats either side of the gingham-clothed table and Ottmar played with the rim of the salt pot.

'Did I do something wrong?' Anna asked.

'Leonard is my friend.'

'I know.'

Ottmar could not bring himself to look at her but his hand crept across the table as he spoke and he caught her fingers gently in his large and dark-haired grip. 'Do you know what he is, Anna?'

'What? Leonard? Oh! Yes. I … Yes.'

Ottmar's gaze rose gingerly until he almost met hers. 'But you would not tell on him.'

'Leonard? No. Why would I?'

'He thinks you do not like him. He is trying to be your friend. He tried to give you tickets, an afternoon out. But you will not have tea with him … Now he is afraid …'

'What? No! The one thing has nothing to do with … I didn't like to ask for time off.'

'He thinks it is because you do not approve.'

'No. I really don't care one way or … If anything it makes it easier to rent from someone, to live beneath someone, who I know is not …'

Ottmar's fingers sprang open and he withdrew his hand. He looked at the tablecloth again. 'So you will let him take you to the theatre?'

'Of course I will.'

'You can have the lunch service off. Not holiday. Just off.'

'Thank you. Ottmar ... I didn't mean to say—'

But Ottmar held up a hand and, rising from the table, pronounced, 'We are fine.'

* * *

Anna had rather hoped that she might get to go to some Shakespeare, or even Ibsen or Chekhov, but these writers were not the kind of writers to set the West End stage alight. Rather the play that Leonard got her tickets for involved a pair of newlyweds living in the house of an overbearing father and failing to consummate their marriage.

In the dress circle with the pensioners and the students Anna felt at first entranced – by the drama of the interior, the brightness of this strange world with its gilt and its velvet and its baroque loveliness. This was not the grimy air of Shaftesbury Avenue or the bus-jammed filth of Tottenham Court Road. This was like a miniature Versailles. A world of angel faces, ribbons and masks; opera glasses in their little cages, pill-box-hatted ice-cream girls in sharply starched black and white. It was a world seemingly unchanged in the past fifty years, a place suspended in time.

Onstage the characters danced and sang their way through a vulgar wedding party. They embraced and argued and traded insults. They were a big, tight, dysfunctional mass of connectedness and frustration and wild, spiralling hopes. Nothing like Anna's family. Nothing like the world she had grown up in or indeed any of the other various worlds she had become privy to in the past ten months. The Covent Garden world of dirty commerce, where everyone was a spiv or an interloper from some unloved foreign country. The insular planet of the Alabora Coffee House, which was governed by Ottmar's wild extravagance and the unstinting need of the customers always to be fed and watered like grubby, grasping children. The world of Leonard's theatre where the ladies all affected a better class of voice and every painted surface shone with a rose-gold light. She honestly could not tell if she loved London or she loathed it. For she could not decide for herself what London was at all.

49

After the show Leonard took her to Bunjies and plied her with Cinzano and asked her if she'd ever thought about leaving the Alabora because as much as he loved Ottmar he thought that she must be rather bored waitressing when she had a good head on her shoulders. Anna allowed herself to get rather drunk and by the bottom of her second glass she had somehow agreed to give notice at the coffee house and spend a month on probation as a dresser to the leading lady who could not – to quote Leonard – 'focus around the young male staff'.

That evening, after the other waitresses had left for home, Anna sat down with Ottmar over coffee and cake and told him she was running away to join the theatre. Ottmar extended his large dark paws and cradled Anna's hands between his. When she looked, a little fearfully, into his eyes they were tired and dark and wet.

'Will you still come and have lunch with us sometimes, little Anna?'

'I'll be living just upstairs.'

'I know. But life. It rushes by and then you think you'll see people … You think you'll do things and have time for this and time for that … And then there is never time. This is what I have learned, Anna, I have learned that there is never as much time as you think there is.'

'I'll come and have coffee with you every evening if you'll promise not to be so maudlin,' Anna joked.

'Am I maudlin?'

'Yes.'

'It's mostly tiredness.'

'I know,' she said and she reached across and briefly touched his cheek. 'I know it is.'

Let's

Leonard's sitting room was large and white and somewhat bare for Anna's tastes. There were two blue sofas and a tall white bookcase holding what looked like a double layer of paperback books. A record player and speakers stood on the floor against a wall that held one gold-framed picture of the Buddha and an alarming poster for Genet's *The Balcony*. The low coffee table was decorated with orange and turquoise tiles and piled high with papers and files and notes.

'Sit down. I'll fill the coffee maker.'

Anna studied the bookshelves and called through to Leonard who was getting dressed somewhere else in the flat. 'What's happened to Benji's sister?'

'She's in hospital for … women's problems.'

'Right.' Anna was never really sure what this meant.

'They phoned his parents two hours ago. She lost a lot of blood when they operated. They're saying they all have to go in and be with her. We weren't really expecting … It just came out of the blue.'

Anna slumped into a ball on one of the sofas. 'Everything seems to come out of the blue at the moment. The policeman was nice enough but he didn't have a single idea what had happened to Lanny and he's meant to have been looking for her for a week.'

'If there are no clues, there are no clues.'

'Well, she's gone somewhere. What about that boy that got taken from the station in Manchester? The one the Brady couple beat to death. If the brother-in-law hadn't gone to the police would he have been found? And the little girl in the moor? She'd been missing ten months. Why did no one find her sooner?'

Leonard was back now, dressed and peering into the little silver coffee pot that perched on the stove. 'No one's suggesting she's dead.'

'Well, why aren't they? Just because there isn't a body doesn't mean she's okay.'

Leonard frowned at her. 'Anna, come on. We're all a bit scared but really … She'll turn up. It's just a horrid time.'

'It's a horrid time for us, but what about Lanny? What if we're all sitting round saying, isn't this awful, this worrying is so exhausting, and in the meantime someone's doing something to Lanny? What if they're hurting her? What if she's trapped?'

Leonard shook his head and set out cups.

'I was thinking of going down to the club tomorrow, the one she talked about in the interview,' Anna said, though really it had only occurred to her just now. 'I mean, what was she doing there? Was she meeting a man? Was she buying drugs?'

'Depends on the club.'

'I'm going to start with Roaring Twenties.'

'See, no,' Leonard said, putting a couple of teacakes under the grill to toast, 'I don't see Iolanthe in there. They're playing reggae and ska and all sorts of weird Caribbean stuff. It's mostly a club for coloured kids.'

'I've never been in. What's it like?'

'Not really my kind of place. I'm not a nightclub man. It was white when it started. White-owned, white-run. You know … Jewish kids down from Hampstead pretending to be cool. Coloured musicians on the stage, whites only on the dance floor. Not overly popular with the musicians, as you can imagine. I went there a couple of times in the early days and it was fine. Quite small. Good for a night out and an ounce of weed. Few years went by and it shifted. Musicians hated the colour bar, got antsy. They got themselves a coloured manager for real. Count Suckle, playing all this Caribbean music from his enormous sound system. Honestly, it was the size of a car and the floors would shake underneath you, the whole place bouncing and rolling. He disappeared a while back. I heard he got sick of all the drugs being sold and got himself another gig up on Praed Street. So now it's Duke Vin but very popular with the pop music lot. Ringo Starr's been seen drinking there, Daltrey, Keith Moon, Freddie Garrity. Whoever owns it must be raking it in.'

Leonard carried over plates of teacakes and tiny black enamelled cups of coffee, while Anna shifted in her seat. She herself had long ago learned to avoid any mention of a person's skin or nationality, and she wondered at the carelessness of Leonard's language.

Leonard was talking again. 'You know the big coloured guy on the door, Charlie Brown? He was John Christie's landlord.'

'At Rillington Place?' Anna asked.

'London's much smaller than you think. Everyone is somehow connected to everyone else. Even if they do all hate each other.'

There were no curtains at the windows, only offices overlooked the room and Anna searched the sky for signs of light. She hated winter mornings, that irresistible pull back to bed. 'Do you really think we all hate each other, Leonard?'

'D'you know what I think?' Leonard plonked himself down on the sofa next to her. 'I think it's all about money. I think we all come for the same reason and we call it jobs or houses or culture but what we really mean is money. Money makes places shiny. It makes them glitter. The rich come flooding in because they have things to do with their money. They can spend, show it off, make more of it. The poor come flooding in because poverty is terrifying and they gravitate to the place where there's the most work. The immigrants come here because if you don't head for where the money is you're going to be going back on the next boat. My parents came here because the pogroms laid waste to their town and there were Jewish boarding houses and Jewish companies. Why's Ottmar here? Why are you? We all come looking for the shiny and then we find that there isn't very much to go around. And if all that's binding you together is a search for shininess … well … those are very dangerous ropes to bind any group of people together.'

Anna stared, perhaps a little too intently, at Leonard's face. 'You never said you were Jewish.'

Leonard looked taken aback. 'I assumed you knew.'

'I think I thought you must be but then you never mentioned it.'

'I don't practise.'

'There just … there weren't any Jewish kids at my school. I think sometimes I just assume everyone who seems English is English.'

'I am English,' said Leonard. Pointedly.

'I know … but I meant Anglo-Saxon Protestant English. Fruit scones; Book of Common Prayer; Henry-the-Eighth-had-six-wives English. You know. English English.'

'You're eating a bloody teacake; what more d'you want?' Leonard worked a currant out from between his teeth. 'Nothing can ever be too English, can it? Nothing can ever be too pure. It's like there's an entry test for Englishness and only twenty people pass it every year. Are you clever? Are you virtuous? Are you kind? It doesn't fucking matter. All that matters is that you're English.'

Anna made an apologetic face but Leonard was now in full flow.

'It's like the bloody countryside. Benji's English, of course. Went to the right school. Carries the right blood. And we're all meant to love the countryside. Wellingtons, dogs; all that bollocks. Of course we never get invited anywhere. Too queer for country houses. Too faggoty for gaudies or hunts. We have to do it ourselves. Discreetly. He makes me go on driving holidays to Wiltshire and Somerset. And I sit there, with my sunglasses on, blocking out the scenery, reading Barthes just to piss him off. "Look at that view!" he cries. But no, I will not look at the bloody view. It's all the same anyway. Vulgar, garish greenery. Ancient oaks. God, I hate it. It's so small. So unimportant. So fucking parochial. I hate it and it hates me back.'

Anna looked at him. There was a manic grief in his expression, alongside the annoyance and humour. She realised suddenly that she didn't know Leonard very well at all. At work he was professional and friendly and precise but there was so much messiness to this other Leonard, this angry Leonard who lived in a half-bare flat with his city-suited lover and his odd neuroses. Anna knew the kind thing would be to hug him; to tell him to be any way he wanted. But even that little outpouring of intimacy seemed too great a leap. For a little outpouring of intimacy could easily become something more, something familiar, something desired, essential, habitual.

'I've made you uncomfortable, haven't I?' Leonard said.

'No. No!' Anna assured him.

'Shall we be English again?' Leonard asked with a small, watery smile.

And Anna smiled back. 'Let's.'

Going Out

The wind blew fiercely down Regent Street and the secretaries and shop girls in their black and white winter coats squealed and skittered, handbags swinging wildly, hands reaching out and grabbing for a friendly arm. Hayes watched them all bowling towards the tube stations as the lights in the department stores went dark. Then he crossed the street and headed into Soho. It was half past five and he'd soon be off shift but he'd been warned that the clubs didn't open until early evening. He wanted to have an informal chat with Charlie Brown or anyone else he could find before the evening rush started.

He was frustrated by the lack of urgency in the office. Inspector Knight seemed convinced that Iolanthe had left of her own accord. He had gone to speak to his boss that morning, to ask for backing in investigating the multiple bank accounts, but Knight had dismissed him without thought.

'Dead end, Hayes. Not worth your time. She'll be off her head or knocked up. That's why women run. She was seen at Roaring Twenties, which says to me she didn't care much what happened to her. Older woman. Single. Lonely. Probably sleeping around. She'll have been buying dope or worse and getting herself felt up by the lower classes. We'll get a call, sometime, you mark my words … She'll be found dead. Overdose. Heroin. Suicide. In the stained sheets of some coloured's bed.'

'But how can we be certain, sir, that it wasn't about money? She was earning well. It could be robbery or extortion or kidnap.'

'Trust me, she's just another low-rent Monroe. Childless. Looks going. Nothing to live for. Waste of our bloody time.'

Two hours later, as Brennan pored over the meagre round of witness statements for the fifteenth time, he was called to the phone.

'Detective Sergeant Hayes? It's Anna Treadway. You interviewed me yesterday.'

'I remember it well, Miss Treadway. How can I help?'

'Well, I was talking with someone last night and it sparked in me a realisation … silly, really … and you probably know this. But Yolanda and Iolanthe are the same name.'

'Oh …' And then there was silence on DS Hayes' end of the line.

'I know … I felt very silly when I realised. And since you hadn't said anything about this in interview …'

'No. Of course. From violet. And flower. I even did Greek at school.'

'And there's something else. The last day, the Saturday, she got a phone message from an American man by the name of Cassidy. Second name I'm guessing.'

'What was the message?'

'Well, nothing really. Just to say he'd called. And the boy on the stage door said that it wasn't the first time he'd rung the theatre.'

'Do you know who Cassidy is?'

'No idea. Sorry. Someone from back home, I guess. If I can be of any more help, Sergeant Hayes, please let me know.'

'Of course, Miss Treadway. Thank you for calling.'

And now Hayes stood on Carnaby Street in a light drizzle and watched a young coloured man unloading equipment in front of the door of number 50. An older man in a rumpled suit was scooping up wires and helping him through the doors. Brennan drew himself up to his full height of Barnabyness and approached the suited man.

'Good evening, I was wondering if you were Charlie Brown?'

The suited man gazed quizzically at Brennan. He nodded, a little noncommittally. 'I'm Charlie.'

Brennan held out his hand. 'I'm Detective Sergeant Barnaby Hayes. I'm with the Metropolitan Police and I'm working on a missing persons case. I'm looking for Iolanthe Green. Do you know who that is?'

Charlie nodded. 'Actress. She came in here a few times.'

'Was she with anyone?'

'I don't think so. I think she came on her own. Couldn't swear to it though.'

'Did she leave alone too?'

'Couldn't say. I'm watching them coming in more than going out. They pass me by, I say goodnight, that's all.'

'Was there any gossip about her, do you know? Was she seeing anyone? Was she drinking a lot? Was she behaving wildly, perhaps?'

'So many people, Sergeant. They come, they dance. We get musicians and actors in here sometimes. Not such a strange thing. Mostly it's just very chilled. You know, the whole place is just quite chilled. We don't go in for violence.' Charlie smiled broadly and Brennan found himself smiling back though he didn't know quite why. He had a momentary impulse to ask Brown about John Christie but Barnaby stamped on that quite firmly.

'Thank you, Mr Brown,' Hayes said.

'My pleasure.' Charlie nodded him away. Hayes walked slowly through the rain, back towards Regent Street, then he turned north towards Oxford Circus and started to walk as swiftly as he could into the wind. All along Oxford Street commuters were waiting for their buses and women in expensive coats with fur collars were hailing cabs. Hayes wondered at this great sea of the oblivious. He wondered at so many people tripping gaily through life when so much in the world was wrong. And then he wondered, as he often did, which of them was out of step. Was he the freak? Choosing to know, to actively seek out the unpleasant and the animal and the cruel. He stopped to pull on gloves and button his coat by the window of John Lewis. His reflection was half visible, laid over the headless form of a man in an argyle golfing jumper. He tidied his hair and watched in the reflection how men in mackintoshes queued to get on their bus. How foolish of him to assume that they were all happy. Of course they felt pain. Each one of them might well be spilling over with grief or self-loathing. But, still, their misery was all their own. The misery he dealt with was other people's; which can often seem more terrible than the kind you know.

The tall figure of Barnaby Hayes, with its neat, short hair and clean-shaven face gazed back at him. He liked Barnaby more than he liked Brennan. Brennan was good but Barnaby was admirable. Brennan was idealistic but Barnaby was effective. Barnaby looked like the men in the adverts for cigarettes; he was an English gentleman: beautiful, polished, refined.

At Marble Arch he headed north-west up Edgware Road. Pages from the newspapers blew past him. Cigarette packets, paper bags, the cord from a bundle of *Standards*. Sussex Gardens flashed by. Sale Place.

On Praed Street Hayes searched the signs above the shops for Cue Club. He found it at last: a little door beside the Classic Cinema marked 5a. Hayes climbed down the unlit wooden stairs.

The club was quiet but not deserted. A man with a quiff stood behind the bar restocking the shelves. On the little stage at one end of the room a boy in T-shirt and jeans sat surrounded by speakers cleaning the jacks of a handful of wires.

In a dark corner of the room a tall, well-built man sat at a wooden table drinking tea with a woman in a coat. He looked over at Hayes as he entered and nodded his head.

'Can we help you?' he asked. The woman in the coat turned and stared at Hayes. She was Anna Treadway.

'I was looking for Count Suckle.'

'That'd be me. I'm having tea with the young lady. Can you wait? Martin'll get you a drink.' Count Suckle – whose real name was Wilbert – nodded towards the bar.

'Thank you. But I won't drink, I'm on duty. Are you licensed to serve me at ten past six?'

Wilbert stood and straightened his suit. He approached Barnaby, his hand outstretched, his wide eyes open and intense. 'Yes, as it happens, we are.'

Hayes took his hand and shook it. 'Barnaby Hayes. Detective Sergeant. I hope you don't mind me asking but did the young lady come here to talk about Iolanthe Green?'

Anna stood and faced Hayes. 'I didn't want to tread on any toes; I just thought I'd seek out the opinion of someone who knew Roaring Twenties. Because Lanny had been going there. So we were chatting … about clubs and suchlike. Clientele. I mean, she didn't just vanish, did she?'

'Have you spoken to anyone else who might be a part of this investigation?'

'One or two. Duke Vin. Lester Webb. Pete King at Ronnie Scott's.'

'When? When have you seen all these people? You said nothing about this at interview.'

'I only started talking to people today. There seems to be a lack of urgency in this investigation. What if it is murder? What if she's been kidnapped? What if she's lying in a hospital somewhere and can't remember who she is?'

'But this is a police investigation and you're not a member of the police. You could be prejudicing the enquiry. You could be putting yourself in danger. You don't know … I'm sorry – I am sorry – but you *have* to stop talking to people about this.'

Wilbert had been watching things bubble over with an increasing sense of enjoyment but now he felt the need to interject. 'Sergeant Hayes, Miss Treadway's just worried about her friend. She's doing no harm. Anna, my dear, can I get you a drink on the house? We have a live set starting in an hour. You can stay, listen. Sergeant Hayes, if you want to talk to me I'm here. Let's talk.' Wilbert smiled at them both like an indulgent mother then he called over to the man behind the bar. 'Martin! Get the lady a drink. On us.'

Anna nodded to Count Suckle and – giving Hayes a wide berth – went to take up one of the seats by the bar. As it was she didn't really want to drink, nor did she particularly want to stay, for she was having one of her antisocial patches. But she couldn't leave now. Not when Hayes had suggested that that's what she should do.

'What'll it be?' the barman asked.

'Single Scotch, thanks.' Anna watched Hayes as he talked to Count Suckle. There was a lot of serious nodding going on and Count Suckle was struggling to explain something, his hands conjuring in the air between them both.

The Scotch was a little harsh but it did its job; Anna sank lower in her chair. She was vaguely aware that a second person had joined her at the bar but she refused to take her eyes off Sergeant Hayes.

'Are you here for the band? Or are you with the band?' Anna looked up to find that a tall, thin black man in a moddish suit was leaning against the bar looking at her. His neatly cut hair held the suggestion of a quiff and he wore thick, dark-rimmed spectacles.

'Neither,' she answered, 'I was speaking with Count Suckle.'

'And having a drink.' The man sat down two seats away from her and the barman, Martin, handed him a tall glass of something.

'Are you a friend of Wilbert, then?' the man went on, drinking down half his glass in one great gulp. He saw Anna watching him and laughed: 'It's Coke. I haven't got the legs to drink rum like that.'

Anna smiled, embarrassed, aware now that her judgement had been written on her face. 'I'm not really a friend of Wilbert – is that Count Suckle's name? I'm more of a friend of a friend of a friend of a friend. I'm asking around because someone I know went missing.'

'Oh. I'm sorry. Can I help? Would I have seen him? Or her?'

'It's Iolanthe Green. The actress. I was her dresser at the theatre and eleven days ago she walked down Charing Cross Road and …' Anna gestured a little wildly and slopped Scotch down her skirt.

The tall, thin man drew a handkerchief from his pocket and offered it over: 'It's clean.'

Anna wiped herself down and replaced her glass on the bar. She handed the man back his handkerchief. 'Sorry. I don't drink very often and I'm not very good at it when I do.'

The man laughed and repocketed the damp hanky. 'My name's Aloysius. I'm Count Suckle's accountant. Pleased to meet you.'

Anna shook his hand and as she did so her eyes slid over to the table in the corner where Count Suckle now sat alone.

'When did the policeman leave? I didn't see him go.'

'I've no idea. You know, I read about Miss Green in the newspaper. It's a strange thing. Why d'you think Wilbert knows where she is?'

'Lanny – Iolanthe – had been going to Roaring Twenties before she disappeared, but when I went and asked the men there, they just didn't seem to want to answer my questions. And Leo … my boss told me that Count Suckle used to work there and I thought maybe he could help me.'

'What did Wilbert say?'

'He said he hadn't seen her and yes, there were drugs, but he couldn't imagine her getting herself into much trouble at the Twenties unless it was maybe with a man.'

'D'you think she ran away?'

'In a way, I hope she did. Every other possibility just seems so bleak.' Anna stared at the band setting up on the stage and figured that it was probably time to leave. She felt out of place here and she certainly wouldn't know what to do with herself at a proper night-club when the music started and the crowds arrived. She glanced over at Aloysius, who was watching her with a strange and thought-ful expression on his face. 'I think it's time I went home,' she told him and she stood.

Aloysius put out his hand and touched hers briefly. 'It was nice to meet you, Miss …'

'Treadway. Anna. I'm sorry. I really need to go. I barely slept last night.'

'Take care of yourself, Miss Treadway,' Aloysius called as she disappeared up the stairs.

Outside, Praed Street was bitterly cold. Buses shunted slowly past in a queue of traffic. Anna stared at the bus stops but she didn't know the routes, and the crowds of people huddling about the shel-ters put her off. She started to walk towards the Edgware Road with an idea of finding her way home along the least windy thoroughfares.

She stood at the traffic lights at the top of Edgware Road in a crowd of people waiting for the little man in green to appear. Fingers plucked at her shoulder but she pulled herself further inside her coat and ignored them.

'Miss Treadway.' She recognised the Jamaican accent without quite being able to remember who the voice belonged to. The lights were changing and she was pushed and shuffled into the road amongst the other bodies.

'Miss Treadway!' There was the voice again. She turned but could only see the man and woman directly behind her, forcing their way forward with grim-faced determination. Anna started to trip, righted herself and kept on towards the pavement.

Once safely on the other side, she pushed her way over to stand under an awning and survey the crowd. A man bundled into a great grey army coat sat in a little shelter behind a pile of newspapers. He was shouting the name of the paper from behind his hands, which he'd cupped over his face to warm himself. His fingers were filthy and Anna found herself disgusted by the sight of the blackened nails. Did he have a wife? she wondered. Did he touch a woman with those filthy hands? Did he touch himself?

Aloysius's figure appeared to the right of her. With his face shaded from the sodium by a wide-brimmed fedora he looked to Anna as if he had arrived from another time. He reminded her of men of her father's generation, the gentlemen of the thirties and forties with their smart, conservative clothes and their smart, conservative lives. What kind of a name was Aloysius anyway? Had he been to Eton? Well, obviously not, but he seemed to be playing up to something. Standing there in his mackintosh and his fedora, looking for all the world like some fellow from a black and white movie, he reminded her of Jimmy Stewart ... if Jimmy Stewart had been black. The image of a coloured James Stewart momentarily confused her and Anna realised that she didn't quite know how to think about black men, for she really had no frame of reference. As he stepped under the awning Aloysius took off his hat. 'Miss Treadway, I don't mean to gossip. But I might have an idea of what has happened to your friend.'

Dr Jones Is Having Supper

Wednesday, 10 November

Ottmar's eyes followed every woman who walked past the cafe window. Samira had not come home from school and it was dark already. She's still so small, he thought, my baby girl. He could see her at once as a baby and a five-year-old and a young woman of thirteen. He saw every part of her, every stage, every moment of strength and rage, determination. She was her mother's daughter.

Ever since she'd turned sixteen, she'd been going out in the evenings, staying out late, school nights, every night.

'Where have you been?' they asked her as she wandered up the stairs to the flat at midnight or one o'clock.

'Becky's house.' 'Mary's house.' 'I went to the late show with Bernie.'

'Who's Bernie?' they asked.

'Short for Bernadette.'

'Where does she get the money?' Ekin asked and Ottmar shook his head, too scared to suggest any of the possible answers that presented themselves.

Back in February, during Ramadan, Sami had told them that she would no longer be attending the mosque. Ekin, the only one of the family who bothered to fast during the day, screamed at her daughter: 'Idiot! Do you want to burn in hell?'

'I think I want to be a Marxist,' Samira told her.

'Then be a Muslim and a Marxist.'

Samira thought about this for a moment. 'I don't think I can.'

Ekin's hands rose in the air and marshalled a heart suspended in space. 'How can you turn your back on the love of Allah when nothing in the world is more beautiful?'

Her daughter stared back at her with a look of sheer bemusement.

Ottmar thought of Rashida in her posh girls' school. And Samira, poor clever Samira, who hadn't quite made the grade. He blamed himself, he blamed Ekin, he blamed the whole world. Neither Ekin nor he had been able to read English when they arrived so Sami had had to pull herself through school. Struggling and failing and making all the mistakes so that Rashida might succeed after her. Yet she was the clever one, Ottmar always felt this – Samira was the talker, the thinker. It was their fault she'd failed the eleven-plus and a piece of supreme injustice that Rashida had passed. Samira, who would have loved that girls' school so much, who would have sucked up every piece of knowledge available, who would have carved a greater path in the world than the one she would carve now.

She's only sixteen, he told himself: there's time. But a terrible, sick part of himself said it was already too late. He'd had a clever uncle and a good mind but without the right education, without the private income, he'd had nothing to protect him. When the hard times came he had lived without a shell. He told his girls that in the Alabora he had built himself a little world from his dreams and that was – in part – true. The Alabora, with its turquoise walls and sunset-coloured chairs, its silver-framed mirrors and red and gold embroidered bunting was a vision from a dream he had; but it was a dream of childhood. It was a dream of visiting his uncle in Istanbul and sitting in the coffee shops watching the men smoking and playing chess. It was not, as Ottmar would have them believe, a dream that he wished to recreate in adult life.

He was a cafe owner – little more than a serf, what with business partners and taxes and the local council. His daughter did not tell her fellow students what her father did, though she did sometimes mention her great-uncle who had lectured on the epic poets in the great university at Istanbul. He would, he thought now, become the forgotten generation. *Oh, Ottmar – he was the one who came from Cyprus to England.* His great achievement: a boat ride across the sea.

* * *

Aloysius insisted on paying both their fares. 'I'm dragging you across London. It's the least I can do. Really. We'll have a little walk at the other end unless we change but I love this journey, there's this view over the river and … You don't mind a little walk?' Anna shook her head with a smile, the bell clanged, the 2A drew into a stream of traffic and they went to find themselves seats upstairs.

For the first few minutes neither of them spoke. In that strange and hurried conversation on the corner of the Edgware Road Anna had found herself caught up in the excitement of chasing Iolanthe. At last she had a clue, a lead; she knew something Sergeant Hayes did not. She had sped through the streets to Baker Street, Aloysius taking her arm as they crossed each road. She had felt daring and unconstrained. A single woman running through the darkness with a handsome black man at her side. She hoped that people would see them and wonder who they were. She hoped that people thought they might be lovers.

But now, under the unromantic glow of London bus lighting, she felt sweaty and unkempt. The two men travelling at the front of the bus had turned round and stared at her and Aloysius and then they'd laughed a hard and dirty laugh that had no hint of generosity about it. Aloysius himself seemed much more uncomfortable now that they had settled in for the journey and when the men started making monkey noises he asked her: 'Would you like me to go and sit in the seat behind? Then no one would think anything about it.'

'No!' said Anna, though a little part of her wanted to answer 'Yes'. Aloysius touched her hand very briefly then he picked up his brief-case and slid quietly into the seat behind her. Anna turned, knowing that she should say something but Aloysius smiled a weary smile at her.

'It doesn't matter,' he said. 'We can still talk.'

Anna turned in her seat so that they would be face to face and she'd feel less ashamed in her acceptance that they should sit apart.

'Will you tell me again what the man in the club said? It was so loud on that corner I only caught half of it.'

'I was in Roaring Twenties to discuss business with Mr Peters who's over from Jamaica wanting to buy houses up on Brixton Hill.

66

And it was late and loud and we were joined by a lady: Mr Peters' girlfriend. She was called Melody or Melanie – I couldn't hear. And she says how that actress is over there again and how she's had too much to drink and she's crying. And that she'd asked her – the Melody, Melanie woman – about doctors who helped women who got themselves into trouble. And that Melody, Melanie had told her about Dr someone in Streatham Hill. Who has a surgery on Drewstead Road. And I remembered it because I live just across from there and was curious. Anyway, it didn't seem like something I should be asking about so I kept quiet. Then a few days ago I'm doing the books in Cue Club and Martin – he's the barman – Martin says how his girlfriend says she is late and how this is the end of the world and how he's going to send her to Dr Jones. And he nods at me as if I know what he's talking about. And he says, come on Louis, you must know Jones, you practically live right by her.'

'And this Dr Jones is a woman?'

'I guess so. I know she's a doctor and she lives just near me and that she helps out women who ...'

'Who are late?'

'Yes.'

'And you think the actress was Iolanthe?'

'I don't know. I can't swear to it but then you said she'd been in there around then ... I wouldn't have rung the police because it doesn't seem enough. But then she's disappeared and you seem so anxious to find her. You must be close to her.'

'I don't know. I think I felt some kind of ... She was funny and a bit vulnerable, you know. I worried about her even before this happened. She went missing on the Saturday and no one even knew she'd gone for two days. Isn't that awful? I kept thinking what if I disappeared tomorrow ... Who'd notice? Who'd come looking?'

'Maybe we all have to look out for each other.' Aloysius smiled. His expression betrayed a mind and sensibility so free of cynicism that Anna felt quite taken aback. A little part of her wanted to be persuaded by his apparent goodness but she could not help wondering if his gentleness was feigned as part of a seduction.

Aloysius's eyes creased with pleasure as he watched the view through the window; they were crossing the river now. Anna looked out but they were over the best of it already and crawling to a halt behind a line of buses at the southern end of the bridge. A line of advertising hoardings blocked the view of the empty land to their left. Anna took in the pretty pictures, as bright and unreal as the illustrations from a children's book.

When it pours, we reign

Avoid the squeeze, please

Bond drives an Aston

Life is for living. Don't be stuck on 'DRUGS'

"'She looked as happy as a rose-tree in sunshine.'"

'What?' Anna turned to Aloysius and then back to the adverts. What was he reading from?

"'I should only be *de trop*: I'd best go and talk to the hermit.'" Aloysius nodded his head to the great stretch of wasteland beyond the advertisements. 'The Vauxhall Pleasure Gardens. That's where they went.'

'Where who went?'

'Becky Sharp. On the night Mr Sedley was meant to propose. When I realised that that was what had happened to the gardens I think a little piece of my heart died.'

The bus moved off and Anna craned her neck to see the jumble of earth beyond the hoardings and to understand what it was Aloysius was trying to tell her.

'Becky Sharp?'

'Dr Gillespie used to make us read that chapter out loud. It made him laugh.'

Anna stared at Aloysius. She felt as if she'd gone to sleep and woken up in another conversation entirely. 'I have no idea what you're talking about.'

'*Vanity Fair*.'

'By Thackeray?'

'Yes.'

'I've never read it.'

'Oh,' said Aloysius, looking quite deflated. 'Sorry. I didn't realise.'

'How have you … This is coming out quite rude. But how have you read it?'

'I was a Knox College boy in Jamaica. Head prefect. Dr Gillespie, fifth-form literature, made everybody read *Vanity Fair*.'

'What an odd choice.'

'Why?'

'Well, did that world make any sense to you?'

'Of course. Why wouldn't it?'

Anna had literally no idea how to answer this politely so she let it pass. Aloysius, who'd been holding on to the bar on the back of her seat, withdrew his hands and laid them in his lap. Conversation stopped. The bus chugged down to Stockwell and on to Brixton.

Aloysius watched the darkened terraces pass by. For the most part he had done away with his romantic notions about London. It was very much colder, dirtier and more unfriendly than it had been in his imagination. But he retained a romanticism when it came to English girls. He had been captivated by Anna's voice, with its English accent with a capital E. She didn't look like the working-class white girls he saw on the way to and from work, with their stocky legs and cheap-looking minidresses. Anna was very tall – as tall as an Englishman, he thought; perhaps even five foot ten. Her frame was muscular with long, powerful legs and wide, strong hands. Her mouth was broad, her nose almost Roman and she had very large dark grey eyes. She reminded him of the women you saw carved in wood on the front of old ships in Kingston Harbour. She looked like a goddess from another place and time and he had wanted to impress her with his education, with his reading.

He had gone out of his way to present himself well since he moved here. He had bought a briefcase like the ones he saw the English accountants carrying in Kingston. He had invested in a fine suit, made to measure from a tailor's shop in Croydon. He polished his shoes. He shaved meticulously. The boys in the back rooms would tease him about his appearance, calling him a fop and a nancy boy. A gentle man by nature, he had forced himself to suppress every instinct he had to answer back or defend himself from slander. When people laughed at him in meetings he smiled and allowed them to have their moment of humour; when he was refused service in a pub or cafe he packed up his things and left quietly; when men made monkey noises on the bus he moved his seat. He was fighting the assumptions of the English with every weapon in his arsenal but nine times out of ten he was left feeling empty, exhausted and defeated.

Anna, meanwhile, was staring at the landmarks she knew and desperately trying to find a literary connection between them and something that she'd actually read. She realised that the conversation was broken and she wondered if Aloysius would now abandon her somewhere in darkest south London. If she could only think of a connection between Brixton Town Hall and Dickens she might be saved. Anna turned to Aloysius, who seemed to be deep in thought. 'Have you read *The Ballad of Peckham Rye*?' she asked.

Aloysius thought about this. 'No. I don't remember reading anything called that,' he said at last.

'Oh. I only asked because we're quite close here.' Anna gestured vaguely at the world outside the window. 'It's about the devil,' she went on brightly.

'I see. And what does the devil do?'

'Well, we don't really know if he is the devil. He just turns up and experiments on people. He tries to influence them.'

'Do you recommend it?'

'Well, yes, maybe. I liked *The Prime of Miss Jean Brodie* better but that's about girls in a girls' school so …' She trailed off.

'I shall keep an eye out for both of them,' Aloysius said with a nod of his head.

Anna searched her mind for something else that might rekindle their spark of connection earlier in the evening. Of course she didn't know this man at all and really had no idea how to begin talking to him; though she had begun quite nicely when they'd had Iolanthe to talk about so perhaps things would get easier when they got off the bus. They rode on in silence.

They were on Tulse Hill when Aloysius stood and rang the bell. Anna stood too and he motioned for her to precede him down the staircase. They stepped out into the cold and Anna looked around her to see if she recognised the road.

'We can cut through down the street over there.' Aloysius nodded over the road and they crossed, though this time he did not take her arm.

They walked in silence for several minutes, Aloysius leading the way, and then Anna asked: 'What are we going to do when we get there?'

'You mean, what will we say?'

'Am I going to have to pretend that I'm in trouble? She might want to examine me.'

'No. No. We'll just say we're friends of Iolanthe's and we don't want to make trouble but has she seen her.'

'Do you think she'll tell us the truth?' Anna asked.

'I have absolutely no idea.'

Anna looked around here. Here was a neighbourhood of red brick houses, a park bordered by box hedges. Clean and anodyne suburbia, fathers and husbands passing with swift steps on their way home from work, rows of Morris Minors broken up here and there by the flashy lines of a Ford Cortina. Aloysius touched a hand to her elbow, they turned another corner and the houses seemed to rise and tower above them. Oversized chimney stacks, decorative gables, turreted roofs and circular windows: houses for the newly and glee-fully wealthy, the Edwardian rich. Each new street a neighbourhood, Anna thought, a level of success. They turned again, onto Streatham Hill, crossed at the lights and started up Drewstead Road. The style of the houses became hushed once more, pre-war semis for the modestly affluent. Cautious buildings for cautious families. They came to a large semi-detached house, much like all the other semi-detached houses except it had a brass plaque on the gatepost.

Drewstead Road General Practitioners
Dr P. Jones
Dr A. Matthews
Surgery hours:
9:00 a.m. – 5:30 p.m.
Monday to Friday

'But it's closed,' said Anna.

'There's a light on round the side. Let's see if there's another entrance.'

They walked up the gravel driveway and round the side of the house where they found a second front door with a small brass plaque announcing: Dr P. Jones. Aloysius rang the bell and looked at Anna. His good humour was returning; Aloysius clearly liked an adventure.

The lights came on in the hallway and a figure came to the door and looked through the frosted glass. A middle-aged woman in navy trousers and a beige jumper opened the door to them.

'This is outside surgery hours,' she said.

'We know,' said Aloysius, 'and we're sorry, but we heard that Dr Jones was a very special kind of doctor.'

'Dr Jones is having supper,' said the woman.

'We've come a long way,' said Anna, trying to make herself seem smaller and more vulnerable than she normally looked. 'We don't mind at all if we have to wait. We only wanted to have the very briefest of words.'

Another figure appeared at the top of the stairs, though they could only see her shoes. 'Who is it, Carla?'

The middle-aged woman went to the bottom of the stairs and leaned heavily on the banister. 'They want to see you now.'

'Have you explained it's out of hours?'

'I have,' replied Carla, evidently annoyed but without the absolute authority to shut the door on them.

'I'll give them five minutes after supper.'

Carla turned towards the door. 'You both hear that?'

Aloysius and Anna nodded enthusiastically. Carla closed the door with some force and turned off the hallway light.

Anna could see their breath rising in the air. They looked at each other in the near darkness, the orange glow of a remote street light leaking into the space where they stood. Aloysius laughed and then bent down towards Anna's face. She started back a little but then felt the warmth of him against her cheek as he whispered: 'I thought she was going to let us wait inside.'

'Do you think she realises how cold it is?' Anna whispered back.

'Oh, I think she realises very well.'

They stood for a minute listening to the far-off sounds of cars on Streatham Hill. Anna put her hands inside the collar of her coat to warm them.

'Don't you have gloves?' Aloysius asked.

'I left them at home today. I went out this morning and I thought: I know, I'll pop across to Carnaby Street and see if anyone's about at Roaring Twenties. And there wasn't so I went across to the Marquee and then when I'd finished there I went back to Roaring Twenties and somehow I just kept walking and asking people if they'd seen Iolanthe until I ended up at Cue Club and then here.'

'Don't you have work to go to?'

'The theatre's dark. They got a flood of cancellations when Iolanthe went missing. Then there were articles suggesting that it was bad taste to keep the play on when no one knew what had happened to her. Then the insurance company wanted it settled one way or the other. So now they've pulled Iolanthe's play – *The Field of Stars* – and they're looking for another show to bring in. Until something else opens I'm not even getting paid.'

'Oh …' Aloysius's face fell a little in sympathy. 'What was it about anyway?'

'What was what about?'

'*The Field of Stars*. I've never heard of it.'

'It's this melodrama about a woman who's invented this other version of who her parents were to create sympathy for the things she's done. It's set in America, in the South, and she's a kept woman living in a big house that was bought for her by the governor. And almost everyone sees her as a whore and she has no friends. So she makes up this version of herself where she's Spanish and her parents were killed walking the Way of St James and she was brought up by nuns and then sent over to America all on her own.'

'Why the Field of Stars?'

'Santiago de Compostela is the town that you get to at the end of the Way of St James. Compostela means field of stars. It ran for a bit on Broadway fifteen years ago but it never made it over here. I don't know. It's very … florid. Not modern at all. But people like the costumes and the big sets and the histrionics.'

'What happens to the lady at the end?'

'She shoots herself on a balcony behind a fluttering curtain.'

'What a depressing evening at the theatre.'

'Well, yes.'

They stood in silence for a moment. Anna shivered in her coat. Aloysius opened his mouth and asked a little hesitantly, 'Would it be odd if I offered to warm your hands?'

'Oh. Well. No. Not odd, exactly.'

Aloysius held a gloved hand out towards her. Anna, consciously making her hands as stiff and unalluring as possible, pressed them together and placed them on his gloved palm. He closed the second gloved hand on top of the first and they stood there together in the cold, very aware of how they were almost touching and not quite sure what to do about it next.

After a few minutes they heard footsteps on the stairs and the hall light came on again. Anna withdrew her hands from Aloysius's clasp and thanked him quite formally.

The woman – Carla – opened the door. She was obviously disappointed to find that they were still there. 'You can come up for five minutes. Dr Jones needs her evening.'

They followed her up the carpeted stairs and into a large sitting room with a dining table at one end. The walls were covered in cream woodchip and decorated with sculptured art made from metal and nails and cord. Spider plants sat on the top of every bookcase and baby spiders cascaded like bead curtains in front of the hundreds of serious-looking tomes on medicine and history and art.

Dr Jones sat at the dining table. Her finished supper plate had been pushed away. A second sat across from her, a fish skin sunk fatly into a pool of grey gravy. Dr Jones was smoking a cigarette and reading the *Guardian*. She was a diminutive woman, well built and smartly dressed. She wore glasses and her thick black and white hair was cut into a bob. She put down the paper unhurriedly and looked first at Aloysius and then at Anna.

'We were about to have coffee. Would you like some?'

'I would, actually,' said Anna. 'If you don't mind.'

'Yes, please,' said Aloysius, the seriousness of the room somehow quieting his voice.

Dr Jones waved her hand towards two low armchairs and the visitors duly sat, or rather perched, like small children, their knees drawn up in front of them. Carla picked up the finished plates and went out into the kitchen.

'So,' said Dr Jones. 'How can I help?'

'It's not about me,' Anna started in, 'it's about my friend.'

'And why isn't your friend here talking to me herself?'

'Because we don't know where she is. Nobody knows where she is.'

Dr Jones nodded but said nothing.

Aloysius held a hand up to signal that he was ready to take over. 'Both myself and Anna here are under the impression that you are a doctor who helps women in trouble. Is that right?'

Dr Jones studied Aloysius for a few seconds. 'Are you the boyfriend?'

'Me? No. I'm just helping Anna.'

'And are we talking about who I think we're talking about?'

Anna nodded. 'Iolanthe Green. I worked with her. We think perhaps she came to see you.'

Carla came in with a coffee pot and a stack of mugs and started to pour. She moved with the quiet concentration of someone who was listening to every word being said.

'Miss Green did come to see me.' Dr Jones drew a cup of coffee towards her. She and Carla exchanged a look.

'Was it the last weekend of October?' Anna asked. 'She went missing on the night of Saturday the thirtieth so I thought perhaps she came here on the Saturday or Sunday.'

Carla passed them two half-full cups of black coffee, briefly blocking from their view the sight of Dr Jones. Aloysius and Anna were each aware of the other one holding their breath until the shadow had passed away.

'I saw her on a Thursday morning,' Dr Jones said slowly, as if struggling to recall the details. 'I believe it was the Thursday before she went missing. We had a conversation. I didn't treat her for anything.'

Anna felt a rush of relief when Dr Jones said this. Without the spectre of discussing what she might have done to Iolanthe, Anna felt free to use the actual words. 'She was pregnant?'

'She registered as an emergency patient. I owe her my confidentiality.'

'But she's disappeared; she might be dead. Surely there comes a point when you can break confidentiality.'

Dr Jones just shook her head. Aloysius reached across and touched Anna's knee. 'Dr Jones, I respect that a doctor has a duty but Miss Green came here to ask you about an illegal practice. And if the police end up here and they question you, then you might find yourself ending up in all kinds of trouble.'

Carla, who had been hunched over her coffee listening, leaned back in her chair. 'Don't threaten us,' she said.

Aloysius held up both his hands, a gesture of surrender. Anna finished her coffee and put the cup down on the floor by her foot. She started to speak again but she didn't look up at the two women.

'I have no desire to see either of you get into trouble. I'm guessing that something else happened between the meeting here on Thursday and her disappearing on Saturday night. But if she has run away it makes sense that it was about the pregnancy, so anything you can tell me will help me to find her. And if I find her then the police don't have to.'

She glanced up at the women to see how this was going across. They were both watching her intently.

'I give you my absolute, solemn word that I will never say that I came here and never mention your name to anyone. And if I'm lucky enough to find Iolanthe, I'll make sure that she understands the same. Nobody here wants to threaten you.' And Aloysius held up his hands again, wordlessly.

Dr Jones lit another cigarette. She cast Anna a sharp look and said, 'Why don't I tell you some of the reasons that women find themselves in trouble. Sometimes, as I'm sure you're aware, young women don't understand about contraception ... or indeed about reproduction. But sometimes it happens at the other end of the spectrum. Sometimes women who are quite fertile believe themselves too old to have a child; they may be unmarried and thus barred from being prescribed the pill; sometimes they're just unlucky. Often these women have good jobs: they work as doctors, headteachers, manageresses. They know that they will lose their position if they have a child. There may well be no way back for them. But ending a pregnancy can be tricky. There are various methods and women find some more palatable than others. Sometimes women want to take a pill or a herbal concoction. But if the pregnancy has gone beyond, say, eight or ten weeks then the pill method becomes less effective. The only sure route is to perform a small operation. Many women do not want to hear this. Many women run away from hearing such a thing.'

'Iolanthe wanted to take a pill but you told her she was too far along?' Anna asked.

Dr Jones smoked and said nothing.

'And she didn't want an operation?'

Dr Jones didn't meet her eye.

'But you gave her somewhere else to go?'

Dr Jones frowned.

'So she just went away again still pregnant and still not wanting the baby?'

Dr Jones looked over at Aloysius.

'Yes?' he asked.

Dr Jones looked at Anna and then looked again at Aloysius.

'What? The baby was going to be the wrong colour?' Anna asked.

'I'm still not the father!' Aloysius said.

'Nobody thinks that you're the father,' Anna told him, quite sharply. She turned back to Dr Jones. 'Do you know where she is?'

Carla leaned across the table and touched the doctor's arm. 'You've said enough. They're going now.' Anna and Aloysius stood at her command but as they did so Dr Jones started to speak.

'She would have had to have the procedure very late on Saturday night or early on Sunday morning. She would have had a day or so in bed to rest but then there was a risk of her bleeding while she was onstage. I told her to take the normal precautions. But she panicked. She was panicked by the whole thing. She was in a state of extreme distress.

'She gave me six or seven reasons why she couldn't carry on. Said someone had mentioned something, someone knew something. She was going to lose her job. She didn't have the money, couldn't afford it. She thought the baby might be dark-skinned. She was alone, had no one with her for support. She didn't want to be a mother. She'd been drinking heavily for the past few months, she'd taken drugs. She thought the baby might be damaged. She was … distraught and confused and hysterical. I hate that word. But she was … beyond reason.

'I tried to help but she didn't want to hear what I had to tell her. In the end I suggested that she take some time and think it over; that she could come back and see me whenever she needed. I … I didn't mean to let her down. But I'm a doctor. I have a duty to tell the truth.'

Carla put an arm around Dr Jones' shoulders. 'It's not your fault,' she told her, 'but you need to stop. They're going now.'

Dr Jones peeled herself away from Carla and walked into the kitchen. Anna and Aloysius let themselves out and walked back in silence onto Streatham Hill.

A Library for Naval Men

Nathaniel watched the birds on the lawn. Right now there was a pair of red-breasted orioles, an American redstart and a tiny green and black bird that he was hoping was an Acadian flycatcher. He wheeled himself to the corner by the window where he was allowed to keep his books and papers and drew his *Birds of America* from its case. On the desk beside it lay the pamphlet of poems by Tao Yuanming he had been trying and failing to read.

> *I wasn't fitted for the common crowd*
> *My more basic nature drew me to the hills*
> *And yet I fell into the worldly net*
> *Which held me fast for thirteen years.*

Twice a year Briggs would send a parcel of books to the Naval Library, odd texts and beautiful editions that he had found on his days off and sent home for safekeeping. Always at the top of the bundle would be a little note for Nathaniel.

How you keeping, Nat? Ever read The Odyssey? *Try it now. B*
Or:
You would be amazed by the things I found in Seoul. Not much Korean lit. here in English. Try the Chinese poets next? Briggs

Nathaniel remembered his green and black bird and pushed himself onto his hands to see the grass. But he had forgotten about it for too long and now it was gone.

Ever since the accident in Japan he had struggled to concentrate on any one thing for too long. He had to write his errands down on the backs of his hands. He read poetry and newspapers because he couldn't keep his memory together long enough to finish up a book.

He chastised himself for forgetting and then took solace in flicking through the thick pages of Audubon prints. He loved most the birds that he would never see: the flamingos and the spoonbills and the great auk on her rock. He had joined the Navy to see the world and everything it had within it. His brief spell in Japan had been wondrous and terrifying to a boy of eighteen, but he had only been there twenty days before his Jeep turned over. He had arrived in the spring of '46, when the fields were bright with flowers and there was still blossom on the trees. His ship was carrying troops and food packages, and khaki-covered bodies flowed from the mass of vessels like lines of a spider's web, each one stretching back beyond the sea to home.

Commander Briggs had spoken to them that first night when they were all safely ashore.

'The hatred of the past five years has no place here today. You have come to a country on its knees. A thousand children will die out there tonight without the food we bring. We are here to feed a nation because those children didn't choose to bomb our men. Those children didn't kill or maim; they didn't try to cut our legs from under us; they didn't torture us in camps. The vast majority of the people out there are blameless and we must minister to them as if they were our fellow Americans. We have taken their cities and their roads; their emperor is prostrate before us. In Nagasaki and Hiroshima they are dying still, hundreds more every day. Know when to be humble; know when to be compassionate.'

'Shit, Green,' said Franco, the oldest of their unit, 'who does he think he is: Jesus Christ himself? Kill the lot of 'em, I say, murderous, slit-eyed cunts.'

Nathaniel hated Franco and he loved Briggs but he never really knew whose Navy it was he'd joined. Everyone seemed to have a different idea of what they were for and yet they were all – supposedly – following the same orders. He had planned to grow up in

80

Japan. He had planned to grow up in the Navy. But instead he broke in half within a month.

Two birds lay prostrate on a hill of earth. Their eyes closed, their heads slack. The duck hawks paused in the act of ripping apart their prey and met the gaze of the reader, tails and wings aloft, talons splayed.

He'd been given the Audubon by a lieutenant commander who'd taught here for a while in '59. Like most of the officers who worked at the Academy, Lieutenant Commander Johnson had assumed that Nathaniel was simple and had given him the lovely book of birds much as one would reward a ten-year-old boy for trying hard at maths. Even his boss at the library, Henry Morgan, treated him like an invalid. 'Nat? Tell me, Nat, do you think you'd be up to taking these papers back to the archives? You don't need to file them, I'm sure I can do it later.' 'Nat, do you mind, Nat, are you busy? I've just got the smallest number of books need taking across to the main counter.'

Nathaniel was never busy. He was lucky if they gave him three tasks to do each day. But they paid him twelve dollars a week and gave him a room on the ground floor which had been a supply closet before Commander Briggs had told them to take out the shelves and fit it with a bed and a washbasin and space for his wheelchair at night. Commander Briggs remembered him from before he'd lost his legs. He knew that Nathaniel was the same man he'd always been.

It was four o'clock. Nat went into the little kitchenette, pulled himself higher against the counter and moved the kettle to the sink. He lowered himself back into the chair, wheeled himself to the edge of the sink and pulled himself up again to turn on the water. He slid the kettle towards the stove and then lowered himself down into the chair to wheel himself along to where the stove was connected to the wall. His arms feeling the strain, he pulled himself up again, picked up the matches, lit one one-handed and started the gas. As he pulled the kettle onto the stove the phone rang in the office. Nat dropped back down into his chair and manoeuvred himself out of the tiny kitchen.

'Naval Academy Library. Nathaniel Green speaking. How can I help?'

'Nathaniel Green?'

'Yes.'

'My goodness. I've been ringing round for two hours and now here you are!'

'Here I am indeed. How can I help?'

'Sorry. My name is Barnaby Hayes. I'm a detective sergeant with the Metropolitan Police in London. Are you free to talk for five minutes or so?'

Nathaniel's mind went to the kettle on the stove but it would take a few minutes to boil. 'Of course. Always happy to help the police.'

'I'm terribly grateful. Now I need to ask: are you related to a lady by the name of Iolanthe Green?'

Nathaniel dropped the phone to his chest so that Hayes could not hear his breathing. He wanted to hang up but the policeman knew where he worked, was obviously looking for him. What on earth had Lanny said? He brought the receiver back to his mouth. Somewhere very distant a man in London was saying something to him but he couldn't hear what it was.

'Excuse me, Detective Sergeant Hayes, but has something happened to Iolanthe Green?'

'Well, yes. I'm sorry to have to tell you but Iolanthe Green has gone missing. I'm in charge of finding her. You were aware that she was in London?'

'No. I didn't know she was in London.'

'Mr Green, is Iolanthe your sister?'

Silence again. Nathaniel stroked the cover of his *Birds of America* with its beautiful print of crossed feathers. He thought again about the Acadian flycatcher. It probably hadn't been one of those at all. He wouldn't have been that lucky.

'Mr Green?'

'Yes, sir.'

'The day of her disappearance Iolanthe gave an interview to *The Times* in which she said that she had had a brother named Nathaniel Green. I also know that Miss Green sometimes deposits money in savings accounts in that name. One of them being in Boston, the other in Annapolis. So I'm right in thinking that she is your sister, aren't I?'

'Yes, sir, you are.'

'Are you in regular contact with your sister, Mr Green?'

'No, sir, I'm not.'

'Can you explain to me why Miss Green would claim that you were killed in a car accident in 1946?'

'Did she tell you that?'

'No, she told *The Times*. It was part of the interview.'

'Sweet Jesus!' Nathaniel spoke more to himself than to anyone else.

'Had you fallen out with your sister, Mr Green? Because I can't quite understand how she could have claimed these things about you and yet was depositing money into your savings accounts.'

'We didn't fall out exactly. We had a parting of the ways. I was injured, very severely, in a car crash in Japan in '46. Iolanthe had already lost our father and our mother and she assumed the worst. She'd been making plans for a new life in New York. She wanted to go on the stage. So when I was shipped home ten months later without … the use of my legs, Iolanthe had already upped and left.

'We came to an agreement, whereby I would let her live out her plans and she would offer me a bit of financial support if she ever made anything of herself. She didn't come back to Boston and I muddled along. When my commander came home on leave he checked up on me and saw that I wasn't able to find employment so he pulled some strings at the Naval Academy in Annapolis and found me a job and a room and I've been here ever since.'

'When did you last see Iolanthe?'

'1947. She came back to Boston to sort out the sale of our mother's house. I was still living there but I couldn't cover the mortgage so Iolanthe decided to sell. She used the money to set herself up and I put my share into my savings account.'

'So your parents owned their own home?'

'Well, no sir, not exactly. My mother was a cook. She was left the house by her employer when he died.'

'And what did your father do?'

'Oh, this and that. My mother was the steady one.'

Nathaniel was vaguely aware of the kettle whistling behind him. His mind wandered back to the book of birds. He opened it to a random page. An American hen hurried through the brush with her young at her feet.

'Mr Green, are you still there?'

'Yes. Sorry.'

'Oh. I thought we might have been cut off. Was the inheritance from the sale of your mother's house substantial?'

'No, sir. I'm afraid that after the death ... after my mother's employer died we had to re-mortgage the house twice. When Iolanthe sold it there was only a little bit of money left in it. We got about six hundred dollars each.'

'But if you'd been left six hundred dollars why did the Navy feel the need to offer you a room and a job a year later?'

For the first time in the course of the conversation, Nathaniel raised his voice. 'Because nobody would employ me, sir. I couldn't get a job. I have no legs. Iolanthe assumed – she's not a monster, sir – Iolanthe assumed that I would be okay because I had a bit of money. But I had no way of replenishing that money. I *needed* someone to employ me.'

'Of course. I didn't mean to ... I apologise for what may seem like very intrusive questions, but I really do want to discover what has happened to your sister. What part of Ireland were your parents from?'

'What part? Somewhere around Dublin I guess. I don't really know. I've never been.'

'They weren't from County Cork, then?'

'Is that where Iolanthe said they were from? She was always better at family stuff.'

'Were you ever aware of your sister being in a relationship? Did she have a boyfriend? A fiancé? Someone she was serious about?'

'If she did I wouldn't have known. I knew she did a film because it came and played in the cinema here. And I knew she was doing okay because she was generous with her deposits. But that's about it.'

'I hope you don't mind me asking, but what are your savings accounts for, exactly? Do you have a grand plan?'

'I live how I live by the charity of the Navy and at some point I have to expect that that charity will end. I make plans for a time when I will depend only on myself, on the money I have managed to collect. I am warding off my future poverty, sir, that's all.'

'I see. Thank you, Nathaniel. I'm very grateful for your honesty in this matter. I can assure you that we are doing everything we can to find your sister.'

Behind Nathaniel the kettle was screaming wildly, fit to burst.

'Is there a suggestion that she may have been hurt, Detective Sergeant Hayes?'

'No, sir. We have no reason to believe that she's been hurt. But we don't really understand what's become of her. If she's a runaway, she may well come back eventually. I'm hoping we can track her down sooner rather than later.'

'If you find her, will you call me and let me know? She's really the only family I have.'

'Of course, Mr Green. Of course we'll let you know. Oh, wait, one more thing. The names Maria and Yolanda Green … Can you tell me who they are?'

'Well, Maria was our mother's name, sir.'

'And Yolanda?'

'I really couldn't say, sir.'

'You're aware that Yolanda and Iolanthe are the same name in different forms … I was wondering if your sister had ever gone by the name Yolanda.'

'Not to my knowledge, sir. She's always been Iolanthe to me.'

'Right. Well, okay. Thank you very much, Mr Green. I'll be in touch when I have some news for you. Goodbye.'

In the quiet and the darkness of his office in London, Barnaby put the phone down and felt a surge of satisfaction. If nothing else, he could follow the money. He looked at his watch. It was quarter past nine. He'd missed supper now and bedtime with Gracie and he hadn't even rung home to say he'd be late. Orla had long ago stopped checking up on him. She just assumed he wouldn't turn up for anything. All the same, it was liver and bacon for tea and it would be horrible cold. Maybe he would eat something here instead.

He searched the drawers of his desk for food, then gave up and went through Detective Sergeant Potts' drawers instead. Potts lived for his chocolate. A pristine pack of digestive biscuits sat in the top drawer alongside a bar of Fruit and Nut, a packet of Munchies and two bars of 5 Centre. His fingers hovered over the 5 Centres but then he made the healthy choice and pinched the digestives instead.

Four thousand miles away Nathaniel had burned his fingers on the shaking kettle and was holding them in cold water. When the pain subsided a little he made himself a cup of black tea with sugar and wheeled it back to the desk.

Like the Layers of an Onion

Wednesday, 10 November

Anna and Aloysius stood outside his house. He had offered to accompany her back to her flat in town but Anna felt this displayed an unnecessary level of gallantry. Now that they came to say good-bye neither of them seemed terribly keen to part. Anna wavered on the pavement occasionally asking questions, sometimes of herself and sometimes of Aloysius.

'Perhaps she's absolutely fine. If the baby was going to be illegit-imate and half-caste maybe she thought it best to run away and start again.'

Aloysius stood and listened, his breath misting the air in front of him, his nose slowly losing all feeling. Anna danced around in an effort to keep warm. 'Or she went somewhere seedy to get help and something else completely happened to her.'

Aloysius glanced, a little longingly, at the crescent window of his room on the top floor. As much as he liked Anna, as much as he was intrigued by the chase, he would be so much happier if they were warm right now.

'Or maybe, maybe she had the procedure and then that engen-dered a kind of breakdown. What a depressing thought,' Anna said as she bounced up and down on the spot on the edge of the kerb. She didn't seem very depressed. She actually seemed quite exhilarated by the whole thing.

'Anna,' Aloysius said at last, 'I am very cold. Can we please go inside?'

Anna stopped bouncing and narrowed her eyes. Aloysius raised a placatory hand. 'Or you can go home. I'm not trying anything. But I cannot feel my toes. And we are standing outside my house, which is nearly always warm.'

The temperature had dropped noticeably since they had waited outside the doctor's office. There was frost in the air. Anna contemplated her walk to Tulse Hill and her wait at the bus stop. Now she came to think of it she was terribly hungry.

'You know,' Aloysius continued, 'I have a very nice landlady who would make us tea and toast. It would all be perfectly correct. And I would walk you to the bus stop before the last bus of the night.'

The mention of the landlady swung Anna, as Aloysius had hoped it would. He found his latch-key and they walked in together.

There was a radio playing in the kitchen and the lights blazed from the back room of the house. Aloysius helped Anna off with her coat and hung it beside his on the hallstand.

'Mrs McDonald? I've brought a young lady for tea. I hope that's okay.'

A tall and rather busty lady appeared in the doorway to the kitchen, drying teacups with a cloth. She wore a jade-green dress and a scarlet hand-knitted cardigan. Her hair was a mass of pale brown curls and her skin was honey-brown and freckled. Anna could see that she must be fifty at least, but she was still strikingly beautiful.

'Hello, young lady,' said Mrs McDonald with a nod.

'Hello. I'm Anna. Aloysius was helping me with something for a friend.'

Mrs McDonald looked at Aloysius while Aloysius ignored her with some intensity.

'We wondered if we could have some tea,' Anna asked.

'Surely.'

'And toast,' added Aloysius, pretending to be interested in something through the doorway of the darkened living room.

'I'll bring them both up.'

Anna looked a little alarmed. 'I think we're quite happy to eat down here, if you don't mind.'

'Don't be silly,' Mrs McDonald said. 'Go on, upstairs now. You'll be much comfier.' And she flapped her tea towel in the direction of the stairs.

Anna ascended first, Aloysius close behind her, and she heard Mrs McDonald whisper to him through the banisters, 'A girl!' and Aloysius answer, 'Hush.'

At the top of four flights of stairs, Aloysius showed her into an oddly angled room, the ceiling sloping under the eaves on one side and the curve of the crescent window looking out onto the street. A large single bed stood along one wall and beside it a bookcase and a little lamp. There was a wardrobe and green velvet armchair and a very small coffee table and almost nothing else. Aloysius picked up a number of socks from the floor and threw them behind the wardrobe door. Without them the room appeared quite tidy. From the evidence of books spread across the bed he was reading *The Odyssey*, *The Mirror Crack'd from Side to Side* and *Black Mischief*.

'Do you like Evelyn Waugh?' Anna asked.

Aloysius smiled at the question. 'Despite myself, I do. But he makes me angry as well.' He shrugged. 'He's clever and funny and crude. I don't know if it's good literature; Dr Gillespie would not have thought so.'

Anna wanted to ask if Dr Gillespie was black but she couldn't think how best to put the question. Aloysius ushered her into the green armchair.

'I will leave the door open,' he said. 'Just so everyone knows where they are.' He kept his coat on and perched on the edge of the bed. 'So, what are you going to do now?'

'Well, the sensible thing would be to go to the police, to go to Sergeant Hayes and tell him.' Aloysius raised his eyebrows so she added, 'But of course I'm not going to do that because we promised Dr Jones. Which means the onus is rather on me to follow it up.' Anna stared at the light from the street, which was bleaching the glass of the lunette window. 'I think, truthfully, I'm a bit scared of going further.'

'Because you're frightened of what has happened?'

'Because I'm frightened of the kind of people I might have to meet. I'm scared to ask people about abortion. I'm happier not knowing.'

'You probably shouldn't become a policewoman then.' Aloysius was teasing her, but the tone of his voice was gentle. She looked at him now, really looked at him. He had long narrow bright eyes and an almost snub nose. His lips and his cheeks were full but the impression his face gave you was of someone long and lean and serious. He wore black-framed NHS spectacles and looked like someone who would grow up to be a wacky professor. Or a man who gives talks on mathematics late at night on the radio. She did not quite think him handsome but he was rather beautiful – though whether his beauty came from his features and his colouring or whether it came from the kindliness he exuded she could not yet decide.

'You know, I never thought how scary it might be to be a police-man,' Anna said. 'I always saw them in their uniform and I think I imagined them to be like robots. They have this thing about them where they seem not quite to be human. But of course they must be human. And they must be afraid, too. Imagine needing to find out the worst thing you could hear? Or wanting to? Waiting to be told something awful in almost every conversation you had at work. What must that do to a person?'

They sat in silence for a moment. 'I want the world to be a gentler place than it is,' Aloysius told her. 'I want to believe the good in people. I don't think that is a manly sentiment to have.' He stared at his feet.

Speckles of black pitted the glow from the light on the window-panes. Anna moved to the window. Outside the world was swirling. She turned to Aloysius and grinned. 'It's snowing.'

Aloysius gazed up at Anna framed against the half-moon glass. She was smiling like a child and her happiness floated through the room and lifted his heart as if in a pair of hands and kissed it. He joined her and side by side they stood, watching the flurry of white flakes blot out the details of the other buildings and obscure the road and cars.

'How will you get home?' he asked.

Anna laughed. 'There'll still be buses. There are always buses.' She had forgotten Iolanthe and Dr Jones and Sergeant Hayes. They stood there, side by side, arms touching, the cold of the glass threatening to burn their fingertips.

'Toast!' cried Mrs McDonald and they turned together. The landlady was standing in the doorway with a large tray covered with tea things and plates of toast and knives and spoons. She watched them for a moment with a look of real gentleness, then she set the tray down on the bed and nodded towards the cups.

'Don't give her anything with a chip in it,' she told Aloysius and left again, pulling the door closed behind her.

They sat cross-legged on Aloysius's bed and ate the toast. Anna sat at the head, leaning back on pillows that Aloysius had arranged for her and he sat beside his little pile of books and poured the tea.

'Did you go to university?' he asked her, not quite knowing if this was a silly question one way or the other.

'No. No university. School. A-levels. I wasn't very happy when I was seventeen. I mucked things up. What about you?'

'University of the West Indies.'

'Oh. I see,' said Anna, nodding enthusiastically.

Aloysius flashed her a knowing smile.

'What?'

'You did the white person nod.'

'Well, what other nod am I supposed to do?'

'Doesn't matter.'

'No, it does matter. You're making fun of me. What did I do?' Anna put down her teacup. She looked quite upset.

'It's just when you say things like University of the West Indies there are two reactions, okay? So the first one is when people say, "Where the hell's that? I didn't even know they had universities where you come from. What's your speciality: boiling missionaries?" and then everyone laughs: "Ha ha ha ha ha". And the second one is the white person nod. That's when the person wants to seem really knowledgeable so they do this fast nod like they were just thinking: "Oh, yes, University of the West Indies; that's where we

91

were thinking of sending Cedric. Excellent cricket team, no doubt. More Pimm's?"'

'So basically I can't win. I'm either an idiot or an idiot with manners.'

Aloysius thought about this. 'Before I came to this country I thought I would see hansom cabs on the streets of London. I thought that all manner of men would speak perfect English and no one would ever swear. I thought that you could get on a red bus at the weekend and it would take you up to Scotland for bagpipe concerts. I thought that I would live in a little flat next to Big Ben. I thought that pubs would be clean and friendly and the beer would come in a metal tankard. I thought I would meet a girl and walk in the Vauxhall Pleasure Gardens and there would be fire-eaters and I would propose to her one summer night surrounded by rose-trees. I thought I would work in an office with wooden panels on the walls and my children would be educated at Eton. I thought I would be welcome in the best restaurants and invited to join the gentlemen's clubs for I had taken a degree from a proper university. We are all idiots, Anna. There's no great shame in that. I think it must be the human condition, because I haven't met a woman or man in my life – not even the wisest soul – who wasn't an idiot in some way or another.'

'It's not exactly a compliment, though, is it?'

'If you want to hear nothing but compliments you must find yourself a liar.'

Anna looked at Aloysius. She wasn't sure any more if he even liked her. She felt foolish and deflated and confused. Aloysius read this in her face and saw that he had gone too far. They'd only met four hours ago and he was behaving as if she were a friend of many years. He stretched his hand across the bed, although what he meant for her to do with it he didn't quite know.

'I didn't mean to hurt your feelings. This has been a very strange evening. I thought I could talk to you like a friend but you don't really know me at all. If it helps you should know that I wouldn't speak honestly if I didn't respect you. I have lived in this country for four years and I have the pleasure of an honest conversation about twice a year.'

Anna gave a small smile. 'Welcome to Britain.'

Aloysius's hand dropped back into his lap and he executed a little bow. 'I'm very pleased to be here.'

'Are you really, though?'

'Most of the time … yes, I am.' Aloysius laughed. 'We are allowed to go back home, you know. Some people even advocate it.'

He was teasing her again and Anna suddenly felt quite exhausted. The tea and the toast were warming her bones. The relentless strangeness of the day had caught up with her and she was realising with a certain abruptness that her world – her city – was filled to the brim with people and experiences that she had thought nothing about. She lay back against the pillows and her eyelids drooped.

'Do we need to get you home?' Aloysius asked her, looking behind him at the snowy curtains falling on the wrong side of the glass.

'Do you think perhaps that you could fly me there?'

'On a magic carpet?'

'I was thinking more of a winged horse.'

'I can lend you a pair of gloves and walk you to the bus stop.'

'That will have to do.'

So Anna dragged herself off the bed and pulled on her shoes and Aloysius went downstairs to fetch their coats. When Anna got to the hallway, Mrs McDonald was standing there waiting for her. She passed Anna a little parcel wrapped in baking paper.

'Oaty biscuits. For the journey home. In case you get stuck in the snow and are tempted to eat Louis.'

'Thank you.'

Aloysius was already hovering in the open doorway. He handed her his gloves – 'just till you get home' – and they made their way outside.

Snow tipped down on them from the skies and stung their eyes when they tried to peer at it. Aloysius took Anna by the hand and they walked as fast as they could manage along the wet pavements, shaking their heads every so often to clear the snow from their brows and lashes and the bridges of their noses.

Amesbury Avenue. Hillside Road. Palace Road. The vast houses flicked by, marking time and space. There were no cars on the roads now. The living-room windows shone yellow and orange in the darkness. Here and there Anna was aware of faces pressed to the glass, watching the snow fall, watching a black man lead a white woman through the streets.

Neither she nor Aloysius said a word; their lips and noses were stinging from the cold. And what was there to say, after all? It was most probably a mistake to be on the streets in this weather but the alternative was spending the night in the house or even in the room of a man she'd just met. A man who she might very well be attracted to and therefore must on no account share intimacy with.

On Tulse Hill Aloysius guided her south. 'There's a shelter somewhere down here. I don't think the bus will be on time tonight.' They made it inside the shelter and stood looking at each other, one yeti figure blinking in confusion at the other.

Anna wiped the snow off her face and front. 'Was this a terrible mistake?'

'I think it probably was.' Aloysius laughed and leaned against the glass wall. He stuck his head out briefly to check if there was anything coming. Every minute or so a lone car would pass them, headlights full glare, windscreen wipers pumping back and forth. The pavements and the roads were already wearing a thick coat of snow. The hedges had turned white and the roofs of the houses formed a long white line against the sky.

Aloysius was trying and failing to wipe his glasses clean. Finally, he gave up and hung them on the front of his coat. 'You know, I'm going to have to come with you into town.'

'Why?'

'Because it's horrible. Because the bus only gets you as far as Oxford Street. Because it might break down and I'm guessing you have no money for a cab. Because I want my gloves back but I can't take them away from you in a snowstorm. Pick your reason.'

'But what are you going to do once you've walked me home?'

'I have a friend in Soho. I can get myself a sofa for the night.' And he stuck his head out of the shelter again to check for a bus. Every time he did this he got a faceful of snow and every time he drew his head back in in its yetified state Anna laughed and liked him more. Aloysius was easy to be with. He was – she thought – comfortable in his own skin and that made her feel more comfortable in hers.

Aloysius wiped the snow off his head for the fifth time and glanced across at Anna, who was huddled into a corner trying to keep warm.

'You know, Dr Gillespie used to say that English people think all the rest of the world are like onions. Like …' He waved his hands. 'Have you read *Peer Gynt*?'

'Yes. The onion seller. He peels Peer at the end of the play. Takes off all his layers.'

'Yes, so, Dr Gillespie said that the English, the British, they think everyone is secretly an Englishman at heart and if you peel all the other layers away – the silly accents and the rotten manners and not understanding the rules of bridge – then at the heart you will find an Englishman.'

'But the onion has no heart. Isn't that the point?'

'Exactly. Englishness is just another layer of swaddling. But the English haven't yet figured that out.'

'Bus!' Anna leapt towards Aloysius, nearly knocking him over and together – almost in each other's arms – they stumbled out of the shelter and onto the kerb. The bus stopped, the exhaust blew smoke. They bought their tickets from the grey-faced conductor who was slumped on a seat on the lower deck.

'Let's go upstairs,' said Anna. 'We might as well try for a view.'

The bus was almost completely empty so they walked down the aisle of the top deck waiting to feel a puff of hot air at their feet announcing a heating vent.

'There it is,' cried Anna and they settled themselves, side by side, as close to the heat as they could manage. The bus continued on its way, the windows misted, the swirling cloth of snow reframing – reimagining – familiar streets into the landscape of another town or time. Anna and Aloysius sat in silence, each holding tight to the metal bar in front, each allowing themselves to thaw from the feet upwards.

95

It took the bus more than an hour to make the journey into central London. By Stockwell, when their bodies had relaxed, Anna and Aloysius fell again to comparing books they'd read and books they'd loved. *Brave New World*: Aloysius but not Anna. *1984*: them both, though Anna honestly hadn't ever loved Orwell. *Brighton Rock*: Aloysius hadn't read any Graham Greene but yes, of course he meant to. Evelyn Waugh: Anna liked *A Handful of Dust* because it was human, Aloysius preferred *Decline and Fall* because the comedy was better. Then Anna pretended to have read *Bleak House* and Aloysius pretended to have finished *Dombey and Son*. Then they agreed that *Shirley* was a better novel than most people thought but only in the first half. They couldn't agree on Austen and Aloysius found himself slightly embarrassed at being the one to champion her so they dropped it and both pretended to have read *Tom Jones* instead.

On Oxford Street, they descended the stairs together and, seeing them, the conductor approached Anna.

'Where you going, love?'

'Covent Garden.'

'I wouldn't be counting on any more buses tonight.'

'It's all right, sir, I'm walking with her,' Aloysius told him and the conductor breathed heavily through his nose like a horse snorting and turned away from them both.

The snow had abated a little but the wind was blowing fast down Oxford Street. There were a few cabs but they were mostly parked up with their lights turned off.

'Do you think the tubes are still running?' Anna asked and they cautiously made their way towards Bond Street station. But as they came to the top of the stairs the lights were being turned off down below. They trudged on towards Oxford Circus, both too cold to speak.

* * *

Just west of Liverpool Street Orla and Gracie lay together on Gracie's bed. Orla had been reading *The Lion, the Witch and the Wardrobe* while they waited for the sound of Daddy coming home. But then Gracie had fallen asleep on Orla's chest, and Orla had been so soothed by the warmth and weight of Gracie's little body that she had wedged herself against a wall and fallen asleep herself.

Hours passed and then Gracie woke, crying, having dreamed about a shoal of tiny fish who were circling her bed and blocking out the light. Orla kissed her daughter's cheeks and settled her back. Gracie's little hand moved to the blind.

'Look!' she said.

They raised the blind together.

'Will Father Christmas come tonight?' Gracie asked. 'Does he bring snow with him?'

'No, darling,' Orla told her. 'Father Christmas has millions more presents to make before the big night.'

'Who brings the snow?'

'Just the clouds, my darling. Just weather and science and all that sort of stuff.'

'Jack Frost?' Gracie asked and Orla couldn't remember what she had said, if anything, about him.

'Well now, Gracie, that's a good point you make. What about Jack Frost? I've never seen him myself. But that doesn't mean he doesn't exist. Maybe Daddy's seen him.'

'Is Daddy home now?'

'I've no idea.'

'Will you go and see?'

'Of course I will.'

So Orla searched the rooms of the house for the man who was never there but when she returned to Gracie the child had gone to sleep, one hand resting on the windowsill as if to stop the snow from running away before it became another day.

Orla and Brennan

They met at a funeral. It was June and the grass in the graveyard shone emerald, a slice of colour beaming upwards beside the churning dust and dirt of the Commercial Road. Orla Keane was wearing a poppy in the buttonhole of her black coat and as she entered the church the eyes of three elderly ladies standing to one side settled upon this single discordant note in a sea of black cloth.

Brennan Hayes arrived late for the service, the doors already closing, everybody seated. Orla, sitting beside the aisle a third of the way down the church turned in her pew and looked to see who had entered. Brennan's eye, dashing madly across the sea of hats and half-turned faces, spied the poppy and above it the calm, strong face of a young woman with short-cropped hair who – just for a very fraction of a second – met his eye. Orla gathered the skirt of her coat and shuffled sideways along the pew. Brennan trotted as lightly as he could along the chequerboard aisle and slipped into the space beside her. The priest spoke.

'May the Father of mercies, the God of all consolation, be with you.'

Brennan was aware of the long, pale face turning towards him. He wondered if he had misinterpreted Orla's gesture and whether he should start to move before the first hymn. He glanced sideways and saw that the young woman was looking at him, not with annoyance or distress, but with what seemed like an abundance of good humour. And when she spoke the words, her dark eyes creased into a smile, letting Brennan know that she was talking specifically to him.

'And also with you.'

After the hearse had drawn off and the mourners had started the long walk to Bow Cemetery, Orla and Brennan lingered on the grass by the side of the church. They had walked out together without speaking and stood patiently as the coffin was carried out and the mourners hugged and chattered and exchanged their blessings. Lorries rumbled past, filling the air with fumes.

'Aren't you going to the burial?' he asked her.

'I didn't have a plan. I thought perhaps ...'

'How did you know her?'

'Oh, everyone knew her.'

'I know, but how did you?'

Orla looked at him and her eyes crinkled again. 'I didn't. It was a morning off work.'

Brennan's face stilled and furrowed. Orla unbuttoned her coat, letting him see a flash of bright blue dress. 'I only have three dresses and none of them black. None of them long, either, come to that.'

Brennan still stared at her, a look of puzzlement fixed in his gaze. 'Why would you come to a funeral? Why would you use a funeral to take a morning off work? If you hate your job so much, then lie. Don't use the rites of a person's soul ...'

She made a last-ditch attempt at charm. Drawing herself up tall, she faced him straight on and offered him her hand to shake.

'Orla Keane. I've been in London ten weeks and I know no one. Absolutely no one. Not a soul. I have no friends and my family is four hundred miles away, give or take a bad road. Will you have a cup of tea with me – and a bun, perhaps ...? Else there was no point in playing fast and foolish with souls or rites or any of it. And I meant no harm. So don't be cross. Or I'll have no friends and one enemy and might as well swim home in my clothes.'

In the end they had a cup of tea. And a bun. And Brennan walked her back to the offices of Kavanagh and Hill – attorneys at law – where Orla was newly made a secretary to Mr Hill. And on the following Tuesday, when he was not on duty, he picked her up from work and walked her to Wapping Rose Garden for an early-evening picnic of egg sandwiches and pound cake. And Orla laughed because when they finally arrived there were no roses to be seen. But they sat in their summer clothes and drank dandelion and burdock and then Orla, kneeling in the grass in her dress of green and yellow daisies, performed for him her impression of Mr Kavanagh asking Mr Hill to a dance.

'I shall lead you, Hill, up brook and down dale – I will dance you into next week and you and I will take our little ledgers and live as snug as any two bunnies in dreamland with just our shillings and our pence and our sound contractual services.'

And Orla laughed at her own invention and threw herself down in the grass muttering about bunnies and cocoa and not minding at all that the gardener was staring his disapproval at them both and Brennan knew that he was a little bit besotted with this woman and a small part of him regretted ever asking her to the rose garden for he was only twenty-five and had hoped he had a few years left to himself.

Brennan worried about his family back home in Londonderry. His elder sister had died a year after he left and his younger sister who wrote every month provided a running commentary on their mother's grief and their father's descent into silence. But he had yearned to leave, to fly the nest and all the sleepy blue/grey corners of his youth, so he headed first for St Columb's in the streets of Derry, then on to a scholarship at Queen's in Belfast studying politics and philosophy.

At Queen's he had been befriended by an Anglo-Irish political scientist latterly of Imperial College who longed to return home and who had filled Brennan's head with dreams of London and the expanse of life that waited for him across the sea. To the open disgust of many of his friends he had used his connection with Dr Devlin to make enquiries first about the civil service – not a fruitful exercise as it turned out – and then about a place at the Police Staff College in Warwickshire.

'How do we change the system, Brennan?' Devlin repeated this often. 'How do we change it?' And Brennan would smile at him over his glass and wait for Devlin to give his answer. 'We change it from within. Put one thinking man, one thinking *Irishman*, amongst the lackeys and the sops of the Establishment and we might have ourselves a social revolution.' Brennan smiled and said nothing.

Dr Devlin was just the latest in a long line of men to have inspired his admiration. For Brennan had a weakness for charismatic know-it-alls: lecturers, priests and politicians. He loved a fine, sound, moral idea; he loved the suggestion of a sense of purpose. Above all he loved certainty and the breathless allure of those who have it.

As it turned out, far from being friendless, within days of arriving in London Orla had assembled around her a gaggle of strange and interesting people. There was Marjorie Bendigen who ran a sort of informal home for human waifs and strays. As well as housing and feeding up to fifteen children at a time in her cramped and dark little home off the Commercial Road, she held open house on Tuesdays and Thursdays for the shop girls and secretaries who lived in the rented rooms all around her.

Orla invited Brennan to one of these after they'd been stepping out for a month or more and Brennan – having no idea what to expect – arrived with a bunch of late summer flowers and a small box of truffles. Walking into the dirt and shambles of Marjorie's living room – where old magazines and newspapers littered the floor, a boy was drawing dogs in crayon on the skirting board and Mrs Bendigen's underwear hung on strings in front of the fire – Brennan knew he had misunderstood the nature of the invitation. A clutch of young women in nylon suits turned to look at him from the orange velvet sofa as Marjorie hauled herself up from the floor and enacted a wobbly curtsey. Orla, who was sitting on a stool by the fire, laughed into her tea so hard that she spurted some across the room. But that was Orla's way. Nothing mattered so very much and everything was funny.

Then there was Eddie Miller, who worked as a runner for ATV and who got Brennan and Orla in to watch recordings of *Take Your Pick* at the Hackney Empire. The chance to watch television 'from the inside', as Orla put it, was quite a novelty for two young people who'd never lived in a house with a TV.

'The month I left home,' Orla told Brennan, 'my parents took in a lodger and used the money to hire a television. My father hasn't left the lounge since.'

Sitting on the top deck of the 106 on the way home, Brennan found himself dwelling on the way that Orla had laughed and flirted with Eddie after the recording.

'Do you like Eddie Miller?'

'I like that he gets me in to see the television being made. I like that he's funny and gossipy and he tells me things about the women in the studio. I like that he fancies me because it makes him nice and kind and I'll never say no to a bit of nice and kind.'

'Well, that was honest.'

'Ask me another question,' Orla said.

'Do you really like me or am I just a good prospect?' He had thought he could make it sound like a joke but when it came out of his mouth his tone was all wrong.

Orla was silent for a long half-minute. When she spoke her voice was quiet and filled with pain. 'You're a Mick in the Met, Brennan Hayes. The idea you're going to get anywhere is a bloody fantasy. But up to about a minute ago I really liked you and respected you because you were trying to do something proper with your life. I earn my own wage. I always have. I pay my own way. Live on my own terms. I ...' But she couldn't finish the sentence because her voice had broken.

She swung herself up on one of the poles and pressed the bell. She pushed roughly past Brennan's knees and juddered down the stairs. Brennan watched as she burst out onto the pavement and walked back the way they'd come. He had her bus ticket in his wallet. He wondered if she had enough for another fare. He didn't get up or try to chase her. He rode the bus all the way to Commercial Road and then on to Poplar and Barking; far past the stage his ticket would allow. And as he rode the bus he watched the people outside the window and he thought very, very carefully about what he would do next.

At Chitty's Lane in Becontree Brennan got off. He had made a plan to find a little cafe or a pub where the bus drivers would welcome him in with a silent nod and the possible offer of a cigarette but he found instead that he had been marooned within a large housing estate where all the little windows stared blankly out at him and there were no shops or pubs or greasy spoons to be seen. Brennan walked the streets of the strange new town thinking about Orla and trying to separate out what part of him just wanted to sleep with her and what part of him actually liked her enough to consider making a life with her.

He wondered to himself why he had asked her the prospect question. He wasn't the kind of man to believe that all girls wanted was a ring on their finger and the excuse to stop working. He knew for just about certain that Orla Keane was not a girl like that. But all the same, the men that he worked for in the Met seemed to be married to women who lived to play house and spend their monthly allowances on clothes and wallpaper and magazines and shoes. Or at least that's what his colleagues told him their wives were like. He remembered Mary Lawler, a student from his time at Queen's, whose eyes had shone with a kind of rage when asked one evening by his friend Barry Dunne if she was on the lookout for a husband.

'What makes you think I want a husband?'

'I thought that's what all you clever girls wanted. Three years away from home to hook your fish then back to the countryside to make babies and take up sewing.'

'Why would I give my life away so lightly?'

'For the money, Mary – it's always for the money.'

'And what happens when I can earn my own?'

Barry Dunne refilled their glasses as Mary's cold eyes watched him think.

'Then society crumbles for there'll be no more bairns.' Mary smiled and Barry added, 'But it isn't going to happen. You can only keep up a front for so many years. By the time you're thirty you'll have got tired of all the anger. Your looks will go. You'll realise that having a job is harder work than having babies and you'll take your pick from the stragglers and the fags who never quite got round to it the first time. You're all front, Mary. All front and no follow-through.'

Brennan sat in silence and listened to them fight and when Mary started to look tired he picked up her coat and bag and offered to walk her home.

'Another offer you think I can't refuse?'

'I just think maybe we'll leave Barry to argue with his glass.' Mary took back her coat and together they left the bar.

It was a warm night – warm for Belfast, anyway – and they walked for a while in silence along the paths by the Botanic Gardens. They paused near the palm house and Mary sat and shared a cigarette with Brennan.

'I don't really know what to do with the likes of Barry Dunne. It's like he thinks that all the knowledge in the world has been transported to his head and nothing he can ever hear or study will change it. He's a dinosaur. A nineteen-year-old dinosaur. And some poor bugger will up and marry him one day and then her life will be well and truly over.'

'The thing is …' It was the first time Brennan had spoken since they'd left the pub but it was too soon for Mary. Her head swivelled sharply. 'Yes?'

'The thing is, Mary, I'd put money on the idea that he was flirting with you.'

'Flirting with me?'

'It's what he does. He thinks it's charming. He thinks you'll get really angry and then rip off all your clothes and supplicate to him.'

She was still staring at him and he wondered if the ripping-off-clothes image had been a step too far. Mary thought about this for a moment and then she shrugged and slumped back onto the bench.

'How is this ever going to work, Brennan? How are we ever going to make things work if men are walking round with these idiot ideas branded into their very soul and womankind is dividing herself up into those who will play the game and die inside and those who cannot even imagine making a life with a man because they say things that make you want to put their eyes out?'

'Dr Devlin would say you have to change the system from within.'

'Jesus, does that mean I have to marry Barry Dunne? I'd sooner die.'

'I wish …' Brennan started and then stopped. 'I wish I had the answers, Mary. But I don't.'

'Well, at least that's honest. If nothing else stay honest, Brennan.' She paused, looked at him and stretched her back as she stood. 'You're one of the better ones. We need you to stay as you are.' And Mary walked off into the night, blowing smoke signals up into the air.

In Becontree, Brennan found himself outside a tube station so he bought a ticket and took a train heading west. He allowed the joggling of the carriage to soothe his body. He felt parts of it unfurl. If he really wanted he needn't see Orla again. She didn't have to be the one for him, but he had a suspicion that she was.

Orla was funny and clever, in a sharp-toothed kind of a way. She didn't care much for convention and even less for religion though she never laughed at his faith. She said once that she accepted faith in God as a kind of 'common affliction or sign of the norm'. She was the one with yellow eyes while everyone else had blue or brown.

Between Gunnersbury and Kew he rattled across the River Thames, the calm expanse of water reflecting a deep blue sky shot through with shards of white. The river was low this evening and the muddy banks led his eye up to the half-timbered houses on either side, the vast chestnut trees, the fat black cars sitting outside the fat white houses. Did he want success? Did he want a home and a child and a car of his own? He had taken on a job that had already started to change him. Was he ready for a marriage that would restrict his choices?

At Richmond station the train came to its conclusion. Brennan got out and stood on the platform wondering where he could go next. He glanced up at the station clock. It was six fifty. In twelve hours and ten minutes he was back on shift. The thought of this made his heart rattle unhappily in his chest. These hours with Orla, they were meant to be his escape.

Some days he felt as if he were drowning. He didn't understand where the acts of violence came from but there seemed to be a great wave of malevolence that washed over the whole of the city each and every evening. Working men pounding the bones, chopping and mincing the cartilage of other men: on the steps of pubs, in the yards beside the high-piled kegs of beer, on the shore of the heaving, reeking river. Of course you didn't see anything like that round here. The colours were brighter at the western end of the lines, the sounds of affluence sharper and clearer, the screams almost entirely muffled by thick and well-made walls. He was starting to learn London. He had written this in a letter to his sister Maggie a year ago and she had written back that he was Dorothy trying to understand the topography of Oz, never properly realising that it wasn't real.

Brennan got back on the same train, still idling on the platform, the lighted sign indicating that it would shortly be leaving for Upminster. He rattled back across the River Thames and in the twilight he could imagine Orla in her dress of green and yellow daisies dancing with a bottle of beer along its narrow banks. He could imagine Orla in one of the fat white houses singing to a child in a cradle as she sat with her feet on the windowsill reading the evening paper. He could imagine Orla welcoming him into bed, surrounding him with heat and love and kisses. He could imagine Orla dancing in the garden on a warm, spring day – swinging their child into the air, both of them screaming with glee. She would be a good mother, he could see that already. She had a light inside that shone on the people around her. Everyone loved Orla.

He got off the train at Whitechapel and walked south, arriving at the front door of Orla's block at a little after nine.

Orla opened the door. She was wearing her dressing gown and carrying a towel.

'Yes?' she said.

Brennan opened his mouth to speak but then the words wouldn't come.

'I'm going to have a bath,' Orla said and she turned on her heel and walked up the stairs to the bathroom. It seemed too forward to let himself into the bathroom itself so Brennan climbed the stairs to her bedroom and sat down on the bed.

Orla was obviously in no mood to hurry. By half past nine Brennan was so nervous that he started to tidy the room just to give himself something to do. Having established a clear patch on most of the surfaces he went through her small collection of books and selected *The Water Babies* as something neutral to read.

At a quarter past ten Orla pushed open the door.

'Oh!' She nearly dropped her towel when she saw him.

'Sorry.'

'What are you doing here? I thought you went away.'

'I can't follow a woman into a bathroom.'

'Did you tidy my room?'

'I'm sorry. I was nervous. I don't know why I said it. The prospect thing. I don't think ... You're not like that. You know that Eddie Miller likes you and maybe I was jealous or scared or something ...'

'So you're apologising.'

'Yes, I am.'

'Anything else?'

'Our children would have to be Catholic.'

'What?'

'Do you think you can do that?'

'We don't have any children.'

'Yes. But if we stay together we might. And I know you don't believe and I think ... I think that I can live with that. But not my children. I need to know that they'd be Catholic; that you would let them believe.'

'Why are we talking about children?'

'Because if we stay together then I think this is it. Don't you? I think we do this or we don't. In or out. I need to know if you're serious.'

Orla threw her towel down on the bed. Brennan stared at her, too shocked to turn away.

She crossed her arms over her breasts. 'Could we at least do things in order?'

'What?'

'Could we at least sleep together first?'

'Well, I don't really believe—'

'Yes, I know that, you idiot. But I'm saying let's just go about this like two human animals. Let's go to bed together. And tomorrow to the pictures. And then to bed again. And then let's see what we feel for each other. I can't promise to marry you. And I can't promise to baptise children I haven't had. But if you will treat me well I will try to do the same. Two grown-ups. Doing what the other grown-ups do.'

Five months later Orla Keane and Brennan Hayes walked again down the chequerboard aisle of St Mary and St Michael, this time amongst a congregation of six, and as Orla stood before the priest and made her vows, she kept one hand firmly pressed onto her stomach. For the vows that she made that day weren't simply to Brennan, they were also to her baby, her new-made friend, her love, her very fire and light inside, growing second by second, fruitful and adored, inside her womb.

The Duke Vin Sound System

Snow was piled high in the corners of the windows and Ottmar decided to close early for the night. The last of the customers had left at half past eight when the weather made its turn for the worse. Helen had gone home already, worried about her buses. Rachel could finish the cleaning on her own; he'd put some extra shillings in her pay packet to say thanks.

He turned the sign on the door, letting his fingers rest on the glass as he did so. The door fizzed with the cold outside. He ran his broom very quickly round the edges of the tables and retreated to sit by the hatch and drink tea while Rachel worked. He felt lonely tonight, lonely and downhearted.

Leonard was upstairs waiting for a phone call from Benji about his sister. Rashida was in bed and Ekin was sitting up, sewing name tapes inside a hockey kit and waiting for Samira to come home.

They had tried to stop her, he told himself. Tried to reason with her. Tried to pin her back down. Just last weekend they had told her she could not go out at all and she had stayed in the flat all Saturday and Sunday, which meant of course that Ekin could not go out either. Samira had pretended that Ekin didn't exist, ignoring her when she walked into the room, preparing food as if Ekin was not standing right beside her.

Ottmar had been watching his little family fight and fall apart for so many years now that he no longer knew if there was any other way. In many ways he lived a life quite separate from his wife and daughters. He had his little world downstairs which consumed his time, his attention and his money. The women's intensity frightened him. He regarded them as a line of boiling pots whose lids might blow into his face at any second. They seemed to love each other, though as the girls grew older he saw more love flowing from Ekin than back the other way. He watched his daughters' cruelties, their indifference to their mother's feelings, and racked his brains to ask himself if he had been the same when he was still a boy. He had felt pain – actual, real, unimagined pain – when he contemplated the way that he had destroyed his mother's life, disregarded her opinions, fled from her arms.

'I was a terrible son,' he said to himself out loud. He had sat down to write a letter to her and had got more than a dozen sentences in when the futility of his gesture had overwhelmed him. He folded the little piece of airmail paper and tucked it away in his inside coat pocket. His mother had been dead six years already. He had not seen her in the nineteen years since he'd left Cyprus. He had not attended her funeral.

Rachel was finishing cleaning.

'Will you be able to make it home?' Ottmar asked her.

'I'm going to walk,' she told him. 'I'll be home in thirty minutes and it'll keep me warm. Don't worry. I'll see you tomorrow.'

'Rachel. Wait. If the snow is worse tomorrow please telephone first. I might not open for lunch.'

'Okay,' she called to him, already halfway out the door. Ottmar noticed how the darkness and the snow seemed to flatten the mood, the temperature, of his little cafe. He noted how the bunting over the hatch was looking ragged; how people had picked mosaic tiles of mirror off some of the frames around the room; how the red and yellow paint on the chairs was starting to crack and peel and chip away. A cold wind was blowing through his little slice of Istanbul and he realised with annoyance that Rachel had not shut the door.

He was hurrying over to secure it when he spotted her standing in the falling snow and talking with two tall, coated figures whose shoulders, faces and heads were almost entirely white. As he watched her he heard Rachel call 'Goodnight,' and walk quickly away. The shorter of the two figures approached Ottmar, waving to him through the glass. The figure wiped her eyes and nose and he saw that it was Anna.

The figures entered, shaking snow onto the mat and then onto the floor. Ottmar helped Anna to peel off her coat as she shook her hair out and wiped clean the rest of her face. The man beside her was attempting to clean his glasses with his shirt.

'Allow me.' Ottmar handed him a napkin from the nearest table and the tall figure thanked him in an odd accent. Ottmar went into the kitchen to heat a pot of coffee and from the safety of the little room he watched Anna's friend unpeel his coat and shake his hair free of snow. The man Anna was with was not white.

When the coffee was ready he brought it through to them and they all sat round the table furthest from the doors and windows.

'This is Aloysius,' Anna explained. 'Aloysius is an accountant. And this is Ottmar. I used to work for him and both of us live in the flats upstairs.'

'How do you come to know Anna, then?' Ottmar asked.

Aloysius thought about this for just long enough that Anna stepped in. 'I went and talked to a lot of people today about Iolanthe. I met Aloysius at the Cue Club and he had some very helpful suggestions, which we followed up. But then the snow came and Aloysius insisted on seeing me home.'

'Well,' said Ottmar, adopting a fatherly tone, 'I approve of that.'

'She has my gloves. I'm really just hoping to get them back,' Aloysius joked and Ottmar frowned a little, not appreciating levity in anyone who was lucky enough to spend the evening with Anna.

Aloysius knocked back the rest of his coffee and choked violently. Anna reached out and grabbed his arm. 'Don't drink the grounds at the bottom! They're disgusting.'

The way she said the word disgusting made Ottmar's heart burn in his chest. He saw how Anna touched the coloured boy, how she leaned in towards him with concern, brushed his shoulders with her hand. His stomach ached with self-loathing. He rose from his chair and nodded to them both. 'Forgive me, but it has been a long night and I promised I would go up to Ekin.'

'Sorry, Ottmar. We'll be on our way.' Anna signalled to Aloysius that they were leaving and Ottmar fetched their coats and helped Anna on with hers. He noticed as he stood behind her that Anna's hair smelled of the same shampoo that Samira used. He had forgotten who he was waiting for. Please God, any god, let Samira still be his little girl.

Aloysius opened the door for Anna and they slipped outside.

'What a strange man,' Aloysius said.

'I think he's just tired tonight.' It was still snowing but only lightly now. 'Where does your friend live?'

'Just beyond Soho.'

Anna held out his gloves; they were soaking wet. They looked at the sorry things lying in her hand and laughed.

'Keep them,' said Aloysius. 'No use to me tonight.'

'I feel as if I should walk you home now. Or at least to Soho.'

'Don't be silly. Go in and get warm.'

'I feel stupidly awake. I shouldn't have drunk all that coffee.'

'You know you can call me again,' Aloysius told her. 'I'd like to help. Any way I can.'

'Can I? I want to go to Roaring Twenties, perhaps tomorrow night, and I don't really want to go alone.'

'It would be my pleasure. Or I could always put my head in now. On the way past. It'll still be open.'

'Will it?'

'For another hour. Maybe more.'

Anna stood in Neal Street and looked up at the falling snow. Her shoes and tights were soaked through. But somehow she couldn't stop herself. She needed tonight to carry on; she felt the momentum of its action, felt as if the night itself were willing her to stay up that bit longer and find out how much further she could go.

'You know, if you'd let me change, we could go to the club together. It's just I'm so wet, I need some drier shoes.' She laughed and felt her laughter catch in her throat because she feared the hesitation she saw in Aloysius. He looked at her and then glanced over at the cafe as he thought. His brow wrinkled.

'Are you sure?'

'Deadly sure.'

'That's very sure.'

'You can come up and wait for me in the warm.'

And so they went inside. Aloysius sat on the stairs while Anna changed quietly in the living room. Her Oxfords were soaking and the only other shoes she had were heels, meant for interviews or smart occasions. She hated wearing them, though she thought perhaps they'd be more appropriate at a club. She'd never been to a club before.

She knew the girls up Carnaby Street wore their bright little dresses or their black and white minis. She had a green corduroy skirt whose waistband she could pull up around her ribs and safety-pin to make it shorter, and a black polo neck jumper. She couldn't imagine going without tights, though plenty of girls did even in the middle of winter, so she pulled on her thickest black pair. She went into the tiny bathroom and brushed her hair. Kelly's make-up was sitting on the shelf. Anna spat in the little pot of mascara and ran the brush through her lashes a couple of times. The face in the mirror looked like a picture from a magazine. She ran the water and washed her face, getting most of the blackness off. Then she put on her coat and her uncomfortable black heels and made for the door.

At the last moment, for reasons she didn't quite understand, Anna left Kelly a note.

Have gone to Roaring Twenties. Expect to be back tonight/morning.
A

She collected Aloysius from the stairs and together they walked back out into the snow.

Ottmar had not gone upstairs to Ekin. Instead he was sitting by the hatch in the darkness of his little cafe, waiting for Samira to appear. He saw Anna and Aloysius pass by, Anna stepping high to keep her heels out of the snow and holding on to Aloysius's arm to stop herself from falling. Where were all these young women going? The ones who walked out into the snow or out of sight with other men?

* * *

Carnaby Street was quiet tonight, the snow had frightened most of the young people indoors. Charlie Brown was standing where he always stood at the door of Roaring Twenties, half inside half outside, a thick black overcoat and gloves protecting him from the cold.

'See,' said Aloysius, 'I told you they'd be open.'

'You won't leave me on my own?' Anna asked.

'You can stick to me like glue.'

The bass ebbed up to them from the space below as they squeezed down the stairs and into the hot, dark interior of the club. They shook their bodies free of snow. The air was smoke, beer, sweat, rum and sweet, sweet perfume. Down one end there were tables where groups of women and couples on dates hunched over their drinks or shouted to each other or watched the dancers dance. There must have been a hundred bodies on the dance floor, the room was thick with them, the young women ducking and weaving as men squeezed through the crowd carrying drinks from the bar, cigarettes hanging from their lips.

They looked around them, getting their bearings. A man to their left knelt up on a bar stool and raised a hand to Aloysius. Aloysius slipped off his coat and silently unbuttoned Anna's for her too.

The rhythm was not a rhythm Anna knew. A low bass line pumped like an unsteady urgent heartbeat, an incessant entreaty that tickled the blood in her veins and unsteadied her nerves. Over the bass line a melody tugged at her clothes, nipped at her skin, wound itself around her like a snake. Aloysius touched her arm and she jumped. The music felt like another pair of hands on her, hundreds of hands, and the heat of the room was shooting through her body like a fire. She hadn't had a drink in seven hours but she felt drunk now.

She pushed her hand into the crook of Aloysius's arm. 'Find us a table,' she told him as they moved through the crowd. The throbbing bodies separated them and she stood for a moment alone, jostled and pushed in the midst of the dresses and the suits. She turned around and then around again, panicking at his absence, and then she raised a hand, one long black-sleeved arm, and waited for him to find her. A long-fingered hand wound into the air six feet away and she danced towards the sight of it. When she found him she laid one hand on his white-shirted chest and pushed against it as if to test his presence for herself.

Aloysius covered her hand with his own and they moved together, rocking backwards and forwards until the song had exhausted itself. The heartbeat stopped only for a moment and then the music shifted sideways and the trombones played and a soft rasping Jamaican voice sang, 'I'll be glad when you're dead, you rascal you …' and Aloysius smiled with a kind of surprised wonder and raised her hand to his mouth to kiss her palm. Anna watched him do this and though she felt his mouth on her hand it was the sight of him – his eyes closed, lost in the sensation of the moment – that seduced her. Here was a man who could both think and feel and it occurred to her that such a man would be the kind of man to marry. They stood there, Anna watching Aloysius watching her, lost in the narcissism of desire.

Anna was the first to break away and, taking his hand, she led him out of the crowd and towards the tables. One table stood lonely in the far corner and Anna threw herself into one of the chairs and arranged their coats around her. Aloysius stayed standing, watching the room, allowing a flush of embarrassment to pass. He cleaned his glasses and sat, refusing to look at Anna.

She leaned across the table and laid her hand on his wrist. 'Are we okay?' she asked him.

Aloysius nodded but said nothing. The music bucked and surged. Aloysius sat up very straight and watched the dancers dance. Anna felt the blood tingle in her face and lips. She wanted to kiss him. She wanted to take off his suit jacket and unbutton his shirt. Her fingers moved unconsciously, tracing the rise and fall of the melody, creeping along the lines of a body so real in her imagination she could feel the hardness of the muscle and the line of the ribs.

Piano keys jangled over a snaking bass line and someone somewhere far away could be heard riffing their way trance-like through 'Summertime' as if playing in a dance hall of the undead. Couples moved closer, so close that no darkness could be seen between their bodies, and the room rocked together to a twisting line of synco-pated notes. It was, Anna thought, as if the more the music strayed and twisted and confounded them the more they moved together as one, catching at the beat below to guide them, grinding through the strangeness as if hypnotised. She looked at the shiny, open-mouthed faces; they looked like a room of people drugged, high as flying kites on heat and proximity, their hearts tripping and racing just as hers was doing within her chest.

She was sweltering. Sweat tickled her collarbone and ran down her sides. Beneath her sweater she wore a cotton camisole so she peeled off her polo neck and tugged the body of the camisole down over her safety-pinned skirt. Aloysius glanced briefly across at her and then stood up with such force that he knocked over his own chair. 'I'm getting drinks,' he shouted, not quite meeting her eye and certainly not meeting her chest. 'Scotch?'

'No. Get me a martini and remind me to drink it slowly.'

'Okay,' he called over his shoulder and then he was gone.

Five minutes passed and then ten and then fifteen. Song flowed into song; shaking, shifting beat melted into lion's roar and then into the pulse and growl of jazz piano. When men tried to catch her eye Anna scowled her fiercest girls' school scowl. The music rocked and pounded through the floor and the table and her limbs. The sweat dried on her back and chest and brow; she felt the hairs on her arms prickle and stand aloft; she was very aware of the ache between her legs. Had she really been left alone? she wondered. Had she disgusted him? Her hands scrabbled on the floor below her chair and she pulled her sweater on again, put away her flesh, turned off her body and turned on her mind.

The white girls in the club wore pale dresses cut high on their thigh; dresses that shimmered with a pearly blue light, and gold and mustard thread. The black girls wore red and black, green and purple, bold bright colours which moved with their long, dark limbs. The women swayed their hips, backs curving sinuously, arms hovering in the air, grazing shoulders, stroking hair. Men in long, slim black trousers and white shirts rolled up their sleeves and danced with the same fluidity as the women. The more Anna watched the more she realised that there were no men and women in here but only bodies, a strange luminous tribe of humans lost in a single swell of sensation. Mostly hidden by the turntables, a thin black man in a dark shirt drank slowly from a bottle of beer and lifted discs to the light to read the labels. He chose one and Anna watched him move and sway as he fitted it to the turntable. Flown here from over the ocean a voice cried, 'I'm going down to girls' town!' and the tempo lifted and rocked, shaking the dancers in their reverie.

Aloysius edged his way back to her carrying a martini and something short in a round glass. He noted her redressed form and straightened his jacket.

'I was asking around.'

'And?'

'Martin – the barman at Cue Club – his flatmate Derek is in the kitchen so I talked to him. Iolanthe was here most nights the past month. Three, four times a week. He said she might have been with different guys, he wasn't sure. But two, three weeks ago she was seeing this guitarist, played for some of the little acts that came through here.'

'And he was black?'

'No. White.'

'Then he can't be the father.'

'Maybe the white guy found out that she was having an affair and did something to her.'

'Does he have a name?'

'Mark something. Derek's seen him around Soho late at night. There's an Italian coffee bar down Kingly Street he drinks in and a pub on Beak Street where Derek thinks he works behind the bar.'

'So, what do we do? Go and look for him?'

Aloysius shrugged. 'This is your adventure.'

'I keep waiting for someone to say, "Oh, yes, I know where Lanny is."'

'Yeah. I don't think anyone's going to do that.'

Anna examined how much of her martini she'd consumed. 'You know, I wasn't even going to go after the father. I thought we'd try and find out where she went to get her … pills or whatever. She went somewhere in the days after she saw Dr Jones, she must have done. She must have slept with someone or visited someone or I don't know …' Her voice was getting hoarse from shouting above the music.

'Do you want me to go back and talk to Derek again?'

'No. You're right. I'm meant to be looking for Lanny myself and now I've just given up and handed over to a man.'

Aloysius laughed. 'That must be very humiliating for you.'

Anna rose and straightened her safety-pinned skirt. She needed to use the lavatory and time in the lavatory was time to think. She made her way over to the ladies and joined the queue. She glanced back over her shoulder to see if Aloysius was watching but the crowd of dancers blocked her view. She thought of Iolanthe coming here every night after the show. Dancing, dating some man in secret from her other life, her other world. This was an easy place to feel secret in. In this world of black faces Anna felt oddly invisible, as if she'd entered another country and nothing she did here mattered to the girl who lived on Neal Street. She might very well strip naked and make love to Aloysius while the others watched for she had no need to be Anna any more if she didn't want to be. She wondered briefly if she might change her name again. She lived an assumed identity anyway – why not strip off her flesh, like the skin of a snake, and start over?

On the sound system a man's voice could be heard chugging, chuffing and blowing in rhythm with the trumpets and someone shouted 'Guns Fever!' Bullets whizzed and wailed above a beat that ran like a horse, all four legs lifting off the ground for a second at a time. A woman on the dance floor laughed and spun her girlfriend round, their faces glinting in the light. 'Guns Fever!' they shouted.

The queue inched forward. Anna fiddled with her skirt and tights. Her shoes were hurting her. She watched the women at the sinks do their make-up, scrape through their hair with their fingers, adjust their bras and their stockings, rub the mascara from off their cheeks. A young woman in a dark orange minidress exited a stall and caught Anna's eye just for a second. Anna was about to move past her when some strange mathematics of recognition started working inside her brain and she knew she had seen someone who was out of place. The girl in the terracotta minidress hadn't stopped to wash her hands but was already moving for the door when Anna's head came up with its result and she spoke the word aloud: 'Samira!'

A Suit-Wearing, Tea-Drinking
Man of London Town

Wednesday, 10 November

In West End Central Barnaby Hayes was still making calls. After his conversation with Nathaniel he next called the two main banks in Boston to ask them about mortgages held in the name of Maria Green. The man he talked to at the first bank gave him very short shrift about asking for client information but the lady at the second bank pronounced herself charmed by his accent and said that 'yes, of course' in the case of a missing persons enquiry at Scotland Yard she would be happy to take a look at their records for the twenties and thirties and she'd see what she could find before close of business. Hayes did not correct her when she made the assumption that he was calling her from Scotland Yard. He knew that romanticism had a part to play in all acts of policing and he had learned not to stand between people and their prejudices just as long as those prejudices helped him along in his work.

He tried quite fruitlessly to track down the New York bank that held account details for Yolanda Green and was well into the second half of the packet of digestives when the switchboard rang to say he had a call waiting from Boston.

'Miss Pettifield, how kind of you to call me back,' cried Hayes, pulling himself up to his full height of Englishness. Miss Pettifield laughed immoderately.

'Detective Sergeant Hayes, I have been through our records and I have found your mortgage. Would you like to hear the details?'

'Miss Pettifield, I would *love* to hear the details.' More laughter on the end of the line.

'Well now, our bank first granted a mortgage against the property in 1926 to a Mr Harold Green who paid $14,550 for the property, of which we loaned him $9,270. In 1942, on the death of Mr Green the house and mortgage passed to Maria Green, who I assume was his wife. On Maria Green's death in 1943 the property passed jointly to her children Nathaniel and Yolanda Green. Between June 1943 and June 1944 we received no mortgage repayments, but after that month they resume. In 1945 the house was re-mortgaged twice, both times with us. And then in November of 1947 the house was sold and the mortgages repaid in full. Would you like me to repeat any of that?'

Hayes had been writing furiously as she spoke. He tried now to re-read his notes.

'No. I think I'm clear. I'm just going to check … you said Nathaniel and Yolanda Green?'

'Yes.'

'Not Iolanthe Green?'

'No. Definitely Nathaniel and Yolanda.'

'And you think that Harold Green was married to Maria Green?'

'Well, I honestly couldn't say. I'm making an assumption based on the shared name and leaving her the property. She might well have been his sister or someone else entirely.'

'And you said the house cost fourteen and a half thousand dollars in 1926. That sounds like a lot of money. Was it?'

'Well, yes. That's an expensive house we're talking about. You don't know Beacon Street, I'm guessing, because the houses down there are lovely six-storey brownstones. You'd pay $40,000 for one of those now. Way beyond a mortgage clerk's salary, I can assure you.'

'One more question. Can you tell me anything about the name Cassidy?'

'Do you have a first name?'

'I don't. I know that a Mr Cassidy had been in touch with the missing woman and I believe he was an American. I wondered if you were aware of a connection.'

'I'm sorry, Detective Sergeant. This is Boston. I could pitch a handful of paperclips out of my window now and be pretty sure of one of them hitting a fellow called Cassidy. Without another name …'

'I understand completely. Miss Pettifield, I am already indebted to you, but can I ask another favour?'

'Anything you like, Detective Sergeant.'

'Would you happen to have a telephone book for Boston somewhere in your office? I was after the phone numbers of some of Mr Green's former neighbours.'

*   *   *

Over in Roaring Twenties Aloysius was waiting for Anna to return. It had begun to occur to him that he had rather overcommitted himself to a group of people whom he hardly knew. He was attracted to Anna but he'd had flirtations before and as often as not they were driven by a sudden rush of hormones, a desire to release some tension within himself. He lived in fear of becoming trapped by a girl's unwanted pregnancy; lived in fear of committing himself to a woman whom he liked but did not love. He had a life to build for himself and it was easier done alone. He didn't want to explain why he took this job or that; didn't want to feel that he was needed back at home at six o'clock; didn't want to be tied to a house or a street or a particular city.

He had willed himself to England and into the life of a middle-class gentleman even if he was still not perceived as such by others who shared that description. He had drawn a thick, dark line between himself and those parts of Caribbean culture that might seem to reclassify him as something different from the man he wished to be. He was a suit-wearing, tea-drinking, *Financial Times*- and Evelyn Waugh-reading man of London town. He was as English as toast. And when the time came – when he was fully formed – he would take an English wife in whatever colour she happened to arrive.

But in following Anna he had been led into the lives of two people: Anna herself and the missing Iolanthe. He had accidentally taken some responsibility in this unknown actress's fate and he couldn't help feeling that the course of his relationship with Anna would somehow be determined by the benign or malignant nature of Lanny's disappearance. Moreover he was struggling with the fact that he didn't actually care at all for the missing woman. He couldn't even picture her. She was a name connected to a puzzle presented by a girl who he would like to see naked.

He closed his eyes. The heat and the music and the brandy were working on him like medicine. He saw his mother dancing in an orange dress with wide full skirts, smoking long thin cigarettes on a Saturday and Sunday night, drinking a glass of brandy when the rest of the family came over. He remembered his cousin Philip taking him to one of the grown-up dances when he was thirteen, watching the full-breasted women in their loose tops and pedal pushers pump their arms in time to the music in the rich, hot swell of a June night. They played American music then, rhythm and blues and honking rock 'n' roll and the Alpha Boys down in Kingston played their marching band tunes, which became jazz and ska and blues after school was out. But he was a Knox College boy, a scholar, an aesthete: he sat in the audience, he didn't play the music.

'Louis'll get himself buried in a square box,' his Auntie Pauline said, 'the better to fit in the ground. What all them people doing with those arms and legs, he thinks. Why you all so untidy?' And everyone would laugh at him.

'Aloysius!' Anna's voice was calling him back to the club. He opened his eyes and there she was, walking towards him, clutching the arm of a young girl in a minidress.

'Aloysius, this is Samira. She's the daughter of Ottmar, the man in the cafe. She's only sixteen and I know for a fact she isn't allowed out this late. I'm sorry – this has nothing to do with Lanny – but we need to take her home. For Ottmar. Just so we know she's safe.'

Samira held out her hand to Aloysius. 'I'm actually fine. Anna's going crazy because … I have no idea. I'm here with friends and they'll walk me home when it shuts.'

Aloysius looked at the two women, both of whom had turned the full intensity of their gaze upon him, and stayed silent.

'Right. Everyone get their coats,' Anna commanded. 'We are going to take a very quick detour and then we're walking Samira home.'

The young girl grimaced. 'Samira thinks you're making a fuss about nothing. I'm not drunk, I'm not stoned, I'm not having sex in an alleyway.'

'It's after midnight and Ottmar and Ekin will be scared to death. Come on. It's school tomorrow anyway.' Something of the head girl had crept into Anna's voice as she marshalled her followers together.

Aloysius picked up his coat and walked behind Samira to the table where she'd been sitting with a group of girls in jeans and bright-striped tops. She rolled her eyes at them. 'I'm being walked home,' she said.

And then they turned and climbed the steps up into the white world of the street.

It wasn't snowing any longer but the cold was bitter at this time in the morning. Samira's coat was short and her legs were bare; she shook as Anna led her through the streets.

'Where are we going?' Aloysius asked.

'To see if we can spot this Mark. Maybe ask him a few questions. Since we're here.'

'Is it a good idea bringing her along? Shouldn't we try this another night?'

Anna looked at him. 'Iolanthe isn't getting any younger, is she?'

Almost all the bars on Kingly Street were dark, as was the Italian coffee bar, but Anna pressed her nose to the glass door nonetheless. And there in the back of the bar, sitting near the counter, were a group of men in black jackets smoking and playing cards lit by the light that shone through from the kitchen out the back. Anna reached behind her and without looking gestured with her hand for Aloysius to join them. The three of them peered through the door together.

A single face shot up from the crowd of heads and shouted out: 'We're closed.'

'I'm looking for Iolanthe Green,' Anna shouted through the door.

Now all the heads turned round to look at them and a dark-haired man sitting at the end of the table called out to her, 'She isn't here!'

'I know. She's missing. Please, can you tell me if one of you is Mark?'

'Who's asking?' shouted the dark-haired man.

'I'm Anna. I'm a friend of Lanny's. I'm worried about her.'

The man nodded his head towards Aloysius. 'Who's the coon?'

Anna licked her lips. 'We're all friends of Iolanthe. Do you know where she is? Do you know if she's safe? If she doesn't want to be found, we'll understand. I just want to know she isn't in trouble.'

The man with dark hair stared at her and then turned back to his cards.

'I've no idea where the bitch is. Probably fucked off with someone else.'

'Is there any chance that you would let us in?' Anna asked.

The dark-haired man, who presumably was Mark, nodded to an older man who came over to unbolt the door. He opened it and stood there looking at them, blocking the entrance with his body.

'I don't think I really want these people on my premises.' He pointed a finger at Aloysius. 'And I don't like the look of him.'

Anna hesitated and looked at Aloysius, who had made himself very still. 'Well, you see, we're all friends of Lanny's and we're all together.'

'You girls can come in. Blackie there stays in the street.' The man stood back to allow the women to pass and Anna looked inside, into the dark cafe and at the eight or nine strange men sitting with their beer bottles and their cards, and decided that she and Samira weren't going anywhere on their own.

'We're all together,' she repeated. 'We'd be grateful if we could all come in. Please.'

The man pointed his finger again, first at the girls, 'You,' and then at Aloysius, 'Not him.'

'Hey, Nick, you all right?' The call came from behind them in the street and they all turned to look. Two policemen, dressed in capes and hats, were watching them from a little way up Kingly Street. The taller one, the one who'd spoken, nodded towards Aloysius. 'That one giving you trouble, then?'

Aloysius held his hands up and walked away from Anna and Samira, putting space between himself and the man in the doorway. 'No trouble here.'

The policemen walked towards him. 'What you doing then? What you doing with these young ladies?'

'He's helping—' Anna began but she was shouted down immediately.

'I wasn't talking to you. I was talking to your coloured friend.'

One of the policemen paused to observe Samira, shivering in her minidress and bare legs. He looked at Aloysius but pointed to the girls. 'Are they yours?'

'They're friends of mine, officer. To be exact, one of them is a friend and we were walking the young girl home. As a favour. To her father.'

'Turn around,' the officer told him.

'What?'

'Turn around and face the wall.' Aloysius turned towards the wall and the shorter officer produced handcuffs and tethered Aloysius roughly.

'What did I do?' Aloysius's voice quivered a little. The men from the cafe had gathered around the doorway to watch. Samira clutched Anna's arm.

'I am arresting you under the Sexual Offences Act 1956. I suspect you of procuring these women for the purpose of accruing immoral earnings. You don't have to say anything but anything you do say may be taken down and used in evidence against you. Barry, pat him down.' And the shorter officer started to go through Aloysius's pockets.

Anna's thoughts ran straight into her mouth. 'You can't do that. He's an accountant!'

The tall man turned on her and started to advance. 'Shut up! You're both under arrest for crimes of solicitation.'

'We haven't committed any crime. He's an accountant. This girl's at school—' but the officer grabbed Anna by the wrist, momentarily shocking her into silence.

'I am arresting you under the Street Offences Act of 1959: loitering for the purposes of prostitution. You don't have to say anything but anything you do say may be taken down and used in evidence against you.' He signalled to Samira to offer up her arm and then he handcuffed Anna's right hand to Samira's left. Anna watched him do all this with a stifling sense of astonishment. The world had decided it would make no more sense.

Samira was starting to breathe oddly so Anna put her free arm around the girl's shoulders and gathered her into a fierce and frightened embrace. From the corner of her eye she watched the crowd of men drift away from the open door and back into the darkness.

* * *

In West End Central Hayes dialled again and checked the clock. It was a quarter to one now, so quarter to eight in Boston. Too close to suppertime?

A boy answered the phone. 'Butler residence.'

'Oh, hello,' said Hayes, English to the very tops of his 'h's. 'This is Detective Sergeant Hayes calling from the Metropolitan Police in London. May I speak to the gentleman of the household?'

There was a brief silence and then he heard the boy holler, 'Ma! There's someone from the Neapolitan Police on the phone for you.' The receiver went clunk against a table or floor and Hayes waited. A panting woman retrieved the phone and spoke.

'Mrs Butler speaking; who is it calling, please?'

'Good evening, ma'am. This is Detective Sergeant Hayes calling from the Metropolitan Police in London. I apologise for calling so late into the evening, but I am on the hunt for an American citizen who's gone missing in London. Could I ask you a couple of questions?'

'Well, yes of course, officer.' She held the phone away from her and bellowed, 'Bobbie! Turn the dinner off!'

'Thank you so much. I wonder if you ever knew a Maria Green. She lived on Beacon Street from some time in the 1920s until her death in 1943.'

'Maria Green? Do you know where she lived? I mean, what number?'

'378, I believe. Just down from you.'

'378. Oh, okay. That's two doors down. Yes, I know the house you mean, of course I do; I've been here all my life. There was a banker there when I was growing up. An Englishman with a fancy accent. He was Mr Green. Definitely a Mr Green. But there never was a Mrs Green.'

'Are you sure?'

'Well, my mother always used to say she thought him a bit of a strange one. No wife. Nor visitors. Except once or twice a year when he would hold a fancy party and all the windows would light up. They'd post a little note in through the door letting us know the date and apologising for any noise or nuisance. He was ever so polite, you see. And shy. Very shy. And then the next morning, that cook of his would come round with cakes and sweets and puddings left over from the party. She made chocolate mousse with little pieces of orange on the top and I can taste it now. I should have got myself the recipe except I didn't think of it. I used to dream about those little pots of chocolate mousse. I think he must have died the year that I was fifteen. No more chocolate mousse after that. No more parties.'

'I see. Thank you. I'm trying to track down a Maria Green who had two children, Nathaniel and Yolanda Green. They took over the house and mortgage when Mr Green died.'

'Well, I never saw any sign of a wife. The servants lived on there for years and we never did know why. They didn't seem to be serving anyone at all. And then the cook's son went away to war and came back with his legs missing. He was in a wheelchair and he could never get in or out of the house because we're up these steps, you see. I remember that the house became quite dirty – unwashed windows, unswept steps – after Mr Green died. The cook's boy lived there at the end and then it was sold to a lovely family from Connecticut, the Bakers, who've kept it very nice these last twenty years or so.'

'And the cook's boy, did he have a sister?'

'Yes he did, pretty little thing. Quite pale-skinned. Dressed herself up nice, 'specially after she was grown. Always a new dress and matching coat those last few years. Thought herself quite grand. The pale-skinned ones do, I think.'

'The pale-skinned ones?'

'Negroes. Pale-skinned negroes. Very proud of their looks, I find. In their lipstick and their heels, looking almost white. I don't suppose you have people like that in London.'

'Well ... Um, I'm sorry. The cook's boy and girl were black?'

'They were all black, sir. All the servants were. The cook was very dark-skinned with lots of crazy hair. And the boy and girl were quite pale. You wouldn't have known they were related at all. But I s'pose you get that with us too. My Bobby has red hair but my Glenda's blonde. Family's a funny thing.'

Hayes agreed with her that yes, most definitely, family was a funny thing and hung up the phone. He looked at the clock and wondered if he could call Nathaniel back in Annapolis but he didn't have a number for anywhere except the main desk of the library. So instead he opened his notebook and tried to write it all down in a way that would make sense of what he'd learned.

* * *

On Marlborough Street a police car sat and steamed. Anna and Samira had been lodged in the back for nearly half an hour while the shorter officer, Officer Barry as Anna thought of him, turned the key and the tall officer stared at the engine under the lifted bonnet and swore. Aloysius had been told to stand facing a wall and wait so this is what he did. It was snowing again and the snow was piling thickly on the head and shoulders of the tall police officer and Aloysius. Anna could only imagine how cold Aloysius was, how angry. Samira had slumped beside her and Anna half suspected her of going to sleep out of terror. That's what babies do, isn't it? she thought; when they're very scared, they just go to sleep.

She heard a scream of pain from somewhere around the bonnet of the car and the tall officer threw down the cloth he'd been holding and fell to his knees, burying his hand in the snow. By the wall, Aloysius looked over his shoulder at the crouching officer.

'You know,' he said, a little hesitantly and his voice shaking with the cold, 'if it's West End Central you're trying to take us to we could just walk. It's only ten minutes away. And we're all handcuffed. I just meant … if the car won't start.'

The tall officer stared at him from the snow and then he stood up and brushed the powdery white from his legs and cape. Aloysius turned his head back towards the wall. Anna watched as the officer grabbed Aloysius by the back of the head and swung him round until he was facing the car. She saw the way that Aloysius's face had contorted in pain and surprise as he was pushed towards them. And then that vision was gone and the whole car rocked violently as the policeman drove Aloysius's head into the roof. Samira woke and tried to grab at Anna, confused by her surroundings and the handcuff at her wrist. Officer Barry turned in his seat and stared at the roof of the car as if Aloysius's head might come through it at any moment. Outside the darkened window two bodies retreated and the caped figure dumped the suited figure back into the snow beside the wall.

Aloysius's nose and mouth ran with blood. His glasses were missing. When he opened his mouth his teeth were stained pink and red. Anna watched him roll for a minute in the snow, unable to right himself or bring his handcuffed hands to his face. She was, she realised, too afraid to speak. Officer Barry looked at the women in the back, his glance restive.

Aloysius righted himself and bent his long legs to support his weight. His head fell limply between them, exhaustion or confusion overwhelming him. Blood dripped, spotting the snow where he sat, and Anna saw how easily it tainted something that had once seemed beautiful.

Early-Morning Savile Row Blues

Thursday, 11 November

In the end they walked back to Savile Row. Aloysius was marched in front of the women wearing his shattered glasses. He didn't speak and somewhere along the way he'd lost his hat. When he stumbled the tall policeman stood away from him and let him struggle to his feet.

Anna felt dazed. Through her tiredness she would stare down and see a vision of dark drops scattered about her feet. She thought of the bodies of those children lying under a bed of earth and ice up there in Yorkshire. Why had it never occurred to her that snow could be something sinister? Where had she got this idea that snow meant family and cosy Christmases around a fire? No good could come of the earth freezing over. It was the putting out of life, green shoots trampled underfoot. The warm, dark vitality of Roaring Twenties seemed to belong to another life altogether. A dream of pleasure; a hallucination, really. All that desire, all that want. She put it away from her. She remembered who she was.

When they arrived at last in the comparative warmth of the station the desk sergeant was having an argument with a police officer about the acceptability of arresting two men for vagrancy so that they wouldn't freeze to death. The men in question – whose deeply lined faces seemed both ageless and inhuman in an other-worldly way – huddled on the wooden benches at the side of the room, wrapped in blankets, their feet tied up in layers of shopping bags. Anna wondered what had happened to so separate them from the world of men. And then she looked at Aloysius, whose swollen,

131

bloodied face she could just glimpse, and wondered at the way a policeman's blow had transformed him into an unfamiliar creature: the boxer, the hoodlum, the murderer, the thief. They had made him ugly. Perhaps she had made him ugly. After all it was she who had taken him for protection into a world that was not properly his own.

What did she know about him anyway? He was a tall boy, good at maths, needed glasses to see; he read Agatha Christie and Homer and Evelyn Waugh and wanted to propose to a girl in a rose garden that no longer existed. He had not known how to speak to the officers, but then neither had she. Was it all their fault? Was there some trick to dealing with the law that none of them had been taught? How on earth could those men imagine she was a prostitute? She was wearing woolly tights, for goodness' sake. Of course, Anna thought, of course there will come a moment when I will simply explain and somebody will hear and the world will turn the right way up again. Sergeant Hayes, she thought. Sergeant Hayes will know exactly who I am.

The desk sergeant and the young police officer had reached an impasse over the homeless men and they were allowed to stay in the waiting area while Aloysius, Anna and Samira were processed. The tall police officer, who seemed to go by the name of Brent, was running through an account of the arrest with the desk sergeant and fresh forms were being spread out on the counter.

Samira, who had been almost entirely silent since the arrest, squeezed Anna's hand. 'Please. You have to get me out of this. I can't be arrested. It's going to kill them.' She didn't have to tell Anna who she meant.

'Don't worry,' Anna told her, 'I have a policeman friend. He'll understand what happened.'

Samira's face came alive with relief. 'You know someone here?'

'I do.'

'Will he help us?'

'I believe he will.'

Officer Barry pushed Aloysius to the edge of the counter. The desk sergeant looked at him, taking in the broken nose and blood-stained clothes.

'Not your first time in a police station, I'm guessing. You'll know what to do.'

Aloysius licked his lips. 'Excuse me, officer, but I've never been arrested. Can you tell me what to do?' To encounter such a genteel voice emerging from such a dark and bloodied face made the desk sergeant chuckle, though he didn't seem to take much notice of what Aloysius had said. It was at that moment that Anna stepped forward, raised her uncuffed hand and in her best cut-glass tones she called out: 'Excuse me, sir.'

The desk sergeant didn't even glance at her. 'We'll get to you later.'

'Excuse me, sir. I'm a friend of Detective Sergeant Hayes.' All three officers turned to look her in the eye, and so did Aloysius for the first time since they'd been arrested. 'Barnaby Hayes. He'll know who I am. There's been a sort of mix-up. Not anybody's fault, I'm sure. But I think Barnaby Hayes would be rather upset if I was processed before you'd checked with him.'

Sergeant Brent shrugged at the desk sergeant. 'I don't know. She never said anything before.'

Anna exchanged a long glance with Aloysius and she saw his eyes soften and his lips tremble again. She flashed him a very small smile.

'Detective Sergeant Hayes works eight till six,' Brent told her. 'He won't be in for another five hours and I'm not leaving you lot hanging round here.'

'Actually, he's here. Signed back in at seven,' the desk sergeant said. Brent blew air through his nose. He pointed a finger at the three arrestees and told them: 'I'll be back.' And then he was off down the corridor into the heart of the station. Anna could see Samira and Aloysius relaxing just very slightly and she felt a rush of triumph that she had saved them from this mess that was partly of her making.

Brent returned with a rather dishevelled-looking Detective Sergeant Hayes, who stared at the three arrestees and then gave Anna a brief nod. Anna fixed him with a big, confident smile. She had unpinned her skirt while they sat in the police car and pulled it down to its usual conservative length and she certainly cut an odd figure in her woolly tights and librarian's clothes standing handcuffed to a dark-haired, dark-skinned girl in a dress that only reached the middle of her thighs.

'Hello, Sergeant Hayes. There's been a terrible confusion. My friends and I had heard about someone who might have been Iolanthe's boyfriend and we believed that he drank after hours in a cafe on Kingly Street. So we went to see if this was true and while we were chatting with the cafe owner these police officers mistook us for prostitutes … which of course we're not. And they rather assumed that Aloysius here, who's an accountant, was a pimp. Which of course he isn't. And then we came here and it occurred to me that, of course, you know exactly who I am and what I do so you could help straighten this all out.'

'Well?' asked Brent.

Hayes wrinkled his brow. 'This lady is Anna Treadway and she is a dresser at the Galaxy Theatre. She was Iolanthe Green's dresser. I interviewed her on Tuesday morning and as far as I know she has nothing to do with prostitution. But … I'm not sure I can help any further than that. Sorry.'

'But you see …' said Anna, 'I mean, thank you, Sergeant Hayes, but you see I can vouch for my friends. I've lived with this girl here in the flat below me for several years now. She's only sixteen and she's still at school and she comes from a really very observant family of the Moslem persuasion. And this gentleman here, who met with a rather unfortunate accident, he is a trained accountant of very good standing who has been helping me in my search for Miss Green. I mean, honestly, he wasn't meant to be in Soho at all tonight. He was meant to be at home in Streatham except that I didn't know my way home and it was very cold and he lent me his gloves. So, you see, it's my fault that all of this has happened and he really shouldn't be charged with anything at all.'

Hayes stared first at Samira and then at Aloysius. The girl looked to be Mediterranean and he couldn't quite place her age. She was wearing thick black eyeliner that was streaked across her cheeks and pale white lipstick, which had come off half her mouth. Her jacket and dress were ill suited to the weather and displayed a lot of flesh.

The coloured man's face was smashed and bloody. His eyes and nose were swollen, so you couldn't rightly tell what he looked like. He was certainly well dressed in a spivvy kind of way but his collar and his shirt front were stained brown and red with blood. He looked to Hayes very like what Brent said he was: indeed he could just imagine this man as a pimp. He briefly thought of Iolanthe, with her pale skin and her dark curly hair and tried to reconcile her with this man standing here. He couldn't see them as the same race at all. Though, now he thought of it, if this man did know something about Iolanthe's disappearance having him in custody would be useful.

'I'm sorry, Miss Treadway, I'm happy to see you released into my care but I can't possibly vouch for your friends. I know nothing about them.' Hayes looked over at Brent. 'I need another conversation with her anyway. If you hand her over she can be my problem.'

Brent shrugged. 'I'm still booking the other two.' He nodded to Officer Barry. 'Uncuff her. She's going to talk to Hayes instead.'

'Wait. Sorry. I don't understand – am I free to go?' Anna asked.

'Not exactly. You're helping us with our enquiries. I need you to come and talk to me. The Iolanthe Green case has developed over the course of the night,' Hayes told her as Officer Barry released her and handcuffed Samira to himself instead.

Anna took a step away from Samira, placing distance between herself and the indignity of the cuffs. 'But what about my friends? Aloysius was in the Cue Club yesterday evening. He was at the bar. Didn't you see him there?' she asked Hayes.

'No, I didn't. I didn't notice him. I'm sorry.' Hayes raised his hands in a gesture of retreat. 'I just don't know these other people.'

Anna struggled to find a diplomatic form of words that might signal her solidarity with her friends but would stop short of annoying Brent into re-arresting her.

Samira spoke: 'Are you just going to leave us, then?'

Anna played with her hands. 'I don't know what else to say. I'll explain to Sergeant Hayes. I'll explain who we are. I mean, there's nothing to it, obviously. They'll have to let you go. There isn't any evidence.'

'You can't just leave me here! D'you know what will happen if I'm charged?'

'They won't charge you.'

Samira's voice rose in panic. 'D'you understand what this is going to mean … if they don't let me go?'

'You'll be fine,' Anna insisted. 'Just tell the truth.'

'Just tell the truth! I don't have a policeman friend, do I? I was safe in that club. I was *safe*. I didn't offer to go walking round Soho after dark with a fucking black man for protection. What world d'you think you're living in?'

Anna looked at Aloysius but he had no intention of meeting her eye; then she looked at Hayes, imploring him to step in, but Hayes just shrugged.

'What do you want me to do?' Anna asked the room in general.

'Shut up and let me sleep!' cried one of the blanketed men lying on the benches.

'Come on,' said Hayes, 'there's nothing more you can do here now and I've got questions I need help with.' He opened the door that led to the back offices and Anna followed him through. She looked over her shoulder and watched the door slam shut behind them.

'Detective Sergeant Hayes, what will happen to them? What will happen to Aloysius? He really is an accountant.'

'I dare say it will all come out in the wash,' Hayes told her, not sounding at all as if he believed what he said. 'Come on, I can't be bothered to set up an interview room. Let's have a chat at my desk.'

Anna followed him into a large dark office cluttered with desks, filing cabinets, boxes, stools and metal safes. A single lamp was lit above a desk that overflowed with papers and chocolate wrappers. Hayes dragged a chair over for Anna and then he slumped into his own.

'Have you found her then?' Anna asked.

'Goodness, no. Found her? No, no, no, no, no.' Hayes unwrapped a bar of 5 Centre and offered it to Anna. 'Chocolate?'

'Yes. Just a bit.'

He broke off two chunks and ate the rest himself. 'But I did find her brother.'

'Her brother who's dead?'

'That's the one. He works in a library in Maryland. Not dead at all. Lost both his legs. Left in '46, came home again the next year. Lived at the family home in Boston but couldn't pay the mortgage, it seems. Iolanthe came home and helped him sell up. They pocketed a bit of money each and then he went to work at the Naval Library in Annapolis. Says he hasn't seen Iolanthe since '47.'

'Bloody hell.'

'My thoughts exactly. So then I talked to a neighbour who remembered Nathaniel and his sister, the children of a cook who worked for an English banker. Except the girl wasn't called Iolanthe, she was called Yolanda. And none of them were Irish; the cook's family were all coloured.'

'But Iolanthe's white.'

'Is she?'

'Well, yes.'

'The neighbour said the children were light-skinned, not like the mother at all. And then there's the odd coincidence that they all have the same name as the man they worked for. Who, as it happens, had no wife.'

'You think the banker was the father?'

'It would explain the pale-skinned children. It would explain the cook being left the house.'

'And why she thought the baby might be black.'

'What baby?'

The room went very quiet. Anna felt her heart pause in her chest.

'What baby, Miss Treadway?'

'We … Aloysius and myself … think that Iolanthe *might* have been expecting a baby.'

'Based on what?'

'Based on something that Aloysius was told at Roaring Twenties about how Lanny was pregnant and might not have been very happy about it.'

'How pregnant?'

'I've no idea. She wasn't showing but she'd put on a bit of weight. Just round her middle. She couldn't get her jeans to fit. So, three or four months maybe.'

'And she wanted to get rid of it?'

'That's what we heard.'

'And were you going to come and tell me any of this?'

'Of course. It's all just happened this evening. There wasn't any time …'

Hayes cast a glance towards a window blanketed with snow. 'If Yolanda Green is outside tonight she will freeze to death.'

'I know.'

Hayes said nothing but his annoyance was palpable. Anna's stomach tightened. 'Lanny told … some people we know … that she needed an abortion. I mean … I only found this out last night. Aloysius heard it from the girlfriend of someone he was working with. But then she wasn't keen on the method, so I don't know if she had it. I don't think she did. And she might have been worried the baby was going to be the wrong colour. Or … I don't know. I don't know who the father was. We also heard she was seeing a musician called Mark who plays cards after hours in an Italian coffee bar on Kingly Street. And then we went to speak to him but the police arrested us. This Mark man is white and quite bad-tempered and he said he thought she might have run away with someone else. He didn't mention anything about a baby.'

'But the baby must have been conceived back in the summer. Was she even here in August? How long have they been seeing each other?'

'Oh. I didn't think. No, if she was more than twelve weeks gone … She didn't start rehearsals in London until the fifth of September. But Mark was definitely her boyfriend, he sort of said as much. Maybe he found out she was pregnant and got angry.'

Hayes rubbed his face with his hands. 'I'm going to make some tea.'

So Hayes made tea and they sat and ran through Lanny's interview again, trying to untangle the Irish connections from the Boston connections and the story of Nathaniel's death from the details of

Nathaniel's life. And Hayes asked Anna about Cassidy – who she knew nothing of except the phone message – and then he asked her again about the details of the abortion Lanny had tried to procure. But Anna stuck to her story of having heard it all from acquaintances of Aloysius and said nothing about Dr Jones or the surgery in Streatham. At five, Hayes decided to call it a night and send Anna home to get some sleep.

'Am I free to go then?' she asked him.

'Yes. Of course,' he told her. 'No charges to be brought. You need to tell me though. You need to tell me what you're thinking before you run off again to figure it all out for yourself.'

'What about my friends?'

'Your friends?'

'The man and woman you arrested. You know that the policeman did that to him, don't you? Smashed his face into the roof of the car.'

'Was he resisting arrest?'

'He was suggesting that we walk back to the station because the car wouldn't start. That tall one, the one called Brent, he did that to him.'

Hayes looked at her. What on earth did she expect he could do about it? 'Change the system from within.' The very idea, Dr Devlin's little mantra, had been a joke. Of course there might come a day, many years in the future, when he was sufficiently integrated, sufficiently secure and senior, that he could do such things efficiently. But for now he was still a nothing and a nobody. And the problem with the system was that it was entirely made up of people, and many of those people were really quite normal and decent and you couldn't strike at them without making yourself into an arse. In fact, the more that Hayes dwelt upon it the more he could see that it wasn't really the system that was the problem at all. It was the few bad apples, the rotten hearts, who let the rest of them down. There was no grand conspiracy to undermine, no revolution waiting to happen …

'Thank you, Miss Treadway,' he said. 'I'll bear all that in mind. Now I suggest that you go home and get some sleep.'

He opened the door into the reception area and Anna passed through. One of the blanketed men still slept on a bench, the other was gone. Beside the sleeping man a middle-aged couple sat, their hands crossed in their laps. Noticing Anna, the man sprang to his feet.

'Ottmar! What are you doing here?'

'They arrested Samira and then we got a call to come down. We don't know what's happening.'

Ekin was hovering behind him, wrapped in a donkey jacket, her hair and neck covered with a blue headscarf. She looked scared to death. Anna reached out for Hayes and touched his arm. The desk sergeant watched them both carefully.

'These are Samira's parents, Ottmar and Ekin Alabora. I've known them for years. They own the Alabora Coffee House on Neal Street.'

Hayes nodded to Ottmar but spoke to Anna. 'It's not my arrest. I don't know the girl and I don't know what she was doing.'

'But I do,' said Anna. 'She was standing right next to me and Aloysius asking Mark about Iolanthe. And before that she was in Roaring Twenties, also with Aloysius and me.'

'What were you doing out with Samira?' Ottmar asked.

'No! We weren't out together. I just found her. In the club. We were going to walk her home but then we got arrested for … um … solicitation.'

'*Fuhuş!*' Ekin said and though of course Anna did not understand her she could see where Ekin was going.

'No! No one was soliciting anyone. But the policemen saw us and they made an assumption. They seemed to think that Aloysius was our pimp and I think it had to do with the time of night and the fact that we were all … you know … different shades. You see, Aloysius is originally from Jamaica and it was that that really seemed to unnerve them.'

The desk sergeant suddenly decided that he was needed in the back office and left. Hayes shook his head at Anna. 'I don't think you want to make those kind of accusations.'

'I'm not saying anything that wasn't perfectly obvious last night.'

'Nonetheless, I'd rather you didn't repeat accusations of that nature. They have a habit of inciting unpleasantness and they certainly aren't going to help your cause.'

Ekin stepped forward and looked at Hayes. 'Mr Policeman,' she began. 'You have arrested a child – from a good family – and said she is a prostitute. Please could you think if it was your daughter … what would you do?'

Hayes refused to meet Ekin's eye. Instead he gazed over the front desk at something imagined on the far wall.

'My little girl is sitting in a cell and she is very scared and—' Ekin broke off and turned to Anna. 'Why won't he look at me? Am I doing something wrong?'

Anna threw her hands in the air. Detective Sergeant Hayes, who she had just been beginning to see again as something of an ally, was now merging back into the trappings of his title.

Ekin pulled off her headscarf in frustration, the tone of her voice mounting towards anger. 'Mr Policeman? Sir? Can you hear me now? I am asking you as a mother if you could please release my child.'

Hayes stood very still, wondering if, if he slowed his breathing enough, they would all just go away.

'Why won't he look at me?' Ekin knelt down on the floor in front of him. 'I have no pride when it comes to my babies. Could you at least look at me? Please? Come on! I am not invisible!' And she struck the floor with her hand, sending a sharp, wet crack ringing around the room.

Very slowly Hayes turned and walked back towards the doors to the offices. Ottmar, Anna and Ekin watched him go. Ekin pulled herself to her feet and rewound her headscarf. She shook her head at Anna. 'A policeman beat my father to death.' Her voice was quite calm, quite matter-of-fact. 'They banged his head against the wall until his skull cracked. But when I walk into a police station I become invisible. There are people who would pay good money for such a power. I could be like Guy Fawkes. I could blow the whole place sky high and still no one would see me standing here.'

They sat and waited on the little benches as the sky got lighter and the homeless man in the blanket woke from sleep to be ejected out into the winter air of another Thursday morning.

In a white-painted cell in the custody suite Aloysius sat cross-legged on the floor and ran over the events of the night for the eightieth time. He would have been more comfortable on the bench but his body seemed to stop working just after they closed the cell door. He had melted to the floor and stayed there, each of his limbs seeming to weigh a thousand pounds. Completely still he sat for five hours as his mind pored over the details, examining every moment from this angle and then that angle. What had he done wrong? he wondered. What moment was it that had betrayed him? Had he seemed aggressive? Had he seemed threatening? Had he failed to carry himself with gentleness and grace? Had he answered the officers rudely? Had he patronised the policeman when he suggested that they walk? He tried to replay the encounter, inserting different words and phrases. He tried to be silent. But each one of these imagined meetings broke down, for he truly could not understand what had been going on inside the policeman's head.

He wondered if it was a punishment for touching Anna, for daring to kiss her hand. Now and again it occurred to him that he might actually be about to go to prison and his heart would flutter with fright. At six o'clock a man brought him toast and tea on a little tray but he didn't touch them. He couldn't move; he doubted he could swallow at all. He felt as if he was trapped inside the mummified shell of another man, a man who had done something terribly, spectacularly wrong.

At nine o'clock Detective Inspector Knight arrived in his office to find Hayes waiting for him, holding a cup of coffee.

'That wife of yours finally emasculated you,' he said as he accepted the cup.

'I just wondered if I could have a word, sir.'

'And what word would that be then?'

'It's about Brent.'

'Oh, for fuck's sake. Shut the door. What did he do this time?'

'He assaulted a coloured while arresting him for crimes of procuring women.'

'And?'

'And I have it on good authority that the man's an accountant, not a pimp at all. Just in the wrong place at the wrong time.'

'How's that my problem?'

'Well, it isn't. It's Vice's. But the man has information regarding the disappearance of Iolanthe Green and I'd rather like to have him on our side. I was wondering if I could offer to get the charges dropped if he would divulge everything he knew about Miss Green. Just smooth things over and get her found. You know?'

'I still don't see why this is my problem.'

'Because Fellows over in Vice hates me and if I go asking for a favour ...'

Knight put down the coffee. 'Jesus, Hayes. What happened to the fighting Irish?'

'I think I've pretty much figured out what's going on with Green. I just need a couple of people in the know to get me there. And he's one of them. I might even take him on as an informant. You know he does the books for a lot of the coloured clubs in town. Just think how much he really knows about. Tax fraud. Bribes. Girls. Drugs ...'

He left that dangling there, aware that Knight would have to be an idiot not to take the bait.

My Whole Life's Just a
Series of Interviews

Thursday, 11 November

'Come in and sit down, Mr Weathers. I'm Detective Sergeant Hayes. I've spoken with my colleagues in the Vice department and we've agreed that if you are willing to supply information to us, as requested, we would be less inclined to charge you with procuring and exploitation. Do you understand?'

'Yes, sir. I understand.'

'Good. I want to start with the disappearance of Iolanthe Green. Can you tell me how you first became aware of Miss Green?'

'She was talked about by a woman in Roaring Twenties who said she was pregnant and asking around about people who could help.'

'Did you meet Miss Green?'

'No. I didn't even know what she looked like.'

'So, how do you come to be looking for her?'

'Yesterday afternoon, I'd finished meeting with Count Suckle and I was doing the accounts for the Cue Club when I sat down next to Miss Treadway. You were there too. You were talking to Count Suckle.'

'Did I speak to you?'

'No. But Miss Treadway did and then I told her what I'd heard about Miss Green being ... you know. In trouble. And then she asked me to help her find her way on the bus and then there was a snowstorm and my landlady made her toast and tea and I tried to see her home from south London. When we got into town Miss Treadway asked me if I would go with her to Roaring Twenties because I knew people there. I went and talked to a friend of mine,

Derek, who works in the kitchen and he told me that Miss Green had been seeing a man called Mark who drank on Kingly Street and then while we were at the club Miss Treadway met that girl Samira and said we had to walk her home after we went looking for this Mark person. And we were standing on Kingly Street when we were arrested and brought here.'

'And you sustained your fall.'

'Yes, sir.'

'I believe it was very icy underfoot last night.'

'Treacherous, sir.'

'What I don't understand is what took you from Paddington to south London and then back again. Where were you and Miss Treadway going?'

'We were looking for Iolanthe Green.'

'In south London. In a snowstorm.'

'Yes, sir.'

'Mr Weathers, if you continue to withhold information from me I will return you to Vice and I will inform them that you have been uncooperative. Do you know what the prison sentence is for procuring and exploitation? You're looking at two years as an absolute minimum. Young girl, unfriendly judge, you could get five.'

'Yes, sir.'

'What were you doing in south London?'

'We went to see a doctor.'

'A doctor who performs abortions?'

'I think so, yes.'

'And what was this doctor's name?'

'I couldn't say, sir.'

'I think you could, Mr Weathers. I think you remember exactly who it was.'

'I don't know that this person has broken the law.'

'Then they'll come to no harm from us, will they, Mr Weathers?'

'No.'

'I don't like to talk about race, Mr Weathers, because I believe we should all be blind to such things. Human beings are human beings, aren't they, Aloysius?'

'Yes, sir.'

'And the Bible tells us we are equal.'

'Yes, sir.'

'But we live in a fallen world, Mr Weathers. And our prisons are, arguably, the most fallen part of this fallen world. And in prison the colour of your skin matters, Mr Weathers, it matters very much. Coloured inmates are not trusted, Mr Weathers. If something goes wrong, if there's a little theft or a fight, I can imagine who will get the blame. And that's before you think about the company you will need to keep. For your own protection, Mr Weathers, you will need to form a close association with other coloured inmates. Men who have robbed and murdered and imported drugs. Men who sell guns and cocaine and girls into prostitution. And in the course of those two or three or even five years, you will form a strong bond of reliance on these men. A bond of reliance that will follow you into the outside world. That will follow you through all your time in this country, that might even follow you back to Jamaica if that was where you needed to go. These things, Aloysius, these things are the things that shape our lives. Not just our lives. The lives of our wives and children; even our parents. So, I'm going to ask you again. What was the name of the man you met with yesterday evening?'

'Her name was Dr Jones, sir.'

'And where does Dr Jones work?'

'On Drewstead Road.'

'Did she admit performing an abortion on Miss Green?'

'No, sir. She said Miss Green had asked for one but had been unhappy about the way it would be done and after that she'd gone away again.'

'And this was after the thirtieth of October?'

'No, sir. No. Iolanthe Green had gone to see her days before she disappeared and she hadn't seen her since.'

'Has *anyone* seen Iolanthe Green since the thirtieth of October?'

'No, sir. Not that I'm aware of. Miss Treadway was trying to ask this Mark man a question about it but then the police arrived and I fell down.'

'That's enough, Mr Weathers.'

'Yes, sir.'

'Let's move on to some of your coloured clients ...'

* * *

Having spent seven hours in a cell and a further hour being questioned Samira was finally released with a caution at half past ten. Ottmar stood beside his daughter as her caution was read to her, squeezing her shoulder in case she was about to cry. When Anna asked at the desk she was informed that Aloysius was to remain in custody but no, he had not yet been charged.

They walked back to the Alabora in silence. Samira led the way, her eyes downcast. Where Neal Street met Shaftesbury Avenue they stopped. Ottmar stared into the dark interior of his cafe. It was too late to think of running a lunch service now. He heard Ekin inviting Anna to eat with them upstairs. He experienced a moment of utter hopelessness, as if some group of strangers were once again taking control of his life.

If you had asked Ottmar in 1938 where he would live and die, he would have told you Cyprus without hesitation. He had been twenty-four then, helping to run a small magazine in Nicosia. Ottmar was the only Turkish member of the unpaid staff but he mixed happily and freely with his Greek colleagues. They worked out of the house of Melanippus Paphos who had inherited both his father's vast agricultural estate and his mother's bohemian instincts. He shared his palace-like abode with sixteen servants, far more than anyone of his lifestyle might have needed, and his lover, Theodore, with whom he founded ανεξάρτητης σκέψης – *Independent Thought* – which Theo liked to proclaim the voice of modern Cyprus.

Ottmar spent his days working as a secretary to the Turkish policeman Captain Dal in a northern suburb of Nicosia and crossed the Pedieos every night on his bicycle, dreaming of the romantic adventures of the mind which awaited him in his future life as a poet and scholar. His mother begged him to set his eyes on Istanbul and try for a scholarship to the university or even a clerical position in his uncle's department. But Ottmar was in love with his own country and dreamed only of writing epic poems in the Ottoman tradition. Flying down the dirt streets of Nicosia, Ottmar's mind would spill over into verse.

> *... we rose that day and dressed for the bloody hunt*
> *The deer feeling our presence strained against the*
>   *ground itself*
> *And reared on their hind legs as if they might take*
>   *flight*
> *And Anwar spoke of the dragon Evren*
> *Who slayed three hundred men before he was brought*
>   *low from love ...*

And the bicycle wheels spun on and Ottmar's mind raced faster and faster as if his soul and his ambition might through force of yearning and creation break through the barrier of the humble man into which they had been poured.

When war broke out in 1939, the magazine lost half its staff overnight. Ottmar's mother argued that he should represent his community against the Nazis by joining up but Ottmar had no more desire to die than he did to go and seek his academic fortune in Turkey. He had a clear and beautiful sense of his own future and his main goal in the present conflict was to still be alive at the end of it.

But then in 1942, Ottmar found his life turned upside down by a curious succession of events. In January Theodore and Melanippus were arrested on the orders of an incoming chief of police and charged with buggery. Melanippus paid handsomely to have the charges dropped but the reputation of the magazine had been tainted. They suspended *Independent Thought*, rented a house on the south coast of the island and disappeared from view.

In July Ottmar met Ekin Battur, an eighteen-year-old high school student. Her father – a planning officer for the local authority – had been arrested in April in relation to accusations of corruption at the planning department and had been held for weeks without being charged with any crime. Towards the end of his fifth week in detention his family were informed of his death in custody. The body was released without ceremony. The cause of death on the certificate stated only: misadventure.

Ekin wrote a letter making a formal complaint against the police and this she delivered to the offices of Captain Dal and the hands of Ottmar Alabora. Ottmar read the letter she left with him and so stirred was he by her family's evident torment that he proceeded to write an opinion piece on the dangers of turning a blind eye to police brutality and submitted it to the main Turkish daily.

By Wednesday he had lost his job with the police. By Friday the windows of his mother's house had been broken and her doorstep piled with shit. By Saturday his mother was on a bus heading for her cousin's cabin in the rural north.

Ottmar no longer knew where he belonged. He was not a good Muslim; not, according to his mother, even a good Turk. He was in a minority on his own island; he had no job of his own, no degree, no training; he had broken up his little family and he had no firm reason to believe that he would make it as a poet – whatever making it as a poet actually meant.

And so like many young people faced with a big dilemma he chose to run in more than one direction at the same time. In his marriage to Ekin he appeared to run towards his Turkhood while at the same time he set in motion the events and favours he would need to leave his Mediterranean home for ever.

*   *   *

'Mr Wingate, thank you for meeting with me. I've never been in a newspaper office before; it's all quite glamorous.'

'If you say so.'

'It's the clatter of it all, you know. The typewriters all going. Not like our offices at all. The sound of the police station, I used to say to my wife, the sound of the police station is the sound of dinosaurs eating reeds. Chomp, chomp, chomp. Not natural typists, most of us. And yet there we sit, world-weary and footsore, and type our way through the blinking forms wondering if anyone will ever read them. And as the day goes on the chomping gets slower and slower until eventually you hear a great creak at four o'clock and one of the dinosaurs has fallen over. Goodness! Sorry. That was a bit of a digression. My name is Detective Sergeant Hayes. I'm investigating the disappearance of Iolanthe Green. I know you interviewed her on the day she vanished. The interview in the newspaper was quite brief and I was wondering if I could see a transcript of the notes?'

'I could probably find them if you gave me a few days.'

'I don't have a few days. A woman is missing, possibly dead. Go and find the notes. I'll wait. Thank you.'

'I dare say I still have the shorthand pad around somewhere. Oh yes, what d'you know, here it is.'

'How many of those do you have?'

'Dozens. I never throw anything away. My whole life's just a series of interviews. Just one rump-numbing question after another. You'd think after this many I'd have learned a bit of truth.'

'Haven't you?'

'I've learned that humans lie to themselves. And then I sit down and copy out the lies and tidy them into a story.'

'Does everyone lie?'

'Everyone who's anyone. Especially if they were nobody to start with. Nobodies who made it need a story; sob story, fairy story, they need something to explain it. Don't know why. Maybe so they don't hate themselves for having got there.'

'Or because they want people who didn't make it to like them.'

'What did you want from the Green interview?'

'I don't know yet. Let's start with what you left out … I have a copy of the paper here. Can you tell me what else is in there?'

'She talks about her family. She talks about her childhood and being poor.'

'Does she talk about her father? Or her mother?'

'Not really.'

'Her brother?'

'Yes. She talks about him being killed in Japan.'

'Good. Tell me about that.'

'So some of it's in there … how hard it was not having anyone left. Then later on we go back to him and she talks about … Oh, yes …

okay … "Nathaniel was so angry to have missed the war; he was determined not to miss the peace. He went out there as a midshipman on the USS *Missouri*." And then I tell her that my father was a commander in the Royal Navy – and actually I followed him in myself for a while – and I believe he was there in Tokyo Bay at the same time as her brother. And she says "perhaps they sailed past each other". And I ask her how long he was in Tokyo before the accident and she says "only a few weeks. He was with some of his unit delivering grain and the roads were a mess and the Jeep he was in turned over." And then I ask her—'

'Hold on. Sorry. He was a midshipman? That's like a trainee officer, isn't it?'

'Yes.'

'He'd done very well for himself. Young lad from a tenement, no university training, no connections and suddenly he's an officer cadet. Does that sound likely?'

'Oh well, if you're going to start picking it apart! None of it makes sense, Hayes. You read her past interviews and the dates, the details. Every time she tells her story something changes.'

'Did it occur to you that this might be rather helpful in our investigation of Miss Green?'

'Well, it's occurring to me now.'

'Anything about a man called Cassidy?'

'Cassidy … Cassidy. Not in my notes.'

'And did your investigations uncover anything about a pregnancy?'

'A what?'

'A pregnancy.'

'She's pregnant?'

'Mr Wingate, I am speaking strictly off the record. This can't appear in any stories. But I believe that Miss Green may have been or is roughly three months pregnant.'

'Good God. Do you know who the father is?'

'No. Lately she'd been seeing a musician in Soho but the dates don't work.'

'Well, I … Right. I see. Goodness. It's a bit of a mess, isn't it?'

'To be honest with you, sir, at this point in the investigation it really is.'

'You know ... I actually have some other notes if you're interested. The stuff for *Harper's* as well as for *The Times*. Would you happen to fancy a drink, Sergeant? There's a bar just next door ...'

'If it would help, Mr Wingate. Lead the way.'

* * *

'Come on. We'll take the comfy side before someone else sneaks it. Sorry. Hold my pint a moment. There we go. Right. Where were we? Yes. Okay. Lanny Green. I realised some months ago that the Irish thing must be some kind of lie. And if the Irish thing was a lie then where had she come from? I thought for a while that she might be Mexican. Lots of Mexicans pretending not to be in Hollywood.

'I met her at a shooting party in Hampshire where I'd been sent to do a funny piece on brash American actors and the English gentry. She was having a high old time, playing Lady Macbeth in a risible-sounding film where they'd stripped her of most of her lines and all her clothes. She'd been filming around a ruined church or something on Lord Vellam's land and they were wrapping around the twelfth, so he'd invited her and Grisci to shoot with them. Except Grisci is some kind of Trot and flew home to Italy rather than spend the weekend with the blue bloods. So there was Iolanthe, all short skirt and silk knickers, draped over the eighteenth-century sofas and drinking her way through the best wine cellar she'd ever encountered.

'Lord Vellam allowed me out on the shoot on the understanding that I couldn't actually shoot anything and that I was not to mention some of the foreign visitors joining him because they're not the sort of people that the readers of *Harper's* like to imagine in the great houses of England. Iolanthe was much too drunk to shoot anything. She'd been drinking wine like it was water all through lunch and then she hadn't any proper clothes for the countryside and her heels were sinking right into the mud so she had to take them off. By the time we got to a decently hidden spot she was filthy and Lord Vellam and his son were sick of all the moaning and swearing.

'I took her off into the woods, mainly so that we wouldn't both be sent back to the house in disgrace and she squatted under the trees in her nothing of a skirt and moaned about how she was about to be sick and could I get her some water. And I attempted to interview her while she rattled on about her tragic bloody childhood, which would have made excellent copy except that it really wasn't that kind of piece. Just as she said she was feeling better she threw up all over my shoes and I had to clean her up with leaves and a handkerchief.

'Of course then the shooting starts and Iolanthe absolutely goes to pieces because there's bangs all around her. And she starts sobbing and saying that they're killing all the little animals and that she hates men and posh people and the English and guns and war and she'd still have a brother if we hadn't decided to help all the fucked-up people in Japan. God, Hayes, it was a long afternoon I can tell you. Finally, the shooting stops and I drag her back to the house where she goes to sleep in an armchair. I'm staying the night but she never appears at dinner so I listen to how ghastly everyone thinks she is and then I retire to the billiards room and listen to all the men saying they'd give her one anyway.'

'My admiration for these people is not exactly growing.'

'Iolanthe or the toffs?'

'Any of them, really.'

'I'll tell you a secret, Hayes. It's a newspaperman's secret. Human beings are awful. All of them. Complete arseholes to a man and woman. The less effective arseholes float through life on a river of excrement and the really effective arseholes build factories full of people who are forced to supply more excrement to keep the river flowing.'

'I don't suppose you'd like another pint?'

'I think it's time for whisky.'

'Coming up.'

* * *

'Go on, then … Iolanthe had failed to come down to dinner.'

'Right. Well. Never found out what happened to her that night. Probably unconscious and put to bed. But the next morning she surfaces at breakfast, looking a little wan. I take her off into the garden and she tells me stories about Grisci and his boyfriend – none of which I can use. Then there's some awful luncheon with lots of huge carcasses of fish on the table and I'm forced to sit next to Vellam's son who hates newspapermen and won't talk to me.

'That evening there's a hunt ball and Iolanthe disappears in the afternoon with the chauffeur to visit a hairdresser. Vellam's son then informs me that I've had all the hospitality I'm getting and can I please go home. So I do. I drive back home and write up pretty much the same piece that I would have written if I'd never been invited at all. Because really, who cares … Anyway, the editor at *The Times* got it into his head that I was the one who "knew" about Iolanthe Green. So I was sent to write another profile on her and I decided to do a bit of research and I called up some old articles and her story just didn't really make any sense at all.'

Harold Wilson Is Not
a Fascist Dictator

Thursday, 11 November

Anna had never been into Ottmar's flat before. After the colour and decoration of the cafe she found it very sparse and cold. There was a single wall-hanging in bold geometric shapes, but the sofa and the chairs were brown, the rug was brown, the mantelpiece held only a square clock and a picture of Rashida in her first-form class at school. In the corner was a work table with an electric Singer and neatly piled curtain fabric in duck-egg-blue brocade.

Samira sat and brooded at the end of the dinner table. Ottmar disappeared to call the staff and arrange for evening opening. Ekin cooked silently in the little kitchen even though a wide hatch connected her to the women at the table. A swirling torrent of animosity flowed between the table and the kitchen counter. When Ottmar returned he filled the silence with his careful, neutral questioning.

'Oh, lovely, Ekin is doing her cold salad. Are we having cacik, my love? Yes. Yes. I think we are. Samira, you must be very uncomfortable in those clothes. I can see your mama needs another couple of minutes. Why don't you go and change into something cosy. So cold the weather is now. Go on, my darling, tights and a big jumper: yes. Wash your face, wash your hands. You'll feel so much better. After lunch a lovely long bath, I think. We rang school and they know you have a bad headache today so no more questions asked. Go on, my darling.

'Now, Anna, let's get you a drink. We don't have any coffee on the go but I can make you tea. Yes? Lovely. Ekin, I will make the tea. No,

Anna, stay there. You are our guest. Knives and forks, yes? And serving spoons. Where are the mats again? I never eat here, Anna. Isn't that awful? Only on a Sunday and then Ekin does a special dinner. You see, in a way, I blame myself. Never here. One parent, it doesn't work so well as the children are getting older. Anna, you know … I'm not making excuses … But sometimes I think, how can it have been otherwise. We cannot afford to live if I don't work eighty, ninety hours a week. The cafe would not bring in enough money and we cannot live on Ekin's earnings alone.

'I don't know how your father was, Anna, but I sometimes think to have a successful family you have to sacrifice a happy family: at least at first. Maybe the girls can be happy later. Maybe we all can be happy later. Or maybe their husbands will not start from nothing and happiness will come earlier. As far as I can see, the successful family sacrifices happiness to work and the unsuccessful family sacrifices happiness to poverty. I think that I prefer success but some days I cannot tell the difference.'

Samira came back in dressed in tights and a sweater and a very short skirt. She sat at the end of the table and stared out of the window at the houses beyond. 'Why are you looking for her?'

'What's that, Sami?' Ottmar asked.

'Talking to Anna,' Samira said without turning. 'Why's it your job to find Lanny, then? Police are looking for her, aren't they?'

'I don't think they're looking very hard.'

'Too busy shaking down Soho for whores?'

Anna ignored this. She was hoping they weren't going to talk about last night. 'I think Lanny got herself in trouble. I think she was in this country on her own and she found herself in trouble and she was trying to dig herself out of it.'

'She had enough money,' Samira said.

'I don't think it was that kind of trouble.'

Ekin started to load the table with bowls and plates, then she took her place beside Samira and watched her daughter ignore her arrival.

'Anna,' Ekin said, 'we normally say du'a. Do you mind? You can say grace if you wish when we are done?'

'Oh no, I'm fine. Please just do as you would always do.'

Ottmar and Ekin bowed their heads and spoke quietly, each using their own form of words; Samira sat and stared out of the window. Ottmar went to serve himself from the bowl of yoghurt but Ekin stilled his hand.

'Please, Anna, say grace. We want to make you welcome.'

Anna gave her a big, embarrassed smile. 'I'd really rather not.'

Ekin's face fell, at a loss as to how to proceed, so Ottmar leaned across and in a stage whisper told her, 'Anna doesn't believe in God.'

Samira's eyes swivelled in Anna's direction. Ekin looked bemused. 'Really and truly?'

'Afraid not. Not really raised in a faith. My parents had one, but then they gave it up. And my school had another one, but I didn't really like my school. My father's a scientist, you see, of a kind. My mother too. I'm just a bit … empirical for all of that. Respectful, obviously. Empirical but respectful.'

Ekin looked at Anna and then at Samira who had moved to face the table. 'My eldest daughter has run away from Allah also. I think the young today dislike all parents.'

Ottmar started to serve people with great vigour and noise. Anna ate some bread and yoghurt and searched her mind for something to say. She pictured Aloysius standing by the desk in the station. She wondered if she would see him again. Their brief romance seemed a very long time ago, very slight and very fragile. She wished she had put her arms around him in the station. She wished she had comforted him in the street. She had watched him bleed onto the snow and said nothing. How much fear is too much? How much is common sense?

Samira spoke. 'So, you're an atheist?'

'I am.'

'I'm an atheist and a Marxist. My parents are members of the proletariat trying to be members of the bourgeoisie.'

'I see,' said Anna, bewildered as to how to follow this politely.

'Our arrest last night was indicative of the fascist hold that the police – who are the army of the bourgeoisie – have over ordinary members of the proletariat.'

'No, it wasn't,' said Ekin.

'I'm not sure that I would describe the police as fascist,' Anna ventured. 'I think that might be to misunderstand the meaning of the word.'

'Your friend had his head bashed into a police car because of the colour of his skin.'

'Well, yes. But that isn't in itself fascist. It's more incredibly thuggish. And racist. And illegal. And unprofessional.'

'Could we talk about something nicer?' Ottmar begged.

'No,' said Samira, 'it's an example of the police believing they are above the law, much as they would in a martial force obeying the whims of a fascist dictator.'

'But,' said Anna, 'Harold Wilson isn't actually a fascist. In fact, he's nothing like a fascist.'

'He's a product of the bourgeois system. He's a grammar school boy who went to Oxford and now he pretends that just because he was born in Yorkshire he's in the pub every night with his whippet and his pipe.'

'Still not technically or actually a fascist.'

'You know,' said Samira, 'if you identify a system as corrupt then your only honourable courses of action are to flee it or fight it.'

'And which have you chosen?' Ekin asked, her voice dripping with disdain.

'First I have to remove myself from the system. I have to throw off expectations of how I will dress and who I will sleep with and what I will do to earn money.'

'Good God!' Ottmar said. Ekin shot his blasphemy a cold stare.

'Of course, they think that means I'll be becoming a prostitute. When in fact I will merely be throwing off the shackles of society's expectations.'

'But how are you going to live?' Anna asked her.

'Outside the system.'

'Samira. Sweet one,' Ottmar began. 'To live outside the system you will need to go and live in a field and eat grass and drink the rain. You know, like a cow. It is not a human way to be. We are social creatures, my darling. Our systems are flawed but we made them. We were just trying to organise the world.'

'So a black man can be beaten for offering to walk in hand-cuffs and a Turkish girl can be called a prostitute because she isn't wearing tights and if you fail to keep your house you end up freezing to death on a park bench. Is that how we're organising the world? After all the thousands of years and all that philosophy and religion and books and poetry, after the millions of elections and debates, that's as good as we get? Wouldn't you rather be a cow? I'd be a cow out of shame.'

Anna stood, surprising herself as much as the others at the table. She fumbled with her napkin. 'Sorry. Ekin, forgive me. It's a lovely meal but my friend is hurt and I have to go to him. And I can't—'

'See!' Ekin said to Samira. 'See what you've done? You've upset our guest.'

'It isn't her,' Anna said. 'It's all the rest of it. I can't just sit here and not know what's happening to him.'

'Of course no one ever bothered asking me,' Samira said as Anna turned to go.

'Asking you what?' Ekin demanded. 'If Anna was allowed to leave the table?'

'No one asked me if I knew Iolanthe,' Samira said, dipping a piece of bread into her cacik and then glancing around her to gauge the response from the adults.

Anna paused and studied Samira's expression. '*Did* you know Lanny?' she asked.

'I did.'

'Knew her how, little one?' her father asked.

'I saw her at Roaring Twenties. I know her boyfriend. Delbert.'

Anna retook her seat at the table. 'Why didn't you tell me, Samira? When you knew we were looking for her.'

'You didn't ask. You just turned up in the club and ordered me home like a child.'

'But can you tell me now? About Lanny?'

'You could try asking me nicely.'

'Samira!' Ekin banged the table.

'I am asking you nicely, Samira. What happened to Iolanthe?'

Samira put down her bread and pushed away her plate. Then she fixed Anna with a direct stare.

'You go somewhere often enough you get to know the faces. The sound system guys, the barmen, the musicians, the girls who turn up to dance. I saw Iolanthe for the first time about three, four weeks ago. She turned up one night, maybe with a guy, I don't know. When I saw her she was on her own. People recognised her, I think, but there are musicians in there all the time so seeing someone from a magazine is no big deal. I saw her dancing, drinking, sometimes she'd be talking to someone. More than once I'd see her watching Del because he works the sound system there sometimes. Lots of the girls like him. I don't know if he goes with them. A couple of times I saw her go up to the speakers, to the deck and she was flirting with him, laughing, leaning over.'

'What about Del? Did he like her?'

'He liked the attention all right. He's very pretty, Del; knows it too. He'll flirt with anyone but mainly he just gets on with the music and stuff. He likes to look good in front of the older guys. Duke Vin, people like that. That's who he respects. I saw her one night standing up at the sound system with him. Another time, I saw them kissing at one of the tables. One night I'm in the women's toilets and I see her crying. Lanny, right. She's sitting on one of the toilets, bent double and she's just rocking. At first I think maybe she's laughing but then it sounds more like she's choking. She puts her hands round her tummy and she just howls. Like she's in pain. I hear the girls talking about her in the queue. Del's dumped her. Told her to find someone her own age.'

'Nice guy …'

'I know. So the next night she's back and she's on the dance floor every minute and she's touching anything that moves. Dancing with the guys in front of him, black, white, whatever. Dancing with the girls, too. Messing about, showing herself off. Trying to make him jealous. Honestly, she kind of struck me like she was a child, you know. Like the girls at school. I expected her to have a bit more …'

'Decorum?' Anna asked.

'Self-respect. She wasn't trash. She was someone. She was more than those men she was draped all over.' Samira paused. 'This society is so fucked up.'

'Language!' Ekin roared.

Samira's eyelids barely flickered. 'You think she got in trouble with Del?'

'Not if he only knew her this past month.'

'You think she got herself knocked up, though?'

Anna said nothing but she held Samira's gaze. 'Maybe she wants to be lost,' Samira said.

'Maybe she does,' Anna agreed.

'But you can't know that,' Ottmar said.

Anna looked at him and smiled briefly. 'That's the thing of it. She could be in the worst kinds of trouble and no one's coming to get her. One policeman, sifting through papers in his office and all the while she's out there somewhere. It doesn't matter if she's all right. It doesn't matter if this is a waste of time. You can't leave someone in trouble all alone. She might do anything. And then it's all our fault.'

'She might do anything.' What a genteel way of putting it, Anna thought. How careful we're all being. Not ever speaking the worst of it. Keeping our distance, staying safe.

Is that what I did to Lanny? Did I keep my distance? Did I keep her at arm's length? Because I do that. I signal my distance from people. I draw back. I cut them out. I walked away from Aloysius … I left him, alone and bloody. Why couldn't Lanny tell me the truth?

'Pregnancy is the loneliest place on earth,' Anna said – surprising even herself – and Ottmar laughed because to him this seemed the most ridiculous of ideas.

'What makes you say that then, Anna?' Ekin asked.

Anna shook her head and blushed a little. 'Nothing.' She felt tears start to prick in her eyes so she stood. 'Forgive me. I really have to go now.' She paused for a moment and found Samira's gaze. 'Thank you,' she said. 'For trusting me with that.'

Anna made her way back to the flat. In answer to last night's missive, Kelly had left a note lying on the coffee table.

Hope he was worth it!!!! K

Of course Kelly had not considered any of the worrying options when Anna had failed to return home. She simply assumed that Anna had finally given in to her natural impulses.

Anna stripped her clothes off and went into the bathroom to wash herself. There was no hot water for a bath at this time of day, so she scraped the muck and the sweat off with her fingernails, the painful ripples against her skin making her feel more alive. Then she put on her only pair of trousers, two sweaters and tied her hair up. So what should she do now? The number of Aloysius's boarding house … could she remember it? Mrs McDonald seemed like a lady who'd have an opinion about most things.

'Hello? Directory enquiries. What name, please?'

'McDonald. Amesbury Avenue. SW2.'

'Thank you, caller. Shall I put you through?'

The phone buzzed and then rang.

'Amesbury Avenue. Mrs McDonald speaking.'

'Mrs McDonald! It's Anna. From last night. I don't suppose you know anything about Aloysius, do you?'

'He called me half an hour ago; said they were releasing him. What did you let happen to my boy?'

'I didn't let anything happen. We were arrested for no good reason and then they assaulted him while I was handcuffed in the back of a police car.'

'He didn't say anything about being assaulted.'

'They bashed his head against the top of the car. And his glasses are broken. And his face is a mess.' Quite without warning Anna started to cry. 'I told the policeman who interviewed me. I told him who Aloysius was. I'm sorry for crying. I haven't slept all night. I think it's just tiredness.'

'Now look. Aloysius told me he was going round to see you after he was let out because he wanted to ask you something more about this missing girl. Anna, promise me you will send him home. He's in no state to do anything else today. If they've hurt him he needs to be getting better in bed. Not wandering the streets looking like another crushed-up black man with a target on his head.'

'Of course. Of course I'll send him home. You have my word.'

'And don't you worry about crying. If your body's doing it that's because it needs to be done. Have a cry. Have a drink. Have another cry. Then eat something or you'll feel like crap. I'm going to go and wait for my boy.'

'Wait! Mrs McDonald. Is Aloysius really your boy? I mean, sorry if I'm meant to know this, but are you related?'

'We all need some kind of family, even if there's no blood in it. Now you send him home and everyone can get a bit of sleep.'

Anna made herself some toast and sat on the sofa with the flat door open, waiting for the doorbell to ring. 'Released' sounded good. It sounded better than bailed. Maybe Hayes had done something after all. Half an hour passed and no one rang or knocked. She pulled on socks, shoes and her coat and went out into the cold.

Aloysius was standing on Neal Street, his arms crossed, his head sunk in thought. Much of the snow had turned to slush under the feet of the market boys but here and there icy hills and peaks still marked the pavements. Anna crossed to him but he didn't stir. She fished a pair of black wool gloves out of her pocket and touched them to the back of one of his hands. He looked up and she saw his large, scared, bloodshot eyes gazing at her through the cracked glass.

'I dried them out on the radiator while I was being interviewed,' she said. 'I should have left them at the desk for you. I didn't think.'

Aloysius took the gloves but didn't speak.

'I rang Mrs McDonald. She said you were coming over here. She wants you to go home.'

Aloysius nodded, though without really seeming to understand.

'I think you might be in shock.'

Aloysius opened his mouth to speak but no sound emerged. Anna had once seen a picture of a statue of the Czar being toppled during the Russian Revolution. Aloysius looked like a man who was in the process of being pulled down and broken into pieces. She had an urge to kiss him, despite his battered, bloody face, to let him know that she had not meant to push him away. Instead she put a hand out and stroked his arm.

When Aloysius's voice came it creaked with thirst. 'I'd like the chance to help you find Iolanthe. I … I need something good to happen now.'

'Okay,' said Anna.

'Do you know where you're looking today?' he asked her.

'I don't. I mean, Sergeant Hayes told me a lot of things about Iolanthe this morning but I don't really know that they help me to figure out where she is.'

'If you have an errand you can send me on … Someone I can speak to. Can you give me something to do?'

'I still think the most likely thing is that she went somewhere else to get an abortion that weekend. But I don't know where. And I don't know who to ask. Oh … Actually, d'you know … I do. Would you come in? Just for five minutes? I'm going to ask my flatmate.'

'I don't mind it out here,' he said, staring at his feet.

'I know. But I do. I'm not leaving you standing in the snow. Come and have a cup of tea. Have you eaten? We have toast.' And Anna pulled Aloysius gently towards the door to the flats.

Aloysius settled himself gingerly on the sofa while Anna put bread under the grill and went to wake up Kelly.

'Kelly?' Anna knocked at the door.

'Ugh?'

'Kelly?'

'What? Are you okay?'

'I am. But I really need to ask you something.'

'Okay. Wait. I'm not dressed.'

Kelly came out of her room wrapped in a kimono, her hair piled crazily to one side. She stared at Aloysius who tried to make himself look smaller by burrowing a little into the sofa and turning away his face.

'Who's this?'

'That's Aloysius. He's a friend of mine.'

'Okay.' Kelly remained in the doorway of her room.

'He was beaten up by the police. That's why he looks like that.'

'Okay.'

'Iolanthe's been missing twelve days now.'

'Iolanthe?'

'Green. The actress. Who I worked for.'

'Okay. Right. Sorry. Long night.'

'We know she was pregnant and trying to get an abortion.'

Kelly grimaced at this.

'Your friends … the other dancers … the hostesses … They must have someone they go to. You know. When they need to. Someone who can help …'

Kelly raised her eyebrows as if to indicate that this was not an appropriate line of questioning.

'I'm sorry to ask when Aloysius is here but no one's going to judge you if your friends have gone looking for something. That's just … It's just … life. And I'm honestly frightened Iolanthe's lying somewhere sick and no one's coming to find her.'

Kelly blinked at Anna for half a minute and then she walked back inside her bedroom and shut the door. Anna waited for a moment but there was no sound from the room. She fetched Aloysius a plate of toast, and tea with sugar in it. 'For the shock,' she told him, 'and when you've finished I'm going to clean your face.'

'No! Please don't,' Aloysius said, recoiling into the cushions of the sofa.

'Why not?'

'Because it took a really long time to get a bit numb and I don't want you poking at it. I wouldn't say no to some aspirin.'

'Okay. We've got aspirin.' Anna went and got a bottle from the bathroom. 'The thing is,' she said, 'you look a little scary at the moment and if we go looking for Iolanthe people might find you harder to talk to.'

'Oh,' was all Aloysius said in reply. He swallowed four of the pills with his tea. 'I'll go and have a wash.'

The bathroom was a tiny, white-painted cube; just about four foot by four foot. There was a half-bath, a sink and a small toilet which a person could sit on sideways with their knees jammed against the pedestal of the sink. Aloysius closed the door with some difficulty and ran the water. It was cold. His image in the mirror was blurred and fragmented. He took off his glasses gingerly and laid them on the shelf. They were cracked but none of the glass had been lost from the lenses. He didn't know what he'd do if he couldn't see.

The lower part of his face was smeared with a brown crust of blood and the end of his horribly swollen nose now pointed to the left. Despite what he had told Anna it was extremely painful, even now, and he didn't dare touch it. There were cuts across his brows and a lot of dried blood in his eyebrows. The skin all around his eyes was swollen with a layer of black blood beneath the skin so that he looked like a boxer after a fight. He washed his hands and carefully cleaned his chin and neck and cheeks. He tried to wash some of the blood out of his brows but the pain was too much to deal with. He would try again when the aspirin had kicked in.

Aloysius had never felt more profoundly unconnected to the person he appeared to be. He realised now that the man he had become inside his head was far whiter and more handsome than the outer Aloysius. The man he had become inside his head would never have been beaten because he would have talked himself out of a dangerous situation. The man inside his head would never have had the experience of handcuffs. He would pity criminals and wonder at their mindset.

Though not technically a criminal himself – and he needed to remind himself of that quite fiercely – he had nonetheless been inducted into the role of informant, a role that carried a very strong suggestion of criminality about it.

He had informed on Dr Jones. This lady – who he had never met before last night, who had confided in himself and Anna, who had stood there in tears at the thought she had failed one of her patients – this lady might now be going to prison because of him. He would be expected to stand up in a court of law and give evidence against her. He would have to look in her face and see his own betrayal, to know that her life was quite undone because a policeman had succeeded in scaring him.

He had answered questions about Count Suckle and half a dozen of his other clients. What books did he keep? What income might exist not shown in his accounts? What sources of income were available outside the law? What tax arrangements did each of them follow? These were honest men, men he looked up to, business owners. How many of them might fail because he had given the wrong answer?

In a matter of minutes, while the world had spun unsteadily around him, he had found himself stripped of his role as a suited professional and recast as a member of the criminal underclass. How fragile his connection had been to everything that he held dear. And how fragile the connection of Dr Jones and all the rest of them. First he had been cut from his position and now he was to help in cutting down these others.

Any idea of a romance with Anna now lay by the wayside. He wouldn't even have blamed her if she found herself revolted by his current state of dishevelment though he had felt an unmanly pang of betrayal when she had so easily left him and Samira standing at the front desk of Savile Row. He had worked hard to flatten that emotion as he sat in his cell, knowing full well that a woman was not expected to save the man she was with; nonetheless Samira's words to Anna rang in his ears.

'I didn't offer to go walking round Soho after dark with a fucking black man for protection.'

The way she had said black had stilled his heart a little even in the awfulness of that moment. Drawing out the sound of the letters; pouring so much ugliness into them. He had fancied himself one of the good, brave, handsome men in an Agatha Christie novel. But the handsome man was never tinged with blackness, for what possible use would he be with skin like that? He wasn't Captain Dobbin or Gabriel Oak or Robert Jordan. What model had he in any book at all? Was he supposed to find an echo of himself in the Emperor Seth or Chokey Cholmondeley? He was invisible – ghostly white, transparent as a wedding veil of silk – within the pages of the books he loved.

There was a tap at the door. 'Aloysius?'

'Yes?'

'Are you okay in there?'

'Yes. Sorry. Out in a minute.'

He opened the door and Anna pressed her fingers to her lips and held a piece of paper up against her chest. Then she pointed to the bottom of Kelly's door and mimed it being slid under.

It read:

High Street, East Ham CLO 6784
Arnold Circus, Shoreditch SHO 7526

They slipped on their coats and shoes and crept out of the flat.

Colonies

Thursday, 11 November

There was a Mark. And a Cassidy. A Yolanda who was really Iolanthe – or was it the other way around? There was a brother alive in Annapolis when Iolanthe said he was dead, holding a whites-only naval commission even though he wasn't white. There was a pregnancy which might or might not have been ended from a completely unknown relationship. And still nobody – absolutely nobody – had seen Iolanthe Green since she walked away from the theatre on that Saturday night in October.

Hayes stood on Kingly Street and scanned the shops for coffee bars and cafes. It was violence. He could feel it. Inspector Knight thought she'd topped herself but why should she? You didn't kill yourself just because you were pregnant. Not when you lived in a place where pregnancies could be ended.

'Why do women normally go missing?' Anna Treadway had asked him.

Men, thought Hayes, and his heart sank a little in his chest. Mark or Cassidy or the father of the baby had beaten her to death.

He'd never seen so many men cry until he'd joined the police. Men who'd slit the throats of their wives and children. Men who'd bottled their friends in a drunken row. Men who'd destroyed their own careers through crimes both big and small. And those were just the criminals. Policemen cried as well. He had discovered this early on. The sergeant in the dark office, filling in the paperwork of another brutal domestic, shoulders hunched, back to the room. The constable in the alley, guarding the body of a woman frozen to death, helmet down, face to the wall. Brennan cried too. Silently, in secret, until the numbness came upon him and he could cry much less. It was a relief and a sadness to him, to see death and to remain untouched.

Sometime soon, in the next few days, he would sit across the table from the man who had killed Iolanthe Green and that man would admit the crime, bewail his short temper and then he'd fall forward, his head in his hands, and sob. 'She should have been faithful,' he would say. 'Shouldn't have fucked around. Should have told me about the baby.' And Hayes would nod and listen patiently because that's what he'd been trained to do. You couldn't feel angry all the time, anyway. It was exhausting. You'd never do your job.

He chose a likely-looking coffee bar set on the right section of the street and stepped inside. The air was thick with smoke and every table was occupied by men baring their forearms in shirtsleeves or else wrapped in heavy wool coats. No one wore a jacket. No one wore a tie. The only member of staff to be found was out the back frying bacon for sandwiches.

'Excuse me,' Hayes called through to the kitchen. 'Metropolitan Police. I need to have a word.' Behind him, he could sense a dozen heads turning to look at him and the level of the conversation dropped.

A heavyset man in an apron came to the counter. His face was bloated and stubbled but punctuated by a pair of remarkably blue eyes which Hayes couldn't help staring at. 'We got trouble, then?' the man asked.

'Just questions,' Hayes told him. 'Detective Sergeant Hayes. I'm working on the disappearance of Iolanthe Green. I believe there were some arrests outside the cafe last night.'

'Whores and a coon.' The large man paused. 'A coloured.' He eyed his clientele over Hayes' right shoulder. Barnaby could hear the door opening and closing behind him but he didn't turn.

'They were looking for someone called Mark. A musician. Believed to be the ex-boyfriend or boyfriend of Miss Green.'

'What if they were?'

'I need to ask this Mark a couple of questions. He isn't in any trouble. There's a woman missing. We just need to be thorough.'

'You trying to pin something on him?'

Hayes shot the man a large, fake smile. 'Absolutely not. He's not a central line of enquiry, just someone I need to say I saw.'

'He does bar work sometimes. Filling in. Said he'd been working the Colony Room on Dean Street. Don't know if you'll find him there. Don't keep his diary.'

'Much obliged,' Hayes told him with a nod and left, watched by two dozen pairs of eyes.

The Colony Room Club. Hayes knew it, though he'd never been in. Run by a Portuguese-Brummie Jew called Muriel, it had a reputation for filth and encouraging alcoholics to destroy themselves with drink. Soho could be so depressing.

He made his way to Dean Street, the snow and the sludge seeping through his shoe leather, the wind cracking the skin on his face. He'd had ninety minutes' sleep last night. Ninety minutes on a bench in the canteen between talking to Anna Treadway and tidying himself up for Knight's arrival. The warmth from the pints he'd drunk with Wingate had worn off now and he was left cold, tired and wary of Orla's resentment when he went home.

The stairs up to the Colony Room stank of urine and uncollected rubbish. The walls around him were painted a deep unpleasant green. Half this city lives in squalor, Hayes thought. They live in the kind of filth I never once saw back home and yet it's us – he corrected himself: it's the Irish are said to be the filthy ones. He paused outside a black door. 'Colony Room Club' was painted there in a swirling cursive, 'Members Only'. He eased it open.

The room inside was large, dark and full of people, even though it was only half past three in the afternoon. At one end was a short bar behind which a dark-haired man was pouring glasses of vodka. In front of the bar stood a gaggle of men and women, old and young, white and coloured. A man in a copper-coloured brocade suit and pork pie hat was playing jazz at an upright in the centre of the room, a cigar hanging from his lower lip. The pictures on the peeling walls hung crooked. Curtains were pinned limply to the side of archways.

The floor was awash with a sea of ash. It reminded Hayes of a saloon bar or speakeasy, the kind of place he had imagined when he read adventure stories as a boy.

'Members only, cunty,' a woman cried from the bar. Hayes turned to find the owner of the voice.

'Never seen him before,' a man's voice shouted.

'You new here, Lady Jane?' Hayes found that the voice was coming from a small, dark-haired woman hunched on a bar stool in the corner. Her eyebrows had been drawn on in a strong black line, her lips applied in the same manner but in red and she wore a garish emerald and blue checked dress.

Hayes fumbled in his pockets for a warrant card and held it out to her, not sure if this was Muriel.

The lady leaned a little forward, threw up her eyebrows and then announced to her courtiers at the bar, 'It's a fucking copper.' Half the room turned and stared at Hayes, the other half kept drinking.

He took a step forward. 'My name is Barnaby Hayes. I'm a detective sergeant at West End Central investigating the disappearance of Iolanthe Green. I believe you have a man called Mark working as a barman here.'

The lady with the drawn-on eyebrows – who was in fact the aforementioned Muriel – turned to the man behind the bar. 'Who d'you murder now then, Mary?' The barman didn't speak.

'Is your name Mark?' Hayes asked him.

The barman nodded.

'You were dating Iolanthe Green?'

'Wouldn't call it dating,' the man said.

'Fucking her?' Muriel asked. 'Shtupping her? Nailing her bones?' There was an edge to Muriel's tone. This incursion was bothering her. Mark eyed her nervously. 'Can I have a minute to talk to the copper?'

'You can have thirty years,' Muriel told him and poured herself a drink.

Mark came out from behind the bar, rubbing his hands on his jeans. 'We can talk on the stairs,' he said. 'Loud in here.'

Hayes nodded and together they went back through the black

door and stood uncomfortably close together on the top steps. The man called Mark looked to be in his thirties, swarthy with a slick of gelled black hair. He wore wide navy-blue trousers and a pink shirt open at the collar. Hayes drew a notepad and pencil from his breast pocket.

'Can you tell me your full name, sir?' Hayes asked.

'Mark Chapel.'

'And your current place of residence?'

'73C Berwick Street.'

'Thank you. And can I ask first of all if you have seen Iolanthe Green since her disappearance on the thirtieth of October?'

Mark pressed himself back against the wall of the stairway. 'I don't have a clue what happened. I would have come forward and said if I did.'

'Were you dating Miss Green?'

'We had a thing, sir. A few weeks ago. Like a fling.'

'And how long did that fling go on for?'

'Ten days. Something like that. I was covering the bar at Ronnie Scott's when she came in start of October time. We got chatting. I took a night off, took her out a bit. I play in bands – session guitar – and I took her along to some rehearsals and she loved all that. Not the theatre. Different world, right? There was a rumour The Who were going to play Roaring Twenties at the weekend so we went there after her show but it wasn't the right night. She liked it though, stayed there for hours, they had to throw us out. We went out three, four times that week and then the next weekend she blows me off and a few days later I hear she's seeing this coloured guy, Del or something, works in the Twenties. So I see her, just in passing, late October. 'Lanny!' I say but she walks right past me. Didn't want to know me. Bitch.'

'She was rude to you?'

'She was stuck up. Used to tell me to talk less, 'cause I was boring her.'

'And you were angry about this.'

'I wasn't *angry*. I was annoyed. She was a cow. That doesn't mean I hurt her.'

'I have to ask you a slightly odd question. When you were dating Miss Green were you aware of her protecting herself?'

'Protecting herself? From what?'

'From pregnancy.'

'Oh! Oh. No. Well … I don't think we talked about it. I just assumed …'

'So you never spoke about contraception … pregnancy …'

'Mostly we got drunk, danced a bit, fucked. Sorry, screwed. Had intercourse.' Mark was sweating now. He struck Hayes as being nervous and also rather stupid. He made no attempt to square up to the policeman, seemed more frightened than anything.

'Do you remember her knowing anyone by the name of Cassidy?'

'Cassidy? No. I don't think so. She was never with any friends. Said she wasn't meant to be out all hours. She had to look after her voice, not get sick, all that actress crap.'

'As far as you know was she in a relationship with this Del person when she went missing?'

'No idea. Maybe. You know the Twenties isn't that nice any more. All gone quite jungle, if you know what I mean.'

'Do you think I might find Del there?'

'Maybe. I don't know.'

Hayes stood in silence and watched Mark sweat. Was this a violent man? he asked himself. He seemed to be something of a shambles. If he'd killed Iolanthe then why hadn't he run? He wasn't married, not rich enough to own his flat. He could have just left. He was probably guilty of something, Hayes thought. Drug use, petty thievery; he certainly hung around with a few thugs. Did he hate Iolanthe enough to have her killed by someone else?

The sweat from Mark's face was soaking into the top of his shirt. He started blinking furiously, had to wipe it from his brows and eyes.

In frustration, Hayes broke the silence. 'You know the penalty for murder is a mandatory life sentence. If it was manslaughter … an accident … you'd be better off speaking up now. Give you a chance of seeing the outside world again.'

Mark's eyes had grown rather pink, either from the sweat or tears. 'I didn't hurt her,' he said at last. 'I might have said some shitty things about her but I wouldn't punch a woman, let alone kill her.' He held his hands out towards Hayes, palms up. They were shaking. 'I'm not a violent man,' he said. 'Don't have it in me.' Hayes met his eyes. Do I believe you? he thought.

Very slowly Hayes put away his pad. Mark watched him for a second, then seized the moment and barged back through the black door into the club. Inside the room Hayes could hear Muriel crowing with laughter. He walked back down the stairs.

Out in the street two coloured men in khaki suits were arguing about the quickest way to get to Muswell Hill. This city, Hayes thought. There is life but no gentility.

The Strength of Weeds

Anna didn't want Kelly to hear them making the calls to the numbers on her piece of paper so they went to find a call box. She already felt quite badly for leaning on the woman in such a personal way. These were not things that any of them wanted to talk about – sex, pregnancy, abortions. These were the dirtiest of subjects, like menstruation or defecation: the rank, unpleasant workings of the body that had to be denied. She felt herself flush at the thought of it, the thought of her body in all its slippery reality, the way she had ached for Aloysius in the club the previous night. How was a woman meant to stay something lovely to a man when her body and her workings were so base? How could she, Anna, who kept herself so clean and clever, hope to hold the respect of a man once she had stripped for him?

A girl walked past them both, black boots, bare thighs, navy skirt cut high on the leg. Anna looked at her and then at Aloysius. Had he noticed? Aloysius attempted a smile. She couldn't tell.

'Thank you,' Anna said.

'For what?'

'For doing this with me. For not wanting to give up. No one would blame you if you wanted to go home.'

Aloysius shook his head. 'Not till we find her. When we find her then we can all go home.'

They walked into the call box together, Aloysius spread some coins out on the shelf and Anna dialled the East Ham number first.

'Hello?'

'Hello. I was given this number by a friend of mine. I hope it's okay to call out of the blue. My name is Anna …' and then she wasn't quite sure how to continue.

'Hello, Anna. Can you tell me what you're after?'

'I'm actually not sure. I think there are …' Anna's brain would not cooperate. What was it you were meant to say? She remembered a picture of a smiling woman with a shopping basket from an advert in her mother's magazine. 'What's regularity of cycle?' she'd asked. Her mother had laughed uncomfortably. 'For when your period stops and you need it to start again,' she'd said. And at the time Anna hadn't understood what it was she meant.

'It's in regards to regularity of cycle. Pills, maybe a tonic, for regularity of cycle. Does that make sense?' she asked.

'It does. Do you need to come today?'

'I'd be grateful if I could.'

'Do you have my address?'

'High Street?'

'That's right. I'm at 118B. South of The White Horse and the park, above the bookies. The cost of medicines is between fifteen shillings and one pound six.'

'I see. Okay. Thank you very much. I will try and get there this afternoon.'

She hung up and rested her forehead on the receiver. 'Well, that was scary.'

'You're doing fine,' Aloysius told her. 'Just sound confident.'

Anna picked up the phone again and dialled the number in Shoreditch.

'Hello? Shoreditch 7526. Marion speaking.'

'Hello, Marion. My name is Anna. I'm ringing up regarding regularity of cycle.'

She paused, hoping that Marion would jump in and help her but there was silence at the end of the line.

'I was given this number by a friend. I was after perhaps pills or a tonic.'

The phone went dead.

'She hung up on me!'

'Maybe they went out of business.'

'Maybe I was too direct. Do I call her back?'

'Not if she doesn't want to talk. Let's go to East Ham and meet the other one.'

'We'll need a pound. Or fifteen shillings at least. That was the cheapest thing she had and I don't have any money.'

'Are we going to buy pills?' Aloysius asked.

'I don't know. I feel like we should. I think they'll be more inclined to help if we've paid them something.'

'I'll draw some money. Listen, I need to make a phone call. I have appointments this afternoon. I have to let them know I'm, you know … sick.'

Aloysius sat in the seat behind her on the number 15 and Anna didn't say a word in disagreement. They had received some very alarmed glances from the driver as they boarded and had gone to sit as far away from other passengers as they could manage.

Anna found his face difficult to look at now. His beauty was entirely hidden and in looking at him she only found herself going over the events of the past night. So they stared out of the window and watched Fleet Street roll past. The roads were less busy than usual on account of the snow. There were fewer shoppers hurrying to railway stations, fewer visitors flowing to the Royal Courts of Justice and St Paul's. The snow reminded Anna that it would soon be Christmas. She wondered if Iolanthe would be found by then, or whether the Galaxy would have taken in another show and her wages would be paid again. The sense of a very mournful time spread itself out before her and she wondered if she might not see Aloysius at all after today.

The bus trundled on, past the Bank of England where naked stone figures holding bundles of keys and weighty chains made Aloysius avert his gaze. Anna stared at the figures of the women pouring down showers of coins on the heads of those who passed beneath them and at the naked boy and little girl who they clutched against their legs. Such an odd sight, those little naked children always on the edge of falling. And she too looked the other way.

What did it profit them, all the great institutions of the kingdom? Life wasn't lived in churches or banks or the Houses of Parliament. It was lived upon the street, on buses and in the carriages of trains, in ordinary houses and ordinary living rooms. It was lived by people who arranged their lives around the meals they ate or what was on television on Thursday or whether their team was at home at the weekend. What were the institutions for at all? She knew they had names, little badges, signifiers that gave them a purpose. Churches were for faith. Police stations for safety. Courts for justice. Banks for the wealth of all the nation. But these were not buildings she ever entered. These were not people she knew. She was reminded of some of the elderly women whom she had come to know in her time waitressing at the Alabora. In the days after she had left to work at the Galaxy she would pop in for coffee with Ottmar and wave to Rose, to Enid, to Millicent.

'Come to the theatre,' she'd say. 'I'll see if I can get you cheap tickets for a weekday mat.'

'No!' they'd tell her, alarmed by her kind offer. 'No! Theatre's not my thing, dear. I wouldn't know what was going on.' Having never stepped inside the doors of a theatre they found themselves terrified by the idea of doing so at the age of seventy-five. Anna would laugh at them with Leonard, rather snottily she realised in retrospect. 'What do they think will happen? Culture will gobble up their bones?'

A child of a good school and clever parents, she had run away to hide herself in penury but retained the idea that institutions somehow belonged to her. She had a sense of ownership of the buildings of the kingdom that had been bred into her by all the adults that she knew. But now, in the moment of needing something ... some kind of institution to sweep down and rescue her, she found herself quite alone. The police had beaten Aloysius and walked away from it. And somehow the overturning of one institution had cast all the rest into doubt. If the police were not what she supposed them to be, were the lawyers, were the priests, were the politicians? After a lifetime of laughing at the kind of people who feared walking into a theatre or a museum or even a grand library she found herself mistrusting each great and stony building she encountered. A sense of general hostility had seeped into her world and was colouring everything like a bloody finger smeared across a lens.

Aldgate station next and out along Commercial Road. Past the vaulting snow-capped might of St Mary and St Michael, where a smiling, bearded Jesus dressed as a king sat on a throne above the door. One cold and lonely pigeon huddled on the orb in his left hand. *Ave Rex Christe*, the words proclaimed. Hail King Christ. A circle of poppies lay half obscured by snow on the pavement by the gate. Remembrance Day, Anna thought. Where had they been at eleven o'clock? Aloysius had still been in his prison cell. She'd been walking with Ottmar, Ekin and Samira. She had not heard the bells, had not thought to keep the silence.

Poplar. Canning Town. The heat on the bus was lulling them into sleep and now and then Anna's forehead would bounce against the cold glass of the window as exhaustion overwhelmed her. Upton Park. East Ham. This was not the London she knew well. 'Last stop,' the driver called as they neared a corner of the park and a line of other buses, windows dark. They walked slowly down the stairs and stood on the snowy pavement, stunned into silence by tiredness and the shock of the cold. On the far corner stood a cafe and through the window Anna could see seven or eight workmen gathered around a table all looking at something in the paper and laughing.

'I don't think I can do this much longer,' she told Aloysius.

'One more visit. While we've still got a chance of something. Come on …' he told her. And he took her hand and led her across the roads. There was something formal, parental in the way he led her now, such a long way from how they'd held hands in the street last night. She felt as if she was being told off, that she'd let him down, and in a way perhaps she had. But hadn't other people let him down far more? She wondered if he thought she was on their side, the side of the police, the side of the white world? Did her skin colour manifest itself as strongly to him as his did to her? Did her skin even have a colour? Perhaps he saw her as she saw everyone else: the pale complexion signalling the blankness of the slate.

They stood at the front door beside the betting shop and Aloysius rang the bell. A window creaked above them, and they heard a child's feet running on the stairs. The door opened on a chain and the face of a girl around twelve years old looked round the crack.

'Hello,' she said.

'Hello. I'm Anna. I rang up earlier. Perhaps I talked to your mum about coming over?'

'Who's he?'

'He's my boyfriend.'

The child unchained the door. The hallway inside had been burned a rich, sulphurous yellow from years of cigarette smoke and the thin carpet on the stairs was ripped with holes and slashes. The child herself wore a red cotton sundress with just a white vest beneath. They followed her slim, bare legs up the stairs.

The flat above could only really be described as a factory of the cottage variety. In the living room there were various tables and desks set about the walls, each one piled with white boxes and bottles and sheets of labels with scrollwork and lots of writing on them. There was a tiny television standing in one corner, a sad-looking pot plant in another, and the walls up here were as ochre yellow and brown as the ones below. A young woman of about seventeen was sitting at one of the desks labelling the boxes and the child went over and joined her, sitting beneath her on the floor from where she filled the boxes with little paper wrappers full of something dark.

Anna could see through to the kitchen where yet another table was piled with paper packages and labelled bottles and large brown boxes sealed with tape. A woman finished taping up a box and came out to them, wiping her hands on her apron.

'I'm Hen. You must be Anna. We're a bit short on chairs but you can take the one at the empty desk.'

'Thank you,' Anna said and, remembering that she was supposed to be pregnant, slumped into it gratefully while Aloysius hovered by the stairs.

'You the boyfriend?' Hen asked and Aloysius nodded, suddenly terribly aware of his smashed glasses and boxer's face. 'She do that to you?' Hen laughed.

'No. Her father did,' Aloysius told her. Hen raised her eyebrows. She had a clever, mobile face and a small, skinny body. She reminded Anna of a bird, all alertness and bones.

'How far along?' she asked Anna.

'I don't know. Maybe twelve weeks. Is that a problem?'

'Doesn't work as well as the pregnancy goes on. Just have to tell you that. Works best early, though I've known women use it at six months. Just a bit more hit and miss. You might need to take it a few times.'

'Okay,' Anna told her.

'So, the tea is cheap but it's on the mild side. The pills are stronger. You can try a couple a day, going up to three at a time if it hasn't worked after a week. We have an oil that's extremely potent but you have to be very careful not to overdose. It's the same with all the stronger stuff. You gotta treat it with caution. Minimum dose then build up slowly. Never double up. Never take two kinds at once. If something isn't working and you're on maximum dose then you try something else. If pennyroyal doesn't work for you, you come back to me and I'll send you in the right direction for something with blue cohosh in it. Different women react differently to the preparations. We're all particular. For twelve weeks I would suggest pills or failing that the oil, if you promise me to go easy on it.'

'I don't know. What do they cost?'

'You can get twenty-five pills for eighteen shillings or a little bottle of the oil for a pound.'

The room was rather warm and the chair comfortable. Anna felt her lids flutter. Hen looked at Aloysius.

'You paying?'

'I am.'

'Got an opinion?'

'Not really. This is a woman's world, you know. All a bit mysterious to us.'

'It's men thinking like that keeps me in business,' Hen said, rather sharply. 'Never mind. Shall we start you off on the pills? Simpler to get the dosage right with those.'

'Okay,' Anna said, aware that she was meant to be asking questions but at a loss as to how to start. 'I, um, I was a bit nervous because a friend of mine, she took a preparation a couple of weeks ago and I heard it made her quite ill.'

'Did she follow the instructions?'

'I've no idea. I haven't seen her since.'

The teenage girl turned and glanced over her shoulder at Anna. Hen's face creased up.

'Well, did she get it from me?'

'I've no idea. I'm not accusing you of anything. It just made me nervous. She was a bit further along and she couldn't face having … you know, a procedure. So then she was going to try something herbal. But I think she got sick.'

'Did it work?'

'I don't know that either.'

'Not a very close friend, I'm guessing, then.'

'Well, she was. I don't know. It's just a bit of a scary time.'

Anna looked towards the older girl who was watching her quite intently. Hen's face relaxed a little bit.

'Maybe your friend needed a little break. We all need a bit of space around these things; you shouldn't jump to conclusions. If you follow the directions you'll be fine. Just don't go necking the whole packet thinking it'll speed things up.'

Hen gave Aloysius a meaningful glance and he drew his wallet out of his coat and produced a pound note.

'We'll have the pills, please.'

'I've got some change in the kitchen. Give me a minute.'

She disappeared into the kitchen and Anna heard a key rattle in a lock.

The older girl was watching Anna still. 'Did your friend go and stay with someone, then? Sometimes they go home to their mums … time like that.'

Anna shook her head. 'I don't know. I honestly don't know where she is. I don't think anyone does.'

'She's gone missing?' the girl asked.

'She has.'

The girl's eyes grew very wide and then she looked away.

'You know,' said Anna, ostensibly to Aloysius, 'I really have to eat something before I keel over. Can we go across to the cafe? Just for a sandwich or something?'

Aloysius shrugged and creased his brow. His face had become extremely hard to read in its swollen state. Anna nodded at him, willing him to understand what she was doing. 'Yeah,' she said, 'yeah, let's go and get some lunch. Have a bit of a rest before the journey back.'

Her eyes slid left and the older girl was watching her again, her broad face tense with thought. Hen returned with a labelled box and two shillings for Aloysius. She had lit a cigarette and it rested between her lips.

'Mind what I say now,' she told them. 'Don't abuse it. Build up nice and slow. Hot bath. Cold bath. Alcohol. Anything you like to help it along a little bit.' Hen showed them down the stairs.

The temperature had dropped even lower; the sky had become more grey; afternoon was creeping past. In the street, Anna gestured silently for Aloysius to follow her across to the cafe. When they were standing outside he asked her: 'Why didn't you just tell her about Iolanthe?'

'Because I didn't want to panic her. And then because I didn't know what to say. And then because her daughter definitely knew something. I could tell she knew who I was talking about.'

'You got that from a look?'

'Yes. And she looked panicked. So, I thought we'd give her a bit of time. Slip over the road. Give her an hour to come and find us. If I'm wrong ...'

'Yes?'

'If I'm wrong we walk back over there and ask Hen straight out.'

'Okay. But I'm thinking this is a waste of time.'

'One hour. We both need a drink. I need the facilities. I hope they have facilities.' Anna looked up at the dirty windows of the caff. 'Come on. Let's get me a sandwich.' And she pushed open the door.

The café's walls were as brown with grease as the flat's had been with nicotine. The radio was playing the Walker Brothers; a man in a butcher's apron was cooking eggs on a giant griddle at the counter. Anna ordered an egg sandwich for herself, a bacon sandwich for Aloysius – who sat at a table in the corner and turned his broken face to the wall – and mugs of coffee. The man grudgingly allowed her to use the disgusting toilet in the back yard.

They sat and ate. Outside a few flakes of snow drifted down from the clouds. The towering red buses arrived and departed, their exhausts steaming in the cold air between times. The park beyond looked brown and barren. On the radio a man with a Home Counties voice told a news reporter that the abolition of the death penalty would see a surge in the number of murders and molestations. Anna asked herself again if Iolanthe really had gone missing.

'We are all capable of the most terrible crimes,' her father had told her. 'Everything is context. Everything is … mutable. Man is not capable of absolute good or absolute evil. He hovers in between the two and most of us beat our wings harder and harder as the years go by, fearing how far it is that we might fall.'

Someone was singing. Paul McCartney telling her there was no time for fussing and fighting. He made it sound easy. Music made love sound easy. Poetry made love and friendship sound possible, attainable. Why had the policeman beaten Aloysius when it would have been so easy not to beat him? Surely not committing acts of violence was the easy road.

She watched the line of shops across the high street, studying the peeling windows of the flat above the bookies. Had the girl under-stood what she was meant to do? Aloysius took off his glasses, laid his swollen head down upon his folded arms and slept. Anna took his crusts and wiped up the yolk on her plate.

The bell above the door clanged and there she stood: Hen's daughter, the older one, dressed in jeans and a blue hand-knitted sweater. She stared at the sleeping Aloysius. Anna rose and beckoned her across to a free table.

'Can I buy you something? A cup of tea or some toast?' she offered.

'I can't stay. I came down to get Mum some fags.'

'Did you know? Who I meant?'

'The older lady? Older than you. Beautiful. I saw her picture on the front of the paper.'

Anna was speechless for a moment. Now that it came down to it she was scared to ask. 'Her name was Iolanthe Green. What happened to her?'

'She rang Mum on the Friday, asked if she could come over Saturday, late. Mum says fine. The lady's offered her five pounds so Mum and me stay up. She comes after midnight. Lots of money in her purse. She lays it all out for us. She says she's three maybe four months along – she's not sure of the dates but it's about that – and she buys the pills and the tea and the oil. Mum gives her all the stuff about not mixing and not going over the dose. The lady offers us another five pounds if we can find her a room for the night. She says she doesn't want it happening where she's staying and she wants a bed for Saturday maybe Sunday night. Says she's expected back in work on Monday and wants it over with. Mum tells her it might take more time but we'll sort her out with a bed.

'So, Mum knows the Barkers up Rancliffe Road and they run a B & B. They're not up that late but Mum sends me out with her to knock them up and see if we can get her in there. So I walk her down and she gives me another pound and we bang on the door and finally Mrs Barker gets up and lets us in. They've got a single free. No bath. And the lady's not happy but says it'll have to do. I leave her there and off I go.'

'What then?'

'So then I think nothing of it until Mrs Barker rings up on Sunday afternoon and says we're to come round and talk to our friend because she's sick. Mum's with a lady so she sends me down and tells me to smooth it over. I get there and Mrs Barker says the lady has been crying out in pain but when Mrs Barker tries to call for a doctor the lady goes mad at her, swearing and cursing her and all that. The place reeks of sick – sorry to be disgusting but it does – and I go in to see the lady and she's curled up in a ball on the floor. So, I know she's overdosed, right, 'cause it happens. We get overdoses bouncing back to us every few months. I ask her what she took and she says lots of pills, but she needs it to happen now; she needs to get it out of her before she goes back to work. She's crying. It's … just really scary.'

The girl stares at Anna and shakes her head, seemingly lost in the memory of it.

'So what did you do then?'

'So, obviously we don't want people going to the hospital 'cause then everyone's in the shit. When stuff gets bad my mum calls her sister-in-law, 'cause she's a nurse. She gives us advice and stuff. If it's really bad she comes over. So, I tell the woman this and she says she doesn't want to stay … she wants to go and see my aunt herself. Except my aunt lives up in Essex outside Clacton and that's a hell of a way. The lady gets us to call a cab and she tells him she has fifty pounds to spend and to take her out to my aunt's at Holland-on-Sea and off she goes.

'I go back and I tell Mum what happened and she's fucking furious – pardon my French – because she says we don't send people off like that without my aunt's permission. She calls my aunt, warns her, and then that's that. We wait to hear if the lady's got there.

'On Monday we get a call from my aunt to say the lady's very weak and she's worried she's got liver failure and it could be time to take her to a hospital. Mum's going nuts because she's so scared and she begs my aunt to carry on nursing her. Then we don't hear any more for a few days, except when I go to get Mum's fags from the newsagent there she is – the lady – on the front of the *Daily Mirror*. I didn't even tell Mum that, she gets so stressed. I thought: what's the point? But I've kind of been waiting for the police to come.'

'Is she dead?' Anna asked then wished that she hadn't. Now that it came to it, she didn't want to know the truth.

'The lady? No, I don't think so. She was still at my aunt's on Sunday. Haven't heard from her since then. Thing is: if you go and find her, you can't tell anyone about Mum 'cause that wouldn't be fair. 'Cause I helped you, right. So, you can't tell on us.'

Anna laid a hand gingerly on the girl's clenched fingers. 'We won't tell on you. We just want to find her alive. She doesn't even have to come back if she doesn't want.'

'Okay. You want the address?'

'I do. I really do. I don't even know your name.'

'Don't worry. We're better off that way.'

Barnaby Hayes

Thursday, 11 November

Carnaby Street. Roaring Twenties. No sign of Charlie Brown this time. The door was firmly closed. Barnaby Hayes knocked. After a minute there was running on the stairs and a young man levered the door open with his foot, a cluster of empty beer bottles seeming to hang where his fingers should have been.

'We're closed.'

Hayes pulled his warrant card from his pocket and showed it silently. The man with the beer bottle hands held the door open and let him through.

The room downstairs was dimly lit. One side was piled with tables and chairs. A heap of rubbish lay beside a broom near the stage. Two men were examining a speaker the size of an industrial refrigerator, the younger of the two sitting right on top of it. By the bar two other men were debating the order of a set.

Hayes tried to judge the pecking order, the hierarchy of this place.

'Excuse me,' the young man called to him from on top of the speaker. 'Can we help you?'

Hayes pulled his belt tightly around his waist, straightened his lapels. 'My name is Detective Sergeant Hayes. I'm investigating the disappearance of Iolanthe Green.'

The young man frowned deeply. 'She went away.'

'Are you Delbert?' Hayes asked.

The young man paused. 'How do you know my name?'

'A man called Mark Chapel told me you were dating her. Is that true?'

Delbert paused. He pulled a tissue from his pocket and wiped something from his hands. 'Maybe. I got nothing to say about her going, though.'

'You've got nothing to say,' Hayes repeated. He thought about this. 'What's your full name, Delbert?'

'Watkins.'

'Mr Watkins. You are the third, maybe the fourth person today to tell me that Iolanthe Green is not your problem. That she's not important to you. That she doesn't matter.'

'I didn't say she didn't matter.'

'Iolanthe Green has been missing for twelve days. No one's seen her. No one's heard from her. She wasn't homeless, wasn't a drug addict. She had a life and a family and a job. So something bad has happened to her. At this point we start to think murder. But it could be kidnap. Or assault. Suicide. Maybe manslaughter. There are dozens of possibilities, none of them good. And yet everywhere I go people wash their hands of her. Iolanthe Green. Oh yes, I knew her. I took her to bed. Had my way with her. But she's not my problem. Not now.'

Delbert climbed carefully down from the speaker and stood facing Hayes. He was a young man, dressed in jeans and a T-shirt, slight, with delicate hands and long limbs. He had a boyish look about him, all dark lashes and smooth skin, teetering on the edge of beauty.

'She was a fantasist,' he told Hayes in a quiet and insistent voice. 'One story after another. Said she'd been sleeping with a sheikh from Arabia in some big house in the country. Said she'd been sleeping with the blue bloods, stealing their wine. Said she'd had it off with journalists, with anyone and that she was this black girl from Boston, her mother dark as me. She got it in her head one night I could rescue her. Make some life in the country. Buy her a cottage. She was crazy.'

'So you had a relationship with her?'

Delbert shrugged. 'We slept together.'

'Were you still seeing each other on the thirtieth of October, the day she disappeared?'

'We split before that. Like a week before, maybe. I couldn't cope.'

'She was annoying you? Bothering you?'

'No. She was just mad.'

'Mad in what way? Was she frightened?'

'She just … She couldn't stop talking. Always talking, all this stuff she was telling me. I couldn't tell what was true and what was lies. Was there a baby? I don't know. Her stories didn't make sense. In the end she was just this sad lady, tripping out.'

'She told you she was pregnant, though?'

'She told me every fucking thing. She told me black was white. I just … It was meant to be a bit of fun, you know. And then all that … female intensity.' Delbert shook his head. 'I got no ill will to her. I just couldn't do it.'

'Do you have any idea where she might have gone?'

'Found some man to buy her a house? I don't know. In the end … I just felt sorry for her.'

'When's the last time you saw her, Delbert?'

'Five, six nights before she went. She was in here. But we weren't talking, so …' Delbert shrugged.

'Do you know a man by the name of Cassidy? American. Might have been an acquaintance of Iolanthe's?'

'Cassidy? No. We were together, like, two weeks. I didn't know any of her friends. Didn't even know if she had any.'

Hayes nodded. He thought about Mark and then he thought about Delbert. These were not – on the surface of it – violent men. But then perhaps their nervousness was the key to understanding them. In his experience insecure men fell to violence when they couldn't cope. Iolanthe had ended things with Mark. Violence, in that case, would make some kind of sense. But Delbert had broken it off himself, so what would be his motive?

I'm doing it again, he thought. I'm trying to make her fit inside a narrative. Battered women make sense to me. They are predictable, unexceptional.

'I'll be back, Mr Watkins.'

'You know,' Delbert told him, 'I'll help you if I can.'

'I'll be in touch.'

Hayes escaped up into the street and started to walk back towards the station. On the corner of Beak Street a couple leaned against the wall of a pub. The man had his hands up under the hem of the woman's skirt. Hayes stopped and looked at them for a moment. One of the girl's stockings was rolling slowly down her leg. The man's body was pressed so far against her that he couldn't see the woman's arms and her face was hidden behind his head of hair. It's like he's eating her, Hayes thought, and a flood of images came tumbling back into his head from the sermons of his youth.

He had done his best to adjust his morals to the place, he'd done his best to accept that people had union out of wedlock. *He* had had union out of wedlock. An ember of resentment burned in him still, in spite of Gracie, in spite of the good that it had brought. Orla had promised him her body, her vitality … she was to be the life and spark of their family.

They'd been happy in those first few months after the wedding. Orla's belly got big and she gave her notice at work. Brennan found them a place to live, a flat on Sun Street so he could walk to work. They joked about their differences. Their child would be outgoing like its mother but disciplined like its father.

Gracie's birth was a bad one, long and scary. Orla came home to their cold flat stunned and tearful, unable to talk about anything except the horrors of it all. When Brennan came back from work, tired and anxious to enjoy his wife and daughter, Orla raged at him for his absence and his uselessness about the house. She barely left the flat as far as he could tell. Just sat in the living room nursing Gracie and watching her sleep. There was never milk in the fridge or bread in the bread bin. He learned to live on biscuits, which he kept at work.

That autumn, as Gracie turned six months, he passed his sergeants' exam. They celebrated his promotion with pound cake and a bottle of cider. The wages weren't enough to get them a house out of town but they made the flat a little nicer, bought a sofa, put a gas fire in Gracie's bedroom.

Brennan had hoped that they might start to sleep together again after that terrible first year. But Orla always had other things to do, other ways to fend off the loneliness of motherhood. She sat up late reading, sewed into the early hours. If Gracie was sick or had a nightmare, Orla would get into bed with her.

As Gracie turned two, Brennan was transferred from a station in the East End to the Criminal Investigation Department at West End Central, which was seen by those around him as quite a step up. Inspector Knight, his new commanding officer, did not like his accent or his provenance.

'I hate the Micks, Hayes. You're lazy and you're deceitful and you're unpatriotic. You come here with a flowery fucking reference and it makes me think you've been playing girlfriend to your last inspector. Shall I start calling you Nancy – little Fenian Flower – or will Mick do for now?'

Brennan stood and listened and said nothing. He needed Knight to like him, to want to work with him. Was it time to give in? To accept that success always came with compromise? He made a decision and he made it on his own. He took himself to Knight's office and announced that from now on he wished to be known as Barnaby Hayes at work. Knight accepted his decision with a nod.

Barnaby Hayes sloughed from his skin every last trace of Irishness. He never mentioned his childhood, the names of his parents or his wife. When he arrested a fellow émigré he made sure to draw a clear distinction in the minds of everyone around him between himself and the faithless Mick he was arresting. Some nights he walked through the door and winced at the sound of Orla's brogue.

Brennan never told Orla about his change of name. She would not have been sympathetic. As Gracie grew she was recovering herself – he could see that – but in her recovery she only seemed to grow away from him. To shape herself as a new Orla, different from the one she had been before. He no longer found her crying in her chair when he came home from work but she didn't share her joy with him. Some nights he would stand outside the door of Gracie's room and hear the two of them together, giggling and whispering like schoolgirls. He felt jealous of his tiny daughter, jealous that she had stolen a connection which had once belonged to him.

Life as a newly made sergeant was hard. If the coloureds weren't rioting in Notting Hill then motorcycle gangs were terrifying people on the fringes of London; brawling on the promenades of southern England, knives stuffed into their boots, razor blades sewn to their lapels. Soho was awash with drugs: with heroin, which appeared as if from nowhere. The streets teemed with girls and boys who could be bought and used for pennies. Barnaby Hayes, in his new-found Englishness, felt himself rising a little higher above the mess. His new voice commanded more respect, his new name spoke of privileged beginnings. He didn't belong anywhere, he was aware of this, but he looked like he belonged, sounded like he belonged. The police were a family and he was learning to fit in.

Summer and Washington

Nathaniel Green wheeled himself along the long, white corridors of the library building, a pile of returns held in his lap. When he reached the cases in the far room he started to shelve the books, barely even glancing at the numbers on the spine. He knew the position of most every book in the place. He knew the colour and the feel of all the favourites. He knew what every shelf should look like full, each one stretching before him like an old, familiar painting, the ripples of the tops like hills from a memory of boyhood that he did not own. He wheeled himself back into the central aisle, moved further down the rows. His eyes scanned the titles of the books remaining and he found, as he often did, that the words made pictures in his head.

The Influence of Sea Power bobbed like a bloated galleon in a sunlit bay. *Ossian, Son of Fingal* strode like a giant over rocks.

I will never have sex again, he thought. It occurred to him almost as if it were a new idea.

He had come inside a woman just once. Margot Brewers, who had developed a crush on him the year after his mother died and who wanted to fix him. They had courted, chastely at first, for nearly a year. When she heard about his place at the Academy she had wanted him to say that he'd go steady. She'd wanted him to do it with her once, so they could both remember it when he went to sea. If he had known that it would be the one and only time he'd be inside a woman he would have made the whole experience last much longer. He would have been kinder to her too. He would have kissed her and touched her and made her happy by way of thanks.

But that had been the crazy year. When he and Lanny spent till they were broke.

In the back office the phone was ringing. Nat turned the chair and wheeled himself towards the sound.

'Naval Academy Library, Nathaniel Green speaking. How can I help?'

'Good morning, Nathaniel. It's morning with you now, I think? I'm Detective Sergeant Hayes. We spoke yesterday.'

'Good morning, sir.'

'I have ever such a quick question for you. Was Iolanthe right when she told a *Times* reporter that you served as a midshipman on the USS *Missouri*?'

'That is correct, sir. That was my rank.'

'That's very impressive, Mr Green. It takes the recommendation of some very senior people to make it to the Naval Academy as a cadet.'

'Yes, sir, it does.'

'Was this something that your mother's employer helped you with?'

'In a manner of speaking, sir. I had the chance to meet a lot of very senior men in Boston society because of who my mother worked for. I gained entrance to the Academy in '45 and I served as a midshipman for eleven months.'

'That must have made you quite unique.'

'I don't understand.'

'I'm asking because I checked with a naval friend of mine and he seemed to remember that coloured sailors in the US Navy were confined to the post of steward's mate ...'

There was silence at the end of the line.

'Mr Green? Mr Green? Are you still there?'

Nathaniel gently replaced the receiver. What had Lanny done to them now? He looked around the little office, out of the window at the trees beyond, as if at any moment he would be dragged bodily from the building. Perhaps, he thought, this is what I need. I am trapped. I can feel it in my bones. Though whether I am trapped by this building or this chair I cannot tell.

Dad died. Nathaniel's breathing slowed. Mom died. And then we were alone.

He and Lanny had been sitting in the kitchen having lunch. Their mother had been upstairs in bed. When Lanny went to take her her medicine she wouldn't wake. Lanny rang her father's friends the Cassidys. 'Mom's gone,' she said. They called the undertaker.

Nat and Lanny hadn't gone to their father's funeral, didn't know how to arrange one for their mom. 'We can have her cremated for you,' Mrs Cassidy said. 'Sprinkle her ashes in the garden. It avoids the problem of where to put the stone.' The garden was their father's place, as were all the upstairs rooms. They had the kitchen and the utility room and the two basement storage rooms they had decked out as bedrooms. The house and the garden were somewhere they visited 'on holiday', when their father suddenly took delight in playing with his family. They would sleep in the big beds, ride bicycles in the garden, study their father's globe. If it was Christmas there'd be a party and his friends would come. Some knew who the children were, some simply thought they were the cook's. The Cassidys brought them presents and called them by their father's name. Yolanda Green. Nathaniel Green. 'Not their fault,' Robert Cassidy always said. 'Harold should have thought it through.'

The holidays never lasted. Sooner or later things between Harold and Maria would cool off or there'd be some big fight and the three of them – Nat, Lanny and Maria – would be back downstairs again. No parties. No steak. No comfy beds. Just sitting and waiting to see how the wind blew next.

Maria had left him once. Just once. Out into the street one night after they'd had a row. Under the stars. Standing at the bus stop. Two suitcases, two kids. 'We're free,' she said to them. 'We're free. We can be anything we want.' But they had no money, no car, no family to fall back on, so five days later they were back, standing on the steps of the house, Maria in tears.

No one else was like them in the neighbourhood. You were black or you were white and it felt like there was nothing in between. Not that that mattered so much if you never went to school. And Nat and Lanny never went to school. Their mother taught them to read and write as best she could; their father taught them geography and maths when the fancy took him.

They were Mackley – Maria's name – until the last two years. When their father knew for sure that he was dying they were all allowed to take Green – he even had a pastor come to the house and marry him and Maria just for the documents. Harold asked that they stay living in the basement after his death so nobody could suspect their true parentage. Maria agreed. She outlived him by a year.

After Maria's death, Robert Cassidy and the solicitor had come together for the reading of the will. Nathaniel was by then fifteen and Yolanda had turned eighteen just the month before. They escaped the need for an official guardian by weeks.

Nat and Lanny had been left the house, with its mortgage still to be paid off. They were to have the interest from their father's stocks for an allowance. Did they understand? Cassidy had asked them. They nodded. Will you call me if you're struggling? he asked. They nodded again.

The house was very quiet with Harold and Maria gone. Some mornings they forgot to pull the curtains and just turned on all the lights. Lanny wasn't much of a cook, she hated it. Nathaniel heated up things he found in the cupboards until all the supplies ran out. They phoned Mrs Cassidy. 'You have to place an order from a food store,' she told them. 'Didn't Maria teach you what to do?' But Maria had refused to train her children to be servants. She had taken the work only upon herself, protected them from everything she could. Yolanda found the number for a butcher in the phone directory. For months they lived on nothing but sausages and bacon and ham. When letters came they put them in a pile on the hallstand. Almost nothing was addressed to them anyway.

In November the refrigerator broke. Yolanda put on her coat, summoned her courage and walked all the way to Filene's department store on the corner of Summer and Washington to ask if she could buy another. The clerk took some details from her. Did she want to use Harold Green's account? he asked. There was credit of more than $1,000 available and it was also authorised to a Maria

Green. 'Yes,' Yolanda told him. 'Thank you. That's exactly who I am.' Did she need anything else for the house? he asked.

Yolanda came home very late, having bought a television set (one of only two available in Boston), a new sofa, nine dresses, two coats, four pairs of shoes, three handbags, four suits for Nathaniel, a gramophone, a stand-up piano and a radio. When Nathaniel asked about her day she told him that the ladies at the store had given her tea and cakes in a little room and shown her lots of things in a catalogue of goods. Nathaniel was particularly excited about the television.

The house filled up with boxes. Dresses lay unworn on the sofas. The piano sat untouched, for neither of them could play. On week-day evenings, Nathaniel would put on one of his suits and walk down the block to the nearest bar where he would sit and drink on his own in a booth in the corner. It was here he met and courted Margot Brewers, who had an eye for a fine suit, and it was here he would take her on dates when her mother thought she was out babysitting. Yolanda rarely left the house. She had no one to take her, no sense of where it was she belonged. She did not understand the rules of the outside world, did not know when to modulate her voice or how to make small talk. She danced alone to the radio, watched white women behave beautifully on television, stood silently in the back garden after dark when no one could see her and she couldn't shame her father. On one of her many evenings alone, Yolanda decided on an impulse to open all the letters they had been sent. But when she found that most of them contained demands for money, she stopped and remade the pile on the hallstand as if it had never been touched.

One morning in May the lights would not turn on in the bath-room. The television set sat darkly in the corner. Yolanda rang the Cassidys. 'Nothing in the house is working!'

Mrs Cassidy sighed. 'Have you remembered to pay the electricity bill, Yolanda?'

'I don't know how,' the girl admitted.

Mr Cassidy came to see them after work. They sat at the dining-room table and opened all the letters from the hallstand. 'You're eleven months in arrears with the mortgage,' he told them. 'You're a year behind with electricity and gas. You haven't paid taxes on your income or the water rates. And you owe $1,061 to Filene's department store, much of it interest.' Yolanda and Nathaniel stared miserably back at him. 'Children!' he said. 'Children! What were you thinking?'

'But there's money coming in,' Yolanda told him.

'$1,425. That was your income last year, before tax. There's a war on, Yolanda. If you had paid the mortgage and the bills you might have managed, but as things are ...'

'What do we do?' Nat asked him, almost in a whisper.

'Well, first of all I will call everyone and explain your circumstances: discreetly. Then we pay off what we can. We return what Filene's will take. We figure out how you're going to live. I am willing ... for a year or two ... to sign over to you my profits from your dad's old company. Just to get you straightened out. You can pay me back one day when everything feels easier. Don't worry,' he told them. 'We won't let you sink.'

So calls were made. Payment cheques sent out. Tax documents filed. The television set returned. Mr Cassidy had been at school with the head of the Naval Academy in Annapolis. He rang him and explained the situation (omitting only the colour of Maria Green since Nathaniel could almost pass for swarthy white). The two men agreed that a discreet entry into a military institution could be the saving of the boy.

Yolanda was to stay home and find herself an occupation outside the house.

'Anything you like, Lanny. This isn't for money. It's just to give you a bit of purpose in the day.'

With a reference from Mrs Cassidy, Yolanda got herself a job at a theatre and dance academy a couple of blocks from the house. She worked as a receptionist and secretary, though her typing skills were non-existent. After a few months she was allowed to help out in class, to prompt and to read in parts. She chaperoned the serious theatre kids to their auditions, she helped them learn their lines. She had a pretty face. She started to play little parts in academy productions, she started to find her feet. One Monday morning Lanny – opening one of the tabloid papers that the parents left on the waiting-room chairs – read about children who had been brought up in a cult.

'That's us!' she wrote to Nat. 'We grew up in a cult. Except we had nothing to believe in. It was all fear, and nothing shiny or bright. I am playing the Blue Fairy in the Christmas show. It's *Pinocchio*. It was a film in the cinema a few years ago. I have started to go to the cinema! It is magical. Do they let you go at the Academy? I hope they do. Please try and go if you haven't yet. When I sit in the dark and watch the pictures everything else goes away. It's like it all never happened. Please go. You will find it so lovely. Sometimes it is better to forget.'

The phone started to ring again. Nat watched the receiver twitch on its stand. Slowly his hand advanced towards it.

'Naval Academy Library.'

'I think I handled that rather badly, Mr Green.'

'Sergeant?'

'Yes, it's me. I didn't mean to make it sound like a threat.'

'Did you not?'

There was a pause on the end of the line and then Hayes said, 'No.'

'What was it then?'

'It was a question. And … Look, in the great scheme of things it probably wasn't the most important question. May I ask you something else? On another matter …?'

'You can try.'

'Do you know anyone by the name of Cassidy? An American. Somebody that Iolanthe knew.'

'Cassidy?'

'Yes.'

Nathaniel thought about this. 'No, Sergeant,' he said at last. 'I know no one of that name.'

Modern Holidays

Thursday, 11 November

Aloysius watched Anna watching the snowy fields go past. They were facing each other in a drab third-class compartment of a virtually empty train to Clacton-on-Sea. It was four o'clock and no one, it seemed, was travelling home or taking a trip to the seaside. Now and then Anna's mouth and brow would wrinkle slightly and Aloysius became aware that he was watching someone in the process of having a waking dream.

'Where are you?' he asked her and she glanced across at him and made a face.

'I was having a conversation with myself.'

'Well, naturally, if you have no one else to talk to …' he told her and this made her laugh. But when that sound evaporated she returned once more to watching the changing scene.

Aloysius was trying to distract himself from the memory of that interview with Hayes. That moment, of speaking Dr Jones' name aloud, replayed itself to him over and over again. He wondered if Anna, less distracted, might notice the guilt written on his face.

Outside the little window the houses and the building sites had ebbed away and they were travelling through a kind of countryside now. Large modern houses stood near the train tracks surrounded by square gardens bedded down with white, and young oaks lined the streets. Fewer cars out this way; no people on the roads. Dusk was arriving and the heavy, grey snow-clouds crowded the roofs of the estates and cul-de-sacs.

'Sometimes I feel like I have landed on another planet,' Aloysius observed.

Anna blinked at him. 'Why? Because of the snow?'

'Snow just makes you notice it more. The differences. The telegraph poles. The rows of cars. The factories and the great fat houses.'

'You don't have factories in Jamaica?'

'In the town we do. But I lived in a village until I was eight. Did my homework by lamps. No electricity. No running water. My first two years of school I had no shoes. Uniform but no shoes.'

'But how do you walk to school without shoes?'

'You walk. Grit roads. Dirt roads. It was normal. When my father came back from the war – he was a very able man – he'd been working in the engine room of his ship. He came back with all this knowledge, engineering, mechanics, electrical repair and they'd started up the buses then: "buses for everyone". He got a job as a mechanic in one of the depots at May Pen, this big town near where we lived. I'd hardly ever ridden in a car and suddenly I was riding the buses any time I wanted. Single-decker, green and white, pink sometimes, little windows that lifted up in front and always breaking down, doors coming off at the hinges. We got everyone else's cast-offs. Buses from Miami, from Kenya, South America. All the buses the world no longer wanted.

'We moved to this five-room apartment with blue flowers on the living-room wall. Electric light in the kitchen, a proper bath. I could read anytime I wanted. I could do my homework at nine o'clock at night. We took our lunch to school with us in a little box. Rice and peas, rice and fish. We were the rich kids then – Daddy working in the depot, Mama helping in the nursery – destined for the big big school. We had it all in front of us.' Aloysius looked at the haze of white and grey outside the window. 'It made me believe things could always change, always get better.'

'What do you think would have happened to you if your dad hadn't got that job?'

Aloysius frowned, insulted somehow by the remark. 'I'd still be me.'

'But you didn't want to stay in Jamaica? Didn't want to be a success out there?'

'I was in love with the idea of England. It was all I read about. It seemed more real than May Pen or Kingston or Mandeville. The Thames was this extraordinary thing and in my thoughts at night I could see Pip and Herbert rowing past the steamers to get Magwitch more clearly than I could conjure a scene upon the Rio Minho. In all those books there was England again and again and again, so fine and complicated. Until Jamaica seemed a carbon paper place, a weakened version of something else.'

Anna thought about this. 'When I was a child my father taught at a university in Wales. Some of the men he worked with would speak Welsh in the senior common room, Welsh in the corridors, Welsh everywhere except in class. And it made my father feel quite lonely because he struggled with his English for years and Welsh was just a step too far. And I remember my mother saying to him one night at supper: "Why are they all so ungrateful? Why wouldn't they want to speak the language that Shakespeare spoke? Why aren't they grateful for those books and plays?" And my father said, because he was a thoughtful man, "Every child in the world knows Shakespeare and perhaps a few thousand know Taliesin. But if they all recite 'To Be or Not To Be' and no one ever speaks the words of Schlegel or Taliesin or Racine then what is the point of culture? Shakespeare speaks and through the power of the sword and the pocketbook his words fly round the world. And Shakespeare becomes another Bible. This set of stories – perfectly fine in their own right – but nothing else is allowed to have such sway. Is that the world you want to live in?"'

And Aloysius smiled because he heard that she was listening – that she understood, that she could feel something of what he was feeling. He opened his mouth to ask about her father – what language he had spoken if not English – but Anna leaned her head heavily against the window and closed her eyes, her mouth drawn up in pain.

'What's wrong?' he asked her.

'I didn't mean to … I don't like to talk about them.'

'Did they die?' Aloysius asked.

'No. They're still alive. I just don't talk about my childhood.'

'Why not?'

'I think because I tried to be someone and I failed.'

'Who were you meant to be?'

'I was meant to go to Oxford. I was meant to be a success.'

'What happened?'

'I screwed up my life. I was angry at my parents. I moved away. Went to Birmingham. Then London. Secretary. Waitress. Dresser. I couldn't tell you if I'm working my way up or down.'

'Do you see them?'

Anna shook her head.

'You never made up?'

'We just haven't seen each other.'

'But don't you love them?'

'I try but I can't do it. I hate them. But I wish I didn't.' She rested her head against the cold window. 'Sorry,' she said. Though she wasn't sure to whom. Aloysius gently touched her knee. Anna didn't move.

'I think sometimes it is very hard to go back home,' he said. 'When I was first living with her Mrs McDonald told me that I had come so far so that one day I could go back home. She said that children have to cut themselves away. They have to grow and make new lives and that when they know who they are meant to be, only then can they comfortably go back home and say to their parents this is me and that is you and we are on a level.'

Anna gave a dark laugh. 'So it's all about power? Just wanting not to be children any more.'

Aloysius shrugged. 'Maybe. Do you want to be a child again?'

'God, no.'

'Me neither.'

'Do you plan to go back home?' she asked him. 'In ten years, if you had the money and the success would you go back home?'

'There are people that I know say we should be going back right now. I left before independence and now there's this idea that things are changing, Jamaica is allowed to be anything she wants and we should all be there: making this new country.'

'But will you go?'

'I have a dirty secret, Anna.' Aloysius's eyes twinkled with humour above his puffed, misshapen face. 'I don't want to change the world. It sounds … impossible. Who am I to make a country good again? I want a house, Anna Treadway. I want a garden. With rose bushes in it. I want two children in school uniform coming in at four o'clock to do a jigsaw on the living-room carpet. I want roast beef on Sundays, crumpets at the weekend. A ticket once a year to watch the Proms.'

Anna was laughing now. Properly laughing. 'You sound like the village spinster!'

Aloysius grinned at her. 'I don't care! I don't care if I'm old-fashioned. Why should I want what everyone tells me I must want? I don't like drugs, I'm not good at drinking and I don't want to sleep with everything that moves. I'm just me. Boring, ordinary Aloysius. When I first came here I wanted to be an upper-class gentleman and I cannot be that. I understand. I get it. But I'm allowed to want a simpler version of that. I don't want to be an anarchist or a Rastafarian. I want a paisley dressing gown, velvet slippers, a subscription to the *TLS*.'

Anna couldn't tell if he was teasing her but she rather thought he wasn't. 'I don't think I have ever before liked someone so whole-heartedly conservative.'

'I'm not greedy, Anna,' Aloysius told her. 'I just want a small piece of success. That's all.' And his face grew cloudy.

By the time they arrived at Clacton-on-Sea darkness had settled over everything. They asked the station master about getting to Little Holland but the man looked so deeply alarmed by the sight of Aloysius that he was forced to wander off a little way and study a poster about seaside holidays. It was an old-style railway poster displayed beneath a painted sign: '100 years of fun and frolics'. A woman in a knitted swimming hat lounged on a stretch of bright yellow sand, smoking a cigarette. A handsome man lay on his belly beside her. 'Clacton-on-Sea – For Modern Holidays'.

'Is he bothering you, miss?' the station master asked.

'Aloysius! No. He's fine. He's my friend. He was in an accident. That's why he looks like that.'

'You sure?' he asked, speaking very low. ''Cause if he's got something over you just nod very slightly and I'll take you somewhere safe.'

Anna smiled sweetly at the man – who was a good four inches shorter than herself – and told him: 'Actually, Aloysius is my protection. I'm starting to think of him as a bodyguard who's good at maths.' She glanced across at Aloysius to see if he was smiling. He was not. 'We just need to get to this cottage – Squaw's Cottage – somewhere outside Little Holland. Do you think there's a bus?'

'Last one left at five, miss. I can call you a cab.'

'Could we walk?'

'I suppose so. You're looking at about three miles but it's along Marine Parade most of the way. When you get to Holland-on-Sea you'll want to turn inland. But you'll have to ask directions after that.'

'Thank you very much. Aloysius, we're walking!'

'Oh, goody,' came back the dry response and he followed her out of the station and down the road to the front. It was another cold night, but very sharp and clear and the air tasted icy in their mouths. The clouds which had gathered so thickly inland were parting here to expose little patches of a starry sky. A fat quarter-moon hung above the sea. Aloysius put on his gloves and then caught Anna's sly sideways glance. He pulled the right one off again and handed it to her.

'This time we're sharing,' he told her, not ungraciously. Anna put on the single glove.

'Do you think we'll see each other after tonight?' she asked him. Aloysius stopped and looked at her, his face quite impossible to read behind the bruises and the swelling.

'I don't know,' he told her. 'I'm not going to assume anything. I mean, I'm not going to expect anything.'

'Me neither,' she told him. 'But … Are we just going to work it out at some later point?'

'I think we find Iolanthe and then we see what happens.'

'Okay.'

'One thing at a time.'

They walked on but after another couple of minutes Anna felt Aloysius's bare right hand brush hers and she took hold of it.

There weren't many other walkers out on the parade that night. Occasionally, they passed someone walking their dog or a woman returning home with her coat pulled up about her ears. To avoid odd glances they passed down the stone steps and walked the lower path for a while, in the shadow of the sea grasses and the stony banks, level with the churning sea.

Miles of sand stretched out in front of them, hugging the banks of the town, and for a while they forgot where it was they were going and who it was they were going to see. Without really meaning to they had come on holiday for a single night and walked like any other pair of lovers along the beach, enjoying the feel of the other's hand in theirs. Anna thought of the old poster Aloysius had stared at in the railway station. Look at us, Anna thought, being modern.

At Holland-on-Sea they turned to face the town and walked inland. A lone fish and chip shop still showed its lighted windows to the world and Anna went inside to ask the way. Aloysius stood in the cold on the seafront, watched the waves and waited.

He could no longer extrapolate the feeling of physical numbness from the psychological numbness that had settled over him in the police station. He had thought that in finding Iolanthe he might rescue his sense of self but now he wondered whether he wasn't just pushing himself to stay awake, to keep walking so he didn't have to go home to Mrs McDonald and the silence of his bedroom and the reality of everything that had happened to him since he'd last left the house. He thought of Mrs McDonald and he wanted to cry. Then he thought some more and realised that it wasn't Mrs McDonald he wanted but really just the privacy to shake and cry and howl out all the pain. He felt as if some small part of him had been killed. No, he told himself, not a small part. Why are you embarrassed to admit this, even to yourself? He felt wounded, mortally wounded, quite undone.

It was foolish to think of seeing Anna again, not simply because he wasn't entirely sure what he felt about her but also because he had a new life now as an informant and that to extricate himself from such a life would be something he would need to do alone. And yet the thought of burying himself in her embrace, in warmth and sympathy and kindness, was so deeply beguiling that it made his stomach turn and his heart beat a little faster.

She was walking back to him now, long, dark legs striding, hair swinging, face serious and bold and beautiful.

'It's the house of the district nurse. About fifteen minutes away, they think. Take the main road through town, up past the hall, then there's a track where the country starts … At least it'll be warm at the other end.'

'If she'll let us in.'

'We're being pessimistic, are we?'

'I come and go.'

She took his bare hand in hers and led him at a steady clip back onto the main road and then past a rather grand building with a lake in front of it. Beyond this the town ended abruptly and it was all hedgerows and profound darkness. Their eyes adjusted slowly to the absence of light. The stars were out tonight and the moon shone above them. After a few minutes a car passed by and its beams showed them the gap in the hedge they had failed to find. Through it lay a dark track between two fields pale with snow. That was all they could discern and they had to trust the darkness to contain a path. They held hands and slid their feet in front of them, patting with their toes to check the firmness of the path ahead. After a long ten minutes they saw a glow of orange light behind a tree. There it was. A bungalow set to one side of the track, a bicycle tied to a tree and a large curtained window from which spilled soft light. A little hand-painted plaque by the door announced Squaw's Cottage.

Anna knocked and waited and peered at the curtains, trying to make out shadows.

A woman opened the door on a chain and a nose and eye peered through the gap.

'Hello?' she said. 'Were you after the district nurse?'

'Yes. In a way. My name is Anna Treadway. I was Iolanthe Green's dresser and I think you might have been looking after her while she's sick.'

'What makes you think she's here?' the woman asked.

'I spoke with a lady called Hen in East Ham and then with her daughter. I haven't brought anyone with me. Well, I have a friend called Aloysius. But no police or anyone from the theatre. I haven't told anyone I'm coming here. We only want to know that Lanny's okay. Is she?'

The door opened wide. A tall, bony woman of about fifty stood holding it; she wore a nurse's uniform covered by a thick blue jumper and her feet were in slippers.

'She's gone,' the woman told them, with a note in her voice somewhere between relief and despair. 'I went to deliver a baby this morning. The midwife called me. Twin birth. And I left her in a little lean-to out the back with a hot water bottle and some lunch made for her and when I got home at three she was gone. She left me a note.'

Anna took a moment to register all of this. Lanny was alive but she was also gone. Found but not found. She looked at Aloysius.

'At least she's alive,' he said and Anna nodded.

'What did the note say?' Anna asked and the nurse stood in silence for a moment as if struggling to remember.

'I'm very tired,' she said at last. 'Would you like to come in? I was going to have some tea. My name's Geri.'

'Thank you,' Anna told her and they stepped inside. The kitchen of the little cottage had pea-green cabinets and a pea-green set of table and chairs. Geri put the kettle on and Anna and Aloysius seated themselves as noiselessly as they could around the table and waited for her as she went about her rituals of tea-making.

'You know, she's really quite sick,' Geri told them as she sat down at the table and slowly tilted the pot from side to side. 'She poisoned herself thoroughly. There were a couple of days there where I thought it was all shutting down. I've seen women die before like that. Horrible death. Horrible. They do it to themselves with pain pills or with herbs. Seen it a hundred times and I still don't understand. I took two days off work – two days as holiday – just so I could be with her. Didn't want her to die alone.'

She poured milk into some cups and then the tea. The room smelled briefly of bracken and shoe leather.

'What did the note say?' Anna asked.

Geri didn't reply. Anna and Aloysius watched as the nurse slowly folded in upon herself almost as if she were an umbrella. She pressed her chin to her chest and let out a gasp of pain. 'Ayyyy.' Her hands went to her face and she rocked forward, letting out one sob, then another.

Anna rose and went to her, took her arm and squeezed it. Geri was motionless for a moment, barely breathing. Then she prised Anna's hand from where it held her and pushed the younger woman away. She breathed deeply, sat erect and swirled the tea in the pot. When she spoke her voice had been wiped clear of all emotion.

'The note said something like: "Thanks for all your help. Cannot stay. Have made lots of long-distance calls. £10 note under biscuits for the bill."'

'Do you have it?'

'No. I tore it up. I was feeling a bit angry at her just then.'

'So you have no idea where she was going?'

'No.'

'Was she well enough to travel?'

'Not really. She needs to be under a doctor. I've been feeding her glutathione but I've nothing here that can assess the state of her liver. If she goes into renal failure … Well, that's it. And then there's the termination. I couldn't find any evidence the foetus had left her. She hadn't bled at all. So, she might still be pregnant. Though what state any foetus would be in after all that pennyroyal I wouldn't like to say.'

Geri poured herself another cup of tea while Anna and Aloysius sat and waited, quiet and a little horrified.

'Sorry to come apart on you like that,' Geri continued, her tone quite conversational. 'One of the little boys died. The second one. They were twins we were delivering. The second little boy didn't make it. Sometimes it gets you like that. Even after all these years.'

'I can imagine,' Anna said. Though of course she couldn't. 'Do you know who she called abroad?'

211

'I was only here for a couple of them. I imagine she made most of her calls when I was out. And they must have been in just the last few days. She didn't get out of bed for the first week she was here.'

'Did you hear the conversations? Do you know who they were with?'

'They were about money. I got that much. She talked about transferring money. I didn't like to listen to the rest. Amounts and all that. Names. I was trying not to pry. I'm pretty sure they were business calls, though. Not personal. She didn't have a personal kind of a voice on, if you know what I mean. She just didn't really talk to me at all. I brought her food and drink. I checked her pulse, her blood pressure, her temperature. She didn't offer to explain about the baby or who she was or when she was going. She was distracted mostly. Caught up in her worries. That's what I'd say about her. She was a woman tangled up.'

The walk back to Clacton seemed to take much longer than the walk to Squaw's Cottage had earlier in the evening. They were deflated. Filled with thoughts of the unfairness of their failure. If Geri hadn't been called out to that birth ... If they had only been a few hours earlier catching the train out here ...

They kept their hands in their pockets – Aloysius neither offering his gloves nor putting them on himself – and they turned their faces down against the cold. There were no dog walkers now; no one at all on Marine Parade but them.

As they came into Clacton there was the odd car on the road and the pubs were lit up on the corners but the icy roads were otherwise deserted. They made their way wearily to the train station and Anna went in search of the station master but found only a train guard with his jacket off sitting on a tool box and drinking a cup of tea outside the dark doors of the refreshment rooms.

'Sorry to bother you. I can see you've finished work. Are there any more trains back to London tonight?'

The train guard cast his eyes about the darkened platforms. 'What do you think, love?'

Anna smiled and feigned abashment. 'Sorry. One more question. There was a lady who possibly came through here today.

Very beautiful. About forty … Lots of dark curly hair. She might have been in a black coat and heels. I don't suppose that rings a bell, does it?'

'Not a clue.'

'Okay. Sorry. I'll leave you alone.'

Anna turned to go, spying as she did so Aloysius who waited in the shadows by the entrance.

'You could try Tom,' the man called.

Anna turned back. 'Who's Tom?'

'He works the ticket counter. He'll be drinking in the Railway Club. It's round to the right as you're going out. Behind a little fence. Private members so they won't let you drink.'

'That's okay,' Anna told him. 'Thank you.'

The Railway Club was really a glorified shed behind a wire fence beside the taxi rank. 'I'll wait outside,' Aloysius told Anna and she didn't disagree.

Inside, the shed was set with tables and there was a large wooden bar at one end. A thick cloud of smoke filled the room from shoulder to roof and the club buzzed with chatter and complaint. A number of heads turned as Anna walked in; she and the barmaid were the only women in there. Anna ignored the attention and focused her gaze above the sea of heads. She fixed her eye on the barmaid and made her way towards the bar. Before she'd even got there the young woman, barely more than a teenager, raised her hand. 'Sorry, love. I have to serve them in turn.'

'No, It's not that. I have to find Tom. Who works at the station. Sorry. Quite urgent.'

'He's normally at the corner table, just on the right, back of the room. Yeah. He should be over there.'

The table in the corner was crowded with men, most of them in uniform. There were station staff and porters and what looked like conductors in a livery she didn't recognise playing at something with matchsticks.

'Tom?' Anna called, to the table in general.

A man of about sixty looked up. 'Lucky night!' he said.

'Sorry to disturb you …'

'Don't be silly, chick. Sit down!'

'Sorry. I can't. I'm on urgent business. I need to know if you've seen someone. A woman of about forty but very glamorous. Lots of dark curly hair. Black overcoat. Black heels. Handbag with lots of gold on it. She might have bought a ticket from you earlier.'

Tom smoothed the front of his waistcoat. 'I might know who you're talking about.'

'We really are very anxious to find this lady. I have a fiancé, you see, and this is his aunt. She hasn't been well and she's set off on a journey without her medication and now everyone's frantic.'

'She didn't look right, I'll tell you that.'

'No, she really isn't. Do you remember where she bought a ticket for?'

'London, pet. If it's the same woman. Not our normal sort. I said to Pete here,' and here he nodded across the table to a youngish porter who was watching Anna's chest most intently, 'I said to Pete here, she looked just like that actress type they think got herself murdered. Lanthy Green? Is that her name?'

Anna shot them her most winning smile. 'London, you say? Very grateful. Do you remember what time?'

Tom fingered his pint. 'After lunch. Might have caught the two o'clock for Liverpool Street. She bought first class. Lanthy Green. She looked like her. But funny-coloured skin …'

Anna rejoined Aloysius outside on the pavement where he seemed to be involved in a staring match with one of the taxi drivers.

'She caught the two o'clock to Liverpool Street. She'll have arrived at half past three. Just as we were catching the Clacton train out of there. We might almost have walked past her.'

'For goodness' sake!' Aloysius's exhaustion was starting to show. 'I don't think the universe wants us to find Iolanthe Green.'

'I don't think Iolanthe Green wants us to find Iolanthe Green.'

'But here we are. Carrying on as if she does!' Aloysius stuffed his hands deep into his pockets and kicked the pavement.

'She's sick! She's sick and alone and trying to get rid of a child. Think about it. Think what that would be like.'

'I don't know what that would be like because it would never be me.'

'Yes. Because you'll never be pregnant and you'll never have to make those kinds of decisions. Aren't you the lucky one.'

'We don't have abortions in Jamaica,' Aloysius pointed out.

'Neither do we.'

'No. We *really* don't have abortions. A woman gets pregnant, she has the child. She lives with it. She lives with her decision.'

'Every time?'

'Every time.'

'Is that what your mummy told you?'

Despite the bruises and the swelling Anna could see the look Aloysius gave her. Oh God, she thought, don't leave me here. 'Sometimes reality wins out over belief,' she told him quietly. 'There's nothing neat about it. Real things happen and they're brutal.'

Aloysius gazed at his feet. 'It's been a very long two days.'

'It has.'

'I didn't mean to start a fight. Do you think we could maybe go and get some sleep?'

'Of course.' Anna reached out a little cautiously and took his arm. They turned and walked back into town.

A single car was driving round and round the central square. The woman in the passenger seat pressed her cheek and the edge of an A–Z to the window, trying to read her map by the dim glow of the lights. Anna watched them pass by once, twice, three times. She and Aloysius were standing outside a B & B which showed the notice: 'Vacancies'.

Aloysius squeezed her shoulder. 'I don't think I have the energy for this.'

'They might be fine about it.'

'I have no money left. I'm going to have to write a cheque. Are you going to say we're married? Will they even take a cheque from me? We might be better off if I slept on a bench.'

'It's fine. We just give them a story. The worst they can say is "no".'

So Anna rang the bell and when the owner opened the door they walked inside together. As they had predicted the lady of the house looked deeply alarmed at Aloysius's swollen appearance, and possibly also his very existence. She was an older woman of fifty or sixty, dressed in a rather bobbly coral-pink twinset and a long tweed skirt. Her hair was neatly set in curls and she wore a pair of reading glasses on a little gold chain about her neck.

'Please,' Anna started in, 'I know you must be frightened by the Reverend Weathers' strange appearance but we've had the most awful day and I really need someone to show us some kindness. You see my name is Anna Treadway and I am the daughter of the Reverend Victor Treadway who ministers to a flock in the area of Walworth Road in London. We have a brother church in Nairobi and it's there that Reverend Weathers normally preaches. Reverend Weathers is here on a cultural exchange and he's been meeting with some young miscreants in a boys' home just up the coast. A number of the miscreants reacted very badly to Reverend Weathers' pronouncements on the existence of hell. The reverend was then attacked quite brutally and my father sent me out here to fetch him home. Except of course we missed the last train to London. Reverend Weathers does not have any money on him but he does have a chequebook and I can give you my father's home address by way of a guarantee. We wondered if you might have two single rooms that we could take for the night. As you can see we are very much throwing ourselves upon your mercy.'

The woman didn't speak for at least a full minute though she blinked a number of times. Anna examined her face and noticed at last that her eyes seemed to have become rather wet. The lady rubbed her hands together a few times and then she spoke directly to Aloysius.

'This area used to be such a nice place, Father. I cannot think … We have seen a terrible amount of violence in the past few years. I am full of shame that you should come to this country—'

Aloysius raised a hand to stop her and when he spoke the voice that emerged was a strange one, approximating – Anna assumed – what he imagined to be a Kenyan accent. 'Please, ma'am. You have done nothing wrong.'

A tear rolled down the lady's cheek. 'My husband was very badly injured last year in the violence along the front. The mods and all that nastiness ... He's a policeman, you know. He *was* a policeman,' the lady corrected herself. 'He had to retire. Head injury, you see.'

Aloysius shot Anna a brief and somewhat angry glance but there was no way that Anna could back out of their story now.

'I am sorry to say that we only have one room vacant at the moment. It's quite a large double. The one on the front. I could try to arrange a second bed on the floor. Or perhaps you'd like to try somewhere else.'

'A double and a bed on the floor will be perfect. Thank you. We're most obliged,' Anna told her. 'Will you be able to accept a cheque from us in the morning?'

'Goodness, child, there'll be no charge. Would the Good Samaritan have asked for money?'

'Oh no!' Anna cried. 'We insist. We have to pay.'

'I will not hear of it,' the woman said. 'Let Reverend Weathers take his money back to Nairobi with the knowledge that there are still some good people left in England.'

Liverpool Street Station

It had been a cold day on Sun Street and Orla had lost track of time playing hide and seek under the beds with Gracie while their flap-jacks had burned to black in the oven.

'Never mind,' Orla said, scraping the remains rather crossly into the bin. 'They weren't our favourite anyway.'

They put on coats and scarves and gloves and walked to the grocer's to see if there was anything tasty going cheap. On the way they held hands and Orla swung Gracie round in circles while they waited for the lights to change and usher them across the road.

'What's a cousin?' Gracie asked as her mother pulled her along.

'A cousin?' asked Orla.

'Debbie has a cousin. Called Rory. And he's coming to visit.'

'Cousins are the children of your aunt or uncle,' Orla told her.

'Do I have cousins?'

Orla thought about this. 'Not on your father's side. He has a little sister but she doesn't have any children. But, yes, you do have cousins.'

'What are they called?'

Orla thought again. She had three brothers who she hadn't seen since she left Ireland. They had written to her once or twice in the early years, though their letters had mostly chided her for leaving. She had not invited them to her wedding, nor told them about Gracie. It was easier, with the whole of the Irish Sea between them, to pretend that they didn't exist.

'How many do I have?' Gracie prompted. 'Are they girls or boys?'

Orla stopped in the street and stared at her daughter. How do you explain to a child who likes everyone in the world that adult life consists to a great extent of cutting people away?

'I'm not entirely sure, my darling. I've never met them either. When I came here, Gracie, it was a very long way to come. And in a way Mammy had to start a new life. Because I didn't know anyone. Not at first.'

'Were you lonely?'

'Was I lonely? No. I don't think I was. Not then. I think I was just excited to be out in the world on my own.'

'Didn't you miss your mum?'

'I didn't have a mammy to miss, darling. She went when I was eight.'

'Where did she go?'

'I don't know,' Orla told her little girl. 'But she didn't take us with her.'

* * *

As Tom the ticket man was later to attest, at quarter to two that afternoon Lanny Green had bought a first-class single from Clacton-on-Sea to Liverpool Street station.

It had taken a great deal of strength and determination for her to climb the path up to Little Holland, to beg the man in the pub to call her a cab, to make it to the station and the train. Along the way people had stared at her, though whether it was because they recognised her or because she looked like she had bathed in turmeric she couldn't say.

She sat in the silence of a first-class train compartment and examined the skin on the back of her hands. 'Curry yellow,' she said to herself aloud.

Geri had explained. The pain, her tight-full stomach, her yellow skin: her liver was trying to shut down. She had fourteen pills remaining in her bottle of glutathione; for now it was doing the work of her liver, keeping her alive. When she got to Liverpool Street she would take another one. Three a day, she thought. That's another four days. I can keep going for another four days.

She opened her handbag to search for powder and stared at the array of letters inside. Half of them she hadn't even opened. What would Cassidy be thinking of her now? Would he have found Nat? She had to warn her brother, to tell him to be on his guard. The thought of speaking to Nat after all this time made her stomach turn over. Out of nowhere she felt homesick for her mother's lap.

Lanny pressed the letters to one side, took the powder and mirror from her bag and tried to tone down the colour of her face. There wasn't much else she could do except perhaps to disguise her hair. She had a silk scarf with her. She tied it now around her head and lay down across the seats.

'Liverpool Street. Final stop!'

Someone was shouting near the window. Lanny woke, prone on the first-class seats, her face half covered in drool. She waited for everyone else to get off the train then she levered herself up and wobbled to the door. Her heart was racing. She didn't know Liverpool Street at all but there must be a cafe or a waiting room where she could stop for half an hour.

She walked gingerly down the platform, stopping to lean against columns as she went. The concourse was busy with people. She eyed jealously a pair of benches near the stairs but they were full. A lighted sign announced a buffet and waiting room on the far side of the concourse between the timetables. She made her way towards it. The station tilted oddly and she stopped. Her heart was banging in her chest and the scene before her was splitting into pieces, each of them disappearing in a different direction. She took a moment and allowed her breathing to settle. The space recomposed itself. She set off once again.

A tiled passage held the promise of a cafe beyond and Lanny's steps quickened, longing for the security of a quiet room and a cup of coffee. Then she was on the floor, her legs gone from under her, her knees telegraphing pain. She raised her head and saw a large man in a city suit and winter coat staring down at her.

'Sorry,' the man said to her, not seeming sorry at all. 'But you weren't looking where you were going.' He glanced towards the departures board and then hurried away. Lanny stayed for a moment on all fours, still confused as to what had happened. Then she slid onto one hip and looked at her knees. Her tights were torn and her left knee oozed blood.

'I can't believe he just walked away like that!' a voice behind her said. 'What a pig!'

Lanny felt in her pockets for a handkerchief but she couldn't find one. A small child appeared in front of her and fished a handkerchief out of her coat sleeve.

'I haven't blown my nose on it,' she said. It had a little picture of Mickey Mouse sewn in a wonky fashion on one corner. Lanny took it and thanked the child. She spat on the handkerchief and dabbed at her knee. The child watched her, fascinated.

'Your tights are all torn,' the child said.

'I know.'

'I don't think that man was very nice.'

'No. I don't think …' Lanny had to stop; everything had started to swim again. She propped herself up and waited for everything to settle.

'I hope you don't mind me asking but are you ill?' a woman's voice asked. She had an accent, not an English accent, though it sounded familiar nonetheless.

'What?'

'Can I help you up? Shall we get you a cup of tea?' The woman with the accent had appeared by the side of the little girl and was bending over and holding out her hand. Lanny turned her face away. She was meant to be getting through here without being spotted. Her hand went to her hair. She couldn't feel a scarf. She searched the floor around her. The mother of the child walked behind her and picked it up, then she squatted down in front of Lanny and handed her the scarf.

'It's okay,' the woman said, very quietly. 'I know who you are.'

Iolanthe paused in the act of tying up her hair and stared at the woman in front of her. She had short-cropped dark hair and a wide,

221

beautiful face. 'I won't tell anyone. As long as you're all right. I don't have to say anything.' Irish, that's what she was. Though her accent sounded different from the Bostonian hum of Lanny's youth.

'I'm just a bit out of sorts,' Lanny said. 'I have to catch another train. But I don't know where I'm going.'

The dark-haired lady cupped Lanny's shoulders and helped her gently to her feet. 'Do you want to go to the ticket office?'

'I need to sit down. Just for five minutes. My legs aren't great.'

'Okay.' The dark-haired woman nodded. 'Let's find you a table in the buffet.'

She led Lanny towards the lighted door and her little girl followed behind. The buffet was less than half full and the woman steered Lanny to a table in the corner where she could face away from the door. Lanny settled herself and unbuttoned her coat. The warmth of the buffet and the hiss of the tea urn were comforting.

'Can I get you anything?' the lady asked. 'Would you like me to go and ask about trains at the ticket office?'

'I don't know where I'm going,' Lanny confessed. 'Would your little girl like a scone or a cake?'

The lady glanced towards the doors. 'We don't really have the money this afternoon.'

'No. My treat. To say thank you. I made her handkerchief all mucky.'

'Can I have a cake?' the girl ventured. Her mother looked at her. Lanny fished in her handbag and drew out a pound note. 'Why don't you get us all some tea and a cake for the young lady and some toast for me and something for yourself.'

The woman took the pound note but she stayed where she stood.

'You know,' Lanny said, 'it isn't kindness at all, if that's what you're thinking. I actually need to ask another favour. I need someone to go to a pharmacy for me ...'

'Okay,' the woman told her, 'if you're sure. That's very kind of you. And in return we'll go to the chemist for you afterwards.' She went up to the counter. Her little girl stayed behind and slid into a seat across from Lanny.

'I'm Gracie.'

222

'Hello, Gracie.'

'That's my mummy. Her name's Orla. What's your mummy's name?'

'My mom's name was Maria.'

'What's your name?'

'You can call me Lanny if you like.'

'Okay. I've got a bear called Hodge. But he's at home.'

'Were you and your mummy coming back from somewhere, Gracie?'

'We just sit and watch the people and the trains.'

'I see.'

Orla started to bring things over from the counter. There was a pot of tea with two cups and a glass of milk for Gracie. Gracie shuffled across and Orla sat down with them at the table. Lanny was staring at the table so Orla poured the tea and Gracie added milk very carefully from the little jug.

'Would you like some sugar?' Orla asked. 'You look like you could do with some.'

Lanny nodded and Gracie added sugar and stirred the tea with great solemnity. Then she pushed it gently across the table.

'I'm not involved in anything shameful, you know,' Lanny said. 'I kind of went missing by mistake.'

'You don't have to tell us,' Orla reassured her. 'It's your life. If you need a break from things ... I can't imagine what it's like having everyone staring at you like that. Up on a stage every night.'

'Oh, it wasn't that. It wasn't the work. I like my work.' Lanny sat and thought about all the things she couldn't say. 'Do you know – Orla? yes? – do you know how it is when you realise that one part of your life needs to end and another to begin?'

Orla's face creased a little. 'Yes.'

'Sometimes the ending of one chapter ... you want it to be gentle and it isn't. It feels like setting off a bomb.'

A lady in an apron brought them two plates of toast and an iced finger for Gracie.

'What d'you say to the lady, Gracie?' Orla asked.

'Thank you.'

'There was this journalist,' Lanny said. 'He came to the theatre two weeks ago, talking about Ireland and how I should go there … You're … I think your accent …'

Orla nodded. 'I'm Irish. Gracie's a bit of a mixture.'

'Mummy calls me a mongrel,' Gracie said cheerfully.

Orla blushed. 'In a nice way, darling. Mammy meant it nicely.'

Lanny smiled. 'You see, I've been sick these past two weeks. Liver problems. And all those hours lying in bed … I started thinking that maybe I should follow his advice. Maybe it is time for me to go. And why not Ireland?'

'I think the question should be: why Ireland?' Orla said.

'What's wrong with Ireland?'

'I didn't suit it, that's all. We're a bad fit.'

'But it looks so beautiful. Like a giant wood. Or something from a fairy tale.'

Orla smiled. 'If you say so.'

'I think that you could get lost in Ireland and no one would care. No one would ever find you.'

'That might be true.'

'Do you think? Do you think you could disappear there?'

'You or me?' Orla asked.

'Well … me. I saw this poster for ferries to Rosslare and I thought maybe I'd just get on one of those. Course I'd need a passport. And I left my passport …'

'Where?'

'I think the police have it now. I don't know … Are they strict? When you take the ferry? Will they want all my papers?'

'If you're not Irish or British they will. Me and Gracie would be allowed on with a birth certificate, a driving licence, anything. But you'd need something else.'

Gracie finished her bun and licked the icing off her palms. 'You can come and stay at our house. If you need somewhere to sleep.'

Lanny found that she was smiling, though it hardly seemed the time. Here in this smoky little room with this mother and her daughter she felt a brisk wave of normality wash over her. How nice it might be *not* to be Iolanthe Green.

She watched Gracie, gazing upwards at her mother. The baby, if there was still something that could be called a baby, was real to her only for a few seconds at a time. Sometimes she forgot about it. Sometimes it became this awful parasite, trying to eat her from the inside. She imagined holding its little hand. And then she imagined that it had never existed. She both wanted it and didn't want it; feared it and marvelled at its very existence.

Tears started to spill down Lanny's cheeks. Gracie stretched a hand across the table and patted Lanny's fingers but Lanny only drew her hand away, not wishing – in this painful moment of adulthood – to be infantilised by the touch of a child.

'I want to start again,' Lanny said. 'Forty isn't any age to …'

'It's no age to give up,' Orla said. 'But then I'm a one to talk. Thirty-two and I'm pretty sure I gave up at twenty-seven. Everything just … You think you're walking into something beautiful and then the shutters come down. I still find it amazing some days how you become completely imprisoned in your own life. Things that on the surface look so sweet and so benign, they trap you. They pin you down.'

'You have a lovely baby girl …'

'I'm not a baby,' Gracie pointed out.

'Nothing wrong with Gracie …' Orla leaned over and kissed her daughter hard. 'She's the bit that keeps me going.'

Lanny's face fell and Orla stopped herself in her tracks. 'Forgive me,' she said, 'this isn't about me. I forget that. Talking to other adults. I forget the give and take of it. You're my first adult conversation in two days.'

'That must be very odd. Not to talk to other adults.'

'It sends you gently mad, Miss Green. It pickles your brains. Come on,' Orla said. 'Come on, Gracie. Let's move our bottoms. The lady needs something from the pharmacy. Tell me what we're getting.'

Lanny opened up her handbag. 'It's called glutathione. I can give you the bottle to show them. You'll need to tell them it's for a friend with an injury to her liver and she's going away and forgot to get enough pills. I have a five-pound note you can take as well. Are you sure? You don't mind?'

Orla stood. 'Not at all. Can you give me twenty minutes or so? The chemist's shop is a little way from here.'

Orla led her daughter by the hand out of Liverpool Street station and round the southern side. 'Now, listen. I need to drop you off at Debbie's house. Just for a couple of hours. I'll pick you up before tea. Is that okay? Do you want to go and play with the doll's house?'

'Okay. Are you going to get the lady her medicine?'

'Trust me, chickadee. I will sort it all out for her.'

Orla dropped her daughter off on Pindar Street to play at dolls and servants. There were two chemists she could try but she found herself walking instead towards the flat on Sun Street. She stopped outside and looked up at the dirty windows.

Like a bomb, Iolanthe had said. It feels like setting off a bomb.

She had felt so trapped back home in Ireland, so out of place. London had felt like freedom itself – everyone here was an oddity and a misfit, abnormal was the norm. She had thought that by marrying in London, by having her child here, she would escape the isolation and confinement that her own mother had clearly felt. But then the walls had come down around her. And Brennan and she had gone from two people who said everything to each other to two people who never spoke a word of truth.

Shopping, cooking, ministering to Gracie. It didn't matter how much you loved your child: it was hard. She missed her work. She missed her friends. I have no adults in my life, she thought. I wanted Gracie to be my little love but now she is my everything.

Back in the buffet, Lanny sat and tore her toast into pieces. She didn't have much of an appetite after all and her stomach hurt. As the time passed and Orla didn't return she started to wonder if she'd made some sort of awful mistake. She gathered her things into her handbag but her legs felt heavy and she couldn't find the strength to move. Where was she going anyway? Did she really have to do all this alone?

More than an hour had passed when the buffet door opened and Orla's shape appeared. She hurried to Lanny's table and sat down opposite her. In one hand she held a white paper bag and in the other a little dark blue book.

'I got your pills. They let me have twenty-four – emergency supply. Said you had to go back to your doctor.'

'I didn't think you were coming back.'

'I know. I'm sorry. I had to drop Gracie off with someone. I brought you something else.'

Orla pushed the little book across the table. 'I want you to have it. It's got another six years to go.'

Lanny opened the cover. There was a small, slightly blurry black and white photograph of Orla. Her birth date. Her place of birth.

'Orla Jane Hayes,' Lanny read. 'This is … This is your passport.'

'I'm giving it to you. So you can be me. If you want. If you need. Our colouring is close enough, face shape. You even have some freckles. You'd need to cut your hair, maybe … And be careful how you used it. But they'll glance at it for two seconds at the port and then you'll be in.'

'But what if you need it?'

'I'll say I lost it. I can apply for another if I have to. Look. I know you don't know me. Not really at all. But I want to do this. You're making me jump. I want to jump.'

Lanny fondled the little book.

'You can do anything with it you want,' Orla told her. 'You can go back to America. You can cross to Ireland. You can start up a new life. Bank accounts in my name, maybe. I can go back to being Orla Keane. It won't hurt me, Iolanthe. It won't hurt me. It's a gift.'

Lanny shook her head. 'I don't know what to say.'

'Don't say anything. Just take it. We've got your pills. We've got a passport. I can go and draw money out for you if you like …'

'Wait!' Lanny pleaded. 'Wait! I'm not ready. Please. We need to figure this all out.'

*   *   *

When Hayes returned to his little flat that night it was already after nine. He stood in the living room and listened for the sounds of Orla moving around but heard nothing. He checked the sofa but she wasn't there and her quilt was still in its cubbyhole. In the kitchen a piece of paper was propped against a bottle of squash. He picked it up.

> We've gone. I am doing this for myself but also for Gracie. She has a right to a happy mother. I am not a happy mother.
>
> In a way, it's not your fault. This was a disaster we both made. At least Gracie came out of it.
>
> When we are settled I will write to you so you know that Gracie is well. I'll get her to do you a picture. When she's better with her letters she can write to you as well.
>
> I've taken as little as I can. I hope you have everything you need. Sorry. Try not to hate us.
>
> Orla

A Chill Night on the Steps

Thursday, 11 November

Brennan sat at the kitchen table for a long time. He thought of Gracie's bed upstairs, empty of Gracie now and in the future. His bones felt cold.

He ate some slices of bread and cheese, put on his overcoat and left the house. It had snowed again and the pavements were pristine white, stretching out before him like white lines drawn on a dark map. The air in Sun Street was excessively cold and a wind whipped against his face, burning his eyes and nose so that he briefly retreated into his own doorway and wondered what to do.

He couldn't think about finding them tonight. His head was scrambled with the immensity of what was happening. He hated her. He hated Orla. He wanted to find her and hurt her and he knew he wasn't allowed to do that. He had to walk away the anger. To channel it into something worthwhile. He thought about James Wingate sitting in that saloon bar this afternoon on Fleet Street and feeding him little pieces of poison about Iolanthe. And then he thought about Delbert and his account of Iolanthe's 'madness'. 'Said she'd had it off with journalists, with anyone …'

Wingate had said something about heading for his club to round out the evening. Hayes set off.

* * *

In a large rose-wallpaper-covered room in Clacton Anna lay under a quilt fully dressed and watched the shape of Aloysius who lay in a long, dark, knobbly line on some cushions on the floor. Like a fallen branch in a forest, she thought to herself.

'You need to sleep,' she told him.

'I can't,' came the tired reply.

'We'll find a way of leaving her some money in the morning,' Anna said.

'Do you think that will keep us out of hell?'

'I think the non-existence of hell will keep us out of hell,' she countered, though she felt oddly crushed by the kindness of the landlady and her own mismatched deceit.

'My mother doesn't believe in hell either,' Aloysius said. 'She says a kind God is a kind God. And you can't throw hell into the mix or she'll stop believing.'

'What about you, Reverend Weathers? Do you believe?'

Aloysius sighed. 'I think there is a thing called goodness that is larger than us. And I think that some people call goodness God. And some people call it goodness. And some people lead lives so terrible that they never get to believe in good at all. I am thirty and that is as far as I have got.'

'Will you know if there's a God when you're forty?' Anna asked, only half joking.

'I've no idea. I used to think you did all your learning in school. And when you came out at eighteen or twenty-one that was it. You were all filled up.'

'I was an idiot at eighteen,' Anna noted. 'Though I didn't know it then. Now I'm not sure about any of it. I feel like I'm a grown-up. I feel educated. But I have this creeping worry that I'll get to fifty and realise that thirty-year-old Anna was a moron.'

'What about seventy-year-old Anna? What will she think of that baby of fifty?'

'She'll probably find her frighteningly naive. Ottmar says it never stops. Learning, experience. It never stops. And yet we are all meant to go to university and choose our careers and our husbands and have our children …' Anna stopped in her tracks.

Aloysius waited patiently for her to go on but instead Anna lay back upon the bed in silence. Aloysius crept across the floor on his hands and knees. He waited for Anna to signal to him that he could climb onto the bed but she just lay on her back, her breathing unsteady.

Aloysius rose and seated himself carefully on the edge of the bed so she would not mistake his intention. He put one arm on her shoulder. Anna rolled onto her side and drew him towards her. They lay together on the bed, nose to nose and knee to knee.

'Some nights,' she told him, 'I feel as if I'm disappearing. I wake, I work, I eat, I sleep. Nothing connects me to anything. Nothing anchors me. No family, no great career. I could disappear tomorrow, like Iolanthe. But not because of a pregnancy or illness or anything like that. I feel like I could disappear because I'm not real to other people.'

Aloysius smiled at her in the darkness. 'I think you're real,' he whispered. 'You're real to me.'

Anna cried a little in silence and Aloysius kissed her forehead. She curled a hand around his cheek, to feel him, to know that he was there. And then she slept.

Aloysius lay awake and stared at her face in the darkness. Why did you leave me in the police station? he wondered. And will you leave me like that again? I'm coming apart, he told himself, but she doesn't know that. Maybe if she doesn't know who I really am then she can hold me all together.

* * *

In the darkness of the Alabora after midnight Ottmar sat and watched the lights move down Shaftesbury Avenue. Samira was home. Ekin was heartbroken. Which was greater, he wondered: the weight of shame at Samira's disgrace or the joy and relief at her safe delivery home? And did it even matter? In a couple of days it would be part of the blur.

* * *

Detective Sergeant Hayes reached Fleet Street at half past eleven and decided to ask at the offices of *The Times*. The young receptionist was reading a paperback Christie and biting her nails.

'Detective Sergeant Hayes. Metropolitan Police. I don't know if you remember – I was here earlier with James Wingate.'

'Different shift I'm afraid, sir. I would have been older and more of a man, probably.'

'Right. Sorry. Would you happen to know where Wingate is now? He wandered off talking about a club.'

'He isn't in the offices now, sir. He might be in again tomorrow lunchtime. Would you like me to leave a note?'

'I really need to talk to him tonight. It's a police matter. Which club is he a member of?'

'I believe he goes to The Rag, sir.'

'The Rag?'

'The Army and Navy.'

'Is that on Pall Mall?'

'Big modern building, sir. On the corner of St James's Square. You can't miss it. It sort of sticks out.'

Hayes set off towards Pall Mall but he found himself wondering if Anna or anyone else had rung him since he went off shift. So he veered north at Charing Cross Road and ended up in the warm foyer of Savile Row where the desk sergeant seemed to be melting into sleep on top of the log book.

'Have I had any calls?' Hayes asked.

'What? You're not on shift, sir. You clocked out hours ago.'

'I'm back. It's the Green case. It won't quite lie down and go to sleep. Any calls?'

'Not at the desk, sir.'

'Well, sign me back in please. I'm going to check the office.'

The office was mostly dark, though Knight was still up and reading some vast sheaf of notes in his little corner cubicle. A note on Hayes' desk read:

Nathaniel Green called. American. Naval Library. Annapolice. Sp?? Asked you call back. Says you have number. Going home now. June.

Hayes found the number in his notes.

'Naval Library. Good evening.'

'Mr Green? It's Sergeant Hayes from London.'

'Sergeant Hayes?' The voice sounded surprised to hear from him.

'Yes. You called me. I have a note.'

'I didn't expect to hear back from you tonight.'

'I'm working on your sister's case.'

'Have you heard from her?'

'I haven't, Mr Green. Sorry. I'm a bit unclear: why did you call me this evening?'

'She called me, sir.'

'Who? Iolanthe? Your sister rang you?'

'Yes, sir. Today. First time in … ten, fifteen years. I didn't know who she was at first. Her voice … She's very upset, sir. She said … She said she was under a lot of pressure over money. She didn't say how. She asked me, sir, actually … I'm sorry. I don't know if I can tell you this. I'm not sure—'

Hayes cut him off in his blathering. 'What can you tell me about your sister and where she is, Nathaniel?'

'Well, she didn't say. I mean she's still in England, I guess. She talked about "over here" and "over there". She asked me to move some money for her. Not her money really. Mine. She was concerned that someone might come after my savings but she didn't tell me how. She seemed to be tired. I wondered if she might be drunk. Or ill. She didn't sound like herself at all.'

'What else did she tell you?'

'Only that things were going quite badly for her and that she was trying to resolve them, sir. That's what she said. "I have to make an end of it, Nat. I have to tie it all back down."'

'What do you think she meant by that?'

'I don't know. We only talked for a few minutes and then she was gone. I don't have a number for her. She didn't tell me where she was. I'm sorry. I should have asked her questions. I was just so shocked. I think I messed it up.'

'You did fine, Mr Green. She's your sister. It must have been very difficult. But … do something for me? If she calls you back, ask her where she is. It's for her own good. Do you understand?'

'I understand, sir. Yes. I understand.'

Hayes headed back out into the snow. Iolanthe was definitely alive: that was something, that was progress. He felt a certain triumph in her continuing existence although it really had nothing to do with his actions. If he could only find her now and bring her back he might be able to salvage something of his sense of self. He crunched and shuffled his way down towards St James's Square.

'It sort of sticks out,' the receptionist at *The Times* had said. The Army and Navy Club – The Rag – was a vast glass-plated, steel-rimmed kind of affair built massively high amongst a cluster of pastel-coloured Italianate townhouses. Gothic black lights burned outside and the building was specked and dotted with lighted windows even though it was well past midnight now.

It had snowed on him again as he walked and he took a moment to stand outside the circle of light and brush the snow from his hat and coat. Places like this always made him anxious.

The liveried servant at the front desk of the club eyed him with a certain amount of lightly concealed disdain.

'Can I help you …' He searched for signs of a uniform or rank. 'Sir?'

'My name is Detective Sergeant Barnaby Hayes of the Metropolitan Police and I am here on a matter of police business. Can you tell me if James Wingate is drinking here tonight?'

'Is he expecting you, sir?'

'No. But we are acquainted. Mr Wingate has been helping us with our enquiries. I need to ask him some further questions as a matter of some urgency.'

'I see. I think it may be that Mr Wingate is a little top-heavy, sir.'
'Top-heavy?'

'Yes. Do you think I might inform Mr Wingate that you wish to speak with him and make an appointment for the morning?'

'I need to speak with him now. It regards the disappearance of Miss Iolanthe Green: a case that is still very much ongoing.'

'It's just that' – the porter dropped his voice – 'he's medicated, sir.'

'Do you have a problem with me speaking to him on the premises? Because I'm quite happy to take him down to the station.'

'I don't think speaking to him anywhere … I … He's *drunk*, sir. I last saw Mr Wingate an hour ago and he was really enormously drunk. I think he may now be asleep.'

'Well, go and wake him up then. I have questions that need answering tonight.'

The porter hurried upstairs, his heels clacking as he went and Hayes suddenly found himself overcome by the heat of the lobby. The whole building seemed quite airless and fuggy and he opened the front door and leaned against the door frame, breathing in the cold of the night. Orla's note had stripped him of his layers of skin. Tonight he felt like the carcass of a policeman, like the boiled remains.

'Excuse me, sir,' the porter called to him from the stairs and Hayes drew his head back inside the club. 'I'm so sorry, Detective Sergeant. Mr Wingate has been involved in a small altercation and we're just having to clean him up. Would you mind waiting for ten or fifteen minutes? We need to find him a change of clothes.'

'The man's a liability!'

'He's normally rather placid, sir. I'm not sure what's come over him. I think you may have caught him on a bad night.'

'Can he walk? Is he sober enough to … Never mind. Never mind. I'm going to fetch a car. Can you tell Mr Wingate that I will be back for him in twenty minutes with a car.' And Hayes threw open the door and walked back out into the snow.

'Bloody man,' he swore to himself as he walked. 'Bloody, bloody man.'

At Savile Row he signed out one of the Morris Minors and when he had finally got it started he drove back to the Army and Navy Club to pick up the body of James Wingate.

We're All Friends to the Police

Friday, 12 November

'Is it about my daughter?' Ottmar asked when he opened the front door to Detective Sergeant Hayes. It was quarter past seven, not even properly light yet.

'Your daughter?' Hayes was confused, 'I'm looking for Anna Treadway.'

'Oh. She lives in Flat B. You want to ring the bell above.'

Hayes stared at the various doorbells down the right-hand side of the door. The top two were both labelled Fleet. Ottmar stood and waited on the doormat in his paisley pyjamas, his hair sticking out in wild white and black tufts.

'Sorry. Who is your daughter? Do I know her?' Hayes asked at last.

'Her name is Samira Alabora. She was arrested two nights ago. With Anna and the Jamaican man.'

Of course, Hayes thought, the Turkish girl in the short dress. 'Your wife was very upset.'

'My wife is still very upset.'

'I'm sorry to hear it, sir. I am Detective Sergeant Hayes. I need to talk to Miss Treadway. Apologies for ringing the wrong bell.'

'I'll give Anna a knock,' Ottmar said and padded upstairs, leaving the front door open and Hayes standing on the step. He came back a couple of minutes later, his brow wrinkled with thought.

'She isn't home. Only her flatmate. Her flatmate seems to think Anna has gone off with the coloured man.'

'Sorry?'

'I think his name is Aloysius.'

'Does that seem likely?' Hayes asked him, genuinely bemused.

'Well, I think they might be *friends*.' Ottmar raised his brows but Hayes ignored the intimation. She's found Iolanthe, that was Hayes' first thought; she's found Iolanthe and they're conspiring together for her to make some sort of escape.

Ottmar nodded towards the cafe window to his right. 'The cafe here is mine. Would you like to come inside? It's a terribly cold morning to be standing on doorsteps,' he said with just a hint of an ingratiating smile.

'I haven't had any breakfast,' Hayes admitted. 'Do you think I could get some toast?'

'Come through the back way. I will make you toast and coffee.' Ottmar spread his arms wide, welcoming the policeman in.

Ottmar seated the policeman at a gingham-clothed table by the hatch and withdrew to put on some clothes. He returned in a white shirt and black trousers to turn on the lights in the kitchen and start the toasting machine, the coffee urn and the grill.

Hayes sat in silence and watched people flow past the quiet cafe. Barrow boys, flower sellers, shop girls, taxi men. He thought of his borrowed car parked up on the pavement on Shaftesbury Avenue and worried that he'd be in the way of delivery vans. He had become, over the course of the night, almost completely numb. Now and again the fact that Orla had left him would resurface and he would push it out again with thoughts of Iolanthe and Wingate and the strange moving of the money.

The smell of coffee started to travel through the air. The grill sizzled and hissed. Somewhere in the depths of the kitchen a machine growled and creaked. Ottmar appeared beside him and laid the table with cutlery and a salt and pepper set. He reappeared with fried eggs and buttered toast and two cups of very black coffee.

'Thank you,' Hayes told him. 'You really didn't have to do this. It smells wonderful.'

'Have something to eat.'

Ottmar seated himself at the other side of the table and sipped his coffee carefully. 'I have an ulterior motive,' he said at last.

'Do you?' asked Hayes, taken by surprise, his mouth full of toast.

'I wanted to tell you something about my family.'

Hayes blinked at him and stopped eating.

'We're not people you need to worry about. We're some of the good ones. Do you see?'

Hayes nodded, still a little lost in his own thoughts.

'We're not the robbers or the thieves or the murderers. We're very straight people, Sergeant Hayes. You think … lots of people think that we do not love this country because our skin is the wrong colour. But what you don't understand is that we love this country more. We weren't just born here. We had to work very hard to get here. You see, you love something so much more if you had to work for it. Don't you think that's true?'

'Well, yes. I suppose. I didn't mean to suggest anything … I'm not sure why we're having this conversation.'

'We're having this conversation because we both live in this city and I want you to know … if you ever have dealings with us again … I want you to know who we are. We are your friends, Sergeant Hayes. We're all friends to the police.'

Hayes frowned at him. 'I'm sure you are.' Why hasn't this man's wife left him? Hayes wondered. And why has mine? Why would God take Gracie away from me?

'I'm afraid Iolanthe may have been lost because we didn't love her enough. When we don't love people enough, you see, we do them harm. Myself and my wife love our daughter very much. That's what made my wife so angry. She is not a bad woman. I think it's better to love than not love. I think if we love people enough that gives them something to hold on to.'

Hayes tuned himself back in to Ottmar's little speech. 'Love?' he asked. 'I thought Iolanthe was a stranger.'

'Oh, yes! I never met the woman. But don't you think there might be different kinds of love? The love you have for your daughter. And then the love you show when you help an old woman across the road. And then the love you show your neighbours when they go missing and you look for them. And then the love a country shows when it says we will not kill. It's just compassion, isn't it?

238

That's the right word, yes? Compassion. It looks different but it's all the same.'

Hayes looked at Ottmar. His eyes seemed to glow from beneath his brows as if he were a seer or a saint or a maniac. This is how the mad talk, Hayes thought.

* * *

Anna and Aloysius slipped out of the B & B and into the dark of morning at half past five, leaving a cheque for a pound on the telephone table before they went. They caught the first train to Liverpool Street, avoiding an early-morning ticket inspector by taking it in turns to visit the toilet. Having evaded the inspectors once, they decided not to risk the tube but caught a bus instead with the last few pence that either of them had, riding it far past the stop they had bought the ticket for. By eight o'clock they were back in Covent Garden, a grey morning sky above them, Anna leading Aloysius towards the Alabora with the thoughts of begging a little tea and sympathy from Ottmar while they made a plan.

And there was Ottmar, dressed already and drinking his coffee, and there beside him eating breakfast was Detective Sergeant Hayes.

Aloysius's heart fluttered in his chest. The terrible fear of that night in the station flooded back inside him. He clasped Anna's arm tightly through her coat sleeve. 'I cannot see that man.'

'It's okay,' she said. 'I'll go in on my own.'

Aloysius found sanctuary in a tobacconist's shop at the top of Monmouth Street where he busied himself taking in the headlines of the morning papers.

CHAOS IN RHODESIA
WAS MAR A MEMBER OF THIS GANG?
HINDLEY'S DEADLY OBSESSION

No Iolanthe Green, he thought. How quickly she had come to bore all those who didn't know her. I still don't know her. I feel like I know her. I think I'm getting her muddled up with Anna.

He wanted to be alone with Anna. He wanted to feel safe and to make her feel the same in return. He wanted to find Iolanthe and be beside Anna when it happened. He wanted to rebalance the wrong that had been done him. He wanted to find himself heroic again. He could not do that when Hayes, his persecutor, was following their every move.

Out in the street he saw Anna exit the cafe and turn in a full circle, scanning her surroundings. He pushed the door of the tobacconist's open and she moved towards the sound. They stood together on the step of the shop, Hayes watching them from a distance.

'I gave him an expurgated version of the truth,' Anna told him in a whisper. 'No Geri, no Hen. But we think that Iolanthe went to stay somewhere in Essex and then came back to London yesterday by train. As far as he's concerned that's all we know. Now, his side of things is that Lanny phoned her brother in the States last night. Long story but it's something about money. Hayes thinks she might be planning to hurt herself and he wants me to go along with him so that she's got a friendly face to meet her. If we find her, that is … I said I'd go with him if you would too.' She clasped his hand and gazed at him imploringly. 'Please. Please. Be my friend and come with me.'

Aloysius could not speak. He could not speak for fear but he pressed the back of her hand to his mouth in assent.

'Thank you,' she told him. 'Thank you.' Hayes did not move. He stood very still and watched them as they moved back towards him.

'We're coming,' Anna announced.

'Right,' Hayes said. 'Okay. In that case I have a little job for Mr Weathers to do.'

Hayes' blue and white Morris Minor was sitting parked up on the pavement and now he opened the passenger door, pulled forward the front seat and gestured to the dark of the back. A tall, skinny man in an overly large blue suit lay passed out on the back seat. 'He's your responsibility now,' he told Aloysius. 'Try to see he doesn't vomit on the seats.'

Aloysius stared at Hayes and then at Wingate. He felt a trap becoming visible around him though he didn't understand yet what

240

it might entail. He glanced back towards the Alabora. A young girl in a fluffy blue dressing gown was standing beside Ottmar, watching them. It took him several seconds to realise he was looking at Samira.

'Wait,' he told Hayes. Anna started towards him. 'Wait,' he told her. He walked at a stately pace back towards the cafe and pushed open the front door.

He gestured to Samira to join him by the open door and then he bent and whispered something in her ear. He straightened, bowed to a baffled Ottmar and returned to where Anna and Hayes stood beside the panda car. 'Just setting my affairs in order,' he told them and then he climbed into the back with the unconscious Wingate.

In the cafe Ottmar and Samira watched Anna and Hayes slam the doors. 'What did he tell you, Sami?' Ottmar asked his daughter.

'Couldn't possibly say, Dad. Much too secret.' Samira watched the police car draw away. She pulled her dressing-gown cord tight around her. 'Good riddance to the lot of them,' she said.

'You're going to be late for school, flower,' Ottmar told her.

Samira looked up at him and smiled a thin, hard smile. 'And why would I be going there?'

Anna, Aloysius and Hayes rode in silence to Liverpool Street station. Barnaby parked in a taxi bay and went to make enquiries. Anna and Aloysius waited in silence for a few minutes while Aloysius perfected a way of keeping the man pinned in place using just his knees.

'Does he know we came through here this morning?' Aloysius asked when the body seemed more steady.

'No. I thought I'd skip the bit about us not paying for our tickets and let him do the asking.' Anna turned in her seat and gazed back at Aloysius whose face had just this morning started to emerge from the bruising and the swelling and to look like itself again.

'What did you say to Samira?' she asked him.

Aloysius pressed his lips together and thought about this. 'Nothing that would hurt you or Lanny,' he said at last. 'But I can't say.'

Anna felt a little stung. It wasn't for him to have secrets from her; that seemed quite the wrong way round. Then she noticed the profile of the body in the back. 'I know that man,' she said. 'He's a journalist. Came to interview Lanny the day she left … Wingate. Smarmy man. Wonder what he's doing in Hayes' car.'

'I think Mr Hayes likes collecting people,' Aloysius said.

'You know,' said Anna, 'I think Hayes is basically okay. I mean … Even given everything that's happened I think he's one of the good ones.'

'Mr Hayes is very much a policeman,' Aloysius noted.

'Well, yes. But I think he really cares.'

Aloysius thought about this. 'People don't care about everything equally,' he said at last.

They turned towards the sound of feet running towards the car. Hayes got in carrying a large hardback book, looked at Anna and exhaled loudly. His cheeks were bright red and his eyes were shining. There was something strangely manic about his whole bearing.

'Well?' Anna asked.

'Right. Okay. So. The thing is … I'm going to have to drive to Wales.'

'I … What? You're driving to Wales?'

'A woman in the ticket office remembers a woman in a black coat and heels with lots of curly hair who fell on the concourse yesterday. She was helped by another woman who then also helped her to buy a train ticket to Fishguard so she could connect with the ferry to Rosslare. So I looked at the train and the ferry times and the earliest ferry to Ireland she could be on is the one leaving tomorrow lunchtime. So that's where we need to be. Fishguard. That's where Iolanthe is right now.'

'Forgive me, Sergeant, but could we not just ring the police in Fishguard?' Aloysius ventured bravely from the back.

Hayes didn't even turn to look at him. 'I don't want her being set upon by some random uniformed officer. She's in a delicate enough state as it is. I think we have a chance to bring her home, gently, with her agreement. If she crosses into Ireland that's a whole other police force to deal with. And after the call to her brother … I'm not even convinced she's safe from herself. I think she just needs a good friend right now. And in the absence of a good friend I'm hoping that Anna will do the trick.'

Anna wasn't sure how to take the last remark so instead she simply checked again. 'You're driving to Wales?'

Hayes handed her the book he was carrying. 'I bought a road map of Britain.'

'Right.'

'Can you navigate?'

'Probably.'

'First things first. Petrol.' Hayes fired the engine and released the clutch.

* * *

The passengers in Sergeant Hayes' panda car sat in virtual silence, interrupted only by the odd direction from Anna. Aloysius stared at Wingate and at the back of Anna's head. Nobody seemed to be challenging the complete insanity of a policeman driving a random selection of people hundreds of miles out of his jurisdiction. Perhaps, he thought, British policing was entirely eccentric. Perhaps it operated quite separately to the rule of law. There was a kind of amateurism about the whole affair which made him wonder how greatly he should be afraid of being made an informant. Did the strange behaviour of the English police make them more or less dangerous? He really couldn't tell.

Anna navigated as best she could. She'd barely been in a car the past ten years and certainly never read a road map. As they headed out of London and onto the byways of the Home Counties she started to wonder if Hayes had lost his mind. He seemed to be sweating quite profusely, almost as if he had a fever, and she found herself watching him carefully. When they passed a lorry outside Reading she imagined for a moment he might be about to turn the wheel into its path. A profound tension ran through him, an air of violence and of misery. Once or twice she allowed herself a glance into the back of the car. She caught Aloysius's eye and they exchanged a look of utter bemusement that the day had taken this turn.

They were past Swindon when Wingate woke with a great howl of pain. He rolled from the back seat and curled into an anguished ball on the cramped floor of the car.

'What's going on?' Hayes shouted back to Aloysius.

'I've no idea. He just rolled onto the floor. Is he ill?'

'He's drunk. Dead drunk. Or at least he was. He hasn't been conscious or awake since three this morning.'

'Should we take him to a hospital?' Anna asked.

'No. He just needs to come round,' Hayes said, an edge of steel in his voice.

'Look, I don't mean to ask silly questions,' Anna said, 'but why are we taking the poor man to Wales?'

'Because I'm pretty sure he's the father of the baby.'

'Of Lanny's baby?'

'Yes.'

'But she got rid of the baby. Or wanted to. Why on earth would she want to see him?'

'I'm not going to show him to her. I'm just waiting to question him more closely.'

Wingate moaned and doubled up violently. 'Has he seen a doctor?' Anna asked.

'He's fine,' Hayes snapped. 'Just leave him alone. He'll soon pull out of it.'

Aloysius gave Anna a look of such deep disgust that she briefly wondered if she was implicated in it as well. Then he crossed his arms, adjusted his coat and sat back to stare out of the window and pretend that he was somewhere else entirely.

Wingate's body eventually slackened and he pulled himself upright and back into his seat. He glanced very briefly at Aloysius.

'Do you have any aspirin?' he asked.

'I don't,' Aloysius replied and went back to staring out of the window. Wingate gazed for a while at the back of Hayes' head and then at the road in front of them. Everyone else in the car seemed to be taking it for granted that they were all meant to be there. His head banged violently and his guts felt like they were weeping blood. He tucked his head into a corner between the door and the seat back and soon began to snore.

As they passed an inn just north of Chepstow, Hayes pulled the car into the little space beyond the verge.

'Rest break,' he announced, took the keys out of the ignition, got out and marched towards the pub. It was two o'clock. Wingate snored. Anna turned and looked at Aloysius.

'What the hell are we doing here?' she asked quite softly.

'It wasn't my idea to come.'

'Do you need to go to the …'

Aloysius did but he didn't really want to find himself alone in a bathroom with Sergeant Hayes.

When Hayes returned Anna and Aloysius were walking up and down the verge. 'I said I was the police and they offered to do us some sandwiches. Anyone want sandwiches?'

Anna and Aloysius mumbled their agreement. Hayes eyed Aloysius rather beadily. 'I need someone to stay with Wingate and I'm afraid you're it. You can use the lavatory if you like. And then we'll bring you something out when we're finished.'

Anna opened her mouth to speak but Aloysius had already set off towards the pub, striding with a kind of ferocity that suggested he didn't really want to talk about anything right now. Anna followed Hayes into the bar and let him choose a table by the window. The pub was pleasantly warm and the windows quite fogged against the cold exterior. They shrugged off their coats.

Anna sat in silence. They were in Wales, land of her almost-childhood. She hadn't been in Wales for eleven years. She scratched at the back of her hands.

'You shouldn't do that, you know. You'll damage the skin,' Hayes said. Anna slid her hands under the table. The barman brought them over a pint and a half of bitter. 'No charge,' he said and winked at Hayes.

Hayes raised his glass as if to toast, and slightly unwillingly Anna raised hers too.

'Your health,' he said. The glasses clunked against each other. They were brought two plates piled high with sandwiches, fish paste and meat paste and ham and cheese and egg. Anna carefully divided her sandwiches in two and saved one half of each for Aloysius. Then they ate in silence.

Hayes drained the end of his pint and ordered another. 'Just to keep me going,' he told the barman. Anna sat and watched him drink. There was something off about him. He was not the Sergeant Hayes she had met earlier in the week. He seemed unsteady, perhaps a little mad.

Hayes finished the second pint quickly then, his fingers shaking, he reached out across the table and laid one hand on top of Anna's. Anna pulled away but Hayes tightened his grip. When he opened his mouth to speak his voice had changed, his Northern Irish tones had started to break back in, unfurling in the spaces.

'I think you're beautiful.'

'Please let go of my hand,' Anna said. Hayes' eyes were pink and moist with tears.

'That man's no good. I don't just mean … the colour of him. I mean you're better than that. Smarter. You stuck your neck out to find Green. You're a truly good person, Anna. I think you should be with a good person too.'

'Could you *please* let go of my hand,' Anna said, speaking slowly and carefully.

'I only want to tell you … that I have a great deal of admiration for you. And if you should ever need a friend … or a champion …'

'If you don't let go of my hand I will scream,' Anna said. She had had more than she was prepared to take of Hayes' lunacy. He had no right to touch her. He had no right to complicate an already quite insane situation. Hayes' fingers sprang up. Anna pulled her hands away and hid them under the table.

'Sergeant Hayes – Barnaby – I am here for Iolanthe. Not for anyone else. I don't need a friend or a champion. I have a friend. He's sitting in the back of your car with his face in pieces. Now, I'm going to take him some lunch. When you're ready to come back and join us we'll be waiting for you.' And Anna swept up the remaining sand-wiches and walked out of the pub.

Left alone, Hayes rubbed at his wet face with his hands. 'My wife is gone,' he said to no one in particular, 'and I'm not even looking for her.'

Anna

'Discuss the symbolism of the house itself in Howard's End.*'*

Anna stared out of the window at cars passing slowly down Stanwell Road. It was July but the sky glowered as if it were October. A grey summer day on the South Wales riviera. Women in wide woollen coats and neat little hats walked the pavements slowly and sedately, handbags swinging from elbows, handkerchiefs stuffed into pockets against the threat of a summer cold. Off they go, Anna thought, to tea with the women from the WI or rummy at the Conservative Club, choosing lamb at the butcher and carrots at the greengrocer, picking up David and Ruth from school at four, then husband home from Cardiff at ten to six, dinner on the table at half past, pinny on, pinny off, a plastic tablecloth hemmed by hand. Lamb on the bone, roast potatoes, boiled carrots, peas; *The Frankie Howerd Show* at five past nine, unless Father found it too risqué. A life for a woman who hadn't been to Oxford; a life for a woman who had chosen to procreate.

'In writing Julius Caesar *was William Shakespeare concerned with portraying ancient Rome or sixteenth-century England?'*

Her mother had brought the papers to the mother and baby home on her last visit. Old Oxford entrance papers for '49 and '50. Anna was due to sit the exam in two months. The plan as it had been presented to her was that she would have the baby, then she would be given two weeks' recovery time and return to school exactly ten days before the exam. This meant her revision had to be complete before she went into labour.

Her mother had passed on a message from her father: 'Do some test essays. A couple a day and post them home to me. Then I can mark them and return them.'

Anna had absolutely no intention of writing practice essays. But then she had had very little intention of giving up her child. It's not that she terribly wanted a child; she wasn't sure she wanted to be a mother at all and certainly not at the ludicrous age of seventeen. But she was horrified at the thought of someone else being allowed to bring up the baby badly.

She lay awake at night and imagined some red-faced housewife in a dirty apron slapping her child and shouting at him. The nurses told her not to be silly: 'Why do you think we'd give the child to someone cruel? The child will go to a lovely home, maybe even to people who can't have babies of their own. You'll be giving them a gift.'

All the same she was determined that her child was not to be mistreated. She had composed a letter, sitting up after everyone had gone to bed, writing by the light of a torch.

> To the new mother and father of my child,
> Please love this child as I would have loved them. Please treat them with gentleness and respect. Please never hit them or humiliate them. Please hold them when they are scared or hurt. Please do not send them away to school or give them up in any way – they will find it hard enough to be given up this once. Please let them read all the books they want to. Please let them ask questions and be tolerant of their mistakes. Please take them to the cinema if you are able. Please let them eat cake sometimes. Please tell them they were made out of love and do not let them imagine anything awful about their origins. Please tell them that their father and their mother were very young and meant no harm to anybody. Please tell them that I will never have another child and that they will always hold a unique place in my heart.
> From Anna, their first mother

'How do Milton's Latinisms affect the immediacy of his message in Paradise Lost?'

Of course she did still want to go to Oxford but her parents seemed to think they could tuck this child into a box and slide it away somewhere out of sight. They reacted to her pregnancy much as one would if one's daughter developed terrible hay fever in the run-up to her exams. They took her to the doctor. They sought out the best advice. In the absence of options to remove the child entirely from Anna's system they came up with a plan of action to move it instead to one side. Anna's path must not be blocked. Anna's dreams must not be denied. Anna was their best-prized sailing ship and they were blowing her towards a brighter land.

She had tried and failed on more than one occasion to write to Ben. He had been expelled from school in disgrace as soon as the relationship had been found out. Both children had been told in no uncertain terms that they were not to see each other.

'He's not exactly destined for Oxford,' the headmaster had reassured her parents. 'He's no chance at all of following Anna there. I've asked his parents to make it very clear to him that he is not to bother her again.'

* * *

On Friday a letter arrived from her father.

> Dearest Anna,
>
> No essays yet. Are you feeling sick again? Please don't worry that I will mind marking them. Nothing could be further from the truth. I want only to help you, my darling one.
>
> I spend four hours of every day marking at the moment. You mother suggested that we might find the extra money for all this summer's expenses by taking on extra marking from the schools. I am now marking papers for subjects I don't even teach. Most nerve-wracking. What do I know of Homer?

Possibly more now than I did before marking all these scripts.

Write to us soon, dear one, and just one or two essays. It will take your mind off it all. Eyes on the goal, my darling, eyes on the goal.

Your loving Papa

But was he her loving Papa? He still talked as if he was but his actions spoke of something different, something steely and determined. Was it he who had first decided that they would give the child away?

Time. She wished she had more time. Decisions of this kind demand a lot of time.

All that afternoon Anna sat by the window, as the strange bundle of limbs inside her shifted uncomfortably about, and she wondered if it were even possible that she could reply to her father. Did she have anything to say to him that wouldn't sound out her pain or hatred?

She thought back to the first letter she could ever remember writing. She had been six years old and her father had been in his third year of internment on the Isle of Man. She and her mother had taken a room in a boarding house on Anglesey, her mother having only escaped internment by volunteering both as a music teacher to the deluge of evacuees on the island and as a part-time engineer's assistant at the RAF base to the west. When the bombs fell on Holyhead they thanked their lucky stars they had taken lodging in the leafy interior. But Anna lay awake at night fearful that German planes were thoughtlessly bombing her papa and believing that if she only stayed awake and thought of him then he would stay safe.

'Father, he is on one little island,' her mother had once told her, 'and we are on another just below. At night we will think beautiful thoughts and send them to him across the ocean and they will move most speedily because there is nothing in their way but seabirds and mist.' It was perhaps the most poetic thing her mother ever said and Anna wondered in retrospect if she had spent a long time formulating the words.

For the Christmas of '43 her mother had given her a writing set, with very thin pieces of paper and a yellow pencil decorated with flowers. 'Write Daddy something,' she told Anna. 'Make his heart swell large.'

'Lieber Papa,' Anna wrote. 'Wir haben Dich lieb und Du fehlst uns. Gibt es viele Vögel auf Deiner Insel? Kannst Du einige Stückchen Deiner Liebe an die Vögel binden und zu uns schicken? Wir sind nämlich ein bisschen traurig hier so ohne Dich und Deine Liebe. Dein Bart fehlt mir. Anna.'

Dear Daddy. We love you and we miss you. Are there lots of birds on your island? Will you tie your love to them in pieces and send it home to us? We have become a bit sad without it here. I miss your beard. Anna

The cars rolled past the window of her bedroom in the home. She would have liked to walk into town, she knew there was a library just out of sight, but she had been discouraged from mingling with the wider community.

She thought back to her father and his time in the camp on Hutchinson Square. No. It was too crass a comparison to make. She hadn't been interned. She was just … She reached for the right words. Confined for her own benefit? Imprisoned in a web of love? She made herself laugh despite it all. How ridiculous these grown-ups were. How misguided their priorities. Still, though … All the same … How exactly was she to escape?

Such a Small Person to
Mean All the World

In London, it was the quiet time between lunch and dinner. Two ladies sat at a table by the window and nursed cups of tea. Long tweed skirts, thick knitted cardigans, handbags neatly placed by chairs. Ottmar watched them, missing his mother.

From a door in the street, outside the cafe window, a figure emerged in a black overcoat. From the colour of her hair he could see it was Samira. Ottmar watched her step off the kerb and walk down the centre of the quiet road. He thought of Iolanthe waving goodbye to Anna in those newspaper reports.

'Rachel! Mahmut! You're both in charge.' Ottmar ran to the hall and took his coat, feeling in the lining for a wallet. 'Sorry!' he called and then he was gone.

Samira headed south through the Garden. It was twilight already. Stalls were packed up, sellers gone home to bed. Boxes stacked eight feet high behind wooden gates at the flower market. Green-painted trollies pushed up against the walls to rest. The theatregoers would be here in an hour or two, pubs filling up, restaurants too. Men in dinner jackets and bow ties, ladies in beaded gowns that glittered below the hems of their navy and cream wool coats. Something was always on at the Opera House on a Friday night. But this was the quiet hour, the waiting time between low- and high-class commerce. Down into the darker streets Samira turned, behind the Opera House, heading for Aldwych. A taxi man stood rubbing his hands on Catherine Street, *An Ideal Husband* spelled out in pink lights above his head. Outside the Opera Tavern, a group of students dressed in graphic monochrome stood without their coats to better show their clothes.

As Samira turned onto Aldwych, Ottmar lost sight of her and hurried through the crowds, desperately scanning faces, aware he might be seen. He paused by Drury Lane and turned in full circles, looking for a small, slight girl in a long, black coat. Such a small person to mean all the world to him. There she was, in a crowd of shoppers, leaning against a bus stop. He stood by the doorway of a cafe with his back to her and pretended to examine the menu. When the number 68 came, Samira got on it with the shoppers. Ottmar waited until they were all well inside and he had seen her climb the stairs, then he ducked in himself and sat downstairs.

The bus set off. Ottmar twisted in his seat and watched the stairs. He had bought a ticket to Elephant and Castle because that's all he'd had a chance to notice on the front of the bus but they sailed past the concrete might of its shopping centre with no sign of a Samira. The light fell fast and the street lamps flickered into life. The roads got wider, the trees more plentiful; they passed hospitals and parks and schools. Camberwell Green, Denmark Hill. On Herne Hill they paused at the lights and he read the boards of the evening paper seller.

WHITE RULE IN RHODESIA

Why was the world so full of places that he'd never heard of? All those sixteen-hour days, never leaving the cafe. That world kept him protected; he even turned the radio down when the news came on. He said it was to protect the ladies and the children in the cafe, but really he didn't want to hear about the killing. So much killing and there he was, just as he had been in 1942, an impotent soul wondering why the love he had to offer seemed to cure nothing at all.

As they approached a sign for Tulse Hill station Samira suddenly appeared upon the stairs in a group of men and women, all descending. Ottmar waited for as long as he dared and then he leapt off the board at the back of the bus and hurried behind the wall of a bus shelter. Samira walked up and down for a couple of minutes peering at the walls and street signs and then she pulled her mother's *London A–Z* out of her pocket and thumbed her way through the pages. Ottmar peered at her from the edge of the shelter and felt quite ridiculously silly. Was this what it meant to follow someone? Surely spies didn't do this in real life. Then she was off again and he behind her, keeping at least thirty yards between them when they were on the same street and running desperately and breathlessly when she turned a corner. Palace Road, Hillside Road, Amesbury Avenue – the streets went on and on, Samira walking ever faster. At Streatham Hill station she turned around suddenly and frightened the life out of him. Ottmar spun on his heels and stood quite still, his head lowered, waiting for the sound of her voice but it never came. When he glanced up and round she was on the other side of the street, turning onto Drewstead Road. Ottmar blundered his way into the stream of traffic, trying to keep his eyes fixed on her, waving madly at the cars in apology. Samira walked purposefully on, scanning the fronts of houses. Eventually she paused beside one and went up the front path. Ottmar crept forward on the road, still twenty yards away, and watched her go in. He moved closer and read the little plaque.

Drewstead Road General Practitioners

Why would she come all this way to go to a doctor's surgery? He could not think of a single happy reason. If she is pregnant we will be kind to her, he thought. We will offer to help her keep the baby. Maybe, if we are kind enough, she will start to love us once again.

He waited on the pavement, hands in his armpits to warm them. Somewhere in the distance church bells rang. Was that six o'clock? Did people go to church at six o'clock? He lived too far away from the sound of church bells to know. Did people go to church at all? he wondered. In London? Still? For all the talk of it being a Christian country he never heard people speak of God. They worked and drove and went to the cinema on Sundays. They swore constantly. If, as Leonard had sometimes wryly noted, Christianity was full of injunctions against hoarding money then the city was surely an anti-Christian one. A city that hates Christ, Ottmar thought. We'd probably have nailed him up as well.

He was so deep within his own thoughts that he was taken by surprise when a girl materialised before him and with a cry of annoyance called him: 'Dad!'

'What!'

'You followed me!'

'I know. I'm sorry. I was worried,' Ottmar managed, having given little thought to what he would say. 'What were you doing at the doctor's?'

'None of your business.' Samira drew Ekin's long wool coat more tightly round her. It was the one her mother kept for Rashida's school events and going to visit clients in Fitzrovia. 'I was doing a favour for a friend.'

'For that Aloysius man?'

'Why don't you just call him what you think he is?'

Ottmar took a step back, genuinely hurt. 'Because I'm not like that.'

'Really? Really? Because you're so bloody perfect. Aren't you? Not like me. Why won't you leave me alone?' Her voice cracked with emotion.

'I don't understand it, Sami. Why are you so angry? All this rage. What is it that you think we're doing to you? We buy you clothes. We buy you food. We love you. We don't hit you. But you treat us like we're nothing. You go out in the evenings ... doing who knows what with your friends. Your mother and I are terrified. Are you being used? Are you taking drugs? You and Rashida, you are our lives. We've given you security: a flat, good schools, money in your pocket. And now you're throwing it all away. Are you going to school at all? You act as if you live alone.'

'But I don't live alone! That's the point. I need some bloody privacy.'

'We're four people living in a small flat, Samira. None of us has any privacy! I live in front of other people twenty-four hours a day. That's just how it is. I would have loved to buy you a big house. I would have loved to buy you everything in the world. I look at these roads and roads of houses and I failed. I know that. I failed. But I didn't do it out of selfishness. This – what I've given you – it's as much as I could do.' Ottmar paused for a moment, and then asked because he couldn't bear not to: 'Are you going to have a baby?'

Samira hissed with annoyance. 'Couldn't you think of anything else I'd be doing at a doctor's?'

'I don't know, Sami. I'm scared.'

Samira thought for a minute. When she spoke her voice was low. 'I was letting a lady know something so she didn't get in trouble. The police like to pick on people. So we look out for each other.'

Ottmar wanted to ask what she meant but he held his tongue. She had trusted him a little; that was enough. He cast around for something to distract them both. 'You know, I was following you on the bus, feeling like a salak, like an old man playing at being James Bond. But I came too far on my bus ticket. I was supposed to get off at Elephant and Castle. And I found myself thinking: what would a spy do?'

'On a London bus?'

'With the wrong ticket.'

Samira's eyebrows rose. 'Baba! You have officially committed a crime. Against London Transport! How d'you feel now?'

'Terrible.' It was the truth.

'Who's in the restaurant?'

'Rachel, Helen, Mahmut.'

'You just left them?'

'I got scared,' Ottmar told her. 'I couldn't keep letting it happen. You walk away, Samira, and I get so frightened that you won't come back.'

Samira caught his eye for a moment and he saw in her a wavering, a flicker of openness. She looked away again. Then she turned and walked a few steps back towards Streatham Hill. At the second lamp post she paused and waited for him to catch her up. They walked together in silence for a while.

'You know,' Samira said, 'no one else is like us. No one's Turkish. No one's Muslim. Half of them have never heard of Cyprus. At school I'm this thing. This thing that doesn't fit. I feel like dirt.'

Ottmar reached out and momentarily touched a hand to his daughter's hair. 'You're the furthest thing there is from dirt,' he said.

The Second Best Hotel in Town

Thursday, 11 November

Lanny was not alone when she arrived at Fishguard and Goodwick station in the dark of that November evening. While Anna and Aloysius were searching for a room in Clacton and Hayes was walking the streets of Westminster, two women and a child were arriving at the single-platformed station beside the port.

Through an iron gate lay a little car park and a weather-beaten kiosk from inside which a middle-aged woman in a green corduroy coat sold cigarettes and newspapers and sweets.

'Do you smoke?' Orla asked.

'Not right now,' Lanny told her.

Orla bought a packet of Senior Service and a lighter. 'Look, Gracie,' she said. 'Senior Service. Like that big sign we always look at in the station!' Her daughter laughed. Orla lit one with a shaking hand and drew a great breath in. Her face crumpled.

'Not good?' Lanny asked her.

'Haven't smoked in years.' A filthy taste like soot and iron filings spread itself across her tongue. They walked together onto the edges of the deserted road.

'You ladies got somewhere to stay tonight?' the woman in the kiosk called to them.

'Not as such,' Orla called back.

'If you head towards the port there's the Fishguard Bay Hotel. Nice if you've got the money.'

Orla cast a glance across at Lanny who shook her head.

'First place they'd look,' Lanny whispered and turned her face away from the woman's gaze.

'What if we don't have the money?' Orla asked.

'Then you'll need to walk into Fishguard. Road you're on takes you to the upper town. Or there's a path round the headland; that'll take you past the upper town and down to the harbour and the lower town. There's a pub with rooms. That'd be my second choice. Pretty place. Lovely and quiet.'

Orla finished her cigarette and picked up Gracie, letting the girl snuggle into her neck. There was no snow on the coast but a fierce wind swept in from St George's Channel. Alongside Lanny she leaned on the railings at the sea's edge and took in the lines of the coast. To the west a fortress of containers marked the edge of the port. Beyond it a stone jetty ran into the sea and above it all a cream-coloured, crenellated pudding of a building nestled in amongst the trees, clinging to the edge of the cliff.

Orla lowered Gracie and they started to walk east. Past the fishermen's cottages with their neat, spare gardens; up the mulch-covered steps between the trees; Gracie clung to her mother's hand. On the steps Orla felt Lanny's hand grasp her wrist. She reached across and circled the other woman's waist, pressed her face close to Lanny's ear. 'Can you do this?' Lanny didn't answer. 'Do we need to find you a doctor? We've got time. We can get you somewhere and still make the boat.'

Lanny rested her head briefly against Orla's shoulder. 'If I can't do this you can leave me, you know. Take the boat without me. If I'm too sick to do this, then … Well …' Lanny gave Orla's arm a sharp squeeze and pulled away.

They rose to the crest of the headland and traced its edges, the sea rustling and clapping the rocks beneath them. The clouds obscured the moon and stars. Orla pulled Gracie away from the cliff's edge and held her on the safer side of the path. She heard Lanny's breathing grow loud behind them. As they rounded the headland the lights of a harbour appeared below them and to their right. A wooden bench sat on the grassy slope above them and Gracie ran to it before Orla could stop her.

'For God's sake, Gracie. We can't go sitting around on benches now.' But Lanny was making her way towards it too, staggering up the little slope.

Gracie sat between Orla and Lanny and gazed across to the cream-coloured hotel, gleaming softly on the cliffs in the distance. 'Why can't we go there tonight?' she asked her mother.

'Money,' Orla said and Lanny laughed.

'We'd be queens,' Gracie said.

'D'you want to be a queen, Gracie?' Lanny asked.

Gracie stared at her for a moment. 'Don't you?'

'No,' Lanny said. She nodded towards the ring of dim lights that surrounded the blackness of the harbour. 'I want to be down there.'

The harbour opened its arms to them, fishing boats bucking softly on the quiet water. They paused by a set of curving steps which wound from the path down onto a sandy beach below. Lanny peered down the slope. 'Which way now?'

'Keep following the lights,' Orla said. 'Follow the houses round.'

Single file they crossed a small stone bridge beneath which a river surged with unexpected force. A sign swung gently from the walls of a stone inn.

The proprietor's wife brought them soup and toast and tea in their rooms. 'Because the poor lady looks done in.' Gracie ate a slice, crawled onto her mother's bed and fell asleep. Orla closed the connecting door and sat with Lanny by a little gas fire, mixing the last of the milk with the half-cold dregs of tea. Lanny unwrapped the scarf she'd tied tightly around her hair.

'How was your brother?' Orla asked, for want of conversation.

'When?'

'When you phoned him. Back in London.'

Lanny stared at the bars of the fire. 'Do you have brothers, Orla?'

'Three young ones. Adults now. With wives and babies that I've never met.'

'Why not?'

Orla frowned. 'I never went home.'

'Nor me.' Lanny studied Orla's face with an expression that Orla couldn't read. She reached out and touched the other woman's arm.

Then she eased herself from her chair, lay down on the bed and closed her eyes.

The proprietress agreed to walk around the bay and buy the tickets. Two adults and a child for the Saturday sailing at noon. Lanny stayed in bed but gave Orla a handful of pound notes to pass on.

Gracie played with her dolls under the bed. Orla sat on the window seat in Lanny's room and crocheted a flower from a little piece of thread with a hook she found in her handbag. When the thread was finished she pulled the work free and started once again. Lanny slept.

The lady brought their tickets up at half past twelve with a tray of hot lamb soup and bread. Orla spread the papers out upon the table and checked them and then rechecked them until she started to dog the corners of her and Gracie's birth certificates. Would the security guard make the connection between the passport for Orla Hayes and the certificate for Orla Keane and her daughter? Gracie's birth certificate recorded under 'mother's name: Orla Hayes formerly Keane'. And my picture, she thought. Lanny will need to look more like me than I do. A momentary ripple of fear passed through her. I'm going to mess this up, she thought. We're going to mess this up.

She stowed the papers and the tickets in the pocket of her handbag, broke the skin on the soup with a spoon.

'Gracie! Come and get your lunch.'

Gracie came with her dolls from the other room and stared at the lamb soup with unguarded horror. Lanny stirred under the covers and Orla went to her, pressing a hand to her forehead, touching a hand to her cheek.

'Do you want me to feed you?' she asked the woman softly.

'Why?'

'You don't look right, Iolanthe.'

'Give me a minute.' Lanny levered herself upright in the bed.

Orla could see her daughter watching Lanny, studying the woman's fragility.

'Gracie! If you don't like the look of the soup, you can take the bread and butter next door.'

Gracie helped herself to two thick pieces of bread and went back to her game.

Orla pushed the connecting door closed. 'I don't think we can travel together,' she told Lanny. 'My name's on Gracie's birth certificate and your passport. And it's one thing you passing for me but quite another me not passing for myself.'

Lanny rubbed her eyes and eased herself to sitting. Her hand went to the bedside table to find her pills. Orla saw what she was looking for and fetched her handbag from the end of the bed. Before Lanny could tell her not to she had opened it and was looking for the little bottle. Orla pushed the stack of letters first to one side, then the other.

'Do you want me to post these?' she asked, still looking for the glint of brown glass.

'No. They're not for posting.'

Orla smiled. 'Are they love letters?'

Lanny's face fell. 'I wish they were. They're demands for money.'

Orla found the bottle of pills, untwisted the cap and handed them to Lanny. 'You don't have to tell me,' she said. 'It's none of my business. I know that.'

Lanny took a pill and swallowed it with water. Then she recapped the bottle and handed it back to Orla.

'A long time ago now … My brother and I got ourselves into debt. Our father had died … Our mother …' Lanny's fingers passed through the air. 'We were gone. Lost.'

Orla seated herself at the end of the bed, signalling her willingness to listen.

* * *

Hayes' little blue and white panda car drew in to Fishguard just as the light was fading and parked up in a street between the station and the upper town. Here in the blustery west the snow hadn't settled and instead the town was covered by a sheen of rain. As the car stilled, Hayes seemed to deflate and he slumped forward, his arms on the steering wheel, his head buried in his hands.

Wingate started to jiggle at Anna's seat with his knees.

'Let me out!' he hissed.

Hayes said nothing to challenge him – he barely even moved – so Anna climbed out and pulled her seat forward. Wingate sprang from the car, almost tripping on the kerb in his desperation to be free.

'That was virtually false imprisonment,' he said to Anna as he passed. 'I'm going to find a train ticket and a bottle of aspirin. Not necessarily in that order. And then I'm going to start wording my complaint.'

Anna watched him stride in the direction of the port. He seemed to be searching in his pockets for something, though he drew nothing from them.

Anna stood on the rainy pavement and surveyed the view. 'There's a big hotel up on the cliffs,' she pointed out. 'Lanny might well be up there.'

Hayes did not respond. Both Anna and Aloysius stared at his unmoving form.

'What are you doing now?' Aloysius asked Anna.

'I think I'm going to try and get us all up to the hotel. Might as well start with the obvious.'

'Would you mind very much if I needed a break?' Aloysius asked her.

'A break from what?'

Aloysius tilted his head towards Hayes but didn't speak.

'Of course,' she told him. 'But will you stay in Fishguard? You're not going home?'

Aloysius climbed stiffly out of the back. 'Anna. Would I come all this way to leave you now?' He smiled at her. 'If you go to the hotel, I'll walk up to the town on the hill. We'll find each other somehow.' He glanced towards the car. 'I can't stay here. I need to breathe some other air.'

'Okay,' she told him. 'Thank you. We'll come and find you later.'

Aloysius strode off towards the upper town.

Anna climbed back into the car and shut the door. Hayes still lay against the wheel. 'Sergeant? Are you all right?'

'What am I doing?' murmured Hayes to no one in particular.

'You're looking for Iolanthe Green.'

Hayes turned his head to look at her. 'But what am I doing in Wales? I don't have permission to be here. I only signed the car out so I could pick up Wingate. Knight's going to go berserk.'

'You're being diligent. You're trying to bring her home.'

'I'm going to get myself sacked.'

'You can't fall apart now, Barnaby. You're meant to be in charge.'

Hayes mumbled something.

'What? I didn't hear.'

'My wife's left me,' he said.

'Oh,' said Anna. What was she meant to do now? Comfort the man? Tell him maybe she'd come back? Maybe she was right to leave him …

'I think I've been behaving rather badly,' Hayes said, with the mournful expression of a chastened dog.

'Well …' Anna thought about this. 'Yes. You have. A bit.' She laid a tentative hand on his shoulder and tried to peel him off the wheel. 'We just need to keep going a little longer. I'd offer to drive but I don't know how. Let's just start by going up to the hotel and asking them if they've seen her. That seems manageable. Doesn't it?'

* * *

Orla woke Lanny at five o'clock and asked if she wanted to eat some tea with them in their room. She'd ordered herself and Gracie sandwiches but Lanny had been asleep so many hours and she'd never really touched her lunch.

'Do you know what, I think I'll take a little walk. Just out to the harbour wall and back. Five minutes at the most. Then, if you think

Gracie will forgive me, I might find a quiet corner of the bar downstairs to eat. I'm sorry if I'm being rude, it's just that I haven't been out of this room all day,' Lanny told her.

She tied her scarf around her head to hide her hair. Then she eased herself down the stairs and went out to see the boats. She sat for a few minutes on a little bench by the harbour's edge. The lights from the houses twinkling in the gloom reminded her of a scene from a Christmas card. Over on the other side of the harbour that long spindly staircase led down to the little beach and she wished she had the energy to walk across and feel the sand under her feet. But it was too wet to stay long outside so she turned back and found a quiet table for herself in the side bar where she ordered a bowl of stew.

'Coming up, *cariad*,' the barman called to her from across the room.

Lanny's mind started to drift. She lost herself in the feeling of heat from the fire. Her senses and her cunning had been coming and going ever since she started to recover. She could be sharp in bursts and then her memory would fail or she'd forget how to speak. Her eyes closed, she melted into the darkness.

The outside door opened with a bang and woke her. A long, pale face stared into the bar through the pane of glass. How odd, she thought to herself, that man looks exactly like James Wingate. She closed her eyes again.

* * *

Anna had managed to get Hayes as far as the lobby of the Fishguard Bay Hotel. They had parked outside and gone in to give the receptionist Lanny's description. The young woman had seemed quite perplexed and swore she hadn't seen anyone who looked like that come in. And no, there was no one staying here under the name of Green. Hayes took himself over to a fake Regency love seat and sat down heavily. He left so little room for Anna that she was forced to bend over him, talking to him as if he were her child.

'I'm sorry your wife's left you,' she began. 'And I'm sure you're having an awful time. But Lanny's in real, horrible, life-ending trouble and you can't just sit here.'

'I've poured myself into this job,' Hayes said. 'I'm good at this job. I thought public service made you a good man.'

'It's a perfectly noble thing to be doing.'

'Then why can't she see that I am good and let that be enough? None of us is perfect. She isn't. Nor am I. Why's she leaving me? Why's she taking Gracie?'

'Is that your little girl?'

'What does she want me to do? She doesn't tell me. I could change. I could be a better husband if she'd tell me how. Everyone has bad bits. But you don't just leave. You stick them out.' Hayes looked Anna straight in the eye.

'I don't know. I'm sorry. I've never been married.'

'I thought I loved her *enough*. But I can't have done. How much is enough anyway? How much do you love someone before you say: yes, this is it. This is the right amount to love someone you're married to.'

'I don't think anyone knows that, Barnaby.' Anna reached down and took his hand. 'You have to get up now. You have to keep going. Don't you? Because she needs us. Yes?'

'My wife is gone and I'm not even looking for her.'

'Then we'll look for her too,' Anna told him, pulling him by the arm as discreetly as she was able.

Barnaby did not move. 'I think I'm letting her leave,' he told Anna, his eyes very wide.

Passengers

Friday, 12 November

The warmth of the pub and the crackle of the fire eased the pain in Iolanthe's ribs. The table jolted beside her. She had the feeling that someone had set something down very near her. Perhaps it was that nice waitress with her meal. Sleep now, her body told her. She leaned her head against the curtains behind her.

'Yolanda.'

'What?' She opened her eyes. Wingate sat across the table from her, looking both angry and a bit triumphant. His face was heavily stubbled and his hair greasy and unkempt. He was wearing a very large dark blue suit, which had obviously been tailored for a completely different kind of man. The whites of his eyes were shot through with red.

'Yolanda,' he repeated.

'Why would you call me that?' she asked.

'Because it's your name. Yolanda Green. Daughter of Maria Green. You would appear to be something of a fantasist, Yolanda.'

Lanny thought about this. 'Not a fantasist, James, no.' She closed her eyes again.

Wingate's hand crashed against the table. 'Wake up, you silly woman!'

Lanny opened her eyes. The men at the next table were staring at them. 'You'll get us both thrown out,' she said.

Wingate dragged his hands through his hair and leaned towards her over the table. His posture seemed threatening but his eyes when she looked at them were fearful. 'You're carrying my child.'

'What?' Lanny said, beginning to rouse.

'You're running away with my child.'

'No, I'm not.' Lanny rubbed her face.

'There's no point lying about it now. Hayes told me.'

Lanny stared at Wingate. She found men in extremis so hard to read.

'It's not *your* child, James. You're not the father.'

'The dates show I am.'

'No they don't. What d'you know about dates anyway? I was pregnant when you met me. Don't you remember how I threw up on your feet? That was morning sickness, you idiot. Why do you think I kept disappearing that weekend? I felt awful. I was four weeks gone at least.'

Wingate sat and stared, looking for all the world as if Lanny had announced that the sky was made of salt, the sea of peas. 'I thought it was mine.' He sounded bereft.

'Oh fuck, James,' Lanny said softly.

Wingate sat in silence.

The waitress arrived with Lanny's bowl of stew and a plate of bread. 'Do you want anything to eat, sir?'

'I don't have any money,' Wingate said.

Lanny raised her hand. 'I'll buy him a Scotch. Since he's come all this way.'

Wingate's face sank further into its deep lines. He looked older. Grey. Cadaver-like, almost. Lanny ate a piece of bread and watched him age.

'Whose is it, then?' he asked.

'I can't tell you that,' Lanny laughed. 'I kind of wish I could. But I can't.'

The Scotch arrived and Wingate drank it in silence. Lanny gave him a couple of minutes to compose himself. 'What are you doing here with no money, James?' she asked.

'I have almost no idea,' Wingate said. 'I think I may have thrown up on myself last night and someone at my club redressed me in this. Then the policeman drove me here.'

'The police?' Lanny asked.

'The policeman from London. He drove me here for God knows what reason and now I can't get home because I haven't got my wallet.'

Lanny opened the handbag at her side and withdrew a clip of notes. 'How much do you need?' she asked.

'How much can you spare?'

Lanny smiled. 'Quite a lot if you'd do me a favour.'

'What's the favour?'

'I am in debt. To a man by the name of Cassidy, whose father once saved my brother and I from … quite a lot of trouble. Cassidy Junior wants his father's money back and truth be told it was a loan. Just one we never thought would get called in.'

'Why don't you pay him?'

'In the past six months I have sold my apartment in the States. I have sold my car. I have closed my personal savings accounts, my pensions. I have offered up everything I have and still it only comes to seventy per cent of what he's asking for. So now there is talk of a court case … and he wants to go after my brother.'

'The one who isn't dead.'

'*Shit*. Seriously? Is that common knowledge now?'

'Well. I haven't put it in the paper. Yet.'

'Are you fucking with me, James?' Lanny asked.

'No. No, I'm not.' Wingate leaned back in his chair and rubbed his face. 'Go on, Yolanda Green. Ask me your favour.'

The barman sat on his stool and watched the interlopers talk. The sallow woman grew more animated by the minute. Her scarf slipped from her head and curls fell about her face as she talked. She really was quite beautiful, even if the colour of her skin made her look a little witchlike. The sleazy-looking gentleman in the dark blue suit eventually drew a notepad from his inner pocket and started to write things down. London folk, the barman thought, swarming across the border, importing their oddness like tins of Gentleman's Relish.

As he watched them parley the door opened again and a very tall coloured man walked into the little vestibule. He was dressed like someone from a 1940s gangster film and his nose was badly swollen. He was wearing a pair of large dark-rimmed glasses in which the lenses had been smashed. He peered at the barman through the glass and the barman stared right back. Then the man seemed to see somebody that he knew and hurried into the bar. He paused by the table of the sallow lady and the note-maker and began to gesticulate with great fervour. Then the sallow lady and the gentleman both stood up, everyone gathered their belongings and trooped out of the bar together.

* * *

In the lobby of the Fishguard Bay Hotel Anna Treadway stood over a love seat shaking the knee of a disconsolate Barnaby Hayes. She had temporarily given up on trying to move him and was wondering desperately where she should go looking for Iolanthe on her own.

'Barnaby? Sergeant Hayes? I'm going to have to go now. I have to go and look for Lanny. Do you understand?'

Hayes sat quite rigid and stared at the far wall.

Anna turned and looked pleadingly across at the young receptionist who was staring very hard at an address book and pretending not to listen. The front door opened and the receptionist glanced up. Then she looked at Anna, then she looked again at the door. Anna turned.

'Lanny!'

A terribly awkward and yellow Iolanthe stood in the lobby beside the triumphant figure of Aloysius. Anna stared at Lanny for several seconds and then she rushed to her and held her tight. Barnaby Hayes quietly took in the scene from where he sat.

Lanny reached her hands up and patted Anna's hair as if to comfort her but Anna did not let go. She breathed in the warmth of Lanny's neck, as if she could remember the smell of her, which of course she couldn't. She shut her eyes tight. I have to tell her, Anna thought. I have to tell her that I understand, that I've stood in her shoes.

She pulled away a little and looked into Lanny's face. More than anything the older woman looked startled and confused by the intensity of Anna's embrace. I've overwhelmed her, Anna thought. She doesn't understand. She doesn't know what we've been through for her.

And still Lanny stared at Anna.

Why doesn't this feel right? Anna thought. Why isn't this what I imagined? Oh God. Oh foolish, foolish Anna. It isn't her. It isn't Lanny that you thought you'd find.

She released her hold on Lanny, took a step away and searched for the words to explain herself. 'I'm sorry. I didn't mean … I've been so worried.'

'I know,' Lanny told her, her gaze sinking to the floor.

'We thought you were dead.'

'I know. I'm sorry. I should have … I was just trying to put things right.'

Hayes rose and took a few steps towards the little group, staring at Iolanthe. 'We found you.' He didn't sound as if he believed in this turn of events at all. He tried it again in a more certain voice. 'We found you.'

Anna shot him a rather sharp glance. 'Aloysius found her. We were just wasting time.'

Aloysius, containing a smile, observed, 'I think it was very much a combined effort.'

Lanny stood there in silence, her frame sagging noticeably. She looked exhausted, older than her years.

'Should we take you to a doctor?' Anna asked.

'No. No. I'll be fine. I just need to sleep. I have a room in town but Aloysius here said we had to find you and show you I was okay.'

Anna reached up and kissed Aloysius's cheek. 'Well done,' she whispered. 'Clever man.'

'Wingate went to see about the last train home. Too late for us, though. We missed it,' Aloysius said.

Lanny raised her hand. 'I'm sure we can all sleep here tonight since this is where we've ended up. I can pay for rooms,' she said. 'It seems to be the the the least I can do.' She walked slowly and carefully over to the desk. 'Do you have a couple of twin rooms, just for the night? Both in the name of Green, please.'

'I do, ma'am. I have two on the first floor.'

'Myself and the young woman will take one of them. The gentlemen can have the other.'

'Any luggage, ma'am?'

'Not really.' Lanny turned and looked at Anna. 'I have some stuff over at the other place but I can get it tomorrow. I just need to make a call. Anna, will you take the keys to the room and go up first?'

'Of course. If that's what you want.'

Anna looked to Aloysius who was still absorbing the fact that he was sharing with Hayes. 'Sorry,' she mouthed at him.

In the room, Anna sat and took in the silence. It's over, she thought. We found her. She's alive. Not dead at all. Just a little ill and battered. We'll patch her up. The play could even go back on. I dare say we can make some story up to protect her from it all. It's all fixable, she thought. Everything is fixable. Even the most terrible of messes.

She sank onto the bed, still in her clothes. After a couple of minutes the door creaked open and Lanny joined her. She seemed to be fiddling with something in her handbag then she stowed it by the bed nearest the door.

Lanny stripped off her coat and her dress. 'Jesus, Anna. It's all been such a nonsense, hasn't it? I'm so sorry. To have worried so many people ...' Her limbs beneath her clothes were iodine-yellow and her veins bulged through the skin of her forearms. She lay down on one of the beds in her underwear and pulled the coverlet over her. 'Do you know something? I was thinking just this afternoon: I've slept with more men in the past six months than in the whole of the rest of my life.' She closed her eyes.

'Really? Did you like any of them?'

'I think I fell into a kind of crazy sadness and I thought I could fuck my way out of it. And I'm pretty sure you can't do that. Fuck your way out of things. So much chaos, Anna. So much destruction. I've been spinning in circles.' Lanny's voice got fainter. 'Spinning ...' She fell silent.

It was still dark when Anna was woken by banging at her door. Outside in the dimly lit corridor stood Hayes, dressed for the outside, clutching his hat against him.

'Is she in there?'

'What?'

Hayes walked straight past Anna, fumbled against the walls by the door and found the light switch. The room, when illuminated, showed two empty beds.

'Where is she?'

Anna stared about her then she walked to the bathroom. No Lanny. No sign of Iolanthe. We did find her, didn't we? she asked herself. I didn't dream it all?

'Where is she?' Hayes asked again.

'I have no idea. What time is it?'

'It's half past seven.'

'Maybe she's gone to breakfast.'

'There's a woman's handbag lying on a beach by the harbour in the lower town.'

Anna's eyes searched the room for Lanny's handbag. She couldn't see it.

'I don't understand. Where d'you think she's gone?'

'I think she's gone into the harbour. I think she's drowned.' Anna tried to absorb this utterly discordant new idea.

'I have to go back into the town,' Hayes told her, 'and you need to come with me.'

'Okay. Just give me one minute and I'll be with you in the lobby.' Anna picked up her key, her coat and her shoes and hurried down the corridor.

Of course, Hayes thought. Of course she would go and fetch him first.

A very grave-faced Aloysius ran alongside Anna down the stairs and with Hayes they set off into the dark outside the hotel. Hayes drove them past the railway station, where a steady stream of worker bees hurried towards their train, over the hump of the upper town and down into the lower. After a couple of minutes travelling in silence Hayes managed to summon his policeman's voice.

'Last night, as a matter of courtesy I phoned the local police and informed them that I was in town and of the reason for this visit. This morning at half past six the night porter wakes me to tell me that the local station is trying to reach me on the reception phone.

'A fisherman had gone down to the little harbour to check on his boat and he'd seen a person standing on the steps by the beach in the darkness looking out to sea. He thought it was a woman because she had a great mass of curly hair. On his way back up from his mooring he decided to make his way across and check that she was okay. He found a woman's handbag lying on the beach but no sign of the woman at all. She'd just disappeared. He didn't hear anyone go into the water but then he'd climbed aboard his boat and checked the inside for a couple of minutes so he says he probably missed it then.'

Anna found herself both relieved and surprised at Hayes' naivety. 'But why d'you assume she went in the water? She might just have forgotten her handbag.'

'There's a letter.'

'What kind of letter?' Anna asked.

'A letter addressed to you.'

'What does it say?'

'We don't know. The local police have it. I need you to come and open it.'

'Oh,' said Anna and Aloysius's hand found hers across the darkness of the back seat of the car. Outside, the sky at the horizon was turning from deepest blue to pink. It was starting to get light.

The local police officer was a man called Iolo Gordon who they found standing with a crowd of locals all discussing the possible fate of the 'poor girl'. One of the fishermen was in tears and was being comforted by a woman who wore a great grey knitted shawl tied about her waist with a dressing-gown cord. Anna wondered where she had seen this before and some part of her mind pulled up an image of the homeless men asleep on the benches in Savile Row, bags around their feet, blankets bound to their waists. She looked at the calm, still water of the harbour. She remembered Aloysius's face. All that blood. Her stomach turned.

A man handed her an envelope. She opened it and stared at the page and then her mouth opened but no sound came out. Someone must have taken the paper from her because a voice close by to her – which might well have been Aloysius's – read some words aloud:

"'Dear Anna, I have so much to ask forgiveness for. Too much for such a little time of knowing you. But life is all uneven. I think we both know that.

"'I have a favour to ask you. Last favour, I promise. Will you see that Nat is left undisturbed? Make sure he has moved his money sensibly. Help him do it if need be. I have asked Mr Wingate to help me too. But you don't have to bother yourself with him.

"'I hope you and the Aloysius man are happy. I like to think of you having somebody after all. Have the best life you can manage, Anna. Don't worry if it doesn't look like any of the pictures in your head. Sorry for the heartache, Lanny Green.'"

Down at the harbour's edge, somebody had sat Anna down on a low stone wall. Somebody else had squeezed her shoulder. Time passed. Everything was quite peaceful inside the silence, she observed. Aloysius came and sat beside her but she couldn't hear what he was saying and after a while he just gave up and went away. Someone in a black diver's suit waded into the water in front of them and started to swim around.

In the bedroom of the inn, Orla sat on the window seat and watched her husband take charge of the scene. Iolanthe had rung her last night to explain that she couldn't come back to the room. She'd warned her that a policeman from London was with her and of course Orla had wondered if it might be Brennan. How predictable, she thought to herself, that her husband should be fifty yards away and yet quite oblivious to her presence. And what were they all doing anyway, crowding round on that tiny piece of beach, peering into the water?

How considerate he looked, bending over to talk to the pale young lady, putting an arm around a weeping man. Behind her on the floor, Gracie played with her dolls, making a hospital for them to run under the bed. He's a good man when he's not with me, Orla thought.

Her father had been a dairy farmer and very clear in his priorities. 'Work, Orla, is not a pleasure or a privilege. The rich will tell you that it is but that's because they never do any. People first. Every time, my darling. Your children and then your spouse and then your parents and then the rest of all the world. Work is what we need to feed the family. But let it into your heart and there'll be no more room to spare.'

How was it that Brennan could put his arm around a stranger but when she had knelt before him, in the early days of Gracie, crying so hard she couldn't speak, he just stood there looking terrified? It's odd, she thought, how men seem to think the act of providing is an act of love – equal to affection, comfort and support. I haven't lost him, she told herself. He just wasn't who I thought he was at all.

An aching sadness passed through her all the same. She looked at Gracie. I am still alone, she thought. She tugged the nets down so she could no longer see her husband's face.

'Do you want to be the patient?' Gracie asked her.

'Yes, darling. I'll be your patient.'

'Your leg's broken.'

'Is it, now?'

'Yes. Lie down on the carpet, please. We're going to chop it off.'

Outside, on the beach, a uniformed policeman led Anna to a car and drove her back to the Fishguard Bay Hotel. A member of staff ushered her into a quiet, empty salon and sat her down with a view of the sea. Someone else brought her a cup of tea but when she put out a hand to drink it, it had gone quite cold. A ferry sailed away in the distance. People asked her questions but got no reply.

The Anna inside her head remarked to the Anna of her body that the peacefulness was actually rather pleasant. Not happy, of course. The happiness had been removed from everything, quite possibly the world itself. But the silence was strangely bearable, if very slow and viscous like sinking into treacle. Things that would not normally have any texture at all, like oxygen and time and mortality were nubbly and fuzzy and discernible. She felt immensely present on the earth. But the earth had changed its nature all around her.

I failed her, she thought. I didn't want her enough, didn't love her enough. That's why she went.

I should have told her that I understood that panic, that need to be alone again in your own body.

I was in the same room as her but I left her on her own. I didn't mean to make her lonely. Oh God, Lanny, I didn't mean to make you lonely.

At two o'clock, just as people were filing out of the dining room from lunch, Aloysius returned to the hotel. He found Anna, her face washed of character. She stared out to sea, glassy-eyed. He knelt beside her and took her hand in his but she didn't turn. He squeezed her fingers and her mouth wrinkled slightly.

Aloysius leaned his head very close to Anna's and whispered softly: 'You have to come with me. Very quietly. Right now.'

She turned to him, blinking her confusion, and he started to help her up before she was even ready.

'I'm so tired. I can't hear properly.'

'Lean on me,' he said and threaded a long arm round her waist.

They walked together, a little unsteadily, down the steps of the hotel and turned away from town, down a path that ran through some trees and then down to the port.

The cold air and the movement woke Anna a little from her trance. She'd come out without her coat. She stopped them both and pulled away; Aloysius's face – very nearly the right shape again – was nonetheless unreadable. 'Hang on. Wait. It's too cold. I don't know where we're going.' Aloysius smiled and took off his coat. She accepted it without a word.

'If I was a more nervous man, I might feel that my role in this relationship was to take off my clothes and hand them to you.' Aloysius smiled at her and his smile had in it more than a small amount of flirtation.

'Do you understand …' Anna's voice was swollen with fury. 'Do you understand that Lanny is dead?'

Aloysius held up both his hands. Then he literally bowed to her, there on the path, in his stained suit. 'I am sorry beyond words,' he told her. 'I had forgotten that one of us was still in grief.' He laid a hand on his chest. 'I have something very beautiful to show you.' He walked a few steps down the path and Anna followed him, speechless, numb.

Aloysius led her a little way up a grassy verge, along the side of the port and around a couple of cement buildings from which the dockers came and went. He pressed a finger to his mouth to tell Anna that they were not to speak. At the end of a concrete path there lay a building of wood and brick painted with the faded message 'Public Lavatories'. There were three blue painted doors, one for men, one for ladies, and the third without a sign on it. Aloysius knocked softly at the unmarked door and it opened almost immediately to show a young woman wrapped in a blue spotted overall carrying a dustpan and brush.

'Megan, this is the lady I told you about.'

Megan placed the dustpan and brush carefully on the floor and wiped her hands vigorously on her apron.

'Morning, miss. Your friend here told me the tale. He said you'd be back to see.'

'To see what?'

Megan started towards the ladies and beckoned for Anna to follow her inside. The room was tiled white and green inside and there were three cubicles and a row of handbasins. The cubicle in the middle showed a little paper sign:

Out of order. Apologies of Manajement.

'Your friend said I wasn't allowed to clean it or let anybody in till he brought you back to see.'

Megan pushed open the door of the middle cubicle and gestured to the toilet inside. The cubicle floor and the toilet bowl and indeed every white surface the eye could see was covered in tiny wisps of black. Anna stared at it and then at Megan.

'What is it?'

'It's hair, miss. A giant storm of hair. It's going to be a nightmare to clear up. Sticks to everything, hair does.'

'But … Okay. So … Do you know when it … how it …' Anna could see Aloysius's thinking but there wasn't strength enough in this to convince her Iolanthe was alive.

'Your friend came down here an hour ago, about half an hour after the lunchtime boat sailed and he was asking some dock hands if they'd seen this woman, lots of black hair. And I said to him that there had been a woman came in here an hour before the boat with a shiny headscarf on, looking quite posh. And she'd been in here ages and I'd been in here too 'cause I was cleaning. And after twenty minutes I gave her a knock and asked if she was ill. Because we're meant to do that if people go in and don't come out. And she says, 'No, no, not ill.' Anyway, she comes out a few minutes later and the shiny scarf is tied round her neck and she's got really short hair, like those boy haircuts, you know. And she says sorry and hurries out and doesn't even do her hands. Anyway, ten minutes later a lady comes and knocks and complains that the middle toilet is disgusting and I should clean it. But I didn't get around to it because then the boat sailed and no one else will be using them for ages.'

'What did the woman look like?'

'She was a bit shorter than you, thin, her skin was quite yellow. She looked like a posh teacher, a shop owner. Someone a bit fancy.'

Anna leaned against the door frame of the toilet cubicle. Her mind chattered nervously inside her head but she was too tired to hear what it was saying to her.

'And she got on the boat?'

'Well, I didn't see her, miss. But she was with that crowd.'

Anna blew out her cheeks and let her mind whir for a minute. Then she spoke. 'You utter shit.'

'Miss?'

'Not you.' Anna walked outside to Aloysius who was waiting for her with eyebrows raised.

'Well?' he said.

'Utter *shit*.'

His face fell. 'You were meant to be happy.'

Anna set off back towards the hotel without a word.

Aloysius waved goodbye to Megan and walked behind Anna, watching her long legs stride across the concrete.

A man in a security guard's outfit noticed them. 'Excuse me, miss. Can I help you?' he called.

'No you can't!' Anna shot back and kept walking.

Aloysius smiled apologetically at the guard. 'We're having a bit of a bad day, sir,' he told him. 'She didn't mean to be rude.'

'I bloody did,' Anna muttered and veered to the side of the path solely for the purpose of being able to kick the stones. They climbed the path back to the hotel, Aloysius at the rear, before Anna paused on the tree-lined avenue, wrapped the borrowed coat tight around her and stared out to sea.

Aloysius hovered at a distance. 'I thought you'd be more pleased.'

Anna didn't turn. 'I *am* pleased,' she said, though she didn't sound it.

'We found her,' Aloysius whispered, fearing to have this moment of triumph spirited away.

Anna ignored him, lost in her own thoughts. 'She could have confided in me last night. *Bloody hell, Lanny!*' she shouted, as if her voice might be able to reach across the sea. '*Can't you think of anyone but yourself?*'

'What are we going to tell Hayes?'

'Nothing. *Nothing.* Let her go. Let her go if that's what she wants. It's not as if we can tell him about Hen because I promised the daughter. We can't tell him about Geri. We can't tell him about Dr Jones …' Aloysius winced.

Anna turned to him now, her face furrowed. 'I didn't tell you the truth.'

'About what?'

'Lanny. She was black. Black mother, white father. Hayes told me and I never said.'

Aloysius thought about this. 'Does it matter?'

'I'm not good at saying things.'

'Did you mean any harm by it?' His eyes searched hers.

A look of confusion passed over Anna's face. 'My name isn't Anna Treadway.'

Aloysius put his head to one side, listening.

'My real name is Anna Wolf. Or it used to be.'

Aloysius smiled at her, both puzzled and touched by her confidences.

'And I shouldn't have left you at the police station,' she went on. 'I'm afraid I'm something of a coward.'

Aloysius thought about this. Now would be the moment to speak. To tell her about his meeting with Hayes, the threats, the promises, how he had informed on Dr Jones. But instead he simply said: 'We are all cowards, Anna Wolf.'

They stood in silence for a moment, lost in their own worlds. Then Anna asked, 'Do you have any money?'

'I can cash a cheque at the hotel.'

'Do me a favour, will you?'

'Another one?'

'Well, you don't have to.'

'No. Go on. It's my week for doing favours.'

'I would like a book. A book and a train ticket. I can pay you back for them eventually. But if you will buy me a book and a train ticket I think I'll be all right.'

'Any book?'

'A decent book. Nothing silly.'

'You're a very conditiony sort of an animal, aren't you?'

'I have standards,' Anna told him. 'We both do,' she corrected herself so that she didn't sound quite so obnoxious. 'We both have standards.'

'How very English of us.'

They started back towards the hotel, walking side by side.

'You can't expect anyone to be a single thing, you know,' Anna said. 'You can't expect me to be something absolute or perfect.'

'I would never see you as something absolute or perfect.' There was a flicker of a smile on Aloysius's lips.

'The me inside of me is disappointing,' Anna told him. 'Sort of corrupt. Or corrupted.'

Aloysius slipped his hand in hers and gave it a friendly squeeze. 'Come on,' he said, 'let's get our things. We shall go and be corrupt together on a train.'

Epilogue

Iolanthe Green

by James Wingate

At around half past six last Friday morning the celebrated and much-admired actress Iolanthe Green ended her own life in the depths of Fishguard Harbour. Strenuous efforts have been made to reclaim the body from the waters but as yet these have all been unsuccessful.

I was honoured to spend a not inconsiderable amount of time with Miss Green during her six months in England and I found her to be charming, thoughtful and marvellous company. Her death, when she was barely out of her thirties, leaves the theatre and the film world a lesser place.

Iolanthe Green was born into an impoverished Irish-American household in Boston in 1925 and went on to lose not just her parents but her sole sibling by the time she was twenty-one. She worked tirelessly to build a better life for herself and the heirs who might one day have been born to her.

She had never visited her grandparents' native Ireland but many have speculated that this is exactly what she planned to do when she took the train from London to Fishguard and booked herself into the Fishguard Bay Hotel. Her family came from Cork, the rebel county as it's sometimes known, and something of that freedom of spirit appealed to Iolanthe Green. We still do not know where she spent the two weeks of her disappearance but something quite compelling must have led her to the Irish Sea and, perhaps, dreams of another life.

Miss Green told me when we met in October that a court action was about to be brought against her in the United States regarding provisions in her late father's will and a friendly loan of money to two destitute, orphaned children in 1944. With the sudden and untimely death of Miss Green this malicious action against her and her family will – one can only hope – be dropped.

I cannot begin to fully understand why Miss Green made the choice that she did. I like to think that she travelled to St George's Channel in the hopes of visiting the land of her ancestors, something that I had encouraged her to do. I think I will remember her as she appeared to me this past autumn: an indefinable and indefatigable flame who burnt a little brighter than the rest of us.

Yolanda Green sat on a hillock of long grass. The sea before her was a deep grey-blue and pale brown birds perched in pairs on every rock as far as the eye could see. Not long ago a ferry had passed by on its way to the harbour at Rosslare, blowing smoke which touched for a moment the low-hanging clouds then disappeared. She wrapped her hands around her thin shoes to warm her feet.

Far out to sea, the dark grey whiskered heads of seals broke the water, making rings. In the air above them one of the pale brown birds from the rocks carried an eel it had caught high into the air and almost immediately was set upon by a dark-backed, white-winged hunting bird. The hunting bird snatched at the eel with its talons and for a moment the two birds spun in the air, the smaller of the two twisting and falling to hang limply beneath the claws of the predator as if shot and tied for suppertime. Three times the smaller bird tried to break away and three times the larger bird increased its grip, flew upwards and broke the balance of its rival.

Yolanda turned her eyes from the sight of them. She didn't need to keep watching to know that the larger bird would win or the eel be split in two. She spread her hands in the soft grass beneath her and raised herself to her feet. Cautiously she stretched her aching body and surveyed the land around her.

A memory caught her by surprise. Dancing in Roaring Twenties, her body pressed firmly against Delbert. The smell of his sweat in her nostrils. The thumping of the floor beneath her feet. She had stood some nights in a crowd of bodies and felt herself at home. As if her adult life had been some terrible extended trip into the body of a stranger. It had felt so good to be that part of herself at last, to feel the comfort of blackness enveloping her, to feel at home in the company of people she didn't even know. How brief that pleasure had been. And how intense.

She still slept late into the morning and napped through the afternoon. But she was eating and drinking like her old self now. She found – much to her surprise – that she thought little of what would happen to the child inside her. She rather assumed that it had died but a part of her, a very small part, was sometimes hopeful that it might yet be born alive. With no career to speak of any more, out of the sight of the press, it no longer mattered if she had a child or not. Though perhaps this was because the child she had created still seemed wholly unreal. She was someone else entirely now. Perhaps she would call herself Maria, her mother's name, or maybe she would stay Orla Hayes another twenty years.

The man at the Iona Hotel had been very good about getting her *The Times* of London every day, though by the time it reached southern Ireland it was nearly two days out of date. She had waited patiently to check that Wingate would write the story he had promised and when at last he did she cancelled her request for newspapers and turned her attention from the English press to the property section of the local Irish newspapers.

She had an idea that she might take the long-distance bus to Waterford and look for a cottage to rent outside a town somewhere. Yolanda was certain that there was a life to be made and some pleasure to be had in the making of it. The money she had with her would last for a little while. And after that she would teach children to dance, or buy a machine and sew curtains. She could cook and clean if she had to. She was only forty. There was still a world of possibilities before her.

She had ridden bicycles in the back garden with Nathaniel and her father a million years ago. Now she would buy one and teach herself to cycle slowly and carefully along the country roads. She would learn to make a fire in a grate and cook stews and soups on top of a kitchen stove. She would disappear into this country like a woodcock or a pigeon in a copse of trees.

Acknowledgements

Thank you to my husband for being there, being kind and making me laugh. And for bringing me poached eggs on a tray whenever I need them. Thank you to my children for your loyalty and enthusiasm and for drawing me *so very many* pictures. Thank you to my dear parents and lovely in-laws for your help and support. And thank you to my friends for cheering me on, cheering me up and pouring a lot of coffee and conversation into me.

Thank you to my PhD supervisors at Cardiff University who have dealt so graciously with a student who turned up on the first day of her first year saying: 'The thing is … I wrote this book … and I assumed nothing would happen to it but now it's been bought. Oh, and I need to write another one.' Thank you to Sonia and Mathias for rendering Anna's letter into German. And thank you to Gus Berger, who sped me a copy of his invaluable documentary *Duke Vin and the Birth of Ska* all the way from Australia.

Thank you to my agent, Caroline Hardman, for communicating her excitement about this book to other people who weren't necessarily looking to be excited at that moment. Thank you to Helen Garnons-Williams, Iris Tupholme and Claire Wachtel for taking the plunge and buying it. And a big thank you to Helen for being the most understanding, generous and thoughtful editor a writer could hope for. I'd also like to thank the whole team at 4th Estate and HarperCollins for their unstinting enthusiasm and love of all things bookish and interesting: I'm so pleased to be working with you.

Lastly, a note on the use of language in the novel. In 1965 the language used to denote a person's race was in flux. The term 'coloured', which was considered polite in England, even liberal, through to the end of the 1950s was in the process of being replaced by the more modern 'black'. But, from my research into the period and from the – often contradictory – responses that racial language used in the novel has produced in some of my early readers, I am aware that the pace of this change was different for different groups of people.

Representing language in its fluid state can be challenging for both writer and reader. However, I hope that I have gone some way towards illustrating the landscape of prejudice in 1965: a landscape within which structural racism could so easily be upheld and acts of racial violence went unpunished. My intention was to underscore some of the ways in which we have progressed in the past 50 years … and the ways in which we have not.